Exploited Blood
Book 2

"The Turn"

R S Merritt

As with all in my life this series is dedicated to my beautiful
wife and family.

Table of Contents

Prologue: Thrown into the Deep End

Chris blinked a few times to confirm his eyes were open. He'd awakened in a room submerged in impenetrable darkness. The muffled sounds of gunfire and screams seeped through the walls. He started to get up, but the world spun sickeningly around him. He couldn't see a damned thing, but he somehow knew the dimensions of the room and where every piece of furniture was located. Breathing deeply through his nose to try and regain his equilibrium he was assaulted by a thousand different smells. He could almost taste the difference in the wood blends between the chairs and the desk. He knew where the mold was growing behind the walls. The places where the wood was slowly rotting away.

Making his way to a wall he put his back to it and slowly inched up until he was in a sitting position. The gunfire outside had begun to taper off. Head spinning, he ran his hands over his body to make sure he still had his pistol. He remembered sitting his rifle next to the chair in the room. That was one of the last things he remembered before Lynn had slammed that syringe full of Voodoo juice into his ass cheek. He knew exactly where the weapon was despite not being able to see anything. He could smell it. How the hell could he smell it?

Too dizzy to go groping around for the rifle he could somehow smell he worked on getting his pistol out instead. Pistol in hand he rested his head against the wall. The very last thing he remembered was a drunken disappointment that being turned didn't require any sort of mutual neck biting. There was nothing after that until he woke up on the floor. Pistol resting in his lap he listened to the bursts of sporadic gun fire slowly dying down outside. Eventually there was quiet.

Chris smelled Benson outside the door. Without thinking about it he sniffed deeply to see what else he could smell. That's how he knew Ortega was with her. The smell of burnt gunpowder and spilled blood came close to overriding everything. By focusing he found he could sift through the aromatic chaos to pinpoint what he was looking for. Other than the handful of weird new party tricks and the severe nausea, he didn't really feel any different.

The door was kicked in a few seconds later. Ortega and Benson ventured slowly into the room. Both of them were shining flashlights around looking for Chris.

"Over here." Chris croaked out. His voice came out sounding funny. Like he was listening to a recording of himself. He could trace the reverberations of the sound waves around the room. Whatever was in that needle Lynn had jabbed him with was seriously potent. Or it was just liquid acid. He was either in a state of hyper awareness or majorly stoned. He had no idea which it was. Either way he didn't know how much more of it he could take.

"Hey man. Are you ok?" Ortega asked squatting down and shining his light into Chris's eyes. Chris blinked rapidly to dispel the sting from the light particles flowing through the air to smash into his eyes.

"He's obviously not ok. He looks like he snorted a gallon of heroin." Benson said squatting down to add her flashlight to the headache inducing illumination already being beamed directly into his brain.

"I'm dizzy." Chris said stupidly. He hated how his voice sounded. It was like he was high, and someone had hit him in the face with a baseball bat. His words were clunky. The tone of his voice was all over the place. He didn't know what volume his words were coming out at. Was he yelling or whispering? No clue.

"Alright. We need to get you out here. Your very scary girlfriend told us you'd be wrecked." Ortega said. The next thing Chris knew he was being hoisted up into the air and tossed over Ortega's shoulder. Chris started to ask someone to grab his shotgun, but Benson was already reaching down to grab it. Ortega mentioning his girlfriend sparked a question from Chris. One of many questions, but he needed to focus on one at a time. When Ortega had scooped him up his stomach had gone into red alert. Ortega wouldn't appreciate being covered in stomach stew after being nice enough to lug him around.

"Where's Lynn?" Chris stammered out. He really wished Ortega would stop bouncing around so much. It wasn't helping in his battle against barfing.

"She's gone. She went into ninja mode and took out a ton of the guys she said were here to kill you. Then she told us to find you and get off the base." Ortega answered. They'd walked out of the office Chris had been laid up in. They were walking down the hallway that'd dump them out into the main part of the warehouse. The part all the gunfire had been coming from.

"When he says ninja mode he's not kidding. You know that right?" Benson added. She was leading them down the hallway. A few steps ahead she was scanning for any threats while eavesdropping on the conversation between Chris and Ortega. Chris smiled remembering how Lynn liked to run sideways on walls while dishing out ridiculously accurate fire.

"Did she say why she was leaving?" Chris asked. He didn't know how many more questions he'd be able to ask. His stomach was on the verge of a complete revolt. His body was on fire. He was really getting sick of being sick all the time.

"Yeah. She lured away the people that'd been sent here for you. She grabbed some other guy and took him with her. It sucks to be that guy if she gets caught. We're supposed to call the number she gave us once we're somewhere safe." Ortega slowed down as they reached the end of the hallway. Benson was peeking around the corner.

"How's it looking?" Chris asked from his perch up on Ortega's shoulder. He felt like he should ask to be set down so he could walk under his own power. He just wasn't sure he had his own power to walk under at the moment. Now that he was already suffering the indignity of riding Ortega like an oversized parrot he might as well keep going. How lame would it be to have to ask to be picked back up again?

Benson didn't answer. Staying low she led them out into the main section of the warehouse. The large open space was a complete assault on Chris's senses. Blood, gunpowder, fire, and decay dominated the gymnasium sized area. Refugees and soldiers alike were randomly splayed out in the obscene poses of death. The lights overhead flickered where they'd been hit by stray rounds. People moved quietly amongst the wounded to offer whatever help they could. Several corpsmen were setting up shop to begin triaging the wounded.

Benson strode purposefully through all of that. Ortega followed directly behind her. They wound their way solemnly through the dead and dying. Chris was lost in a world of his senses. A world where he could slice and dice all of the sensory input in a way that he'd never dreamed was possible. It wasn't that he could smell better or hear better than before. It was more like he was now running all that data through a massive supercomputer instead of the hamster wheel his brain had been prior to Lynn jabbing him.

Chris lost track of all the sensory inputs when he felt himself being lowered onto a flat surface. Ortega was working with Benson on getting him loaded into the backseat of a Humvee. It was one of the armored Humvees without a turret mounted machine gun. The acrid smell of diesel drifted up from the back of the vehicle. Chris assumed that was why Ortega had decided to snag this one. They'd need a whole bunch of gas to make it anywhere in one of these petrol sucking machines.

Chris wanted to ask where they were headed and how long it was going to take to get there. He had a million pent up questions. The last thing in the world he wanted to do was puke all over himself in the tight confines of the back seat. Despite a valiant effort to get the back window open he still managed to soil most of the upholstery as well as his own clothes. Disgusting as it was, he ended up collapsing in his own mess afterwards. Too weak to be bothered by the stench. Overwhelmed by everything he passed back out.

"You think he's going to make it?" Benson asked. She was driving towards the main gate. Lynn had emphasized that they needed to put some serious distance between themselves and the base as soon as possible.

"Yeah. If there's one thing that he's good at it's being sick. I don't think he's been healthy for more than a day or two since I've known him." Ortega joked. He was leaning into the back seat doing his best to wipe the vomit off of Chris. There was a real risk of Chris drowning in a pool of his own puke if they didn't watch him. Scooping handfuls of slimy warm vomit off his young charge didn't even register on Ortega's gross-o-meter. Not after what they'd been through these last few weeks.

"How'd your other mission go?" Benson asked. Ortega had to think for a minute to figure out what she was asking about. The intense firefight with the masked men who'd attacked the warehouse had wiped his memory of the other task from earlier that evening. The one where he'd helped massacre all the infected locked up inside one of the warehouses. All they'd had to do was rig a few trucks to pump carbon monoxide into the tightly sealed underground bunker instead of oxygen.

"Got it done. One of the soldiers broke down. His son was one of the ones locked up in the space. He thanked me afterwards though. Then he just wandered off crying." Ortega answered. He couldn't think of a way to express how seeing that soldier's shoulders slump had affected him. He'd felt the pain that soldier was feeling. Pain and relief all mixed together. Dead kids were an assault on everything that was right and decent. It should be the rarest of occurrences. To have your offspring turned into one of those bald monsters. Then to have their death delayed like that...

They quit talking as they approached the main gate. There were more Marines at the gate than usual. Which was no surprise considering an armed assault had rocked the base less than an hour prior. Although why they thought they could stop it by putting more men at the main gate was anyone's guess. It wasn't like the strike force that'd hit them earlier would've been stopped by having extra guards at the gate. It probably made the commander feel good though. Like he was doing something proactive at least.

Benson rolled up to where a Marine signaled for her to stop. She put one hand on the wheel and the other on the nine-millimeter in her lap. Ortega really hoped it didn't come to that. Enough people had died needlessly for one day. Benson rolled down her window and the Marine asked them where they were going. When Benson told him they'd been ordered to leave the base the Marine told them to wait. They watched as the young leatherneck headed into one of the guard shacks to call whoever was in charge.

"You know they're not going to let us leave right?" Benson whispered out of the side of her mouth.

"Yeah. We should probably go ahead and ram through the gate. I doubt they bother chasing us." Ortega responded quietly. The whole time he was talking he was busy looking like he was resigned to sitting there waiting for the Marine to come back.

Benson slammed her foot down on the gas pedal. The big diesel engine roared to life. The heavily armored truck had no problem smashing through the guard arm. A couple of bullets pinged harmlessly off the back of their armored ride. The Marines shooting more to say that they'd try to stop them than because they thought shooting would accomplish anything.

Benson didn't even slow down. She spun through a few curves and got them the hell out of Dodge. In the backseat Chris hadn't budged since he'd passed out. The Humvee smelled like vomit. Ortega had the air conditioning going full tilt with the outside air circulating through the cabin to try and combat the sickly-sweet smell. They got on Highway 69 and headed north. Lynn had advised them to head north once they got off the base. There were cities in that direction that may still be controlled by regular people. That's where they were supposed to find a phone to give her a call.

Ortega sighed at the vagueness of it all. It felt like the kind of mission a politician would've set up. It didn't help that Chris had been injected with some sort of chemical cocktail that was supposed to turn him into *Superman*. Or maybe it did help. He honestly didn't know anymore. Deciding a nap was in order he told Benson to wake him up if she saw a McDonalds that was open. He'd decided that could be the sign of a still functional city. He fell asleep wondering why Lynn hadn't just handed him a satellite phone instead of making them go through all this hassle.

Chapter 1: The Way of the Dodo

"We're just driving until we get somewhere people have hair and don't try to eat us?" Benson asked. She was wondering how she'd ended up with a ticket on this crazy train. Ortega and Chris might be used to all this supernatural James Bond spy stuff, but she most certainly was not.

"Yeah. I hadn't met the countess before either. Not entirely sure why the hell we're doing what she told us to do. Except that she wasn't trying to kill us, and those other guys were. She said to go north then give her a call once we shacked up somewhere safe. Your guess is as good as mine as to what the hell that means." Ortega answered. He was impressed by the fact that Benson was still with them. In this toilet bowl of a world Chris was a turd magnet.

They continued on in silence. The highway winding through lush overgrown fields. Other than having to dodge the occasional baldie they didn't see anyone. The highway went over a lot of lakes which was working out great for their purposes. They cruised underneath I-40 and kept on heading north. They weren't sure what they were looking for but hopeful they'd recognize it when they saw it. It bothered Benson to be traipsing around so aimlessly, but it was just another day at the office for Ortega.

Chris stuck his head up and moaned miserably as they approached the city of Muskogee. It was the first time that they were going to be driving through a city. Muskogee was nowhere near the size of Albuquerque, but it still made them all nervous. The last time they'd driven into a large city a lot of people hadn't made it to the other side. Speeding through by themselves in an armored Humvee beat the hell out of driving a beat-up Hyundai in the rear of a slow-moving convoy though.

"We're not going around?" Chris asked.

"No. This place barely rates as a city. More like a big town. We'll be fine." Ortega answered without looking back. He was about ninety percent confident they wouldn't have any issues. A ninety percent chance of survival was pretty solid given the current state of things.

"Plus, we're going to have to drive right up the middle of the road in places like this to try and find a phone." Benson added. Chris nodded along with the explanation. As weird as it may be this was his life now. He was way too sick to care much about where they were going anyway. As long as he was in an air-conditioned vehicle that he could recline in he was content. Although Febreze might need to go on the list above the phone if they had to stay in the Humvee much longer.

Chris felt his brain clicking along like the gears in a finely made watch. Things he'd never noticed before were now standing out vividly. It'd never occurred to him to wonder exactly how many hair follicles he had on his forearms but now he knew. He knew without knowing how he knew. He needed to talk to Lynn. How else was he going to know what was happening to him? There was bound to be a lot more to it than being able to spontaneously count his own body hair.

The ability to know where things were in a room that was completely dark was interesting as well. In between pondering if he was about to puke again or not, he wondered if that skill worked something like how a bat does echolocation. Which got him to contemplating the whole vampire mythos again. Discovering he had bat like talents was almost a little too on the nose. On a whim Chris sat up to see if his reflection was visible in the rearview mirror.

"Are you thinking deep thoughts, or do you need to puke again?" Ortega asked looking back with concern. That concern had a lot more to do with a fear of the puke smell increasing than with any actual curiosity about what Chris was doing.

"A little bit of both. Can we pull over for a second?" Chris answered. Luckily Ortega hadn't seen him trying to see himself in the mirror. He'd have never lived that down. There was a good chance he might barf again at any second. Not that he could possibly have much left to throw up. Looking to get it all out of his system Chris stood on the side of the road waiting to throw up. Of course, as soon as he'd stepped out of the car he'd felt fine. He hopped back in immediately when Ortega barked out a warning for him to get back in.

"I guess this isn't one of the towns that's doing ok." Benson said as they drove quickly down the road to escape the small city. Ortega had seen two baldies hobbling out of the woods by the road. Hence the need for Chris to get back in the car.

It was nothing but baldies and the badlands until they got to the Missouri state line. At some point they'd merged onto I-44 which was a much larger road than the two-lane highway they'd been traveling on. Benson slowed down as they approached the bullet riddled cars and decaying bodies haphazardly strewn across the road up ahead. A makeshift barrier of vehicles and concertina wire effectively blocked them from continuing any further along the interstate. They were going to have to get out and hack their way past the wire unless they wanted to risk going off-roading.

The other alternative was to backtrack and take a different route. They had no place to be and no scheduled time to be there. None of them thought that anyone was after Chris to try and create a cure anymore. None of them including Chris could figure out why men kept coming after him and Lynn kept disappearing. It was a hot topic of conversation on the long drive, but they were no closer to figuring it out now than they had been when they'd left the base.

Despite the fact that they could've easily just turned around and headed for anywhere else they chose to get out and cut their way through the blockade. Ortega appeared to consider the blocked interstate a personal affront. Or he just really wanted to use the wire cutters they had in the back. He hopped out as soon as Benson drove through the stalled traffic to park them by the razor-sharp fencing.

Chris was feeling sick, so he wasn't really looking around. Benson was watching Ortega to make sure he got all the sharp pieces of wire out of the way. She could change one of the monstrous tires, but she had no desire to do so. It'd be a hot sweaty job and who knew when they'd get the chance to shower again. Not to mention clean clothes. She watched Ortega snip at wires while wondering if they should get off at an exit to do some shopping. They initially all missed seeing the baldies who'd started crawling out from under the parked cars surrounding them.

It was Chris who yelped out a surprised warning. His new and improved powers of perception had started chiming alarm bells in his subconscious. He pulled himself out of his nausea induced stupor to figure out what was eating at him. The reason for those mental alarm bells coalescing into finally noticing all the baldies emerging from their resting spots. The deathly quiet figures were all silently stalking the soldier obliviously chopping away at the fencing. Normally the monsters would've been howling like cats in heat with prey so close to them. For some reason this group of hunters were as quiet as the grave.

Leaning over the seat Chris shoved the barrel of his rifle past a startled Benson. He fumbled around for a second before he was able to press the horn with his palm. Benson looked at him open mouthed before noticing the shadowy forms surrounding them. The baldies dropped their efforts at stealth and let loose with excited screeches as they sprinted for Ortega. Rather than melting into a puddle of panic juice like Chris was sure he would've done Ortega calmly stood up and put a bullet through the skull of the baldie closest to him.

The horn honk had done a great job of alerting Ortega there were baldies coming for him. The horn honk had also done a great job of alerting the zombies that there were other snacks in the vicinity. Ones other than the guy with the oversized scissors. Chris and Benson weren't in a whole lot of danger in the armored vehicle. It was going to be difficult for Ortega to get back in if they were swarmed though.

A few more bullets right where he wanted them got Ortega within a few feet of the passenger side door. There was a rusting station wagon parked next to the Humvee. The station wagon was riddled with bullet holes. The front windshield was completely missing and the skeletal remains of a family of four were still seat belted in the car. The soldiers who'd manned this blockade must have just started shooting everything that moved when they were bum rushed by the infected. The dead family in the station wagon weren't a problem. The limber monster who leapt on the roof of the car then dove directly into Ortega was an issue they needed to address though.

Seeing Ortega do down under the weight of his assailant Chris flung his own door open to help. A pale kid covered in welts smashed into his door before Chris could step out of the Humvee. The kid bounced off the door and spun to face Chris. Chris already had his knife in his hand to cut the baldie off Ortega. The kid hurled himself into the back seat with Chris. Seized with a sudden clarity Chris swung the knife blade up and into the throat of his young assailant. It was like everything was moving in slow motion except for Chris. The odd sensation only lasted for a few breaths before time began to flow normally once more.

The infected child gurgled a few times before the final mercy was granted. Chris recoiled from the smell of the corrupted blood he'd just spilled. A primal urge came over him. Feeling the need to rip apart his enemies he rolled out of the Humvee to go into battle. The infected outside came at him in that weirdly distorted version of time again. Chris danced among them running the blade of his knife along the flesh of their throats. He plunged the knife deep into the side of the zombie Ortega was wrestling with on the ground. The blade unerringly plunging into the heart to slay the baldie almost instantly. Accepting that he'd just been saved by a ninja disguised as Chris the battle-hardened Ortega once more made for his seat.

Meanwhile ninja Chris turned to kill more of the baldies. He was in the middle of a blood lust like he'd never known before. He wanted to rend and rip the flesh of all that stood before him. He skipped forward a few steps to face off with a sumo sized zombie advancing on the Humvee. Armed with just his knife Chris put the big beast down on the ground in seconds. He'd scrambled the mountain of flesh's brain by shoving his blade through the big beast's eye socket then rocking it back and forth rapidly. Lost in the dance of death he left the knife stuck in the skull of his enemy and turned to see who his next victim was going to be.

The world went back to normal speed. Chris found himself standing on the blacktop without a weapon in hand. A small group of baldies was running straight for him. Disoriented he looked around to figure out where he was. He took a step backwards and felt a pair of arms wrap around him. He was jerked off his feet and dragged back into the Humvee.

"Drive!" Ortega yelled. He pushed Chris off of him and reached for the door to pull it shut.

Bodies slammed into the door as Benson accelerated backwards with the passenger side back door still open. Pulling his pistol Ortega started shooting at the piles of putrid flesh trying to shove their way into the backseat to join them. He put hole after bloody hole into the seething mass of welt covered hairless flesh. Teeth and red eyes flashed at him as new infected immediately took the place of the ones that he was killing. Benson slowed down when the door struck a car next to them. From the sound the door made it was doubtful if they'd ever be able to shut it again.

The firing pin on Ortega's pistol clicked on an empty chamber as he cycled through the last of his rounds. An infected woman with piercing eyes wearing the vestiges of a short yellow summer dress took advantage of Benson slowing down to jump into the backseat with them. Ortega got his hands wrapped around the woman's throat and began squeezing for all he was worth. The woman kept trying to bite him even as her eyes bugged out and her face turned blue. When she finally stopped twitching Ortega pushed her body towards the open door.

Another zombie spun in through the door like some kind of hairless Tasmanian devil. The hitchhiking cannibal knocked Ortega backwards along with the woman he'd just choked to death. Letting go of the body he reached down to grab his combat knife. Before he could get to it the loud boom of a tactical shotgun sounded in the close confines of the Humvee. The Tasmanian terror went flying backwards out of the open door.

Looking down towards the floorboards Ortega saw that Chris was snuggled up next to yet another corpse. That must be one he'd killed himself since Ortega didn't think he'd put it there. A white-faced Chris pressed the shotgun into Ortega's hands and started dry heaving. Kicking the body of the infected woman he'd strangled to death out the door Ortega finally got the rear passenger door to shut. He'd been worried the collision earlier had messed it up so bad they wouldn't be able to shut it. These things were built like tanks though. In this case the government spending a thousand dollars per hinge was totally justified as far as Ortega was concerned.

Other than the occasional hands smacking the windows they seemed to have escaped the baldie ambush. Benson slowed down long enough to turn them around so she could drive in the correct direction. Ortega had her slow down again so that he could toss the other body out onto the road. He also picked up a comatose Chris and laid him out on the backseat once more. A seat that was becoming more of a biohazard by the minute. This machine was going to need a serious detailing by the time they were done with it. Hanging one of those little pine trees on the rear view wasn't going to do the trick.

"Nice driving!" Ortega said to Benson once they were out of the danger zone.

"Nice killing…" Benson responded with a tight smile. Once again, she was seriously questioning how she'd gotten herself into this mess. There were plenty of places she could've holed up. She could be sipping a mixed drink and catching up on her reading instead of whatever it was she was doing now. There was literally no reason for her to be chauffeuring these two trouble magnets across the hellscape that Oklahoma had become. It wasn't like Uncle Sam was still direct depositing her paycheck every two weeks. Or maybe he was. Next time they passed an ATM machine she supposed she could check. A withdrawal might be needed if they started running low on toilet paper.

"Don't worry. I plan on dying with a full head of hair. I'll kill anything that has other plans for me." Ortega said.

"Agreed. Where to boss man?" Benson asked.

"I guess we need to go through Kansas after all. I'm hoping there really are some cities left that haven't been overrun already." Ortega said. He didn't sound very optimistic about it though.

It was hard imagining a city that would've been spared. Especially in the United States. Every refugee center Ortega had been involved with had ended up overrun. Hell, even the McAlester base in the middle of nowhere had taken a serious hit. Albeit the attackers in that case had been regular humans and not the infected. Somehow that made it even worse. If there was ever a time for humanity to come together against a common enemy, then this was it. Otherwise, humanity was going to go the way of the dodo.

Chapter 2: A Close Shave

"What the hell?" Benson asked. Her head was cocked sideways as she stared at Chris's shoulder with a comically confused look on her face.

The first road they'd passed when they backtracked from the Missouri border had been an overpass. They all liked the idea of turning off on a small road and using that to go north versus another major highway. There hadn't been an exit ramp to get on the other road, so Benson had performed a bit of off-roading instead. Once on the smaller back road they quickly drove into the middle of nowhere. When they stopped to answer the calls of nature Ortega had announced they should do a little housecleaning.

While Ortega used an old t-shirt and some water to attempt to clean the nasty gunk out of the backseat Benson pulled Chris aside to check out his injuries. The wound on his hand had healed already. There was nothing there now except for some newly formed pink flesh outlined by a crusty scab. Out of curiosity Benson had Chris remove his shirt so she could see how the wounds on his shoulder looked. Not only was the abrasion that'd been there a day prior now almost invisible she noticed even his older scar tissue had smoothed out noticeably.

"I guess Lynn hooked you up with super healing powers?" Ortega asked when Benson showed him Chris's much improved battle scars. She showed them off like she was standing in front of her third-grade class for show and tell. Chris was floored by Ortega's observation.

"Yeah, I guess so. Maybe?" Chris answered with a complete lack of confidence in his answer. Where the hell was Lynn? He needed to know what was going on. Should he avoid churches? He had so many questions. The way Benson and Ortega were staring at him was making him uncomfortable.

"The way you moved outside the Humvee earlier when you attacked those baldies. You ripped that giant one to pieces like he was nothing. You cut that other one off me so fast I didn't even know you were there." Ortega said. He sounded a little awestruck. Chris would've been embarrassed if he was in any way responsible for those new skills. Having no clue how he'd transitioned to beast mode either he just stared back at Ortega.

"Yeah, but then you wimped out. Like the Hulk turning back into Banner. The fight wasn't even over yet." Benson pointed out. It was very much like her to get to the crux of the matter. Especially if that pivoted around pointing out something lame that Chris had done. It was like she was still harboring some animosity from when Chris had almost killed them all due to his inability to effectively toss a grenade far enough out the window of a moving truck.

"Thanks for saving me by the way." Chris said to Ortega. If the quick-thinking soldier hadn't yanked him back to safety, he'd either be dead or going through another round of intense sickness right now. Although he was already going through some pretty intense sickness right now anyway. Could he still be turned by a baldie? Chris couldn't wait to find a pay phone. Lynn would just have to deal with the per minute costs for a collect call to a satellite phone.

"You'd saved my ass like thirty seconds before that. We're good." Ortega said. He tossed the t-shirt he'd been using to wipe the puke, guts, and blood off of the backseat. The amount of bodily fluids sloshing around back there had been getting excessive. It'd been approaching an amount that might turn them into baldies just by sitting on the seat. How lame would it be to end up a zombie because you didn't have enough Lysol wipes to keep the backseat virus free? Yet another item to add to their next Publix pickup order.

Chris pulled on a fresh t-shirt as they all climbed back into the Humvee to continue trekking north. For a group of people who had no real destination in mind it was amusing to Chris how much of a hurry they were in to get there. Wherever 'there' happened to end up being. It must be the military mindset of his traveling companions. They'd been given a task to carry out and once they'd committed, they were in it to win it.

Windows down to reduce the obnoxious odor that'd permeated the inside of the Humvee they continued on towards the Kansas border. They passed by farms and such but nothing resembling an actual town. As the afternoon morphed into dusk they discussed if they should find somewhere to sleep for the night or keep driving. They were passing by fields full of overgrown crops and long dirt driveways. After driving past a few large agricultural centers, they decided that pulling over and sleeping in the car was the way to go. No need to risk plowing into a mob of the infected in the darkness.

Benson pulled off the road when it got too dark to keep driving without turning the headlights on. Chris advised them they should sleep with the windows rolled up. Benson asked if he meant so the baldies couldn't just reach in and grab them while they were snoozing. That led to an awkward conversation about how Chris could smell everything and everybody around him. Having seen the way the baldies paused to sniff the air before attacking they all got what he was talking about.

"We should be good tonight though. Not much of a breeze." Ortega said before reluctantly rolling up his window. They were going to have to kill the engine to conserve gas, so it wasn't going to be a super comfortable night in the stink mobile. Not that being ripped apart and devoured in the middle of the night would be any better.

Lost in their individual thoughts they set a watch schedule and tried to get comfortable. The energy spent fighting and running over the last day put them all to sleep faster than a roofie smoothie. Handed the first watch Chris struggled to stay awake listening to the deep breathing of his comrades. They'd given him the first watch since he'd spent a considerable part of the day snoozing in the back seat. Ortega had skimmed right over the reason for Chris having spent much of the day napping. It all worked out though. Evidently this stage of the viral gift Lynn had bestowed upon him included a vicious headache. Unable to sleep anyway he'd been fine with sitting in the front of the Humvee staring out into the darkness.

It was a wonderfully uneventful evening. The only thing each of them had to fight all night was boredom when it became their turns to stand watch. Chris had gone as long as he could to give the other two more time to sleep. He felt like that was fair since he planned on sleeping while they drove in the morning anyway. Ortega had spent his time staring into the darkness thinking through their plan. He'd thought of a flaw that he decided to fill them in on as they were getting ready to head out the next morning.

"We're driving north looking for a city that was able to survive the plague right." Ortega stated aloud as Chris and Benson were arranging their weapons around their seatbelts in preparation for another day of random driving.

"What? Yeah." Chris answered. He wondered where Ortega was going with this.

"Any city that's survived must be pretty strict about who they let in. Right?" Ortega let the question linger.

"You're saying that Mr. Puking Everywhere with the bite scars on his arm won't be welcomed with open arms?" Benson tossed out when it occurred to her where Ortega was going with all of this.

"It's worked out ok so far." Chris mumbled. No one bothered correcting him. It hadn't worked out smoothly so far. From being forced to ride on the roofs of RVs to having angry mobs show up to kill him the scars on his arm had been a serious inconvenience at every stop.

"What if we could cover up the scars." Ortega said. The way he said it made it seem like something Chris wasn't going to like.

"Do you mean shave them off?" Benson asked with a thoughtful expression on her face.

"Shave what off?" Chris asked.

"If we shave off the scars the skin will grow back fast based on your other cuts. It won't look like bite marks anymore." Benson answered.

"Or we could not do that." Chris responded immediately. He was perfectly willing to deal with talking his way into places with the number one sign of infection carved into his arm. That sounded way better than whatever butchery Benson and Ortega were contemplating.

It took a good ten minutes of cajoling but in the end, Chris found himself standing outside sipping out of a 'medicinal flask' Ortega produced. He was shivering slightly in the cold air. Benson quizzing him on how cold he felt and comparing his answers to what she remembered from the Twilight movies wasn't increasing his confidence in their bloody science experiment.

"Burn it or cut it off?" Ortega asked. The question was rhetorical since it wasn't like they had a blow torch with them. Not that Chris would put it past Ortega to have a way to make a flamethrower out of household implements though. You never knew with him.

"Cut it. We're going to need to cut off both bite scars. Need to do it nice and even so the skin grows back looking good. We don't want to make it look worse." Benson answered. Chris couldn't comment as he was way too busy trying to force down as much of the liquor as he could before Ortega got to sawing on him. His traveling companions had a lot more faith in his vampiric healing abilities than he did.

With mostly clean t-shirts tightly wrapped around his flayed skin Chris did his best to pass out in the back seat. His skin itched like crazy. If he ripped the bandages off, he was sure that he'd see a bunch of insects crawling around underneath them. The pain from having Ortega filet him had been somewhere between excruciating and birthing triplets without an epidural. He was only guessing on the childbirth pain of course. It wasn't like he'd be stupid enough to say anything like that in front of a woman.

In shock from the pain and well on the road to being inebriated Chris passed out before they'd even gotten back on the road. Neither Ortega nor Benson were talking much either. The butchery they'd performed on their friend had been straight out of a horror movie. They hadn't taken enough skin to make a lampshade, but they could definitely make a nightlight cover. The unpleasantness of the experience would hopefully pay off when they unwrapped the bandages and Chris had baby soft perfect skin in a few days.

"What if the quick healing doesn't kick in?" Benson asked as she navigated the debris covered road.

"Why wouldn't it?" Ortega responded inquisitively. If Benson had a solid reason for why it might not work, then an even better time to have brought that up would've been before they flayed the poor guy in the backseat.

"You saw how he kind of fizzled when he was fighting those baldies. What if he's not strong enough to take care of these this time?" Benson asked. She was making good points. Their vampire knowledge was limited to the movies they'd watched before the world took a nosedive, so it wasn't like they were sure of anything.

"I guess we'll find out. Maybe we should pick him up some antibiotics though. Just to be on the safe side." Ortega said. Now he was worried as well. They'd heated his knife up to clean it before using it as a surgical tool. It wasn't like the hood of the Humvee was a sterile environment though. A splash of vodka wasn't how surgeons generally prepped their operating areas. If Chris didn't have a juiced up immune system, he could be in trouble. It'd suck to have accidentally killed him trying to make it easier for him to survive. In a world where bite shaped scars were an acceptable reason for someone to shoot you in the head Ortega still thought they'd done the right thing attempting to cover up Chris's scars.

"We can hit the next drug store we see. Hopefully they'll have some first aid stuff still on the shelf." Benson responded. She sped up perceptibly. Why hadn't they even considered this possibility before mutilating their friend's arm? Were pain and death so pervasive now that it was causing this kind of ridiculous nonchalance? She'd have never done something this crazy to someone she cared about before all this had gone down.

The small road they were on ended at an intersection with a wider highway. Benson took a right on the highway to keep up their generally northern trajectory. It wasn't long before they found themselves rolling into downtown Galena. The small city center looked like it'd been run down long before the newest members of the hair club for men started developing appetites for the fleshy parts of other people. Having had a head start on looking run down gave the city a real apocalyptic aura.

Eyes peeled for a pharmacy, grocery store, bunches of baldies, or armed militia they cruised through the desolate city. Other than the occasional baldie they didn't see anything of note until they were almost out of the city. Looking to her left as they passed through an intersection Benson thought she spotted a familiar sign about a block away. Slowing down and backing up she pointed out the sign to Ortega.

"First, we skin him alive then we go shopping for life saving medical supplies at the Dollar General. We're the worst friends ever." Ortega commented after looking down the street and shaking his head ruefully.

Unable to disagree with Ortega's assessment Benson turned the wheel to drive down the deserted street towards the Dollar General. Pulling into the parking lot she was doubtful they were going to find anything useful. Had it been a decade earlier and they were rolling with pockets full of dollars she wouldn't have been overly optimistic about finding what they needed. Looking at it now she almost just kept going.

The place was a total wreck. Plywood had been put up to cover the windows at some point. Portions of the plywood still hung over what was left of the windows. The rest of the wood had been ripped off. The rotting wood supported the enormous piles of moldy junk in front of the store. A bemused Benson couldn't figure out the point of looting a place if you were just going to throw the stuff that you'd gathered out into the parking lot and leave it there. Why bother?

"Alright. Let's lock him in then go check for supplies." Ortega said with minimal enthusiasm. Benson shrugged in agreement before putting the oversized jeep into park and opening her door. Observing how dark it was inside the store she reached back in and grabbed the rest of her weapons. Ortega nodded in approval and slapped in a fresh magazine himself.

"Think there's any baldies in there?" Benson asked nervously. No one in their right mind would blame somebody for being wary of hopping into that dark hole on the side of the building. Knowing their luck there was a Walgreens like a block over with all the bandages and stuff sitting right by the door.

"Really only one way to find out." Ortega answered nonchalantly. He'd already slipped into warrior mode. Benson envied how he was able to just snap into it like that. She got a stomach full of butterflies every time they had to do something like this. It was a measure of her willpower that she hadn't blasted her breakfast all over the parking lot yet. Ortega's callous response hadn't been super inspiring either.

Ortega took the lead. He approached the darkened hole at an angle shining his beam of light into the mounds of merchandise littering the store. Benson followed a few steps behind him. In addition to looking for movement in the store she was also responsible for making sure no threats snuck up on them from behind. She'd also just had the brilliant idea of checking the piles of discarded products she was stepping on to see if maybe there were some first aid kits or a bottle of hydrogen peroxide. Not having to step inside the store at all would make her day.

Excited by the sight of a plastic wrapped four pack of toilet paper underneath some moldy towels she yelped loudly when Ortega suddenly shot a burst of bullets into the store. Taking a second to kick the toilet paper closer to the Humvee where she could grab it later, she stepped up behind Ortega to cover the entrance to the store. Ortega was staring through the sights of his rifle. He had his flashlight held along the barrel to shine a beam of light wherever he pointed the rifle. That must be something they covered in super soldier school because Benson couldn't get that to work no matter what she did. Maybe she could snag a bungee cord or some duct tape inside the ravaged discount store to help pull off that trick.

Ortega stepped through one of the holes in the wall to enter the Dollar General. He held his hand up with his palm out to indicate he wanted Benson to remain outside. She didn't think that was a great idea, but if he wanted to walk around inside the discount haunted house all by himself then more power to him. Busying herself with watching the road while simultaneously sifting through the garbage on the ground by her feet she flinched at the sound of more gunfire from inside the store. The sudden surge of hungry howls from up and down the street were a lot more concerning though.

Taking a few steps forward Benson looked down the road. The road that was beginning to fill up with humanoid shapes staggering out of decrepit buildings. The baldies were trying to figure out where the gunfire had come from. Before she could tell Ortega to put a silencer on it, he let loose an even louder and longer outburst from inside the store. The place must be crawling with zombies.

That additional noise was more than enough to let the baldies along the street know where the party was at. The rapidly growing mob started converging on the discount store. A thoroughly freaked out Benson turned to go warn Ortega. She didn't have to go far as he was already emerging from the dark hole in the wall. He'd found a bag somewhere to make his shopping a little more convenient. Benson shouted at him that it was time to go. Without bothering to see if he'd heard her or not, she bent down and grabbed the toilet paper then made a beeline for the driver's side door.

Chapter 3: A Red Road

Ortega gripped tight to the bag full of peroxide bottles and cheap first aid kits. The inside of the Dollar General had turned into an urban warfare training exercise. More baldies had kept popping up every time he thought he'd killed them all. His adrenaline levels had been through the roof. It'd taken every bit of his extensive training to make it to the aisle with the first aid supplies. Returning to the light of day he felt pretty good about having made it out alive with some of the supplies they needed.

Benson's shouted warning was concerning. The way she sprinted for the Humvee ratcheted up that concern. Seeing the mob of baldies converging on the store threw him right back into that adrenaline fueled fight mode. He rode that fresh adrenaline rush to his seat in the Humvee before Benson could leave without him. The look on her face made it perfectly clear that if he decided to dilly dally it was on him. She had her plastic wrapped two ply and was making a break for it.

The speed at which they could evacuate the premises was going to be determined by how many baldies they could smash into before the Humvee ceased moving forward. It was hard to imagine the big machine being crippled by a crowd of naked people. It wasn't like the baldies had a bunch of explosives to hurl at them. All they had was their own flesh and bones to pit against the powerful diesel engine and armored body.

Ortega was still shutting his door when Benson tore backwards out of the parking lot. The thumps as she took out a few of the baldies were clearly audible. The Humvee shuddered from the impacts. Screeching to a stop Benson slammed the shifter into drive. Ortega's eyes grew huge as he frantically worked to get his seat belt snapped on. He was staring out at the crowded street in front them. Stretched out on the backseat Chris was going to be in for a rude awakening if Benson kept up the stunt driving. If she couldn't bash her way through the mob the awakening was going to be a whole lot ruder.

The big tires caught purchase on the concrete rocketing them into the crowd. Benson did her best to hit the mob at an angle. Within a few seconds it was almost impossible to see out the front windshield. It wasn't like they could roll down the windows and stick their heads out either. Not with the hands grasping at every part of the Humvee. Instead, Benson did her best to steer by looking between the legs of the zombie splayed out across the windshield in front of her.

Typically, if you can't see where you're going you stop until the conditions improve. In the middle of a blizzard, you don't just stomp down on the accelerator and hope for the best. Not when your windows are coated with thick ice and snow. When you hit a deer going at a decent speed it damages your vehicle. You stop and check it out to see if the vehicle is still drivable. All of these things were flashing through Benson's mind as she blindly smashed her way through the zombie parade on main street.

Expecting the Humvee to grind to a stop at any second Benson was elated when they began hitting the infected less frequently. She almost blurted out something positive to Ortega along the lines of having made it through the thick of it. Not wanting to tempt fate she kept her mouth shut though. Slowing down slightly she looked out her side window to try to keep them near the middle of the road. She had Ortega staring between the legs of the baldie on his side to see if there was anything in front of them.

"Anything in front of us?" Benson asked. She was hoping for confirmation that they weren't driving through the middle of a zombie marathon anymore.

"I don't see anything. Not that I can actually see anything. Whatever gross shit's leaking out of this dead guy's not transparent." Ortega answered.

"What's going on?" Chris asked from the backseat.

"Go back to sleep." Benson snapped. Lowering her voice, she turned to Ortega. "I need you to jump out and pull the bodies off the windshield. I need to be able to see. Be careful. I think the one on my side's still alive." Feeling bad about making Ortega take on the dangerous but necessary chore by his lonesome Benson stopped the Humvee. No real reason to put it off. The longer she was driving around blind the more likely they'd run into something that'd bring their little joyride to a halt.

Mumbling something that included a lot of vulgar anatomical terms Ortega threw his door open and stepped out of the vehicle. Chris watched open mouthed from the backseat as Ortega dragged the first body off the windshield and let it fall to the ground. The other zombie was writhing around as it tried to get at the prey it could smell coming towards it. Not wanting to cause a commotion by shooting the baldie Ortega pulled it down far enough to stab it in the heart a few times. The cold professionalism with which he accomplished the task was as terrifying as any baldie attack.

Back on the road Benson dodged a handful of the infected that caught up with them and made her way back to the highway. As they were leaving Galena behind, they saw a sign telling them they were going to be entering Empire City. Ortega began cussing out the entire state of Kansas. He would've kept going indefinitely except Benson was familiar with the area. When he paused for a breath, she interrupted his poetic profanity to let him know Empire City was more of a suburb really.

Ortega cursed on autopilot for a few more minutes before gradually becoming less animated. Chris was kind of disappointed. He'd been enjoying the skillful use of Ortega's extensive knowledge of profanity to describe a state. The creative way he'd worked the Wizard of Oz references into his diatribe had been truly inspired.

Empire City turned out to be a whole lot of nothing. Whoever had named it a city had been overly optimistic about its growth potential. If it did ever blossom into a more metropolitan area there was plenty of room to expand. North of the 'city' there was nothing but trees and overgrown fields for miles. Nothing but beautifully uninhabited nothingness. Benson and Ortega were loving the sight of a nice desolate highway.

Chris reminded them he existed by asking what'd happened and where they were going. That question reminded Benson that Ortega had been able to gather some supplies at the store they'd stopped at. In all of the chaos that'd ensued during their departure from the store she'd completely forgotten. Putting off telling Chris what'd happened she asked Ortega what he'd picked up as far as medical supplies. Chris perked up in the backseat at that. The places his skin had been scraped off were itching like crazy.

"You went to Dollar General for my medical supplies?" Chris asked once Ortega had found the bag.

"Yeah, your insurance seriously sucks." Ortega responded gruffly. He'd risked his life for those bottles of hydrogen peroxide. The plastic kits with the big red cross on them were just a bonus. The little plastic cases each had a handful of randomly shaped band-aids in them.

Benson pulled over to the side of the road. Not that there was so much traffic that she couldn't have just stopped right in the middle of the street. Old habits die hard. She snagged one of the first aid kits and a bottle of peroxide from Ortega and got out to look at Chris.

In the back seat Chris dutifully pulled his shirt off and let Benson unwrap the t-shirt strips duct taped over where they'd cut his skin off. Benson half-expected the wounds to be healed already. That didn't turn out to be the case. The hack job they'd done on Chris was very much evident. For scientific purposes she used her smart phone to take a picture of his wounds. If they ended up healing as miraculously as the other ones, she wanted photographic proof that she wasn't crazy. She checked the bars out of habit as she slid the phone back into her pocket. Still nada.

Ignoring Chris's squirming Benson poured hydrogen peroxide over the wounds. In the world they lived in discomfort wasn't something anyone cared about. A handful of pain pills had replaced brushing your teeth in most people's morning routines. Life was going to suck when the ibuprofen ran out. Benson waited for the peroxide to dry off then slapped on a bunch of the oddly shaped bandages and called it a day.

Looking down at the bandages Chris thanked her even though he was thinking the t-shirt had done a better job of covering everything. He'd hoped to see a lot more improvement in his wounds as well. He hadn't been able to hide his disappointment at the sight of his butchered skin when Benson had pulled off the makeshift bandages. What good was it to be a super being with super healing if it only worked every once in a while? Once again, he found himself with questions that only Lynn could answer.

The road they were on went from a two lane to a no lane. Benson began looking for a wide enough space to turn around. The dirt road turned into a driveway that led them out into a homestead. Glancing around Benson noted a few nice-looking houses and a big barn. It looked like a rich dude's ranch. Benson was thinking how nice it must've been to be able to live this kind of life when a handful of men with hunting rifles walked out to block her from turning around.

"Ok." Benson said as she put the Humvee into park.

"I got this." Ortega said. He started to open his door to step out and have a conversation with the locals.

"Armored Humvee." Benson reminded Ortega. In other words, those hunting rifles might as well be sling shots. They could just drive right out of there. Benson could easily scatter the shooters by rolling right through the middle of them. Something she had zero problem doing.

"That'd be the smart way to do it. We need some intel though. Go ahead and let me out. If they kill me run over a few of them on the way out of here." Ortega said grimly. Watching the tense exchange from the backseat Chris could tell Ortega wasn't super concerned about the armed amateurs outside.

"You sure?" Benson asked.

"I've been dropped off with people way scarier than these losers." Ortega answered with a shrug. The biggest badass in the world could be brought down by a bullet fired by the biggest wimp in the world. Life wasn't fair. Ortega wasn't either. Which was why he didn't have a problem stepping up to these morons trying to ambush them.

Benson stopped the car in front of the line of men aiming rifles at them. She was actually impressed that they'd managed to pile out of the surrounding houses quickly enough to threaten the Humvee. She wondered how often the people living here had actually had to defend their position. She doubted they'd ever gone up against someone at the top of the food chain like Ortega. This should be interesting.

"How ya'll doing?" Ortega asked as he advanced on the men aiming rifles at his face. He didn't display the slightest sign of fear. In the backseat of the Humvee Chris felt his blood boil. He wanted nothing more than to see these local yokels lying face down in a puddle of their own blood. If any of the bastards outside pulled the trigger on Ortega, then they'd have him to deal with. Not that he had the slightest doubt Ortega could handle himself.

"Put your rifle on the ground and drop to your knees." The man in charge of the impromptu roadblock ordered loudly.

"How about you put your weapons down and kiss my ass?" Ortega answered diplomatically. He hadn't pulled out a weapon yet. His rifle was hanging from a sling where he could get to it quickly though. The body armor he had on would be a lot more useful if bullets started flying than the western wear the guys facing off with him were wearing.

"I'm not going to tell you again." The man said in a loud, frustrated tone of voice.

"Good. Once was more than enough. My name's Ortega. I'm an actual soldier. If you don't stop pointing those weapons at me, I'm going to start thinking you want to fight. My girl behind me in the bulletproof vehicle wanted to just drive over you all and leave. I was hoping you could fill us in on what's been going on around here." Ortega stood still waiting for them to lower their weapons. At some point during his short speech, he'd swung the automatic assault rifle he was wearing into his hands.

"Or you could just leave." The man answered. None of the men had made a move to lower their weapons.

"Whatever. We'll leave. Guess you guys already know what's going on out in the world and don't want to hear about what we've seen." Ortega said backing towards the passenger door to the Humvee.

"You'll leave on foot without your guns. I need you to leave all your equipment here. Be happy we're letting you leave alive." The man said stepping forward. Seeing Ortega backing away had emboldened him.

Ortega let go of his rifle, so it swung back to his side. The man bossing the pack of would-be bandits around smiled and brought the stock of his rifle into his shoulder a little tighter. His mouth opened to tell Ortega to drop his rifle on the ground yet again. His mouth closed as a small round object flew through the air. Ortega had casually tossed it over in the middle of the line of men. There was no need to order Ortega to the ground as he was already diving in that direction.

A couple of the men pulled their triggers sending bullets into the dirt around Ortega. One of the wildly fired rounds hit him in the body armor. It felt like Mike Tyson had sucker punched him from behind. A big bruise was a lot better than a small hole though. The panicked line of men ran around in circles. A couple had recognized the grenade for what it was. They yelled the information out to the rest of them. Not that any of them had time to take more than a couple of steps before the frag went off. Dirt and rock flew into the air as superheated pieces of metal blew outwards from the tiny bomb.

The survivors who looked up in time caught a glimpse of the brake lights on the Humvee as Ortega and party left to find a friendlier source of intel. Next time an armored car pulled into their driveway they'd be a lot nicer. Especially since the prick in charge of the ranch had eaten a frag sandwich. He wasn't getting off the ground until his band of merry men had time to bury him in it.

Chapter 4: It's Hard Finding a Good Babysitter

"We've got to find a better map." Benson said once they finally turned onto the highway. They'd been in a huge hurry to put some distance between themselves and the place where Ortega had blown up the locals. Running into dead end after dead end wasn't what they wanted to be doing right then. Especially when the dead ends were at a river, and you could see a road on the other side of the river. No wonder Dorothy had needed a tornado to take her to Oz. There sure as hell weren't any bridges where you needed them.

"Why don't we pull over at a gas station then?" Chris offered from his perch in the backseat. A frustrated Benson had been almost as fun to listen to as a pissed off Ortega. Her profanity had been more PG-13 but she'd been hilarious regardless. Her Wizard of Oz puns were on point.

"A visitors center would be perfect." Benson agreed. They needed a better map in a serious way. On top of needing to be able to exit situations quickly they desperately needed to avoid wasting gas. Every time they took a pitstop they were dumping at least a half of a jug into the tank to keep it topped off. They were going to be running out of diesel pretty soon. Humvees are not the most fuel-efficient vehicles. Benson had worked out that the one they were driving was getting about eight miles per gallon. There were units out there using hybrids but those weren't available for the armored Humvees yet. Not that any more would be rolling off the assembly line anytime soon.

"How about a crappy mini mart?" Ortega said pointing out a rundown Stop and Shop coming up on the right side of the road. The parking lot had weeds growing up through the asphalt and the windows had all been broken out. Being on a main road meant it'd been looted multiple times. The hope was that there might still be some maps or an atlas laying around somewhere. Siri had kept right on working for a good while after everything went to hell. There hadn't really been a huge need for maps until the population had been thinned out substantially.

Ortega hoped that if they made it to an uninfected city then their smart phones may become useful for more than taking pictures again. It wasn't like an earthbound zombie apocalypse had made a significant impact on the satellites circling the earth. Regular smart phones would connect to the network via towers that then ran back to switching offices that put the voice or data traffic on their network to transport. Those buildings had a finite amount of time they'd run on generator backup. Once they'd died there was no way for smartphones to connect to anything. A city that still had power should be able to keep those switching offices working. In theory that'd mean people could still use their smart phones.

Pulling into the overgrown parking lot Benson was seriously hoping this wasn't going to be another Dollar General situation. Out here in the middle of nowhere they should be ok. There wasn't any reason she could think of why a bunch of baldies would be hiding out in the decrepit mini mart. Not that anything the psychotic cannibals did made a whole lot of sense. The three of them all exited the Humvee together. Benson cringed when she saw the patchwork of band aids on Chris. There hadn't been a great way to use the generic band aids to cover the large wounds. Some of them were already falling off.

"How do you feel?" Ortega asked Chris. It was a valid question. He was as white as a ghost and wouldn't have been wobbling around much more if he'd spent the morning taking shots of tequila. If a decent breeze picked up there was a good chance it'd knock him over.

"Like complete ass. Does it matter really?" Chris asked with a smile and a shrug. He had a point. It wasn't like anyone really woke up feeling good anymore. Everyone just adjusted their pain thresholds and moved on. If your leg was sore, nobody cared. A bone visibly sticking out of your leg was ok to bring up though.

"I hear you man. Let's go risk our lives for a freaking Rand McNally." Ortega said. Putting his rifle stock up to his shoulder Ortega led the way to the mini mart. Benson and Chris followed close behind.

Ortega stepped alertly into the musty building. Chris was doing his best to shut down his new talent of identifying smells. Most of the odors drifting out of the shop weren't pleasant. It took him a second to catalogue all of the different smells.

"There're no baldies in there but there's at least one dead guy." Chris said lowering his shotgun.

"You're sure of that after a couple of sniffs?" Benson asked incredulously. Up ahead of them Ortega had turned on his selective hearing. He was fine with Chris having superpowers, but he still preferred to clear the building the old-fashioned way.

"Cleanup on aisle seven…" Ortega muttered to himself. The dead guy Chris had sniffed was no doubt dead. It looked like a dozen baldies had descended on the poor guy at once. Each of them taking a few big bites before leaving the man to bleed out on the floor. Chris being able to smell that was more curse than superpower as far as Ortega was concerned. Although if he'd been able to spare himself the image of the chewed-up corpses he'd have happily smelled first. It wasn't like he needed yet another visual to make his nightmares any more memorable.

The store had been well and thoroughly looted. All of the perishables had perished and everything useful that was left had been taken. That included all of the map books. Benson did spot a stained folding map of the state of Kansas on the ground. A good portion of it was stuck to the floor. Knowing they needed the map Benson scraped it up without putting a lot of thought into what the probable sources of the brownish red stains were.

"Got one." Benson held the map up so everyone could see it. Mission accomplished she headed for the promise of fresh air outside. As much fun as it was picking through garbage in a smelly building with a dead body in it, she was happy to be done.

Chris and Ortega followed behind her. Ortega still taking pains to keep an eye on the dark corners just in case. Chris found that he was so certain of what his senses were telling him that he felt completely confident not looking around. Thanks to the bullet to the body armor that he'd taken in the back earlier it took Ortega a little longer than usual to get in the Humvee. Benson and Chris took the opportunity to show their compassion and empathy by making jokes about how old Ortega looked trying to get in.

Ortega had finally finished climbing in when a battered minivan drove by. Caught by surprise the three of them watched as the van disappeared down the highway. Hesitantly Benson backed them out of the parking lot to follow the van. Any kind of intel they could get would be appreciated. There was some information being played on the AM bands that was interesting, but they couldn't be sure how out of date it was.

The prerecorded broadcasts had been edited to avoid giving any location information out. Anywhere that had managed to avoid the infection wasn't trying to advertise for a bunch of possibly infected people to head their way. Even if the newcomers didn't bring the plague with them, they'd still increase the number of mouths that needed to be fed. The supply chain was irreparably broken at this point. Farmers weren't loading produce into the back of trucks to be dropped off at the local grocery store.

Once on the highway Benson sped up. She'd been keeping them at a steady fifty-five miles per hour. That was a good speed to be able to react to something popping up in front of her on the road. It was also the speed at which they achieved maximum fuel efficiency. They'd decided not to try and catch up to the minivan. Ortega had already been shot once that day. If the people in the van had wanted to talk, they could've easily stopped back at the minimart.

Continuing down the highway they kept an eye out for anything that might be a clue that they were getting closer to civilization. They kept listening to the broadcasts coming in over the AM frequencies. Not that the people in charge of those broadcasts were killing themselves to get new content on the air. It was either the same old prerecorded government broadcasts or the static filled ravings of the handful of HAM operators left out there. Those crazies were taking the time to broadcast what they felt was the truth. Nobody in the Humvee could stand listening to them for more than five minutes. Thanks to Chris they actually already knew a big chunk of the unbelievable truth.

"You don't have anywhere else you want to go do you?" Chris blurted out. The question had been buzzing around in the back of his head for a while now. He knew Ortega had nowhere to go. As far as Chris knew they'd never asked Benson though.

"No. The people I cared about all died in the first or second waves. I'm right where I should be. Escorting the savior of humanity to somewhere we can use a phone to call his hot vampire lady to find out what we should do next. I guess that makes as much sense as anything else does." Benson responded.

That answer made Chris feel better. He hated just assuming that Benson wanted to be driving around risking her life with them. She'd said before that she was good with it, but Chris felt a lot better now that he'd asked the question the right way. Honestly if she'd said she had an uncle in Des Moines or whatever then he'd have been happy to go on an uncle hunt with her. It wasn't like they were accomplishing a lot now the way they were driving around without any real destination. If they didn't find some more diesel soon then they'd be walking around without any real direction which sounded infinitely worse.

"What's the map say?" Chris asked. Ortega had unfolded the map and was staring at it.

"That there's a bunch of roads in Kansas. The one we're on runs through Kansas City. We probably don't want to drive through Kansas City." Ortega answered.

"Agreed." Benson said. They'd all had their fill of big city excitement. Even the small cities were death traps. It would've been almost impossible for a place with that many people in a confined area would have been able to stay put without the population somehow getting infected.

"Is that the minivan up there?" Chris asked. Benson nodded and slowed down. Ortega was preoccupied with trying to figure out how to fold the map back up. It made Chris feel good to see that there was a task the super solider couldn't do any better than regular humans.

Giving up on ever getting the map folded correctly Ortega wadded it up into a vaguely rectangular shape and shoved it into one of the pockets on the side of his door. He joined them in staring at the minivan sitting on the side of the road. Benson had slowed way down to give them time to discuss what they wanted to do.

"We should try and talk to them, right?" Chris asked. He didn't see any harm in a little conversation. Especially not when they were riding high in a bulletproof battle machine. If they couldn't handle a couple of civilians in a minivan, then they might as well give up right now.

Ortega grunted in assent when Benson said she thought they should play it by ear. If the minivan folk wanted to talk then that was great. If they didn't want to talk then that was also great. The bigger question was around why the van was pulled over anyway. Odds were it'd either broken down or run out of gas. It'd looked pretty rough when they'd seen it drive past them earlier. Did they really want to stop and chit chat with a crew that may be looking for a new vehicle? Did they want to end up with possibly infected strangers crowding into the Humvee with them?

A middle-aged woman with her hair pulled back into a vicious ponytail glanced up at them from under the hood of the van. She had on thick gloves like you'd use in the garden to pull weeds. Not a bad idea when you're messing around under the hood of a car with no idea what all the gizmos and doo hickeys are for. Benson stopped the Humvee next to her and looked over with a smile. Ortega had already rolled his window down. He waved at her and asked her if she needed anything.

"I think I might need a jump. I pulled over to check on my baby and then this piece of crap van wouldn't start back up. I have gas." The woman said after a long pause. Her long inspection must not have turned up anything she found suspicious since she was ok with them getting out and helping her. Not that she had much of a choice. Ortega had already clocked the Glock she had hanging off her hip. It didn't concern him much. A single woman with a baby out here in all this mess. It would've been a lot weirder if she didn't have a way to defend herself.

"The United States government was kind enough to load this bad boy down with all kinds of tools. Happy to give you a jump." Ortega responded with a friendly smile.

The woman smiled back as Ortega exited the Humvee to go search in the back for jumper cables. Benson climbed out to take a look at the engine and see what she could learn from the lady.

"Hi, I'm Jenn how are you? Just you and your baby?" Benson asked. Staring at the engine never really accomplished anything. She'd typically ask the woman to go try and start it up but wanted to see if she could get her to talk first. It wasn't like any of them were in a huge hurry.

Chris felt sick so he had his window rolled down. It made him feel like a really bad friend that he'd been calling Benson by her last name this whole time. At some point she'd told him her first name and he'd instantly forgotten it. She was going to always be Benson to him. He'd thought at first that Benson was using a fake name in case the woman was a spy or something. Determined not to forget this bit of personal info he continued listening to Benson chat up the woman.

The woman was named Ashley. It was just her and her baby. She was coming from a little tent camp outside of Sheldon, Missouri. The infected had shown up in force one morning forcing everyone to scatter in a hurry. She didn't have a real destination in mind. She was just driving until she could find another refugee camp. Preferably one that someone had figured out how to make sustainable. Life on the road was no fun at all.

Her daughter, Baylee, was in the middle row of seats in the minivan strapped into a car seat. Ashley was insistent no one get near the girl. She was paranoid lest the toddler breathe in someone's contaminated breath and end up a baldie. As far as fears went that one seemed pretty rational to Chris. "Following the science" had never worked out well for the average American. Not when financially motivated researchers skewed the results in whichever direction best filled their bank accounts.

Benson and Ashely continued chatting while Ortega hooked up the heavy-duty jumper cables that he'd located in the trunk. Getting back in the Humvee he started it up and waited while Ashley did the same. The minivan's engine stuttered to life on her third attempt. Ashely thanked them profusely before getting in her van and driving away.

"We're not going to ask her to come with us?" Chris asked when Benson and Ortega both got back in the Humvee. It seemed unchivalrous to Chris to let the mom and daughter duo disappear into the dangerous world. They could easily have asked them to follow the Humvee so they could all stick together.

"I think she wants to be alone." Benson said. She'd tried to steer the conversation towards where Ashley was trying to get to a few times and been shut down. Her assumption was that Ashely was paranoid about being around people. Something must've happened to make her that way.

"I'd want to be alone too if I had a baby baldie in my van." Ortega commented. That shut everyone up. The gloves Ashley had been wearing suddenly made a lot more sense.

Chapter 5: A Penny for your Thoughts

After another night in the Humvee, they got back on the road. Chris still felt horrible from the pharmaceutical cocktail Lynn had shot him up with. It was like the opposite of a flu shot. He was doing his miserable best to learn how to cope with constantly being sick. How Lynn was able to run sideways on walls while always looking like a super model was beyond him. He felt more like a model for Nyquil.

At least they'd been able to find some extra fuel when they passed through Fort Scott. There'd been a couple of pumps by a building where all the service vehicles were parked. Someone had even conveniently pumped a bunch of jugs full of diesel and left them appropriately labeled. All the regular gas was gone. They'd strapped a couple of jugs to the roof of the Humvee when they ran out of room in the trunk. Too much fuel was a great problem to have. None of them had been willing to leave a single drop of the precious liquid behind.

Ortega had spent his watch studying the map to plan out where they should go. He walked the rest of them through his ideas once they'd started moving. He'd boiled it down to a few key variables that he thought would be necessary for a place to still be standing. Basically, it needed to be a military base or have a heavy military presence and there needed to be some form of natural barrier. A service academy would be perfect since it'd be full of young military people who didn't have families. Loved ones were the Achilles heel of secure locations.

"Annapolis? West Point?" Chris asked.

"Those are both on the East Coast. We'll need more gas." Benson said.

"We've got plenty of gas. Fort Leavenworth's right up the road. They have a service academy there with a big river right next to it. We just need to detour around Overland Park and Kansas City. Big cities scare the hell out of me. I don't want anything to do with an Albuquerque part two." Ortega said. Chris agreed. They'd barely made it out of Albuquerque alive.

"Isn't that where all the gold is?" Chris asked. Leavenworth was ringing a bell for some reason. His massive headache was keeping him from remembering what it was though. On the plus side his body seemed to be limiting itself to only one thing being horribly wrong with him at a time. That was a welcome development.

"That's Fort Knox. Leavenworth is where the prison is." Benson answered absently.

"So, we're going to a military jail and that's supposed to be the place where the people have more discipline than your average civilian?" Chris asked. Ortega had spent a good bit of time explaining his reasoning on why a military town was better a than a town full of civilians. More discipline meant less chance of an outbreak. Even if the prisoners were more disciplined than civilian prisoners, they were still people who'd done something wrong. You don't find the cream of the crop in the brig.

"The answer is yes. I checked the map and Leavenworth is definitely on the way to where we're going." Ortega said in a huff. He had a point. They didn't have anywhere else in mind so why not Leavenworth? At least Ortega had come up with some criteria. Chris had been all about driving north and looking for some sort of sign that'd take them to where they needed to go. He was picturing red spray paint on an overpass telling them to take the next exit if they wanted to live.

When Overland Park started getting too close for comfort, they pulled off the highway and hit the backroads. Ortega navigated as Benson took them down the neglected back country blacktop. They passed a few expensive looking housing developments. Other than a badly sunburnt baldie handcuffed to a motorcycle they didn't see anyone. They amused themselves for a little while coming up with reasons why the baldie might have been left handcuffed to a motorcycle for all time. The stories stopped when Chris pointed out they probably should've mercy killed the poor bastard. None of them cared enough to turn around but it took the wind out of their sails as far as joking about it.

The road was straight and boring. Nothing but overgrown fields and equally spaced intersections. Ortega did his best to guide them based off the folding map. It didn't give him much intel about the countryside though. His main job as navigator was to keep them as far as possible from the larger cities shown on the map. As far as the smaller cities and towns he didn't see a problem with blowing through those. For all they knew one of those may turn out to be the place they were looking for.

Barely able to think around his pounding headache Chris gingerly scratched his itchy arms. Benson had removed the band aids earlier to check on the wounds. She'd been impressed with how much they'd healed already. It wasn't the same level of super healing his shoulder had shown but it looked pretty good. She'd wrapped the wounds with strips cut from a t-shirt after dousing the wounds in peroxide. The homemade bandages she put together were about a million times better than the garbage they'd gotten at the Dollar General. Those cheap Band-Aid alternatives either fell off within minutes or stuck like crazy glue. The ones Benson had to pull off took every hair along with them.

When they got closer to Leavenworth, they were going to find a place to chill out until Chris's skin started looking good. They'd been hoping it'd already be there. Hollywood vampires who could wake up looking as good as new after having half their faces burnt off the night before had set a standard that Chris wasn't living up to.

Chris was starting to notice other things though. The changes were subtle. They were hard for him to pinpoint because once they were there, they felt like they'd always been there. The most obvious change so far had been the enhanced sense of smell. Even there though he couldn't tell if he could magically smell better or if he was just interpreting and cataloguing the smells more clearly. Had the shot made his nostrils bigger or heightened the sensitivity of the receptors in his brain that handled smell? Even with the waves of nausea and crushing headaches he could feel himself getting stronger. Not superhero strong but stronger than he'd been before.

Chris was beginning to suspect that this version of vampirism wasn't going to include everything on the brochure. Lynn had called the drug she'd given him an enhancer. The drug was just enhancing whatever genetic gifts Chris already had. The big one being that he should be able to live for hundreds of years now. He wasn't overly excited about that one. The way everything was going he'd be lucky if he survived the week. It wasn't like being able to find his way around in total darkness was a significant superpower. He'd trade his night 'vision' in a heartbeat for some sort of anti-headache power.

Coming close to matching Chris's vision on how they were going to locate survivors a large sign posted in front of a gated community they were cruising past warned them to keep out. They were due for a pitstop anyway, so Benson pulled over near the gate. Ortega hopped out quickly having drank most of a gallon jug of water he'd purified and added lemon flavoring to. Unzipping his pants as he walked, he came close to taking a dive when he tripped on the stop sticks running across the road.

The sharp steel spikes would've ripped the tires to shreds if Benson had pulled up much further. These folks were serious about the no solicitation rule. The spikes had been partially buried by the leaves covering the drive leading up to the security gate. Ortega continued looking around after he finished his bathroom break. He really needed to get his addiction to lemonade flavored water under control. Not only did he spend way too much time whizzing it was also going to suck big time when the world ran out of it.

End of the world and he was worried about running out of Crystal Lite packets. Ortega shook his head back and forth with a grin. If running out of the refreshing lemon flavoring was the worst thing that happened to him then he was doing pretty good. Looking closer at the gate he saw that it extended into a ten-foot brick wall on either side. There were a couple of cameras around the tops of the wall. Ortega walked over to see if the cameras were operational. With that tall stone wall running around the neighborhood there was a chance this may be one of the places that'd survived.

"Return to your vehicle and leave. Do not pull forward. Leave immediately or you will be killed." The tinny voice was coming from an outdoor speaker by the guard shack.

Ortega motioned for Benson and Chris to get in the Humvee but kept walking towards the guard shack himself. The voice spouted out the same warning again. Once again Ortega ignored it. He looked around to see if he could find the man delivering the threats. With the setup he was seeing the guy could be anywhere though.

"We're not here to bother anyone. We have supplies and would be willing to trade for access to a phone line." Ortega said loudly hoping there was a microphone somewhere that'd pick up what he was saying. There was a key entry gate box set into the concrete that had an intercom button on it. Maybe he could try pressing that?

"Leave immediately or die. There are claymore mines aimed in your direction that I can set off at the push of a button. The only reason you and your friends are still alive is I don't want to make a bunch of noise. If you're not out of here in ten seconds I'm going to go ahead and blow you all to hell." The no nonsense voice was back. Now that Ortega had been told what to look for, he spotted the tell-tale signs of the explosives hidden in the bushes by the fence. Ortega decided the bodiless voice wasn't bluffing. It was time to go.

"Make sure you backup without pulling forward." Ortega advised Benson once he'd climbed in. Benson nodded. She'd noted the spikes already. A big part of her training as a driver in war zones concerned spotting anything abnormal on the road. She'd known something didn't look right when she pulled in. That's why she'd stopped closer to the road than the gate.

Annoyed that they weren't being given a chance to make their case they left the expensive looking subdivision to continue on their way. It was a real eye opener though. How many of the other places they'd driven by were still populated? How many other neighborhoods had united together to survive? A group of people who'd made it this far would know better than to let any outsiders in. That was going to be a problem.

"We'll have a better chance of getting in on a military base. They'll have protocols for incoming refugees and military units." Ortega said. He was fuming over being denied access to that last neighborhood. How a bunch of suburbanites had gotten their hands on claymores was a story he'd love to hear one day.

They rumbled through a desolate looking city and then over a bridge that was holding up pretty well all things considered. Travel was going to become a real pain in the ass once the bridges started collapsing. It was a little surprising that the bridges hadn't all been blown up or blocked off to try and stop the spread of the infection. Of course, the infection had spread everywhere before anyone even knew about it, so it would've been akin to closing the barn door after the horses were out. Not that anyone had known that when all of this started though.

Passing around a box of really stale Cheerios they continued on towards Leavenworth. Benson was keeping up a moderate speed knowing that they were going to have to stop and rest up for a day or two before presenting themselves at the base. That should give Chris's skin time to heal. If his super healing didn't kick in, then they might be spending more like a month sitting around somewhere. She didn't much care one way or the other. The idea of sitting around a cabin beside a lake somewhere actually sounded pretty chill. Better than driving into a base full of convicts anyway.

They drove in silence. Only occasionally speaking up if they saw something in the road or a baldie coming towards them. Otherwise, each of them spent the time lost in their own thoughts. There was a lot to consider. Two of them were driving around with someone who was slowly be turning into a vampire. Chris was spending a lot of time analyzing every emotion, feeling, and sensation to try and understand what it meant to be turning into a vampire.

So far, he couldn't say that he recommended turning into a genetically enhanced superhuman. Not unless you were really into nausea and headaches. His new powers kept stacking up in interesting ways. If the others found out about his nighttime navigational prowess, they'd happily put him in charge of gathering firewood every night. Some things were best kept secret.

Chapter 6: An Apocalyptic Getaway

Through some random stroke of good fortune, they stumbled across a massive log cabin overlooking a pristine lake. Driving up a one lane road that turned off of the highway Benson had expected to find a couple of mobile homes nestled in the woods off the gravel coated dirt road. Instead, there was a huge cabin on top of a hill. She hadn't even known that you could build cabins as big as this one was. It looked like the kind of place a CEO would host a corporate retreat. They could easily fit thirty people and still have plenty of room to do random team building junk.

"Please don't let this place be full of baldies." Benson said putting the Humvee in park. Tall weeds covered the driveway. Nature was working overtime to reclaim the picturesque resort. A few more spins around the sun and it'd just be another big pile of rotting wood in a weed filled clearing.

"You just jinxed us." Ortega commented. He knocked on the wooden stock of his assault rifle to mediate the jinx. None of them made a move to get out of the Humvee. It was nice and bullet proof. There could be people using this place as their post-apocalyptic party pad. Those people may be willing to shoot trespassers without any warning. After ten minutes of staring to see if any curtains moved Ortega opened his door and got out.

Shielding his body with the armored door Ortega continued to scan the cabin for any sign it was inhabited. When he didn't see anything after another five minutes of monitoring the place he motioned for Benson and Chris to get out.

"Clear the cabin?" Chris asked hesitantly. The cabin was huge. Clearing it was going to take forever. Even if the cabin turned out to be devoid of men or monsters trying to kill them, he'd still have to endure hours of Ortega criticizing his clearing technique.

"I was thinking we'd use your super sniffer to declare the place safe or not." Ortega responded. He'd still clear everything himself afterwards. Chris's clearing technique was painful to watch. Not to mention all the times he'd looked up to see Chris accidentally pointing his rifle at him or Benson.

The whole operation turned out to be very anticlimactic. The interior of the cabin was spotless. Whatever corporate boondoggle had been held there most recently had been followed by an army of professional cleaners. It was so clean that Ortega felt a little guilty about having gotten broken glass all over the foyer when he was breaking in. While Chris was sniffing around, Ortega went and got a dustpan to clean up the mess. Benson thought that was hilarious.

"This place is the bee's knees." Benson announced once they'd confirmed no murderers were lurking in any of the rooms.

"Bee's knees?" Chris asked with a raised eyebrow.

"No clue. Heard it in an old gangster movie. Always thought it sounded cool. This place is totally the bee's knees." Benson said doubling down on the archaic saying. She'd seen a lot of old movies growing up. Her parents had died in a car crash when she was a baby leaving her grandparents to raise her. Her granddad was a huge fan of the roaring 20's. Her nana used to tease him that it was because he liked watching the flappers dance.

"This place is pretty bad ass. Maybe we just stay here for a while." Chris said.

Neither Benson nor Ortega rushed to argue with that idea. The oversized mountain mansion was a gift from God. It was one of the few buildings they'd seen lately without any signs of disease or death in it. There was even a landing down by the water with a pontoon boat. A small bait ship stood next to the dock. It looked to be equipped with everything they'd need to do some serious fishing. Not to mention the rack full of shotguns they could see through the window. Those were probably intended for skeet shooting but a little extra firepower was always welcome.

As if all that wasn't enough to justify Chris wanting to call this place home, they'd made a really pleasant discovery when they went downstairs. A big room in the basement was stuffed with food. The food was all canned or dried so would last for a while. The stove in the kitchen ran off of propane. The big tank outside was at 100% capacity based on the meter. There were even solar panels on the roof. The place was perfect. It was way more than any of them would've dared to hope for. They lugged in enough weaponry to fend off a small army before settling in to spend their first night

That first night spent in an oversized suite with a dazzling view of the lake below turned into days. It was the most relaxed any of them could remember being. They spent their days watching movies from an impressive DVD collection downstairs. Chris's skin was growing back nicely. By the end of the first week at the cabin, you could only tell where his arm had been carved up if you knew exactly where to look. Even then it was just a slightly higher ridge of flesh. Nothing anyone would point out as a recent injury.

"When do you think we should head over to check out the base?" Chris asked. Him and Ortega had walked down to the little bait shop to grab supplies.

They'd broken into the small building by the dock the first day they'd been there. It was more of a shack than a building. The lock on the door had given in immediately to Ortega's front kick. Inside the shack they'd found the keys to the pontoon boat, a credit card machine, snacks and soda, fishing poles, lures, shotguns, and shells. Not to mention a bunch of other miscellaneous items crammed in on the shelves. Basically, anything that could be sold to rich tourists looking to spend a few hours getting pictures of themselves communing with nature to post on their social media accounts.

"You in a hurry to die?" Ortega asked.

"Not really. I just want to get in touch with Lynn somehow. I need to find out what's happening to me. What other changes might be on the way." Chris responded.

"When you get to a certain age hair starts growing everywhere. Its natural." Ortega said with a grin. He would've kept going but he saw that Chris wasn't in the mood.

"Yeah. I figured out the birds and bees a while back. What no one's told me about is why I can suddenly tell if someone's hiding nearby by taking a couple whiffs of the air. Or why I'm able to walk around in a dark room by listening to where the walls are." Chris said.

"Listening to where the walls are?" Ortega asked. What the hell? The seasoned sniper in him loved the idea of being able to do that though. Maybe he needed to go get himself a shot of Lynn's special sauce.

"Yeah. Makes it super convenient when I have to take a piss at three in the morning." Chris joked. A second later he was serious again. "You know I haven't really been hungry since we got here."

"I've seen you eat." Ortega said arching an eyebrow. He was looking at Chris with real concern now. In a world where you never knew where your next meal was coming from someone losing their appetite was unheard of.

"I eat a few bites, but I don't really feel like I need it." Chris answered the unspoken question.

"You don't have like a hankering to bite my neck, do you?" Ortega asked.

"Maybe if you shaved and put some makeup on." Chris answered.

"Yeah, but do you?" Ortega asked curiously. If Chris was turning into a vampire straight out of every vampire movie Ortega had ever seen, then this seemed like a conversation they should be having. Better to find out now than when Chris started levitating outside his window at night.

"I can smell everybody's blood now. Infected blood smells horrible for some reason. Regular peoples blood smells good though. Like if someone handed me a mug full of warm blood with no chunky stuff in it then it might happen. I don't have any urge to rip your neck apart though. At least not yet." Chris said thoughtfully.

"I'd appreciate a heads up if you do start getting those urges." Ortega responded. He looked at Chris for another few seconds before dropping the subject. There wasn't much they could do about it now. Chris was right. Eventually they needed to try and find out what was going on with him. That was going to require leaving this perfect little setup. Preferably before Chris started looking at them like they were giant Capri Suns.

They spent a few hours in the pontoon boat fishing around an island in the middle of the lake. The lake was really just an extra wide section of a river. The fish practically jumped in their boat every time they cast out a line. Fresh fish tacos were going to be on the menu. Or at least they were if Benson knew how to make tortillas out of the bags of flour in the oversized pantry. Neither Chris nor Ortega had a clue. Worst case they'd be frying up some fresh fish to eat on top of rice instead. It was going to be a million times better than risking botulism by eating random canned food from burnt-out gas stations.

Benson was sitting on a rocking chair on the wraparound porch when they returned. They'd already cleaned and fileted the fish. Benson was doing her best to see what it was they had in the bucket Chris was carrying.

"Men bring back meat." Chris said in his best cave man impression. Benson was salivating at the idea of fresh food. So much so that she didn't even bother pointing out that all they'd done was go fishing. He should save the macho act for when they took down a bear or something.

"Do you know how to make tortillas? There's flour in the pantry. I think you mix it with lard and water or something.... There's a rolling pin involved..." Ortega had been around people making flour tortillas his entire childhood. He wished he'd paid more attention in the kitchen now.

"It's pretty easy. You drive to the grocery store and pick a bag of the ones you want right off the shelf. You thinking low carb or wheat? Do I look like Betty Crocker to you?" Benson answered with her typical sarcasm.

"I already asked Chris and he definitely doesn't look like Betty Crocker. We were thinking fish tacos. Since none of us know how to make tortillas maybe just barbequed fish on rice?" Ortega asked. That seemed to assuage Benson.

"Go grill the fish. I'll make the tortillas." Benson spun on her heel and went back in the cabin. Her rifle swinging from the strap on her shoulder as she did so. Even here they kept up the habit of going fully armed everywhere outside of the shower.

An hour later they were sitting at a big wooden table on the wrap around porch. Two bottles of expensive wine sat uncorked in the middle of the table. The fish tacos had come out unbelievably good. None of them spoke for the first fifteen minutes after they'd sat down. All of them too involved in making delighted noises every time they took a bite of the taco or a swig of the fancy wine. Chris found himself enjoying the meal despite not really being hungry. It was more about the camaraderie for him.

Ortega scarfed down the last of his food and took a big swig of wine out of a fancy glass goblet he'd snagged for himself. Chris could feel the attention settling on him from the special forces soldier. At least Ortega should be in a really good mood. A full belly and plenty of booze with a fairly safe place to spend the night. What else could a man ask for? It turned out a man could ask for the tacos sitting untouched on Chris's plate. Ortega split Chris's extras with Benson.

"Your stomach still all whacked?" Benson asked Chris. She was doing her best not to devour the taco until she was positive Chris didn't want it.

"He doesn't get hungry anymore." Ortega said around a mouthful of tortilla blanketed fish.

"Huh?" Benson asked looking at Chris for confirmation. Her extra taco sat untouched on her plate. Chris went through the explanation he'd given Ortega earlier. Benson was slightly more empathetic. Neither of Chris's travelling companions were going to win any bedside manner awards anytime soon. Halfway through his explanation Benson had started munching on the taco. She was staring at him like he was the season finale of her favorite show. There weren't a lot of entertainment options available.

"That's why we have to get out of here and head over to Leavenworth." Ortega said once Chris was done answering Benson's questions. That hadn't taken too long since he didn't have a lot of answers. Other than the odd new talents he'd picked up and not being very hungry he didn't feel any different. Benson had made him smile to prove that he wasn't growing in a set of fangs. That'd probably been the wine working on her more than an actual concern that he was sprouting canines.

"When should we go?" Benson asked. Chris loved that she didn't hesitate. Both her and Ortega could easily put off his concerns to hang out in this slice of baldie free paradise a little longer.

"Let's give it a few more days at least. We can check every day to make sure we can still see his reflection in a mirror. The slightest transparency and we leave immediately. I'm willing to risk death for more fish tacos." Ortega answered.

"This wine doesn't suck either." Benson agreed.

Chris continued sipping at his glass of wine. They'd gotten into the bourbon the night before and he'd discovered yet another change to his metabolism. Fear of a massive hangover kept him from experimenting too much, but it appeared he'd gone from being a lightweight to a Mike Tyson caliber drinker. The bourbon had given him a slight buzz that went away almost immediately. He'd woken up feeling fine despite going shot for shot with Ortega.

The conversation continued through another two bottles of wine before winding down. With full stomachs and wine fueled buzzes Ortega and Benson locked themselves in the upstairs bedroom and quickly fell asleep. Chris sat up long after Ortega started snoring to stare out the window overlooking the lake. It was hard to sleep with all the thoughts rattling around in his head. He'd also found sleep was like eating now. It was nice but he didn't feel like he really needed much of it. Until he did of course. Then he was a world class sleeper. Yet something else to ask about if Lynn ever showed back up.

Chapter 7: A Deal's a Deal

"Why couldn't the damned phones work? Do you know how easy this would be if the stupid phones would just work?" Benson had tried every phone in the house at least twice. Praying for dial tone she'd been sorely disappointed each time. She'd painstakingly searched the cabin to see if she could find a sat phone hidden away somewhere. Living out in the middle of nowhere the caretakers might've wanted a backup way to communicate in case some psychos cut their phone lines. Considering how ritzy the place was she didn't think finding a backup sat phone was out of the realm of possibility. Admitting defeat after an hours long search, she'd begrudgingly gathered her gear together for the trek to Leavenworth.

"That would've been too easy." Ortega answered. He had his window rolled down. He'd have to roll it up soon to be safe from random baldie attacks. For right now though he wanted to feel the cool air hitting his face.

Sitting in the back again Chris kept quiet. He'd woken up feeling ok for the first time since Lynn had dosed him up. His friends were risking their lives to help him find out what was going on with his body. For the first time in a while, he felt like he had things to be thankful for. Basking in those good feelings he leaned back and listened as Ortega and Benson continued their friendly banter. Driving away from the safety of the secluded cabin meant that the real world would rise up to bite them in the ass soon enough.

They made it back down the long winding driveway to the blacktop easily enough. The driveway had washed out a little more since they'd first come down it. The powerful war jeep didn't have any issues slogging through a few oversized mud puddles though. Not with a trained and experienced driver like Benson behind the wheel. Ortega was an excellent back seat driver as well. He was full of helpful advice that was mostly ignored. Chris smirked watching the two of them arguing like an old married couple.

Turning towards the road that'd take them to Leavenworth everything still seemed ok. It was smooth sailing right up until they spotted a group of vehicles approaching them. A trio of brightly colored F-150s loaded down with armed men. The trucks slowed when they saw the Humvee approaching. Benson and Ortega had a quick discussion about the best way to handle it. In the end they decided to keep driving and hope for the best. It wasn't like they had a lot of choices. By the time they could turn around to make a run for it the trucks would be on top of them anyway.

The trucks slowed as they got closer. The drivers spread out to block off the road. They didn't leave any room for the Humvee to pass them. Benson was getting worried. She'd assumed the pickups belonged to a bunch of random refugees. The smooth way they'd executed the mobile blockade didn't appear amateurish to her though. She tapped the brakes until they came to a complete stop and waited to see what the trucks would do next.

The three trucks pulled forward to park in a loose triangle around the Humvee. The men in the truck beds trained their rifles on them. Ortega scanned the trucks to figure out who was in charge. He was hoping they could talk their way out of this. If not, they could always ram their way out. Those rifles wouldn't do much more than screw up the paint job on the armored beast they were in.

"Rocket!" Chris yelled from the backseat. He'd been keeping an eye on the truck parked behind them. A man had stood up in the back of it with an RPG held up to his shoulder. The sight of that weapon being pointed at them had turned Chris's knees to Jell-O. He'd seen what those little missiles could do back in Albuquerque.

"They're gonna tell us to get out or die. If we get out, they'll kill us anyway." Ortega provided his assessment like he was delivering a book report. No real emotion. He was in super soldier mode. His whole demeanor had changed. Gone was the joke telling, bourbon swilling, fishing buddy. The man causally holding his rifle up in the passenger seat now was cold, analytical, and deadly as hell.

"Screw that." Benson said. She flipped the gear shifter into reverse and slammed her booted foot down hard on the gas. The armored machine flew backwards into the pickup truck behind them. The one with the man holding the RPG. There was the sound of tortured metal and breaking glass as the much heavier Humvee shunted the pickup to the side. One of the pickup trucks in front of them exploded. The rocket guy must not have been good at aiming while somersaulting through the air.

Benson spun the wheel as a hailstorm of bullets pounded their hood. The men in the remaining truck had opened fire as soon as she'd hit the gas. The men who'd gotten out of the truck were all jumping back in now to pursue them. The Humvee's windshield was pockmarked with white marks where bullets had struck. The windshield was still intact though.

"Let me out." Ortega said calmly.

Benson looked at him like he was crazy but brought the Humvee to a complete stop. Ortega hopped out immediately. Bracing his rifle on the doorframe he began sending rounds down range. The F-150 accelerating towards them didn't have bulletproof windows. The driver took a bullet in his forehead. The truck swerved then came to an abrupt stop in the ditch after throwing the men who'd been in the back out onto the road.

Ortega walked over to the men laying on the ground and kicked their weapons away from them. Not really having the time to screw around with securing them he casually put a bullet in each of their forearms. He left those guys moaning on the hot asphalt and walked over to the ditch. Over at the ditch he quickly executed everyone in the cab of the wrecked truck. He glanced over towards the truck that'd caught the random rocket. There didn't appear to be much of a need to check in on the occupants of that barbequed hunk of deformed metal.

Realizing he should be helping versus spectating Chris grabbed his rifle and climbed out the door. Benson opened her mouth to warn him to be careful then shut it again. Chris was a big boy. He'd proven he could take care of himself. That'd been against baldies though. Guys with guns were a whole other thing.

Benson took her seatbelt off to join her comrades. Directly in front of her Ortega was asking Chris to guard the two men laid out on the road. Benson stepped out of the driver's seat to help Ortega. Right as her foot hit the pavement someone started popping off shots at them from behind the pickup she'd backed into. Ortega casually tossed a grenade up and over the wreckage. The shots ceased after the grenade went off.

The only gunfire after that came from Ortega walking around the wrecked pickup to finish off anyone who'd survived. The grenade had finished off most of them. They'd been huddled in a small group right where the grenade happened to land. Ortega would've loved to say he threw it there on purpose but honestly, he'd just tossed it in the air and hoped for the best.

Chris was tasked with watching over the two men on the ground while Benson and Ortega did another round to make sure no one else was going to start shooting at them. A few more shots rang out as Ortega double tapped some of the bodies that didn't look dead enough. Once that grisly task was completed, the three of them gathered around the two miserable looking prisoners on the ground. Chris had already made sure they were disarmed.

One of the men was sitting up while the other one was lying on his side. In addition to being shot in the forearm, the one lying down had a bone sticking out of his leg. Chris had thought he'd had a weapon concealed in his pants at first. It'd totally grossed him out when he wiggled the bone around and the man started screaming in pain. Even grosser had been the sudden urge to lick the man's blood off the end of the shattered femur. The sweet smell of the blood from the open wound was intoxicating.

"All good?" Benson asked noticing the oddly hungry look on Chris's face.

"Oh yeah. Neither of them has said anything yet." Chris answered guiltily. Not that he could control the urges that came over him now. He was just happy he was strong enough to avoid acting on them.

"Well let's see about that." Ortega said striding over. Without slowing his pace, he kicked the guy on the ground in the face. Before Chris could even finish gasping out 'what the hell', Ortega brought his boot down on the prone man's forearm right where he'd shot him earlier. The man screamed in pain. He didn't pass out though. Chris chalked that up to another scary piece of Ortega trivia. The man naturally knew how to bring someone to the brink without pushing them over into unconsciousness.

Turning away from the man he'd just tortured Ortega squatted down in front of the hard looking soldier sitting with his legs crossed. The man had his bloody forearms sitting in his lap. He looked painfully resigned. The man was a professional. He knew what happened next.

"Talk to me." Ortega said.

"Promise to make it quick. For me and Murdock." The man said nodding his head at his squirming companion. Ortega appeared to think it over for a few seconds. Then in one smooth movement he put the barrel of his rifle up to Murdock's head and pulled the trigger.

"Deal." The decorated Delta soldier answered. The man sitting on the ground had barely even flinched.

"I'm Mercado. We were going to take your ride and your supplies and let you go." Mercado stated in a flat voice.

"Let us go?" Benson asked doubtfully. She'd raised an eyebrow when she said it.

"We'd have asked you to come with us darlin'. We were in the DB for a long time." Mercado shot a wink at Benson. Ortega didn't bother hitting the man. Mercado knew he was going to get shot in the face when they were done quizzing him. Smacking him around now would be pointless. At least while he was cooperating anyway.

"DB?" Chris asked. All he could think of was defensive back. He had no idea why a football position would be relevant to the conversation.

"Disciplinary Barracks. It's the unit that houses people who violate the UCMJ. For the bad stuff like murder, treason, and rape." Benson answered. Mercado acknowledged the description with a nod and a crooked grin. He looked like he was proud of his super villain status. Chris nodded along wisely wondering what the hell the 'UCMJ' was.

Prodded along by Ortega to get to the relevant pieces Mercado gave them a quick summary of how he'd ended up where he was. By the third wave the bulk of the prisoners at Fort Leavenworth had caught the virus. Being in a prison they'd been given all kinds of vaccinations. No one wanted a prison pandemic sending all the inmates to the infirmary at the same time. The few dozen inmates who didn't turn were eventually released into another detention center on the base.

The inmates had sat in the new holding facility for months until someone had decided they should be put to work. The officers originally in command of the base had been killed in the first waves. That'd left a man two rungs down the ladder to assume command of the base. He'd been a leader on the leadership academy side with no idea how to deal with the prisoners. Assuming they'd be grateful to be allowed to get out and help he'd authorized them to be sent out with the scavenging parties.

Mercado and the other prisoners had helped as much as possible the first few times they went out. However, the people leading the scavenging patrols hadn't been as progressive as the new base commander. The prisoners noticed quickly that they were the ones constantly being ordered into situations where baldie bites were more likely. Sent in without being given anything but baseball bats to protect themselves with. Talking it over in the secured common space at night they gradually hatched an escape plan.

The plan wasn't Oceans 11 deep or anything. It would never have worked if the base had still been commanded by someone who understood the mindset of the convicts. As it was though a single pair of armed guards were all that were responsible for letting the men out in the mornings. The inmates were ordered to line up then given their assignments for the day. Instead of lining up for the morning muster they bum rushed the startled guards and beat them unconscious. Next, they'd grabbed weapons and trucks out of the warehouse they'd helped stock from the salvage operations. The gate guards never even looked closely at them until the small convoy was almost all the way out.

One of the guards had eventually noticed something was off and yelled out the order to halt while slapping the button to shut the gate. The overly observant guard was shot in the leg by one of the escapees. A firefight had ensued. Mercado had no idea what'd happened on the base after that since he'd been lying prone in the back of one of the trucks that'd made it out. The guys driving the trucks were special forces trained. When they'd seen a Humvee coming their way, they'd gone into ambush mode.

The story rang true. A little more questioning revealed Fort Leavenworth was still standing. Or at least it had been when the prisoners made their run for it earlier that morning. There were multiple fences surrounding the large facility. Rock walls, wooden walls, and chain-link fences kept the bulk of the baldies aways from the fort. Building and repairing fencing had become a primary past time of the forces in the fort. There were refugees housed inside who helped maintain the base as well. Other than that Mercado didn't have a lot of other useful intel. He had no idea if the phones on base still worked or if there were sat phones available.

To thank the scumbag for his cooperation Ortega handed him half a pint of vodka. Mercado drained the whole thing then stared Ortega in the eyes as he lined up his rifle. Chris turned his head to the side. A loud boom echoed along the road as Ortega honored his side of the deal. Chris didn't need to see or hear the gun to know all of that delicious blood had just sprayed out the back of Mercado's head.

Chapter 8: A Well-Regulated Militia

They finished loading all the weapons they could salvage from the escaped prisoners and got back on the road. The mood was much more somber now. It was barley lunchtime and they'd already killed a dozen men. The men they'd killed were felons who'd been prepared to kill them just to jack their ride. They were still people though. It wasn't the same as bashing in some baldies heads. Even for Ortega it'd been an excessive amount of killing.

Signs for Leavenworth began popping up on the side of the road. A road that gradually widened as they got closer to the city that'd grown up south of the base. A grisly reminder of the massive loss of human life began to line the road as they hit the outskirts of the city. The breakdown lanes on both sides of the road were covered in human remains. As the infection escalated the zombified inhabitants had made their way towards the Army side of the highway. The Army had responded with automatic weapons and an almost infinite number of rounds.

The bodies had been moved to either side of the road by the scavenger patrols the fort sent out. The big machines normally reserved for plowing snow off the highways in the winter had been enlisted to clear the roads of a different kind of hazard. The men Ortega and crew had wasted that morning had manned some of the tractors doing that work. The military understood the importance of keeping the supply lines open.

Other than a few stragglers that Benson easily dodged they didn't spot many baldies. That let them cruise along at a good clip as they made their way to the turnoff the big green traffic signs said would take them to Fort Leavenworth. It was nice not to have to dodge all the normal garbage in the roads. The zombie sweeping tractors had shunted aside all the regular garbage as well as the biohazards.

"You think they'll just let us drive in and use a phone?" Chris asked. It was more to have something to say than because he thought anyone was going to have a great answer. None of them had a clue if they were going to be welcomed with open arms or shot in the face. Nothing was for sure anymore.

"Maybe." Ortega answered the question with his usual eloquence. Used to the fact that the super soldier was a crappy conversationalist Chris brought up a topic he thought Benson might jump on.

"How do you think they get the supplies they need to keep going? Especially if they have a bunch of refugees they have to feed." Chris tossed the question out there and let it sit. With her background in logistics, it'd be interesting to get Benson's take on it. Assuming she took the bait.

"They've lost a lot of their original troops. It's hard to tell your forces to standby when their wives and kids are in danger outside the fort. The civilian workers would've been dismissed when it started getting crazy. Some of them might've stayed but most would've gone to be with their families. We already heard what happened to the prisoners. Assuming they'd stocked up plenty of supplies ahead of time, they'd be good with rationing to last a long time. Supplement that with scavenging, farming, and fishing and they should be able to scrape by practically for forever." Benson answered.

That was all the time they had for talk. Makeshift fences now lined the road around them. The fences all funneled into the road. The road ran straight into a heavily secured checkpoint. A few dead baldies were sprinkled around on the road. That told the occupants of the Humvee that there were snipers somewhere around them. Benson slowed down as they passed a sign indicating the base had been around since 1827. Up ahead the gate slid open to let them through.

Nervously Benson gave it a little gas to get through the gate. They entered a section with an even larger gate in front of them. There was a row of guard shacks to the side. The gate behind them rumbled shut while they waited to see what happened next.

A woman with a paper mask underneath a plastic face shield came out of one of the guard shacks. She was carrying a clipboard in one hand and a pistol in the other. A man stepped out behind her holding an RPG. He didn't aim it at them, but the implied threat was very clear. Deciding this wasn't the time to put up a fight they rolled their windows down.

"Good afternoon. Everyone in the vehicle please keep your hands where I can see them at all times. Is that understood?" The woman asked. After everyone indicated they understood she slipped the pistol back in its holster and brought the clipboard around.

The next twenty minutes were a back and forth as they provided the gate guard with all of their information. The woman interrogating them didn't bother asking for identification. Most refugees had long since lost their wallets or purses. There wasn't a whole lot they could do with the identification even if someone did have it. It wasn't like the DMV was up and operational. They had access to computers and satellites and all of that. It was limited access that no one thought was worth wasting on random data entry though.

After answering all of the questions they were ordered to get out of their vehicle and submit to a bite check. Chris loved that he wasn't going to have to explain the scars from old bite marks anymore. The woman took Benson in for her check first. She then had Chris and Ortega enter the small shack where she used a Maglite to scan them for any bites. She also did the hair pull test on them. Once they'd all passed, she told them to get back in the Humvee and wait for the gate to open.

"You think something's wrong?" Chris asked. The woman had picked up a handset to call in their information before ordering them to wait. Chris had asked her if she could call outside the base from the phone and the answer had been an annoyed 'no'.

"If something was wrong, we'd know it by now." Ortega said. He didn't sound as sure of himself as he normally did though.

Before any of them could get overly worked up about the long delay the gate in front of them began sliding open. The face masked guard came out of the shack and waved them through. She'd told them to take the road to the first building with a red roof and stop there. They'd be assigned to a barracks and given work assignments based on how long they were planning to stay. If they had other orders, then they should pass them along there. Ortega had told her they were on a mission but then told her that was all he could tell her. He'd thought he was being cute at the time. In retrospect it might explain why they'd had to sit in the car outside the guard shack for an hour.

They parked at the large building with the red roof as ordered. The interior of the base was well kept. It'd be easy to forget the world had gone to hell if you confined yourself within the walls of the fort. The refugees who made it here would be doing a lot better than the others they'd seen. Even with his heightened senses Chris didn't detect anything suspicious about the prison complex turned survivors compound.

They'd maneuvered themselves into a catch-22. To get in the base Chris had gotten rid of the bite scars. To convince people that Chris should get access to things like sat phones they normally showcased the bite scars. The scars made their story way more believable. Trying to convince the base commandant to give them access to a satellite phone by having Chris demonstrate his enhanced sense of smell didn't sound like a winning plan.

"We might not even need the fancy phone. The regular phones should have a code on them that gets you access to the network." Ortega said. Benson nodded along. The military loved themselves some redundancy. It helped that money was no object when the lobbyists started talking about securing America. Now that money really wasn't an object hopefully those circuits were still in place.

Walking into the red roofed building they were met by a bored looking junior enlisted man. The young private pointed at the corner where a group of seats were. Ortega bristled a bit but joined Benson and Chris on the seats. There was a TV mounted to the wall with a DVD player built into it. Good thing the military had stayed a decade or so behind on updating their media players. In any civilian location the screen would've been hooked to some sort of streaming device that wouldn't work without an internet connection.

"How do you guys get power?" Chris asked curiously.

"Most of its solar. We still have generators we can use if we need to. Any more questions?" The bored private asked. He was standing in front of the screen ready to press play on the DVD player.

"Can we get some popcorn and candy at least?" Ortega joked.

"Yeah, I just need you to watch this then I have to quiz you." The private mumbled trying to get the DVD to start.

"… and then I have to quiz you **Master Sergeant**." Ortega said emphasizing his title.

"Huh?" The private responded without turning around. He'd finally gotten the video to start playing.

"Did you not hear the Master Sergeant part of what I just said?" Ortega asked in a dangerously calm voice. He'd stood up right behind the private. The private abruptly switched his whole demeanor. He wasn't used to refugees coming in and pushing him around. He only ever really paid attention if any of the refugees happened to be female and around his age. Otherwise, he didn't care much for being the orientation video guy. It was a hell of a lot better than being assigned to one of the scavenger patrols though.

"Sorry Master Sergeant. No popcorn or candy here. I can go get you water if you'd like?" Alarmed he may have put his cushy job in peril the private transformed into the model of military courtesy. The tone of voice Ortega had used left no doubt in his mind that he was dealing with a senior enlisted NCO. He hadn't been paying attention earlier or he'd have already noted that Ortega had enough military bearing to starch the shirts of the people standing near him.

"Three waters. Sounds good." A mollified Ortega turned his attention to the screen.

A salt and pepper haired man in an officer's uniform appeared on the screen and proceeded to welcome them aboard. The orientation video started out by detailing how Fort Leavenworth had prepared for the waves of infected. They'd been proactive since the very beginning. It helped that they had nice sized holding facilities readily available. At the first sign of infection people had been locked away. That rule had been nonnegotiable. When the commandant of the base he pulled out a clump of his own hair one morning he'd marched himself over to the jail. That kind of top-down commitment was why they hadn't fallen apart like so many other places.

The man starring in the orientation video was the current commander of the base. Colonel Kubrick had an easy-going manner about him. The reason he spent so much time explaining how the base had come to be safe was because he intended to keep it that way. The walls around the perimeter included a ten-foot-tall concrete block wall. The baldie stopping structure had been largely constructed by the prisoners prior to the third wave. After the third wave everyone pitched in. Their available manpower diminishing over time due to the high number of infections.

There were constant drone patrols along the perimeter as well. The drones were equipped with infrared sensors that allowed them to detect groups of infected moving around at night. Once detected the infected were taken out if deemed a danger to the base. Any zombie wandering around too close to the base was considered a threat. Chris agreed completely with the 'kill 'em all' approach to baldie border security.

Many of the infected prisoners in lockup had been mercy killed to prevent an outbreak. It was also considered the humane thing to do. Just in case there was still some spark of self-awareness in the person who'd been infected. How horrible to be trapped inside your own body. It was the stuff of nightmares. A handful of baldies were still being kept under observation in their cells for research purposes. For that reason, no one was allowed near the disciplinary barracks or other holding areas.

The last part of the video focused on the fact that this wasn't a refugee rest stop. No one should expect to waltz in and be taken care of for the rest of their lives. Anyone wishing to stay for any length of time was required to sign up for work parties. Any active-duty military personnel would be assigned to a unit unless operating under other orders currently. Those orders were required to be vetted before being considered official. Everyone would be assigned a berthing area and a mealtime. Any attempt to disobey the rules would lead to a disciplinary hearing where you would most likely be expelled from the base.

"At least we get to keep our weapons." Benson said as the video wrapped up. Colonel Kubrick had spent a good ten minutes explaining why everyone on the base was encouraged to maintain their own personal weapons in addition to any issued to them for their official duties. The commanding officer was a firm believer in a well-armed militia. It'd been a big part of why they'd been able to successfully fight off the third and fourth waves.

"What do we tell them about our orders?" Chris asked. The question hung in the air awkwardly. The private had chosen that moment to walk back into the room. He'd left them alone after bringing out a tray with plastic cups of warm water sitting on it to enhance their orientation video watching experience.

"You have a suggestion private?" Ortega asked.

"Yes, Master Sergeant. Colonel Kubrick is a real straight shooter. I'd just tell him the truth. From everything I've seen and heard he tries to do the right thing." The private answered. Chris smiled inwardly at the way the private had delivered his opinion of the colonel while basically standing at attention in front of Ortega.

"The truth huh? Yeah, maybe we'll give that a try.
Now can you give us our berthing info? I'm ready for a nap.
It's been a long day." Ortega said standing up. He smirked as
the private executed an about face before running off to get
their info.

Chapter 9: Game Recognizes Game

The barracks they'd been assigned to were inside a long two-story warehouse. The building had a decent number of post-apocalyptic upgrades. There were additions like the lookout tower jutting out of the roof. Multiple layers of fencing surrounded the building. The fencing extended around the parking lot where row upon row of military vehicles sat under cover. A man in camouflage walked out to meet them as they were getting out of the Humvee.

"Master Sergeant Ortega?" The man asked with a barely concealed smile.

"That's me." Ortega answered walking forward to shake the man's hand. Ortega's head was cocked as he tried to figure out what the guy's deal was.

"Awesome. You guys are all more than welcome. We've got some food and a video inside for you to check out." The man still had that lopsided grin on his face.

"We already watched the orientation video." Benson pointed out quickly. She had zero desire to watch it again. She'd agreed with most of what the Colonel had said. It'd just felt like the whole production lasted about two hours longer than it needed to. The base commander turned movie star had spent a good third of the time reading all of the rules out loud. Left to her own devices Benson knew she would've never read the rules, so she got why he did it. No one should end up banished for a rule they'd never heard of.

"Yeah, this one's a little different. LT has one I think you're going to like." The soldier told them they could come back for the rest of their stuff after they'd met everybody. Gesturing at them to follow him inside the grinning soldier headed back to the door he'd come out of. You had to zig zag through the chain link to get there. Chris liked that these guys had secured the building they were living in. The fences wouldn't stand up to a mob of a thousand baldies, but it'd help if a smaller group of the monsters slipped through the perimeter defenses.

"The hell's that music?" Chris asked. The soldier taking them into the warehouse had let out a blast of loud classical music when he opened the door.

"It's that flight of the Valkyries song. You know, the soundtrack to every war movie ever." Ortega answered Chris's question absent mindedly. The Delta operative was preoccupied with peeking through the door to see what was going on. Chris and Benson followed closely behind him.

The space inside was packed with gear. Crates were neatly stacked from floor to ceiling. A couple of electric forklifts were parked in a corner. Gigantic bins were filled with every conceivable type of weapon. A large white screen had been hung about halfway up one of the walls. The inside of the building was dark. Chris couldn't tell if it was dark because they didn't have lighting or if they were just keeping it dark to better show the video they were playing. Considering the blaring war music, they must be good to go electricity wise.

The floor was packed with armed men and women in camouflage. They all applauded and busted out some loud 'hoo-ahs' when the three newcomers walked in. Chris was at a complete loss until Benson poked him in the arm and pointed at the movie screen. Switching his focus to the screen Chris tried to figure out what was going on.

Playing on the homemade movie screen was a video shot from a drone. The green tinted video showed three pickup trucks cruising down the road. The trucks separated to encircle a Humvee. What happened next was a bird's eye view of Ortega and team obliterating the escaped prisoners earlier that morning. The fugitives must not have been very popular with the crowd in the warehouse. Every time one of the escapees was killed another chorus of blood thirsty cheers went up.

When the video finished the crowd surged around the three of them offering up drinks, fierce bear hugs, and bone crushing handshakes. Standing with a beer in his hand Chris flinched back when a blond-haired beast of a man approached the group. The last thing Chris wanted was another bear hug or handshake meant to test his manhood. What he wouldn't mind some more of was the home brew one of the soldiers had handed him.

"Enjoying the baldie brew?" The long-haired man asked casually. Ortega sized up the guy then popped off a quick salute.

"Yes sir. It's delicious. You the CO here?" Ortega asked. He'd clocked the man's bearing and attitude with ease. He had the swagger of a SEAL with the reserve of an officer. The long hair didn't matter at all. Special Ops guys grew theirs out all the time. You wanted to go native and blend in. It helped when you were doing your best not to be captured, tortured, and killed. Ortega kept his short just because he got dandruff otherwise. It wasn't like there was a factory still mixing up vats of Head and Shoulders.

"That I am. Lieutenant Samson. It's a real pleasure to meet you Master Sergeant. Those dirtbags you took out killed a couple of my guys on the way out. We'd have been on them in another twenty minutes if you hadn't taken care of them for us. Delta?" Samson asked.

A bemused Chris watched as Ortega nodded in acknowledgement of his Delta affiliation. How those two had so quickly sized one another up was completely beyond Chris. He'd been around Ortega long enough now to know that's just the way it was though. To reach the vaunted pinnacle of elite military fighting units you needed more than just fast reflexes, and really good aim. You also needed a ton of situational awareness. Rapidly evaluating data to transform it into actionable intel was what being an outstanding special operator boiled down to.

"No barbershops on base?" Benson asked. She couldn't quite bring herself to say 'sir' to the camouflage wearing Fabio.

"A full head of hair is what separates us from the brain munchers. When a couple dozen of them cross over our firing line it makes it easier to figure out who to shoot. That's also why I insist no one goes into battle completely naked." Samson said with a grin. It was a well-polished response that he'd obviously whipped out a hundred times over.

"So, we were told this was our billet. What do you guys do here?" Ortega asked. He didn't mind the idea of keeping a warehouse organized one bit. As a Master Sergeant he'd be put in charge of the work crews anyway. He could spend the majority of his days delegating and learning how to make that delicious beer.

Being on the bottom of the totem pole Chris was a little less excited about being assigned to a warehouse. It absolutely beat being out in the field or being the guy who had to show that orientation video though. He'd sort supplies out of a bin any day. He was hoping that's what 'billet' meant anyway. Spending his days around people who communicated in military jargon he'd learned to base a lot of his understanding on context. Every once in a while, when the acronyms really started to fly, he was forced to call a timeout to get some of them explained so he could keep up.

Samson invited them to follow him back to his office. Benson noted that the Lieutenant had pointedly not answered Ortega's question. That was setting off alarm bells in her head. Her two companions seemed completely at ease though as they drank their way past the slowly dispersing crowd. It was hard to focus when a few dozen hardcore warriors wanted to congratulate you for avenging their friends in such badass fashion.

Samson led them across the warehouse to a set of stairs that went up to a second level with multiple hallways and doors. One of the open doors revealed a large room with bunk beds stacked along the walls. It looked like the rooms Chris had seen in the war movies where they did the flashbacks to the barracks at boot camp. He fought the urge to stop and take a closer look. He had a feeling he was going to be spending plenty of time in the room before too long anyway.

In an office that also held a twin sized bed and an impressive collection of weapons displayed on the wall Samson invited them to have a seat. There was only one chair besides the one Samson had sat in. Ortega had maneuvered himself to be in front of it so he could claim it as his own. That left Benson and Chris to awkwardly plop down on Samson's bed.

"You guys do a little bit more than just organize scavenged goods don't you sir?" Benson asked. It still hurt her to add the 'sir' on for the man with the flowing blond mane.

"The long hair's really bothering you, isn't it?" Samson asked looking closely at Benson. Her mouth opened but no words came out. She hadn't realized she was that easy to read. It was a little ridiculous for her to be worried about someone having long hair when there were rampaging groups of bloodthirsty zombies roaming the countryside. Not to mention the secret group of illuminati vampires that Chris had gotten himself mixed up with.

"Not anymore. Now I'm a lot more interested in why you keep avoiding telling us what you do here." Benson let the statement hang in the air. Belatedly she realized she'd forgotten to tack on the required 'sir'. It was too late now to say it without looking even more disrespectful. Maintaining eye contact she chose to roll with having already addressed him as 'sir' once during the conversation. Saying it too many times always seemed weirder than not saying it enough to her. Although with most officers it was better safe than sorry. Or at least it was back in the old days with the standard stick up their butt's officers she'd dealt with. Fabio here might be cut from a different cloth.

"We're the ones who go out and keep the infected at bay. We do runs as often as needed to expand the buffer area of relative safety around the fort. You were sent here to serve based on what we saw in that video. It'd be a waste to use you as scavengers or guards or mechanics or whatever. You guys have some serious skills. I want those skills on my team. Make more sense now?" Samson asked with a wink at Benson.

"What if we'd rather be something else?" Chris asked. Working the breakfast line sounded better than working the firing line. You had a better chance of surviving the high cholesterol from too many butter-soaked omelets than the mobs of infected psychos waiting outside the perimeter fence. Samson gave him a long piercing look.

"Every man or woman on my team's a volunteer. Everyone has the option to walk away at any time on this side of the fence. Once we roll out on a mission there's no turning back though. If you'd rather go peel potato's just let me know. If you want to be the tip of the spear fighting to reclaim this country from those bald bastards, then I need you to let me know that too." Samson paused to look at each of them in turn. If he was expecting them to rush forward and volunteer all at once, then he was going to be in pause mode for a while. Patriotic speeches were about as meaningful as offering a gift card to Starbucks for the residents of this brave new world.

"The thing is sir we're on another mission right now. One that may or may not allow us to join your team. We need a sat phone or the access code to the sat uplink from a regular phone to confirm." Ortega stated their case matter of factly.

"I'll take what I can get. I'll let you use my phone, Master Sergeant. The little sticker on it has the code to access the uplink. It only works about half the time so keep trying if you don't get though at first. I'll let you have the room for thirty minutes. Make your call and let me know what your decision is. We're heading out on a mission first thing in the morning, so I'll need an answer today." With that the long-haired Lieutenant walked out of the room pulling the door shut behind him.

The three of them stared at the phone for a second before Ortega walked over and picked up the handset. He started to dial then stopped with the handset in hand and looked at Chris.

"We want to let Lynn know where we are right?" Ortega asked. They'd talked about this exact subject ad nauseum. Despite the late nights and copious amounts of brown liquor invested in coming up with a plan for contacting Lynn they still hadn't decided what they should do. It boiled down to Chris wanting to know what the changes in his body were about. He needed to know what he was turning into. Ortega and Benson respected that. They were having a difficult time reconciling it with their initial objective of saving the world by creating a cure using Chris's blood though.

Chris nodded and Benson shrugged. Ortega went ahead and dialed the number that he'd been given by Lynn. Expecting to hear the sultry voice of the beautiful killer herself he was a little let down when he got voicemail instead. The voicemail wasn't even Lynn's voice.

There was no greeting or anything. The robotic message simply asked them to state their location and hang-up. Before he could talk himself out of it Ortega let the machine know that they were in Fort Leavenworth. Hoping he didn't have to press any more buttons or enter any more codes he hung up after delivering the message. Once again, they stood in the small room staring at one another. Chris half-expected the phone on the desk to start ringing.

"Do we want to fight the infected or go be janitors?" Benson finally asked. She'd checked her watch a couple of times. Thirty minutes wasn't very long to be making life or death decisions. She didn't doubt that Samson had been serious about them coming out of the room having decided though. If they didn't have an answer, he'd probably kick them out on principle.

"I'd rather fight. I don't like cleaning. Besides we may need to use the phone again. We'll have a lot more freedom to move around if we stay here than we will pushing mop buckets around." Ortega answered.

"You just want to stay for the beer. I'm good with staying in the fight though." Benson answered.

"I like the beer too." Chris chimed in. Volunteering to go outside the wire when they had the option of nice safe gigs was asinine. He couldn't imagine voluntarily separating himself from Benson and Ortega though. Not after everything they'd been through together. They could've easily stayed at that luxury cabin with all of the supplies in it for the next year. They'd come out because Chris needed them to come out.

The door opened and Samson walked in with an eyebrow raised. When they told him they were staying and fighting for as long as they could he pounded them on the backs and welcomed them to the unit. Then he told them to go grab their gear and get settled in.

"Get a good night's sleep. We're on the hunt first thing in the morning." Samson didn't waste any more time on small talk. Turning on his heel he disappeared back into his office. The three of them were met by a private who offered to show them around and help get them situated. Chris hoped the tour ended at whatever bed he was going to be sleeping in. He was exhausted. It'd been a long day.

Lying in bed later he couldn't fall asleep. Tossing and turning he wondered why he was so sleepy today when the day before he'd barely been able to sleep at all. Theories about rebuilding his strength bouncing around in his head he really hoped Lynn hurried up and checked her messages.

Chapter 10: Thunderstruck

Chris looked up from the hot bowl of fruit covered oatmeal at his smiling mom. Alice was in full on mom mode. She'd made breakfast early in preparation for them spending the whole day together. Smiling to himself Chris looked back down to take another bite of the oatmeal. The strawberries on top had melted leaving a disgusting blood colored coating on top of the oatmeal. The bloody scum smelled delicious. Feeling his stomach recoiling Chris looked up to see his suddenly bald, sore covered mom lunging at him with bared teeth.

"Yo! Sleeping beauty wake up." Benson continued to press her boot covered foot annoyingly into Chris's chest. She'd told him to skip the extra beers before bed, but he hadn't listened. She wasn't getting a lot of enjoyment out of this subtle pre-dawn 'I told you so', but she was getting some. Considering the times that they were living in she'd take her pleasure wherever she could get it.

For his part Chris was happy to have the steel toed combat boot kicking him out of his nightmare. Anything to get the vision of his zombified mom out of his pounding head. The beers had either hit him harder than he'd anticipated, or he was back in the throes of another vampiric metamorphosis stage. Regardless of the source of his headache, nausea, and chills he just wanted it all to go away. Knowing none of the people he was with were going to care about his 'tummy issues' he rolled out of his bunk to work on waking up.

Benson and Chris had been given bunks in the main barracks. The large open space was coed. At one time that would've been considered progressive. The zombie apocalypse had ushered in a wave of equality. If humanity managed to survive then it may emerge better in some ways. Every blacksmith knows it takes a fire and considerable force to forge something of lasting strength.

Ortega chose that moment to enter the barracks. Despite having drank five times as much as anybody else in the room he appeared ready for inspection. The camo pants he was wearing looked like they might have even been ironed recently. Chris would never have suspected you could iron that kind of pants. Smiling broadly Ortega made a beeline for Chris. It was like he could sense how miserably hungover Chris was and wanted to relish in it.

"How'd you sleep?" Ortega asked with the amused grin plastered on his face. For Ortega to be smiling that broadly Chris knew he must look really bad.

"How's your private luxury suite?" Chris asked hoping to skip the part where he had to talk a lot. Talking made his head hurt. Of course, not talking also made his head hurt.

"It's alright. I'm going to ask the butler if I can get a higher thread count on the sheets though." Ortega said tongue in cheek. Seeing the look of confusion cross Chris's face, he began howling with laughter. Chris was so addled he'd actually believed that there was a butler scurrying around right now trying to find the Master Sergeant silkier sheets.

Benson walked over to see what was going on. Once Ortega explained it to her, she couldn't stop laughing either. Chris did his best ignore them both as he tugged on his boots. When he finally looked up it set the two of them off again. Benson had tears streaming down her cheeks she was laughing so hard. Ortega stopped once he realized he was laughing like a lunatic around the soldiers he'd be leading in battle later. Samson would be there, but everyone would be looking to Ortega as the senior noncom to make sure everything went as it should.

"Attention on deck!" The ritualized shout came from the front of the room as Lieutenant Samson walked in. The room grew instantly silent as everyone stood up with their heels together and hands at their sides. The Lieutenant immediately barked out the command for everyone to stand at ease. The troops went into parade rest and waited to hear the details on the mission they'd be going on today. It was a tradition that Samson had established over the last year. Prior to each mission he came in and made sure everyone understood what they were doing and why they were doing it. He was also good about listening to any advice anyone had on how they could do it better.

"The plan for today is to take the boats down to Kansas City for a clearing exercise. Intel points at there being thirty to fifty thousand tangoes in the vicinity of where we'll be setting up. We'll kill as many of them as we can without getting close enough to the bank to put ourselves in danger. We'll use the drones to figure out where to drop mortars. Everyone packs a full kit. I don't expect anybody to come home with leftover ammo. Questions?" Samson waited silently giving his team time to come up with any comments or questions.

"What time do we leave sir?" Ortega asked.

"No time like the present. Let's aim to be on the boats within the next thirty minutes. You'll just need your personal kits. We loaded the munitions on the boats yesterday. They're ready to go." Samson answered looking at his watch.

"Sounds good." Ortega answered wondering why everyone was still at parade rest.

"What are we going to do today?" Samson called out.

"Kill! Kill! Kill!" The harsh battle cry rang out from all the soldiers in the room.

After that last part of the pre-mission ritual Samson dismissed everyone. The patrol leaders worked to make sure everyone had the gear they needed before filing out of the room to head over to the boats. Chris felt like he'd accomplished a lot when he finally got his boots tied. Falling in with the rest of the soldiers in the patrol he'd been assigned to with Benson they walked down the stairs and out of the warehouse.

Once outside they boarded the golf carts in the parking lot to make the trip over to the river. The convoy of multicolored electric carts seemed like an odd way to start off on a mission to mass murder the infected inhabitants of Kansas City. It beat walking though. Especially with all their gear strapped on. Chris supposed the golf carts made sense as a way to harness solar power to move around the base versus using up a finite resource like gas. He felt naked being outside without a nicely armored vehicle wrapping him in its protective cocoon though.

At the river there was a dock with multiple pontoon boats tied up to it. The large boats might not be the most fuel-efficient way to cruise the river, but they'd get the job done. The open spaces in the boats were critical to allow for launching the mortars that were stacked up in boxes on board each of the vessels. A few of the boats had machine guns mounted on them. The ones that didn't had crates of ammunition for everyone to cycle through with their small arms.

Numbers painted on the boats told everyone where to go. Ortega had Chris and Benson join him and Samson in the lead boat. Another soldier on the boat was responsible for navigating them through the mud filled water to the zone they wanted to target. Once there they'd drop anchor and get started on a long day of zombie target practice.

The trip down the river started off as a lazy affair. The banks were heavily wooded occasionally giving way to glimpses of buildings in the distance. Samson used the time to quiz them on where they'd been and what they'd seen. They told an edited version of their adventures where they glossed over the parts where Chris was an immune superfreak. Samson could tell they were leaving parts out. He'd started asking more pointed questions when the sky began to darken. Rain began to drizzle down on them.

Samson gave them a break from his interrogation to hold a hurried conversation with Ortega about whether to abort or not. They were close to the target site and both men hated the idea of wasting all the fuel it'd taken to get them there. Opting to play it by ear and abort if the rain interfered with their baldie bombing the convoy of militarized party boats continued down the river. A miserable Chris shivered in the cool rain as the drizzle gradually notched itself up to a downpour. Lightning bolts began to snap across the sky as Kansas City grew closer.

"How much further to the target zone?" Chris asked. Ortega answered that it was right around the next bend.

"We'll drop anchor once we get there and wait out the rain. Hopefully it passes quick." Ortega filled them in. He was saying the words, but the doubt was written all over his face. This storm didn't look like it wanted to disappear quickly.

By the time they made it around the next bend their visibility was sorely limited. They had running lights turned on so the boat behind them could see where to go. Chris could barely see the shore. Although he found if he closed his eyes, he knew almost exactly where the shoreline was. Or at least he thought he did. If the sun ever came out again, he'd be able to validate if his new sixth sense was accurate or not. For now, he just shivered miserably in his soaking wet clothes. They'd thrown on ponchos after they were already soaked. Chris felt like his was amplifying the cold making him even more uncomfortable.

They tossed the anchors over the side to attempt to maintain their position. Typically, this wouldn't have been an issue, but the river was flowing faster than normal thanks to all of the rain. Completely out of his element Chris did his best to stay out of everyone's way. He may not know much about boats, but it was obvious this was not going well. He set aside his discomfort and tuned in to hear what Ortega and Samson were discussing in hushed tones towards the bow of the boat.

"Can you hear what they're saying?" Benson asked incredulously staring at Chris.

"Yeah. It's kind of like with the way I can smell everything now. I'm just able to sort it better. Like I can filter out the other noises to just hear what they're saying." Chris explained. He'd been caught off guard by the question. He hadn't realized that what he was doing was odd until called out on it. It's not like he was trying to make it happen. It was just happening.

"Ok weirdo. What're they talking about?" Benson asked.

"Ortega thinks we should give up and head back. Samson wants to wait and see if it clears up so it's not a wasted day." Chris answered. There was more to it but that was a decent summary.

The rain stopped. As quickly as the storm had come it was gone. The clouds dissipated. The sun shone down on a watered-down world. The pontoon boats anchored haphazardly all around them came into view. The river was still moving faster than normal based on the pieces of conversation Chris picked up on. The anchors might not be enough to maintain their position, but they could always use their engines. They needed to avoid doing that for as long as possible since fuel for the redneck flotilla was hard to come by.

The men on each boat hurried to setup the mortars once it was announced that the operation was a go. A few drones were launched up into the air to provide eyes in the sky. A familiar guitar riff began pounding out of the speakers of one of the party boats. The volume was maxed out as *Highway to Hell* from AC/DC blasted out of the oversized speakers. Soldiers began bobbing their heads in time to the music as they setup the portable artillery launchers and got on the machine guns.

On the riverbank the loud music was having the desired effect. The infected were emptying out of the nearby buildings to see what all of the noise was about. Forming large crowds, they stared out across the water at the prey filled pontoons. Chris could hear them moaning in frustration at not being able to get out to the boats. There was an intermission after the first song ended. Samson was staring at the video feed from a drone on an iPad to see how many of the baldies had shown up to the party. Nodding his head, he held up two fingers.

The brief silence was shattered by AC/DC launching into *Thunderstruck*. It was an apt song as the rockets began to fly from the boats into the crowded riverbank. After a salvo of rockets the machine gunners took a turn raking the rows of zombies pressed up against the water. The gunfire and loud music captured the attention of every zombie in the city. The bald-headed, sore covered, mostly naked masses converged on the river.

It was exactly what Samson had been hoping for. He watched the video on the iPad as the rockets hit the same spots repetitively blasting the contaminated flesh of their enemy into the air. The men manning the launchers were checking the feeds as well to determine when to launch the next round. Unlike gas for the boats, they had rockets for days. They still tried to be economical with them. It wasn't like the bomb factory was churning out any new ones any time soon. Samson liked to remind everyone that being conservative with the explosive rounds was the ultimate definition of getting the biggest bang for their buck.

Chris had his rifle in his hand. As long as he was standing there he might as well chip in. Looking through the sights on top of his rifle he began sending rounds across the water. He stopped when he sensed someone staring at him. It was Benson again.

"How are you doing that?" Benson asked.

"Doing what?" A half-deaf Chris asked back. At this point they were communicating mostly by lip reading and hand gestures. The background noise had risen to a level where not even Chris was able to make out much anymore.

"Shooting like that." Benson clarified. Chris had to think about that one for a minute. Finally, he put the weapon back up to his shoulder and really focused on what he was doing. Putting the rifle back down about ten seconds later he thought he knew what she was talking about. Most people probably couldn't run through an entire magazine that quickly with that kind of accuracy. It was just easy for him. He was able to focus like never before.

"I just can. Kind of like the hearing I guess." Chris replied.

"Glad you're on our side!" Benson shouted over the sound of the mortars exploding on the shore.

The noise covered up the sound of distant thunder. At first no one noticed the sky darkening again. By the time they did it was too late. Lightning danced across the sky. The wind whipped up. No one needed to be told that play time was over. The munitions were hurriedly put back in their places as everyone got ready to get underway. Samson had the radioman on their boat relay the order for everyone to return to base.

The rain was coming down in sheets. It was ice cold. Visibility had been completely wiped out. Helping pull the anchor up Chris yelped when a golf ball sized piece of hail nailed him in the back of his head. The large hailstones kept raining down on them. The crew without any current tasks gathered underneath the small roof covering the console area of the boat. Chris tossed the anchor on the deck and went to get the other one and pull it in. Ortega had beat him to it. Instead of pulling up the rope he just cut it.

Chris sat down and grabbed one of the empty mortar boxes and held it over his head. It wasn't ideal but at least he wasn't getting pelted in the head by the frozen snowballs. The boat began to make its way back up the river. Chris heard a horrifying new noise growing louder. He couldn't tell if the noise was coming from behind them or from all around them. It sounded like a massive freight train.

"Tornado!" Chris yelled loudly into the storm. Sitting on the deck with a box over his head and hailstones bouncing all around him no one heard him. It didn't matter though. You didn't need super hearing to make out the massive rumbling in the air. The hail stopped.

Chris looked out to see what was going on. He couldn't hear anything over the sound of the tornado. The gigantic funnel cloud was less than a hundred yards away on the bank of the river. A wave of dirt and debris swept across their boat temporarily blinding them. Looking back up after wiping his eyes off Chris watched as one of their fellow pontoon boats was sucked up into the funnel cloud. A gigantic gust of wind pushed them towards the opposite bank. The bank with all of the baldies on it.

The hail started hitting them again. In the moment before it started Chris had seen another massive funnel cloud bearing down on them. This one was rampaging through the city itself. The boat they were on was dipping and swaying dangerously in the wind whipped water. With no warning the entire bow went under flinging them all off and into the water. The boat smashed into the water upside down next to where Chris was struggling to keep his face far enough out of the churning water to breathe.

A powerful storm driven current pushed him around in the water until he found himself able to stand on the mud-covered bank. He felt slightly more secure until he was picked up by the wind and casually tossed about twenty feet through the air. He landed in the middle of the concrete covered courtyard that they'd been happily mortaring the hell out of fifteen minutes prior. All around him the shadowy shapes of the infected flitted through the rain. The baldies were all still shambling around. Knowing the infected were guided primarily by their sense of smell Chris wasn't too worried about them finding anyone in this mess.

The hail beat down on Chris as he sought out shelter. Seeing an opening where a plate glass window had been shattered by looters, he ran towards it. He could taste blood in his mouth. He must've bitten his tongue when he was tossed through the air. He was halfway to the window when something grabbed his arm. Spinning on his heel he swung a wild haymaker. Benson staggered back with a bloody nose and a hurt look on her face. Chris put his fist down and tried to figure out where she'd come from. Disregarding the punch Benson dragged him back to the alley he'd just ran past.

The narrow alley was carpeted with zombie parts thanks to their recent bombing exercise. Chris attempted not to stare at the assorted appendages randomly lining the narrow concrete space. The reek of contaminated blood was strong. The infected blood struck him like spoiled milk hits an unsuspecting kid's nose early on a Saturday morning. Not the kind of chunky goodness he wanted to pour over his Fruity Pebbles.

Kneeling in the middle of the mess was Samson. He was working on immobilizing the arm of a soldier that'd broken it in all of the excitement. Ortega was there as well. Chris let out the breath he hadn't realized he'd been holding. He'd been fearful his friends were dead. It looked like they'd all made it. Not that they necessarily had much longer to live. Not when you considered the only thing keeping the rampaging zombie hordes from eating them alive was the twin tornadoes ripping the city apart around them.

Chapter 11: Tornado Alley

The storm kept getting worse. The alley they were hunkered down in was turning into a nasty little lake. The rain pouring down on them was being trapped by the dam of corpses blocking off the alley. Given the extremely limited visibility they could just make out the occasional baldie shuffling past them. It was only a matter of time before one of the monsters ventured into the sheltered alcove. The rain hadn't slowed down but at least the wind wasn't tossing them around as much anymore.

Knowing that they shouldn't make noise by firing any weapons Ortega had positioned himself towards the end of the alley. He had an axe dangling from his hand. Chris and Ortega had talked about that axe multiple times while arguing about the best melee weapons to lug around an apocalypse. Ortega's preference was more of a tomahawk than a wood chopping axe. He was able to swing it with one hand. It was heavy enough that he didn't have to use the sharp side to put down a baldie. That was important since edged weapons became dulled after use. They could also get stuck inside whatever you were trying to kill. That could be inconvenient when multiple zombies happened to be coming at you at the same time.

"Let's roll!" Samson shouted to be heard over the storm noise. The deafening roar of the nearby tornadoes ripping the city apart giving him the confidence to be a little louder than usual. No one was worried about a little extra noise except Chris. If the infected happened to have abilities similar to his then they'd be able to filter out Samson giving orders even with all the background noise. He hadn't seen any evidence the baldies had that same skill. He'd seen them doing an awful lot of sniffing though which made him wonder if they might also have some version of his hearing capabilities.

Chris was about to ask why Samson wanted them to leave the relatively safe alley when he realized why they couldn't just stay there. The only thing keeping them alive was the storm. Once it died down, they'd be standing in a dead-end alley waiting to be eaten alive. No way could Ortega Paul Bunyan his way through an entire city of the undead. It didn't matter how big his axe was.

Chris didn't even have an axe. He didn't have a rifle either. He'd lost that somewhere amidst all the craziness. He had his pistol and a few extra magazines. The fixed blade serrated combat knife he'd strapped to his chest might come in handy if he opted to channel his inner Rambo. Their survival was going to depend mostly on luck. The freight train sound of the tornadoes hadn't lowered in their intensity. Chunks of concrete and other debris fell out of the sky into the alleyway fairly regularly. The way their day was going there was a very good chance they'd step out of the alley and end up in Oz. Chris had no doubt they'd materialize somewhere way off the yellow brick road.

Ortega got to try out his oversized hatchet when a skinny baldie came stumbling into the alley out of the storm and attacked him. The flabby white creature was extremely excited to have abruptly come face to face with uninfected flesh. The beast lunged forward to take a bite out of the Master Sergeant. Ortega sidestepped the gnashing teeth and slammed the infected man to the ground. In one smooth motion Ortega knelt down and bashed the back of the baldies head in with his hatchet. Without missing a beat Ortega stood back up and continued walking out of the alley.

The rest of them followed the deadly Delta warrior out into the storm. Benson was immediately behind Ortega. Samson was in the middle helping the wounded soldier along. Chris brought up the rear trying to make sure nothing snuck up on them. An almost impossible task in the complete chaos surrounding them. It only took a few steps before Samson was waving his hand in the air and pointing at a smashed-up storefront to their right. Chris agreed completely. No matter how incredibly stupid it would be for them to wait out the storm in the alley it'd be even dumber to stay out in the open.

The massive storm had turned day into night. Visibility was rendered nonexistent by the massive volume of dirt and debris whipping through the air. Every bit of Chris's exposed skin felt like someone had attacked it with a piece of sandpaper. He couldn't even imagine how uncomfortable the butt naked baldies must be. Pressing forward they got to the door of what turned out to be a laundromat. The door was hanging from a single hinge, and it was pitch black inside. Lightning was striking all around them providing brief bursts of semi-visibility.

They crowded into the shelter of the doorway to wait while Ortega stepped inside to clear the space. The beam from his flashlight illuminated at least a dozen baldies standing in some type of stasis. Their trance was broken by the sudden beam of light accompanied by the warm, rich smell of their prey. The storm sweeping in through the doorway didn't bother them in the slightest. As if they shared a single consciousness all of them stepped forward at once with a low growl.

Coming up with a variety of creative new ways to combine old cuss words Ortega blasted away at the wave of monsters threatening to break over the top of him. Chris was horrified to have been caught as flat footed as everyone else. He'd noticed the musk of the massed group of zombies at about the same time Ortega had flicked on his flashlight. Pulling his pistol to try and help Ortega he set aside his self-reproach for later. He absolutely should've been paying attention to what was going on inside the laundromat. In his defense there were a lot of things going on though.

Ortega took small steps backwards until he was in line with the rest of the group. He reached for another magazine when his firing pin slammed down on an empty chamber. Chris stepped to one side of him and Benson to the other. The two of them pulling their triggers as fast as they could to hold back the flashing white teeth of the beasts who wanted nothing more than to rend them apart. Ortega reloaded and continued to blast away as they retreated out the narrow doorway.

The Lieutenant had stepped forward to get on the firing line the next time one of them ran dry. The soldier with the broken arm was staring out into the storm to see if any more of the infected were coming for them. He barely had time to call out a warning before a small group of infected ripped into his exposed skin from every angle. Samson turned in time to see the man get yanked out into the storm by the flesh starved gang of ghouls.

Samson ran to the entrance and systematically shot each of the infected holding the soldier down. The deluge pouring down from the heavens wasn't enough to keep the blood from pooling up on the skin of the badly bitten soldier. One look was all the Lieutenant needed. Benson emerged from the doorway right as Samson put a bullet into his man's face. Understanding flooded Benson's eyes. In a sudden surge of empathy, she put a hand on Samson's shoulder to comfort him. The moment of compassion ended when she spun around to guard the door Chris and Ortega were hustling out of.

Ortega darted to the side and tossed a grenade into the laundromat through one of the missing windows. Yelling for everyone to get down he pulled Chris down to the ground with him. Benson kept up a steady stream of fire into the doorway to kill the infected still coming for them. The blast from the grenade momentarily overrode the roar of the tornadoes. The explosion had the desired effect of stopping the zombies from pouring out the door.

The gunplay and explosions were bound to attract more of the infected. They had no choice but to keep moving. Ortega and Samson spent a few seconds rifling through the possessions of the soldier Samson had just mercy killed. The body wasn't even cold yet. Shoving loaded magazines and an extra pistol into his pocket Ortega bounced up to take point. Everyone fell in as they left the laundromat behind to try and find somewhere more secure to shelter from the storm.

Pistol in one hand and Rambo knife in the other Chris stumbled along behind Samson. Gusts of wind kept driving sand and debris into their eyes. Chris was attempting to wrap a t-shirt around his face to help him to breathe easier. Otherwise, every breath was like eating a mud sandwich. There was a crashing sound off to their left and a wall of bricks and concrete smashed into them.

Rubbing his eyes to clear away the darkness Chris looked around. He was lying on the ground in a pile of bricks, wood, drywall, and concrete. They must have been hit by a wall blown out by one of the tornadoes that was still howling around nearby. Sitting up he felt around for his pistol but all he could find was the novelty knife. Visibility was limited to a few feet between the darkness from the heavy cloud cover, the pouring rain, and the walls that were evidently flying through the air now. Seeing a shape coming towards him from out of the rain Chris called out to see if it was one of his comrades.

Chris realized his mistake when the shape got closer. The shadowy form morphed into a hairless naked man with sores covering his body. The baldie turned its head sideways to regard Chris for a second before leaping for him. Luckily it missed its footing in the pile of rubble and stumbled to its knees before it could get at him. Chris took a careful step forward and rammed his knife into the man's chest. He'd aimed for where he thought the heart should be. He was basing his aim on where he typically saw people put their hands when reciting the pledge of allegiance. He really needed to find an anatomy textbook. Having been a psychology major he'd kind of glossed over a few of the required introductory courses.

When the man didn't immediately die Chris ripped the knife out and stabbed him a few more times. The stabbing kept the baldie from biting him. His assailant wasn't much of a multitasker. Once the ghoul finally stopped flopping around Chris tried to see where everyone was. He still couldn't see crap. Realizing he was going about this like a normal panicked person he tried to force himself to relax. Not so easy when he'd just killed a man-eating monster in the middle of a city being ripped apart by twin tornadoes.

Breathing in through his nose and out through his mouth wasn't helping. It was like it was raining from the ground towards the sky the storm had gotten so crazy. There was water going up his nostrils. He was going to drown standing outside in the street. Assuming another flying wall didn't finish him off first. Giving up on the calming idea he let the panic guide him towards the row of buildings nearest him. At least they all looked like they were still standing.

"You ok!" Samson looked less like Fabio and more like a half-drowned golden doodle. His lustrous locks were covered in dirt and debris. They hung down in a tangled mess over his eyes.

Chris nodded instead of trying to yell back. Somewhere close by another building had just given up the fight. The noise around them was reaching decibel levels that would have the most hard-core Metallica fan reaching for their ear protection. Out of nowhere Benson and Ortega emerged from the chaos. Chris's instant relief at seeing them was ripped away by the sight of a pale naked figure jumping on Benson from behind.

Ortega saw what was happening out of the corner of his eye. Reacting quickly, he grabbed the baldie in a head lock to keep it from nibbling on Benson's neck. The baldies knees hit Benson in the back sending her to her knees. Chris lunged in to stab the baldie while Ortega held it firmly in the head lock. Not an easy task the way it was flailing around to try and get its teeth into the prey that was holding it. The dying monster never even looked to see who was stabbing it. Its focus entirely on getting its teeth into Ortega until its last heartbeat.

Chris debated on whether or not to keep the knife in his hand or sheathe it back up so he wouldn't lose it. For the first time he was thankful for the insane amount of rain. It was helping to wash away the copious amounts of grossness covering his stabbing arm. The poncho he had on was twisted and ripped all to hell. Turning around to see where their fearless leader was going to take them next Chris saw Samson on the ground beating a bald tween to death with a brick.

After doing a real number on the little monster's brain bucket Samson failed to stand up. He stayed kneeling on the ground staring at the kid he'd just killed. It was a valid response to slaying a child. Even if the child was infected with a disease that turned it into a monster. When they were dead that weird light went out of their eyes. That was when they went from being demonic beasts to just being dead people with no hair and horrible skin. Kids were the absolute worst.

This was no time for the Lieutenant to have a crisis of conscience though. The idea was to fight their way home so that he could drink himself to bed every night with a bottle of brown liquor like the rest of them. The hangovers were a million-times better than the nightmares. Although Chris had figured out the alcohol didn't really stop the nightmares, the booze just made it so that you forgot them quicker after you woke up. Either way they needed the LT to snap out of it. None of the rest of them had the slightest clue where in Kansas City they were. Not that there was going to be much of the city left after these tornadoes finished tearing it apart.

Ortega showed his full sympathetic and caring self by reaching down and pulling Samson up by the hair. That served the purposes of getting their leader on his feet and snapping him out of his fugue. Things were hopeless enough without getting caught up in the guilt trap that came with mercy killing the poor possessed souls attacking them. Now that they were out of danger Chris could finally relax and focus. He found that it didn't really help since this was too much chaos for even his newfound vampiric powers to assist with.

A pissed off looking Samson whirled away from Ortega. Hair blowing wildly in the wind he stormed up the debris covered sidewalk looking for a door that hadn't been ripped off its hinges yet. Any building or business that was easily accessible was probably crawling with the undead at this point. It'd be well worth the effort to have to beat their way into a room rather than deal with getting bum rushed by a bunch of man munchers again.

Not wanting to attract any unwanted attention they were all wielding hand weapons. Samson was down to carrying the bricks he'd found on the sidewalk. Ortega still had his oversized hatchet. Benson was sporting a machete while Chris was starting to feel pretty confident in his knife slaying skills. He'd never be as callous about killing as Rambo though. He'd rather shoot from a distance than stab up close and personal any day. If they ever got somewhere that allowed for casual conversation again, he couldn't wait to remind Ortega and Benson that they'd volunteered for this crap. They could be mowing grass or peeling potatoes right now.

Chris brought up the rear as they carefully worked their way over the piles of wind-swept junk in the street. They'd pause to hang onto whatever they could grab when the powerful gusts of wind threatened to pick them up and toss them in the air. Being pelted with random pieces of flying junk was becoming commonplace. Of course, if this wasn't happening then there'd be about a thousand zombies lined up to pick the meat off their bones right now. Chris was too busy wondering how bad the shingle that'd just hit his nose at like a hundred miles an hour had messed up his face to be feeling super thankful for the super storm though.

Up ahead Ortega ducked into an alcove to try and get the door to a FedEx shop open. The small corner shipping center was windowless. That was a huge selling feature in the middle of a *zombnado*. Crowding into the tiny alcove they all stared as Ortega fumbled around with the door handle. Chris expected to see the highly trained special forces operatives he was with whipping out little lock opening kits like you see in the movies. Instead, the SEAL and the Delta commandoes were beating the hell out of the doorknob. They looked like a couple of homeless meth addicts trying to break into an ATM machine to fund their next fix. Samson should seriously consider a haircut.

Benson and Chris did their best to keep an eye on the street while Ortega and Samson tried to beat their way into the FedEx shop without permanently damaging the door. They'd want to be able to shut and lock it behind them.

"Oh hell…" Chris muttered. He'd just noticed a crowd of the infected milling about up the street from them. He could barely see them through the rain but estimated at least a dozen. There could easily be more. What they were doing standing still in the middle of the storm was a mystery. If all the baldies would hang out in the middle of the road while the city was being ripped apart that'd be great. There'd be a whole lot less baldies by the end of the day. It was hard to tell with the rain pouring down his face, but it looked like they might be moving in the direction of the FedEx store they were in front of.

He tried pointing the zombies out to Benson, but she was unable to see them. Shaking her head in amazement that Chris was able to see anything in this weather she turned and prodded Ortega. He turned around to see what she wanted. He had his tomahawk out and ready to fight. He didn't like that he'd been pulled away from trying to open the door to be told to hurry up and open the door. It wasn't like he was taking his time. He nodded his understanding that they should be a little quieter breaking into the building. Even considering the noise levels surrounding them it paid to be cautious when there was a roving party crowd of monsters nearby.

Samson turned around to see what they were talking about. Looking out into the street he couldn't see anything. As far as he could tell there was no way anybody should be able to see what was across the street. He chalked it up to either Chris seeing things or a pause in the storm that he hadn't noticed. By the time he turned back around Ortega had the door open. The four of them rushed out of the storm into the shelter of the cramped facility. As soon as they were inside Ortega got to work on shutting and locking the door behind them. Not an easy task after all the damage they'd done breaking in.

Shutting the door was like locking themselves in a windowless tomb. The sudden quiet was deafening. They'd all become used to the rain pounding against them, the wind-blown dirt grinding away at their exposed skin, and the steady freight train roar of the tornadoes. That background noise was still audible, but it was muted substantially.

Standing there in the darkness with water dripping off of every part of him Chris felt all the various cuts, scrapes and bruises he'd gotten outside. In the pandemonium of trying to survive none of them had paid attention to the damage being done to them on that meat grinder of a road. All of them were bruised and bloody. The rain was no longer washing everyone's blood away. It was free to flow out of the dozens of wounds on each of them. Chris's hyper sense picked it up easily as they huddled together in the small, dank space. His sense of smell was now able to be fully engaged.

The blood dripping off of his friends smelled delicious.

Chapter 12: Surviving the Aftermath

"Now what?" Benson asked after flicking on a flashlight to see if it still worked. It was a wonder any of them had any working gear left after being tossed around like rag dolls by the powerful storm.

"We need to get out of here before it dies down completely." Samson answered after a long pause. He'd been caught off guard by the expression on Chris's face when Benson had turned on the lights. It'd been a savage mix of lust and hunger. Chris had been sniffing the air like an addict huffing a can of paint. It'd been uncomfortably close to the behavior they'd seen so many times among the infected.

"Sounds like we still have a little time." Benson said to fill the awkward silence. She'd noticed the look on Chris's face as well. Getting the conversation moving in a different direction was a priority. There was so much stuff going on with Chris at this point that no one would believe it without proof. He didn't even have the bite mark scars anymore to show people. Not that those would necessarily have helped prove he wasn't turning into a man-eating monster.

The explosive roll of thunder from outside reinforced her remarks. The tornadoes may have moved on but there was still a wicked storm brewing outside. That storm was the cover they needed to escape the city. Better to risk getting the crap beat out of them by golf ball sized hail then wait for the storm to clear. Better weather meant they'd have to fight their way through a city full of zombies. Not a pleasant way to wrap up the day. Especially without much left in the way of ammunition.

"What if we wait until it gets dark?" Ortega threw the suggestion out there. Benson wondered if he was really asking or just trying to cover up for Chris acting like a weirdo.

"We'd make too much noise getting out of here with all the junk in the road. The baldies would hear us and come out for a midnight snack." Samson answered. The question shifted his attention to solving the problem instead of worrying about Chris. No one was fooled into thinking the matter was dropped though. The Lieutenant was a sharp individual. A special operations leader who'd managed to stay alive running missions in this hell hole for well over a year. He may not be focused on Chris right now, but he wouldn't forget what he'd seen.

For his part Chris was doing his best to keep quiet. He'd tried to shut down his urges when the flashlight came on. The cravings that'd come out of nowhere when he'd been abruptly confronted with the overpowering smell of uninfected blood in the enclosed space. His senses had gone haywire. He'd let himself lean into the urge under the cover of darkness. Curious to see where it took him without letting it go too far. He hadn't expected Benson to turn on a light in the middle of his experimentation.

With his newfound ability to parse data like a supercomputer he'd easily noted the reactions of the others when the light came on revealing his face. Samson may have been the most obvious about it, but it was Benson's shocked expression that'd hit him the hardest. She knew what he was going through. To look at him like he was a monster though. Even for a second. Ortega had barely flinched. He wouldn't drop his poker face just because a friend of his wanted to rip his throat out and lap up all that hot, delicious blood.

Not that Chris wanted to rip anybody's throat out. He might be tempted to take a small cup of freshly squeezed warm blood if someone offered it to him. As far as sinking his teeth into somebody's neck though, that was still as repulsive as ever. Although he had to admit if Benson was cool with him licking the blood off her forehead he wouldn't hesitate. Especially not if they were behind closed doors. He was more of a closet blood sucker.

"Earth to Chris." Benson was right in Chris's face.

"Hey sorry. What happened?" Chris answered. He roped in his errant thoughts to focus on Benson. There'd be time to figure out his new dietary urges later. Avoiding being eaten was a bigger concern right now than what he wanted to eat.

"Yeah, we all noticed. You need to tone the intensity down with the Lieutenant here. I'm not sure he's ready for the full story." Benson whispered softly into Chris's ear. Ortega and Samson had wandered over to check the door. With all of the background noise from the storm it was doubtful they'd be overheard. Even if Chris thought she was speaking way too loudly given his superior hearing. He started getting lost in thought again. How long until his enhancements made it so he couldn't be around regular humans without them sensing that something was off about him?

"Dude, game face!" A frustrated Benson punctuated her remarks by punching him in the shoulder. Chris nodded guiltily. He'd been chasing another tangent down the proverbial rabbit hole. Benson was right. He needed to get his act together.

"Lover's quarrel?" Samson asked. He and Ortega had finished their door inspection and wandered back over to where Benson and Chris were.

"He wishes." Benson answered with a smile.

"Door still locked?" Chris asked. The question came out awkward but at least he was trying.

"So far so good. We're going to have to make a run for it shortly though." Ortega answered.

"Can't wait. I was worried parts of my body might dry off." Chris joked. No sane person would want to go back out into that storm. Beating your way through the wind and the rain when a baldie could pop up out of nowhere to bite you in the ass was nobody's idea of fun. Not to mention constantly being pelted with all the crap being tossed through the air by the strong winds. As much as leaving was going to suck it was the right thing to do. The longer they hung out the harder it was going to be to escape the city alive.

"How's everybody looking weapon's wise?" Samson asked. They'd gathered around one of the copy machines to talk. Benson had pulled the top of her flashlight up to turn it into a little LED lantern. Using that light, they did a quick inventory of what each of them had in pockets, bags, and waistbands.

The end result wasn't very encouraging. It was mostly the weapons they'd used to fight their way into the copy shop. Knives, hatchets, machetes, and bricks made up the bulk of their melee weapons. They had pistols and a rifle but were very limited on ammunition. Samson wasn't too worried about the weapons situation. There was no way they were going to fight their way out of the city. It wouldn't matter if they had unlimited ammunition and a hover-jeep. They were going to be relying on stealth to make it out.

"No gunfire at all if it can be helped. The more of those things we attract the less likely we make it. You see one kill it fast and quiet. Keep moving. Hiding like this only works if none of them see us hiding. We get cornered in a building with those things outside then we'll be stuck there until we starve to death, or they beat the door down." Samson paused the impromptu mission briefing to see if anyone had any questions. No one did.

"We'll be heading west. Once we hit the suburbs we'll try and snag a vehicle. If we can't find a car, we may have to ride bikes. The suburbs are spread out all around the city. We get through those then we can just hike along the river until we make it back to base." Samson paused once more to see if there were any suggestions or questions. When there were not, he asked Ortega if there was anything he'd like to add.

"If we get separated don't go back looking for people. Just follow the river to the base. We'll all meet up there." Ortega said. It was good advice. Even though none of them would follow it if they thought one of the others might need help.

"Let's do this then." Samson positioned the sheath his combat knife was in where he could get to it easily. Bricks were great for bashing in heads, but he needed the knife for the kind of wet work he envisioned to make it out of the city.

Their hidey hole not having any windows meant there was no way to see if the coast was clear before cracking open the doors. The lock was all torqued from where Ortega had bent it back to break into the building. Once he opened the door, it'd take a minute to secure it again if they had to. They were betting on the coast being clear. Hopefully the group of infected Chris had seen earlier had moved along while they'd been taking a breather.

Ortega pried the door open while the rest of them stood ready to deal with whatever might be on the other side. Other than a strong gust of wind whipped rain nothing came through the door when Ortega cracked it open. Looking back at them Ortega made sure everyone was ready to roll out. Seeing that they were all waiting on him he pushed the door open far enough for them to squeeze through. The wind grabbed it and whipped it open the rest of the way. No big deal if there hadn't been half a dozen of the infected standing about five feet away.

Whether it was just bad luck, or the baldies had some sort of sixth sense that helped them find people hiding in windowless copy centers the two parties found themselves staring at each other through a translucent curtain of pouring rain. No surprise the baldies reacted first. The monsters didn't have the kind of options to consider that were holding the four uninfected people frozen in place. There was only one option for the monsters once they saw their prey.

Ducking back into the copy center was Chris's first instinct. He'd already taken a step backwards when he saw Ortega charging forwards with his hatchet held high. Samson was right behind him. Benson was stuck in that same paralyzed state that'd been holding Chris captive. Adrenaline pumping though his body Chris was able to clearly see everything as it unfolded. Everyone around him might as well be moving in slow motion. Pulling out his Rambo knife Chris lunged past Ortega and savagely stabbed an infected woman in the throat.

Ortega shifted to focus on the baldie that'd been standing next to the woman Chris had just taken out. Chris was already gutting another one of the infected. Samson hadn't even gotten to the enemy yet. Benson was just now moving forward to engage. Chris could feel her eyes following him as he danced among the diseased souls granting them release with perfectly executed knife strokes.

Ortega and Samson each got one. Despite jumping in after the two special ops studs Chris had taken out four of the baldies on his own. Doing his best to appear casual Ortega motioned for everyone to follow him up the road. Even though it was still early afternoon, it was dark as night outside. The roar of the tornadoes had been replaced by the continuous claps of thunder as bolts of lightning ignited fires across the flooded city. Ortega led them around the corner and up another block at a run.

It wasn't easy jogging in a mess like this. The rain was coming down so hard that they were inhaling mouthfuls of water every time they tried to breathe. Water covered debris lurked in the puddles waiting to twist their ankles if they took a wrong step. It was hard to focus on the water when every shadow they passed might be concealing a blood thirsty cannibal ready to spring.

Chris found himself able to easily keep up with the others. It wasn't that he was necessarily any more physically fit than the rest of them. It was more like he was able to put his feet down in better places to run more smoothly. He was able to moderate his breathing and his heartbeat to achieve maximum efficiency. In the midst of doing that he was able to take in their surroundings and look for threats. He was doing all of that on autopilot. Part of himself was sitting back and wondering how the hell he was doing everything he was doing. Another part of him as wondering how come everybody didn't function this way all the time. He wasn't a supernatural being. He was just an incredibly efficient human.

That realization spurred him on as Ortega slowed to engage a middle-aged monster stumbling in his direction. A hard overhand swing and the skinny baldie slumped to the ground with a massive dent in its skull. A human life ended and none of them so much as spared the dying man a second glance as they continued running. An especially fierce gust of wind blew rain and debris into their faces. Chris had seen the gust coming and closed his eyes in time to avoid the pupil peppering his companions received.

Ortega ushered them another block before ducking into an alcove that opened up to a courtyard. They'd apparently stumbled into the ritzier section of town. One where people used to walk around with a glass of wine window shopping fashion and art. The kind of people who could afford to pay their credit cards off each month. Chris had once aspired to that American dream. Now he just aspired to living. Preferably with minimal dreaming.

"Everybody good?" Ortega asked once they'd gathered together under the large concrete archway leading into the courtyard dining area. He was attempting to get his poncho to drape over him in a way that might keep some parts of his body a little drier than the others. With all of the running in the rain he was expecting to be dealing with a whole lot of chafing in the near future. His pondering where he might find a tube of Vaseline was interrupted by a sudden outburst from Samson.

"I need to know what the hell you people aren't telling me." Samson fired the statement off with barely controlled fury. The frustration evident in his voice. Either that or the chafing was already getting to him.

"There's no time now sir. Wait until we make it out of here." Ortega answered. There was no point in pretending they weren't keeping a secret. Not with Chris openly displaying his super ninja skills on top of his super creepy sniffing habit. Better to admit it and deal with explaining it later. Having that particular conversation would be much easier when they weren't in the middle of a massive storm surrounded by thousands of zombies.

"Alright. But I'm going to hold you to that. Do not die before we make it back to base, or I'll be pissed." Samson said looking at them each in turn. Ortega nodded and guided them back into the breach.

Chapter 13: Embrace the Suck

Most of the baldies had taken shelter from the storm. It must suck to stand around naked with all kinds of crap slamming into you. The baldies may have some of the same enhanced senses Chris had, but that didn't mean they'd be leaping out at them at every turn. Even with his genetic upgrades Chris was having a hard time in the rain. He could spot his companions but that was about it. His enhanced senses were rendered much less effective by the massive storm.

They still stumbled across the occasional baldie. The ones they ran into had taken a major beating from staying out in the metrological madness. That made it easier to gut them and move on. Chris began to wish his ability to quickly pick out and remember details was something he had more control over. The corpses of baldies without the sense to seek shelter were smashed into the rubble all over the place. In death the madness left them leaving behind the husk of what'd been a regular person.

Stepping over a mound of bricks and mud that partially concealed the badly bashed body of a young girl Chris struggled to keep his eyes focused straight ahead. Resentful of the others for their relative tunnel vision he fought an internal struggle to keep his mind open to all the input. What were a few more nightmarish images to haunt his sleep? At this rate he was going to have to start sleeping longer to fit in all the night terrors. Thinking that a lot of the survivors out there would kill to have his 'gifts' he got back to watching his friends backs.

A block later Chris had counted two dozen dead bodies that he doubted anyone else in the party had even seen. Not that they should be too focused on the dead ones. Those poor souls had been granted mercy by mother nature herself. It was the living infected that everyone was on the lookout for. A search that was becoming easier as the storm tapered off.

The weather had gone from the storm of the century to your average bad thunderstorm. It was still the kind of weather where you'd be crazy to go outside. In the old days the local weathermen would've been monopolizing the news pointing out the red bands still moving through the area on the weather map. It'd gone from bricks flying through the air to shingles and hail battering the hell out of them. Heads down they walk-jogged their way as far from downtown as they could get as quickly as they could.

"If the sun comes out, we're screwed." Chris said when Ortega pulled them into another alcove for a quick pow wow.

"We've been screwed since we got on those pontoon boats." Benson commented bitterly. She was miserably wet, freezing, and bruised all over. Chafing wasn't just for men either. They needed to loot some diaper rash medicine on the way back to base. In the unlikely event they made it back alive they'd all deeply appreciate having made the side trip.

"We're still alive. When you're pale, bloody, and covered in bite marks that's when you're screwed. Until then we keep moving." Samson ordered. Good thing he had a government job because he'd never make it on the motivational speaker circuit. The rest of his team were most likely all dead by now. A few of them may make their way back to the base but the odds weren't great. The odds weren't great for anyone to have made it this long into the apocalypse. It was like winning the lottery twice and you only bought one ticket.

"Yes sir." Benson mumbled sarcastically. She was way beyond caring about military protocol. Samson didn't take her tone kindly.

"My men just got blown all over the damned place. They're either drowned or being ripped apart by the undead. There's no way to try and look for them or I would. Right now, I'm doing my best to get us back to base. All I really want to do is go rip this city apart to find my dead men. I don't leave people behind. Do you hear me! Do you get me now! Want to make more smug ass comments? I don't care how cold and miserable you are. You're alive. Suck it up soldier!" Samson conveyed that he was yelling at her without raising the volume of his voice all that much. His words trembled with barely contained emotion.

Chris noted Ortega had taken a step forward to intervene if Samson lost it and put hands on Benson. For his part Chris was pretty sure Benson could handle Goldilocks by herself if need be. Of course, with Ortega and Chris standing right there she wouldn't have to.

"Sorry about your men sir." Benson responded in a much more respectful tone. The sincerity in her voice rang true. Samson took a step back and reclaimed his cool, stoic, special forces face. He looked like he was about to apologize as well then just nodded. He didn't trust himself to speak again quite yet.

"The way I see it we just go north until we hit the river then follow that back to base. Sound good sir? Anything we should watch out for?" Ortega asked. His heavy-handed effort to change the subject was welcomed by all.

"Sounds good. It's mostly woods and suburbs once we get past I-35. It's about thirty miles to the fort from here. Once we get in the woods, we should be good. We'll have to find a bridge to get over the canal though." Samson answered. Focusing on the mission was what would get him through this. There'd be plenty of time for self-doubt and self-medicating once they were back on base.

Taking that as an order Ortega led them back out onto the street. The piles of rubble had been replaced by the typical apocalyptic debris. Most of the buildings they were passing in this section still had windows in them. The more the storm eased up the more worried they all became. By the time they could see I-35 they were double timing it. Running as fast as they could without tripping or making too much noise. The sunlight streaking through the holes in the clouds revealing them to the world.

Longing for the darkness of the heavy clouds and blinding sheets of rain they loped down the road towards the underpass.

"Stop!" Chris yelled digging in his heels. He hated making any noise at all, but it was the only way to quickly get their attention. He had to shout again before they finally stopped. Even then Samson had to bark another quick command to get Ortega to stop. Between the rain still drizzling down and their own harsh breathing, it was hard to hear anything. Especially when everyone kept trying to yell quietly.

"What's up?" Benson asked in between deep shuddering breaths. She'd ran track in high school and make it to the state level competitions. This was a whole different ballgame though.

"They're under there." Chris said. He wasn't even breathing hard. His body was adjusting to new methods of regulating his oxygen levels. The shot Lynn had given him opened up the part of his brain that allowed for better autonomous control of his respiratory system. Or at least that's what Chris had worked out while running behind Benson. It was ridiculous how easy it was for him to run now. If he didn't need to stick with his group, he could easily streak off over the garbage strewn streets and be back at the fort in no time flat. The memories of Lynn giving him a piggyback ride through the bowels of a cargo ship like she was starring in a ninja movie made a lot more sense now.

"What? How do you know that?" Samson asked. He was breathing hard as well. He'd turned around to stare through the rain at the barely visible overpass up ahead.

"It just makes sense that they'd go there to get out of the storm." Chris said quickly. He didn't want to explain how he could somehow see 'around' the rain drops. It was too weird. He had absolutely no idea how he was able to do it. They were lucky he could though. Considering the large mob of baldies huddled together underneath the massive concrete structure. Running under there would've been a death sentence.

"Makes sense, but are you sure? I mean they could be anywhere. Have you seen them under overpasses in storms before or something?" Samson asked doubtfully. The long-haired special operator had good reason to want to verify. The storm was beginning to break up. They needed to be at least a mile outside the city before that happened. Right now, they were standing around talking in the middle of zombie central.

"Let's just go around." Benson said. There had to be a section with an embankment they could go up and over.

The storm picked that moment to lighten up. The rain tapered off completely and the sunlight pierced the cloud cover. It was the exact wrong time for that to happen. They were standing on the side of a road with no cover to duck behind. Samson and the rest of them could now clearly see the danger that Chris had brought up. Unfortunately, that danger could also see them.

The four of them spun around and took off in the other direction. They didn't bother looking back to see if they were being chased. If they hadn't been noticed it was a miracle that they could sacrifice a goat for later. One or two of the infected crowd had to have noticed them. One was all it would take for the whole mess of them to bust out from under the bridge and give chase.

Easily keeping the pace set by the others Chris half turned to look back over his shoulder. Every single baldie under the bridge had joined the chase. It was like a reverse running of the bulls. They'd inadvertently fired off the starter pistol for a massive baldie marathon. Chris felt good about his own ability to survive. His friends were going to have a harder go of it though.

Ortega spotted a building on the side of the road that might give them a chance. There were no broken windows or other obvious signs of it being used as a shelter by the infected. Making a split-second decision the Delta operator swerved towards the front door of the building. The rest of them followed without question. There was no time for questions. When Ortega reached down and grabbed a loose brick the rest of them did the same. Seconds later four thrown bricks shattered a window that'd managed to survive looters, hordes of the infected, and the mega storm that'd just passed through.

A few seconds later they'd cleared the broken glass enough for them to scramble into the building. Yelling for them to follow him Ortega kept running down a long hallway to the other side of the building. It was one of those shared office buildings where there are multiple companies on each floor. Their survival depended on getting out the other side of the building before the first baldie made it through the window they'd just broken. Hopefully that would trick the infected into thinking they were hiding in the building when in reality they'd be scurrying like rats back towards the interstate.

Chris won the race to the opposite side of the building. Sliding to a stop he fumbled around with the door to unlock it and get it open. The business across the street from them was a home and auto insurance company. Those rates must be sky high by now. Especially if you wanted to add the end of the world clause. Getting the door open before the others made it there Chris wondered if he should've run a little slower. His Olympic record-breaking hallway dash was going to further pique Samson's curiosity.

Disregarding Chris's freakish speed for now Samson joined the rest of them in hastily vacating the building. Chris ran behind the others as they desperately searched for a way out of the mess that they were in. Ortega broke off from the others when they passed a parking lot full of rusting vehicles. Several of the rusting cars were sitting on flat tires or missing windows. Finding an old Ford truck Ortega broke the window and let himself in. The rest of them gathered around thinking how great it'd be if Ortega knew how to hotwire trucks.

Samson doubted Ortega would be able to get it started. He understood the logic in picking the older vehicle to try. The new ones all had computer chips and keyless everything. The old ones were a hell of a lot easier to steal. If this one happened to have a charge left in the battery and some gas in the tank, then they might get to ride for a few blocks. That'd be a major improvement over their current situation.

Chris was on the verge of pointing out a few baldies he saw sniffing around the road they'd just come from when Ortega got the truck started. The engine sputtered a few times before roaring to life. Ortega waved at them to hop in. He noticed the baldies getting closer and his waves got a lot more energetic. Benson hopped in the shotgun seat while Samson and Chris jumped in the truck bed. Samson slapped the roof of the little pick me up truck to indicate it was time to go.

With minimal ammunition and a desire to keep the noise down Chris and Samson had both pulled out their knives. They quickly put the blades away to avoid cutting themselves when Ortega fishtailed at full speed out of the parking lot. The baldies who'd been streaming towards them were left eating mouthfuls of dirt. Chris spun around in the truck bed to see where they were headed. As fast as they were going, he wasn't too worried about any of the infected joining them at the moment.

Up ahead on the rain-soaked road a few infected were running straight for the truck. Chris dropped back down into the truck bed motioning for Samson to brace himself. Based on how Ortega had left the parking lot he wasn't in the mood to play. Chris was fantasizing about inventing seat belts for truck beds when they finally made it through the zombies and across the canal. The two men in the back felt like a cat stuck in a dryer. Their bruises had bruises.

Up in the front seat Ortega whipped them down small side streets through suburbia. He was ecstatic to be out of that damned city. It'd been a bloody big meat grinder. Now all they had to do was drive back to base. They might even make it in time for dinner if they hurried. Thinking quickly about the best way to get there Ortega slowed down to let Benson in the driver's seat and Samson in the navigator's chair. It made sense to have the guy familiar with the area feeding the navigational advice to the best driver they had.

A minute later they were back in motion with Benson driving. All of them did their best not to look too thrilled to be alive. Not when they knew Samson's mind was dwelling heavily on his missing troops. If ten percent of them managed to limp back to the base it'd be a miracle. It was beyond belief that the four of them had managed to make it this far. Ortega did his best to get situated in the truck bed. Grumbling to himself he second guessed his voluntary seat reassignment. It'd been much more comfortable riding up front.

Ortega didn't let the garbage filled truck bed get him too down. He was alive and headed back to a base with food and hot water. At this rate they'd be hitting the showers in under an hour.

Chapter 14: What's Normal Anyway?

"Dammit!" Ortega blurted out. He was pissed at himself for jinxing them. It hadn't been a minute since he'd thought about how great a hot shower was going to feel. No way the gods of irony could let that slide. The truck's timing belt had snapped causing all kinds of commotion inside the engine followed by the release of a whole lot of steam. A little post-apocalyptic preventative maintenance would've gone a long way.

The truck jerked to a stop accompanied by Benson's inspired cursing. The noise was bound to attract unwanted attention from the undead residents of the suburb they were driving through. The tract of affordable single-family homes was a forbidding expanse of possible nests of the infected. The slight drizzle coming from the overcast sky would dampen how far the noise traveled. This wasn't the time to wait for AAA to show up.

Samson gestured for everyone to follow him into the rundown subdivision. The trick that had worked for them downtown should work here as well. All they needed to do was go through an empty house or two and disappear into the wooded area. From there they could make their way to the riverbank and hike the rest of the way back to the fort. Hot showers might still be on the table.

They jogged past a large wooden sign that let them know they were entering *Windy Estates*. Chris couldn't help but wonder what kind of idiot developer would tempt fate in Kansas by calling their housing project by that name. Samson was casting about for a way to quickly disappear from sight. They were currently incredibly exposed out on the cracked pavement. Thinking quickly, he ran to a house with a fence around the backyard and hopped over it.

The grass might not be greener on the other side, but it was a lot more overgrown. The Windy Estates HOA must be busy sending out passive-aggressive violation letters over the lack of upkeep. Samson waited in the backyard as the others vaulted the fence to join him. Without even thinking about it Chris leapt over the fence and landed on the other side. Landing in the tall grass he saw everyone staring at him. He'd cleared the fence by at least three feet without even bending his knees that much. Benson shot Samson a glance to indicate that they could talk about Chris's ridiculous vertical leap later. Now was not the time.

The slider on the back of the house had been ripped off. The mummified remains of two medium sized dogs were curled up on the porch. The dogs still had their leashes connected to collars around their naturally taxidermized necks. They saw pets that'd ended up like that so often that Chris had started calling them pet jerky. Euphemisms like that helped reduce the time spent thinking about the sad plight of animals left to starve to death after their owners turned.

Samson gave Chris a long hard stare to remind him that at some point they were going to need to talk. Chris awkwardly nodded back under the intense scrutiny. Samson took that as confirmation that Chris understood why he needed to know the capabilities of the people under his command. Especially when those capabilities were starting to enter the realm of 'otherworldly'.

Once again putting a boot down firmly on his curiosity Samson jogged across the overgrown back yard to hop the short metal picket fence into the next yard. This one was overgrown as well but the windows and slider were intact. There was no telling what the front of the house looked like but from the back it was promising. All they wanted to do was hide out somewhere while any excitement died down from the noise of their truck having blown a belt.

"Looks clear to me." Ortega whispered after staring through the back glass slider for a minute or two.

"Yeah, it's pretty clean in there." Benson echoed. Clean houses meant untouched houses. As a general rule looters, baldies, and refugees didn't worry a whole lot about being tidy.

Ortega and Samson got in position to lift the slider and ram it past the locking mechanism. They'd already confirmed there wasn't a piece of wood shoved in the bottom of the door to repel their effort. Breaking the lock on a slider wasn't necessarily a bad thing. It's not like the baldies got much more advanced than push or pull when it came to doors. Even if the slider was broken the baldies would take forever to figure it out. Plus, they had every intention of thwarting any efforts to follow them into the house by finding something to shove in the bottom of the slider.

Ortega counted to three and the two men lifted the glass door up and over. It made a scraping noise then opened with a loud crack. Ortega went in with hatchet held high followed by Samson with his pistol out. If they were outnumbered the Lieutenant didn't have a problem pulling the trigger. A little noise beat out certain death every day of the week and twice on Sundays.

The doors opened up into a large open floor concept with a couple of couches by the sliders. A pale, bald man in boxers with sores all over him jumped up off the couch. The man spun to face them then tripped when he tried to run backwards to get away from Ortega. Ortega had already gone around the couch to bring the hammer down on the suspected baldie. Something didn't feel right about the situation though.

Ortega wasn't used to having second thoughts in the middle of combat. You moved, you acquired targets, you wasted the targets, and then you kept moving. It wasn't a super complicated concept. Especially when the bulk of your enemies were naked, hairless people who were trying to eat you. Monsters who immediately rushed for you as soon as they saw you.

"He's backing away from you." Samson said curiously. He was covering the baldie while simultaneously scoping out the rest of the house. He'd let Ortega signal if he wanted him to blow the things brains out.

"Don't kill me!" The baldie croaked out loudly.

A picture of Ortega could've been taken and used as a universal WTF meme. Stepping forward the Master Sergeant almost killed the baldie out of habit. It's never a great thing to surprise a killer when he's in the middle of killing you. Although in this case it did end up keeping Ortega from caving in the obviously infected man's skull. The long venetian blinds rattled around as Benson and Chris crowded in to see what was going on. Each of them assumed it was something bad. That's just the way their day was going.

"Did that thing just talk?" Benson asked. Her face crinkled up to mirror Ortega's disbelief.

"I did! Don't kill me!" The cowering man on the ground shouted again. His voice was hoarse and crackly but understandable. Like a seventy-year-old three pack a day smoker with the flu.

"Are you infected?" Samson asked. It was kind of a dumb question, but they all listened raptly to the baldie's answer.

"Just a little bit. It screwed up my skin and made my hair fall out. Then it stopped. I never went mad." The baldie answered.

"Do you eat people?" Benson asked. Chris for one thought that was a very valid question. Probably the one they should've started with.

"No! Never! Canned food and really stale chips most of the time. The other infected people leave me alone as long as I act like them. I think they can smell the sickness on me. I'm Greg Stickel." Greg stuck his hand out like he expected someone to help him up.

"How come you haven't come out of hiding? You know there's a base nearby, right?" Samson asked.

"How close do you think I'd get?" Greg said morosely indicating his bald head and sore covered skin.

"Why are you just wearing boxers?" Chris asked curiously. The infected wore their clothes until they rotted off. Considering the conditions that the zombies clothes were subjected to it didn't take long for them to end up being mostly nude. Greg seemed perfectly capable of pulling on a fresh pair of pants if he wanted to though.

"The blisters hurt. You're lucky I'm wearing boxers today." Greg answered while slowly standing up. He was looking around the room to make sure everyone was ok with him standing up. Ortega wasn't.

"Sit down on the couch over there. Sit on your hands." Ortega ordered. When Greg hesitated Ortega took a step forward and Samson casually adjusted his pistol to point at Greg's face. Greg jumped backwards butt first to land on the couch. He folded one hand under each boxer covered cheek and sat there waiting to be told what to do next.

From somewhere on his person Ortega produced some zip ties and tossed them over to Greg. Greg stared at them like Ortega had just flung poop in his lap.

"Put them on your wrists. I wish I had a muzzle with me too." Ortega said coldly. He was having some trust issues with good old Greg.

Meanwhile Benson and Samson went to clear the rest of the house. There was no telling what other surprises lurked in this musty slice of suburbia. Greg fumbled around with the tie wraps. The problem was a large lesion running across Greg's wrists kept him from wanting to tighten the restraints very much. He'd ended up with a couple of interlocked plastic bracelets dangling off his wrists.

Ortega moved closer to the couch to tighten the bracelets. Chris came around the couch to back him up. When Ortega bent forward to grab the bracelets Greg lunged at Ortega's face with his mouth wide open. Jumping to the side Ortega ended up on the ground. Greg turned to spring on top of him, but Chris had already caught Greg in a headlock. Chris fell backwards onto the couch dragging the mostly infected Greg with him. Now Greg was in Chris's lap on the couch. Ortega sprang back to his feet and turned around to smash in Greg's cranium with his axe.

"Stop! You're going to hit my arm!" Chris yelled when an enraged Ortega looked like he was about to start chopping away.

"Move your arm then." Ortega shouted back. Greg wasn't talking. The humanity had fled him when he lunged for Ortega. He was growling and thrashing around to try and escape Chris's hold on his neck.

"If I do that, he'll bite me." Chris tossed back at his friend. Ortega took a step back to consider the best way to deal with all of this. Chris felt Greg relax when Ortega moved back a few steps.

"I'm sorry! He got so close so fast it freaked me out. I haven't been near regular people in so long. I'm sorry! I couldn't help it." Greg forced the words out past the vice grip Chris had on his throat.

"How are you dealing with Chris holding you then?" Ortega asked.

"He doesn't exactly smell human." Greg answered.

"What the hell does that mean?" Samson asked. Him and Benson had returned from their patrol of the house. Samson was carrying a garbage bag that was heavy with something. Greg's eyes widened when he saw what Samson was holding. Chris could already smell what was in the bag.

"Why do you have a bag full of chopped up body parts?" Benson asked. It was a rhetorical question really. Especially considering Greg had blown his cover by trying to eat Ortega's face mere seconds prior to the zombie picnic basket being revealed.

Greg was completely at a loss for words. Benson tossed the bag down on the ground. A maggot infested pile of meat spilled out onto the floor. Samson stared down at the pile of muck for a second or two. Chris thought maybe the Lieutenant was trying to figure out what do next. This probably wasn't a situation they covered in SEAL college.

Samson's lip abruptly curled up. With a gasp of pure disgust, he drew his knife and took the dozen steps to cross the room. With zero hesitation he plunged the blade into Greg's heart. He stabbed the talkative baldie a few more times to make sure he'd done the job properly. Chris pushed the body off of him and stood up to leave. Samson retrieved his blade and spit on the corpse. Then with his head bowed he walked out of the room.

Chris got up and followed the rest of the team out of the room. Glancing down at the putrid pile of body parts he saw what'd set Samson off. Repulsed by the pathetic sight he hurried out of the room. They left Greg's corpse on the moldy carpet next to his bag of snacks. The tiny recently gnawed arm of an infant plainly visible on the floor.

Chapter 15: Back from the Dead

Chris didn't want to get out of the shower. It felt fantastic to wash away the grime after their insanely long day. Only two other members of Samson's unit had made it back to the base. On the plus side that meant he could use all the hot water he wanted. He'd have loved to stand there with the steaming hot water hitting him all night. He very well might have if Samson hadn't sent someone to drag him out.

The Lieutenant had ordered Chris to report to his office once he was cleaned up. Chris had taken that to mean he should treat himself to a spa day. He'd reached new levels in exfoliation trying to waste as much time as possible. There was always the chance that Samson might blow his head off when he heard that Chris had been infected before. Especially after running into Greg the freak on the way back. That infant munching nut ball had been a prime example of why there wasn't such a thing as 'zombie-lite'. It was like being a 'little bit pregnant'.

"Any day now princess." A familiar voice sounded off from outside the shower door.

"'He's spending more time in the shower than I did." Benson added to Ortega's commentary.

"What are you guys doing in here?" Chris asked. Like he didn't know they'd been sent to collect him.

"It's going to take him a whole lot longer to look half as good." Ortega said completely ignoring Chris.

"How much of that Jack have you gone through since we got back?" Benson asked in response to Ortega's slightly slurred flattery.

"Enough of it to be fine with dragging Chris down the hallway by his private parts if he doesn't get his ass out of that shower in the next two minutes." Ortega answered casually. The threat was real enough coming from him that Chris cut the water off and asked someone to grab him a towel. While he was drying himself off, he asked if they had any ideas on how he should handle the conversation with Samson.

"You mean the questions from the highly trained interrogator from the military branch that popularized water boarding?" Ortega asked.

"We've got a couple of minutes. I guess we could come up with a super elaborate story to explain why Greg the zombie didn't think you smelled human." Benson added.

"We'll need to make sure to come up with a legit reason why you can jump like eight feet in the air like it's nothing. Oh! Let's not forget the way you like to smell people and how you're able to kill half a dozen baldies before Samson can get his knife out of his pocket." Ortega said sarcastically.

"You don't think we can spin all that? We could say it's all top secret or something?" Chris asked nervously. Maybe he should just hop back in the shower and give the loofah another whirl. He loved that the bad ass special forces types had boxes full of Bed Bath and Beyond luxury bathing items by the shower stalls.

"The spin ship has sailed. Time to come clean. Maybe next time keep the superpowers on the down low. A little more Clark Kent and a little less Dracula." Benson said. She was pointing at her watch and motioning for Chris to hurry up. She rolled her eyes when he went behind some lockers to get dressed. There weren't many secrets between them at this point. Modesty was more of an afterthought in the midst of an apocalypse.

Chris threw on his clothes. Still thinking through ways to tell his story he followed his friends out of the bathroom and up the stairs. He was having a hard time coming up with the best place to start his story from. Despite all that'd happened he still teared up remembering his mom getting shot down at the beginning of all of this. There were parts of his story that seemed unbelievable even to himself. He could already picture Samson shaking his head at the weirdness he was going to be presenting.

"Just answer his questions. You'll be fine. I think we can trust him." Ortega said before knocking on Samson's office door. It was a reassuring and nice thing to say. It was so completely out of character coming from Ortega that it made Chris way more nervous.

Samson opened the door and invited them all in with a sweep of his arm. They trooped in and found places to sit. Samson's one guest chair was already occupied. A dark complected man smiled up at Chris from it. The smile brought back memories from the beginning of all of this for Chris. Struggling to contain his confusion he finally blurted out a welcome to his old handler. The man he'd been told was dead.

"Desmond!" Chris exclaimed. With an answering smile on his face Chris took a few steps over to shake hands with a man who appeared very much alive. The man who'd handed him bags of cash and helped set him up in a rental house after he'd survived being bitten for the first time. The man Lynn had assigned to watch over him.

"Hey Chris. You and I need to talk." Desmond answered. His tone making it clear Chris should keep his mouth shut for now.

"We were supposed to be talking to the Lieutenant." Ortega said with only a trace of a slur. The liquor he'd been dumping down his throat since they got back was loosening his tongue. He didn't know who the man was sitting in the corner, but he didn't seem military. He gave off more of a CIA vibe. Ortega had never been a fan of spooks. Those self-serving pricks tended to consider soldiers expendable.

"I'd like to speak with Chris alone for a few minutes." Desmond announced. He clearly didn't care who Ortega thought was supposed to be talking to who. Ortega opened his mouth to provide his opinion of Desmond's remark. Before Ortega could firmly plant his combat boot in his own mouth Samson stood up and asked Benson and Ortega to accompany him to get some coffee. Ortega's mouth hung comically open for a few seconds. Benson had to physically poke him in the side to get him to reset. The three of them exited the room. Ortega cast a long hard look at Desmond as he walked out.

"You're just a regular human." Were the first words out of Chris's mouth once the door to the office was closed. He'd been under the impression that Desmond was intimately intertwined in the dark organization Lynn was a part of. He'd known that wasn't true within seconds of spotting Desmond sitting in the office. Desmond's body smelled just like the rest of the uninfected humans.

"I like to think I'm at least a little bit special." Desmond answered with the dry wit that Chris remembered so well. Desmond had been his lifeline in a very trying time. Chris was happy the rumors of his old friend's demise had been greatly exaggerated. Even if 'friend' might be a pretty strong word to describe their relationship. Desmond had been more like his caretaker.

"What happened? Why did Lynn tell me that you were dead?" Chris asked.

"She lies a lot. It makes things a lot simpler for her. I think she likes the look on people's faces when I show up after they thought I was dead." Desmond answered seriously. This wasn't the first time he'd had to explain he was still alive to someone.

"Why are you here instead of her? Are you like a familiar or something?" Chris was thinking of the *Blade* movies where the vamps kept humans close by to carry out their orders. The humans in those movies were called familiars. They stayed close to the vamps in the hopes of being turned one day.

"*Harry Potter* owl or the movie with Wesley Snipes?" Desmond answered the question with another question. A quirky smile tugging at the corners of his mouth.

"The second one." Chris answered feeling like Desmond was avoiding the question.

"Then the answer's no. I'm not like the *Harry Potter* familiar either. I don't have the right genetic make-up to be turned. I didn't win the biological lottery like you did. I'm a high-priced associate of Lynns. Not that salary really matters anymore. Now I stick to her just to stay alive." Desmond answered.

"Why are you here? Why didn't Lynn come?" Chris asked. He was happy to see Desmond, but the guy wasn't going to be able to answer all of the questions that Chris had. No regular human could explain the metamorphosis Chris was in the middle of.

"Thanks for the voicemail. It made tracking you down way easier. I'm here to check up on you. For instance, did you not get the memo about not telling the whole world you were being inducted into a super-secret organization of genetically altered beings? I could be wrong but I'm assuming your two companions know more than they should. From talking to the Lieutenant, it sounds like you've been showing off for the whole world to see. Did you really jump ten feet into the air to clear a fence?" Desmond shook his head as Chris's eyes revealed that he had indeed done that.

"I got the memo. I was 'showing off' by accident. I don't even know what I'm able to do until I do it. I need to talk to Lynn. I need somebody to tell me why I can jump ten feet in the air. How come I can smell the fact that you're just a regular human. I've got a ton of questions." Chris responded urgently. He needed those answers. He needed someone to tell him what the hell was going on.

"Yeah. Well Lynn's not on this continent so you're not getting her answers. There're others like her on this side of the pond. They'd rip your throat out if they knew where you were. Or more likely send their 'people' to take care of you." Desmond sipped at the closet brewed beer he'd been given by Samson. He seemed surprised by how good it was. Chris could totally relate to that. It was sad to think that there was a good chance the guys who'd been brewing it had been smeared all over Kansas City by the storm.

"What can you tell me?" A frustrated Chris asked. He was happy to see Desmond alive and kicking. That initial surge of excitement was fading rapidly though. Desperation replacing the excitement as he realized he still wasn't going to be able to get his most important questions answered. Desmond would only be able to give him secondhand knowledge of what was happening. It didn't help one bit that Desmond was being dodgy with his answers.

"Lynn's in Europe. I have no idea when she'll be back. She's either talking to the elders or trying to kill them all. I'm not really sure which. I can tell you that the guy she took out of that base down south as a decoy for you had his head separated from his body two days later. I can also tell you that no one else in the last decade who's received the shot Lynn gave you has survived this long. At least not to my knowledge. Other lesser beings have evolved but not any other royals." Desmond stopped talking to once more focus on nursing the delicious local brew.

"What can you tell me about what's happening to me?" Chris asked. That's what he really wanted to know. Was he going to get fangs? Would his feet turn into cloven hoofs? Would he be able transform into a bat? At this point he was beginning to believe anything was possible.

"Obviously I don't have first-hand experience. I don't even have much secondhand experience. Even though I've been around the *Familia* all my life. I'm not a familiar or anything. The *Familia* takes in children from certain lineages where there's been a high percentage of people with the right genetic makeup to be turned. Most of us still don't win that lottery." Desmond shrugged to indicate that was fine with him.

Chris waited while Desmond gathered his thoughts. After another sip of the beer the whole story poured out. It sounded like something out of the *X-Men*. A special school for children with special powers. The children in the school Desmond had attended weren't told they were special though. They were educated in everything from martial arts to advanced political maneuvering. It was very easy to wash out and end up in a regular orphanage. Something that was held over the children to ensure they did their best work. The bottom five to ten percent of the class routinely got kicked out every year.

Desmond had been in the top five percent of his class. The testing to see if you were a good candidate for the DNA enhancement therapy was only accurate after puberty. All of the children were tested in what would have been their sophomore year of high school in the normal world. Due to the advanced curriculum and emphasis on learning or leaving the majority of the kids were on the graduate college level of learning by the time they hit puberty. The ones who were kicked out prior to then were never tested as far as Desmond knew. The *Familia* had no use for those who didn't apply themselves.

It was exceedingly rare for the *Familia* to find candidates this way. The odds were considerably better than finding them out in the wild though. What it did for the *Familia* was provide a steady stream of assistants with all the skills needed to serve their masters once they'd passed through yet more training in an even more secretive school. The top five percent of each class ended up directly assigned to one of the *Familia*. To this point Chris had asked once more if Desmond was basically Lynn's familiar. Desmond had added that to the list of questions he was ignoring and kept on going.

The bulk of the students ended up as managers and executives in the family's global business empire. They never really knew who or what the family, or *Familia*, actually represented. Most of them remained ultra-loyal for the rest of their lives. Including the ones who entered the world of politics instead of the world of business.

The top students underwent a series of tests to see which ones would perform well supporting the *Familia* more directly. Desmond had sailed through the testing with flying colors. Then had come another four years of education. He'd earned the equivalent of multiple doctorates during the grueling process. The most important classes had been the ones concerning the *Familia*. There'd been history classes, finance classes, genealogy classes, and all kinds of others specifically tailored to the *Familia*. An organization that the top students were eventually told had some members who'd lived for millennia.

Only the top students ever found out the details about who the *Familia* really was. Desmond had no doubt there were plenty of details that were left out of the documents they'd studied. What was left was chilling enough. Mass murders throughout history had been carried out as the *Familia* experimented with ways to find more of their own. The Holocaust, the black plague, AIDS, massive influenza outbreaks, and a host of other atrocities had been initiated by members of the *Familia*. Facts that would never see the light of day.

The *Familia* was huge in genealogy, DNA research, and pharmaceutical supplies. Graduates of their training programs ran the biggest research and development laboratories on the planet. The disease control centers for the largest nations on earth were all directly controlled by the *Familia*. Chris had already known all of this at a high level but hearing the story the way Desmond was telling it was something else. Lynn had just kind of dropped these knowledge bombs without connecting the pieces then disappeared. Desmond was giving him a dissertation on it. So much so that they had to shoo away Samson and the others twice.

"Ok. So that fills in some of the blanks. The world's run by a bunch of rich old vampires and their MBA prodigy. Why not. Now what does that mean for me?" Chris asked the question he really wanted the answer to. It was great that there was this whole blood sucking Illuminati thing going on. Good for them. How did he fit into it though? Was he going to start slurping down AB+ on the regular? Were his friends safe? Was he going to live forever?

"You're almost a member of the *Familia*. Once you complete the change and get initiated you will be. Once you're in your pretty much untouchable. Right now, you're still touchable. Lynn's enemies will be coming for you. Otherwise, she'll get more powerful once you're initiated. Assuming you stay loyal to her." Desmond said it like that should all make perfect sense. Chris didn't have Desmond's background in Vampire 101. All that time he'd spent watching TV shows featuring vampires and the slayers of vampires was not proving super helpful.

"Ok. So, what's initiated mean?" Chris asked. Maybe if he just narrowed it down to one specific topic, he could get something a little more useful out of Desmond.

"Humans aren't allowed into the hall to see. It's a ceremony they do in Thessaly. It might include some human sacrifice. It's an ancient ceremony. There'll be a group of the elders there to oversee it. The really old ones look at killing humans as sport. That's really about all I know. No new royals have been initiated in over a decade. It's a big deal when they do it." Desmond held his hands apart and shrugged. He was just a well-educated familiar after all.

"When does the change thing happen?" Chris asked his follow-up. Desmond kept his shrug going.

"Lynn or any of the others will be able to tell. You're already smelling everything differently, right?" Desmond waited until Chris nodded his head to indicate the smell thing was a very well-known new ability.

"I could tell you were a regular human as soon as I walked in. Just by the way your blood smells." Chris said.

"That means you're already turning. It's not just my blood you're smelling. It's a mix of pheromones, sweat, and blood. Your brain processes all of that to figure out what kind of being I am. Lynn or any of the others will know you right away by smell. After the initiation something changes. This is just me guessing but I'm thinking part of the initiation's a booster shot of sorts. You'll come out with more stuff going on than you went in with." Desmond sat back and quaffed down the rest of the beer.

"What other 'abilities' should I be looking forward to?" Chris quit beating around the bush. Samson and the others were standing outside the office door waiting to come back in. There was no telling what lies Desmond had told Samson to get the Lieutenant to give up his office and wait outside like a lackey all this time.

"It's really all in your mind. You won't be getting anything you don't already have. What the shots do is open up your mind to access your body better. Everybody has the ability to dunk a basketball. It's just a matter of getting your legs to do it. Everybody has the ability to constantly be moving every muscle in their body to strengthen and tone them. You're exercising twenty-four hours a day now and you probably haven't even noticed it. That's a part of what keeps you young looking and helps you live forever." Desmond answered. There was so much more to it, but they did need to let Samson back into his office at some point.

"Alright. You're not leaving right away, are you?" Chris wanted to make sure he was going to have time to ask more questions. They'd barely scratched the surface. Desmond had spent years studying the family. No way he was able to tell Chris everything over the course of a single beer.

"I'm not. We need to talk to your friends before we talk to Samson." Desmond said walking over to the door and opening it. He asked Ortega and Benson to come in. Samson started to follow them in. Desmond held up his hand and asked for the Lieutenant's indulgence for another ten minutes. Samson walked away cursing steadily under his breath. It'd been a really long day for everybody. This wasn't an ending any of them had expected.

Chapter 16: Another Day Another Disaster

"I still don't get it. You're going to transform into a butterfly or something?" Ortega asked. Desmond had told them enough to make them even more curious. Then he'd left to get some sleep leaving Chris to deal with the fallout. After instructing Chris not to tell anyone anything else if he valued their lives.

"People who know too much about this stuff end up dead." Chris responded quietly. Ortega had come in way early and gotten him out of bed. It hadn't been difficult since Chris needed sleep less and less these days. If he needed a nap, he was sure his body would let him know. Now that he knew his brain was doing all sorts of things in the background to get ready for whatever changes were coming next.

"How much is too much? What if I already know too much? Are they going to kill me more if I know more?" Ortega asked. Unlike Chris he did need sleep. Especially after the FUBAR situation in Kansas City the day before. It just wasn't in him to keep sleeping once his eyes popped open. Instead, he'd rolled out of his rack, laced up his boots, and grabbed Chris for this early morning coffee chat.

"At least Samson's still clueless." Chris said in an attempt to change the conversation up. He didn't want Ortega to be killed because he knew too much. Right now, Ortega knew just enough that when Lynn finally showed up, they could take Benson and Ortega with them to Greece or wherever. If they let Samson in on the secret, then Lynn might decide they only needed one special operations guy. She already liked Ortega, so it'd be Samson getting left behind for a visit from the vampire hit squad.

"Yeah, he's not too happy about that. Desmond showed up with a signed letter from some high up muckety muck. The Lieutenant's used to working with spooks, so he gets it. What he doesn't get is how you were able to pole vault over that fence without a pole." Ortega also didn't understand how Chris had done that. He sipped at his remaining coffee while waiting for Chris to fill him in.

"I just did it. I don't know how. Desmond says my body's constantly evolving now. My brain has my muscles constantly exercising. It's weird. I've never felt this strong in my life. Not even when I was wrestling. I don't really need food or sleep. Except for when I sleep for forever. You know pretty much everything I know about what's going on with me." Chris was done talking. It was pointless going around and around the same topics and points over and over again.

Ortega didn't think it was pointless. It was standard interrogation techniques. Keep the person talking and they'll give away more information each time you ask. That 'exercising constantly' thing was pretty neat. He'd noticed the weird new eating and sleeping patterns a while back. Not much got past him.

"Ready to head back? The base CO is swinging by this morning to meet with Samson. Let's try and not be here for that." Ortega downed the last bit of coffee in his cup and began walking towards the entrance to the barracks / warehouse.

Not being around for an impromptu visit by the commanding officer sounded like a great idea to Chris. He wasn't as optimistic as Ortega that their absence would be tolerated though. Unless Desmond was working his contacts before he'd even finished his bowl of Count Chocula this morning. It might actually be a good idea to give the CO a heads up that some kind of ninja shock troops might be on their way to kill him. Based on the last base he'd seen attacked the bad guys didn't care how much collateral damage they rang up. The end of the world had greatly reduced the need for them to be subtle.

Benson was in the small downstairs mess hall nursing a cup of coffee when they walked in looking for her. They'd gone up the stairs first to look for her. Stomping up and down the stairs hadn't put Ortega in a better mood. Going over to the plastic food bins he snagged a couple packets of instant grits and whipped up a quick breakfast for himself. Benson and Chris both declined when he asked them if they wanted some. Benson had already eaten some instant oatmeal. Chris wasn't excited by the thought of instant anything at the moment.

"You look like you spent yesterday getting blown around a city full of zombies." Chris said looking closely at Benson. Her dark skin tone made her bruises a little less obvious than they were on the rest of them. Same with the myriad of scrapes and cuts they were each covered in.

"Blow me." Benson took the time to clearly articulate each of the words. She even set her coffee mug down long enough to flip Chris off. He must've hit a nerve. Either that or she was just super irritable this morning. A case of the cranks was a reasonable reaction to what they'd been through the day before.

Before Chris could come up with a lame comeback the doors to the mess hall opened and Samson walked in. Where the rest of them were dressed like homeless people who'd looted an army surplus store Samson was dressed immaculately. His uniform was crisp. It even had those lines you get when you press the iron down really hard. Chris hadn't known you could get those without sending your clothes to the dry cleaners. The Lieutenant had his hair tied back in a severe ponytail. The hair style combined with the crisp uniform gave him a serious Steven Segal vibe.

"Officer on deck!" Ortega barked from where he was leaning on the counter waiting for his grits to cool down enough to eat. He snapped to attention before Samson could get out the requisite response to keep everyone from jumping to their feet.

Benson was in the process of begrudgingly getting to her feet when Samson barked out 'as you were'. Chis was still sitting down so was perfectly positioned to be as he was. He'd gotten sidetracked wondering if Benson might fall over trying to stand up. At the first sign of wobbling, he'd been ready to jump in and help her. He'd put so much focus on her safety that he'd completely neglected to hop up himself. Not technically being part of the military should get him out of whatever corporal punishment neglecting to stand at attention rated. It didn't look like Samson cared anyway.

"Morning sir." Ortega said before digging into his grits.

"Good morning. I wanted to make sure you were going to be around this morning. Colonel Kubrick would like to meet all of you." Samson said. He was well aware of how enlisted men liked to disappear when officers were coming through. No one ever volunteered to show up for an inspection.

"Yes sir." Ortega answered enthusiastically. From the tone of his response, it sounded like he'd never have even considered any other course of action. Who wouldn't want to meet up with the Colonel? He must've put a little too much exuberance into his voice. Samson eye balled him warily for a minute before continuing.

"That goes for each of you. Your buddy Desmond as well. Plan to meet here at eleven for lunch." Samson looked each of them in the eye once more to make sure they'd heard and would comply. The conversation with the base commander was going to be hard enough today without looking like he couldn't control the few personnel he had left. The loss of his men was weighing heavily on him. It was like a nightmare. Only he'd woken up and his men were still missing.

Samson turned and walked briskly out of the room. That left the three of them to stare at one another. Now they got to deal with being debriefed by someone else they weren't allowed to tell the truth to. Having to lie all the time was exhausting. Finishing up their breakfasts they went in search of Desmond. They needed to know what they could or couldn't say. Maybe Desmond could shut down the Colonel's curiosity the same way he'd shut down Samson. A phone call or a fax from someone a few links up the old chain of command should do the trick.

They found Desmond in the officer's suite he'd been given on the second floor. It was the size of a decent walk-in closet. Desmond had his laptop out and was reading a pdf scan of an old document when they walked in. He didn't bother hiding the screen. He didn't need to since the text was in some ancient looking language no one else in the room could even identify let alone read.

"How many languages do you speak?" Chris asked curiously. Knowing how long Desmond had been in school and the caliber of student he'd been he was guessing it was a lot.

"If I answer that I'll sound like C3PO." Desmond replied with a grin.

"Did you hear about the base commander swinging by for lunch?" Benson asked. She was staring at Desmond's screen as well. The writing didn't even use letters. The marks on the page were either ancient hieroglyphics or the musings of a deranged two-year-old with a talent for calligraphy.

"Colonel Kubrick, right? I figured he'd show up. I didn't know we were having lunch with him." Desmond answered. He didn't seem the slightest bit concerned.

"Samson asked us to let you know. We need to know what we're supposed to tell him." Benson answered.

"Could you shut down the weird side of the conversation before it even starts?" Chris asked. Ideally, he wouldn't have to tell the Colonel anything about his freakish abilities. The idea of more people staring at him like he was a monster didn't appeal at all. He'd also like to avoid being executed or locked up. That was a risk anytime someone in charge learned about the source of his abilities. He couldn't really blame them for assuming he might just have a slow burning case of the same infection the baldies had.

"Define weird." Desmond asked with one eyebrow slightly elevated. Considering Chris had dodged dueling tornadoes the day before to escape a city overrun with bald zombies, he understood what Desmond meant. Weird around here was just another name for Tuesday.

"Should we tell him anything at all about what's going on with me?" Chris asked. Then before Desmond could answer Chris tagged on his other thought. "If there's a crew of killers headed this way, wouldn't it be a good thing to let Kubrick and Samson know about it? Those guys who attacked us down south pretty much killed everybody who got in the way."

"Let me think about it. The more people we tell the more people who may need to get cleaned up later. The *Familia* has lots of rules around who's allowed to know about them and what happens to the people who know more than they should. Given the state of things a lot of those rules are getting more flexible. Millenia old monsters don't like change though. The less we blast out what you guys know the less likely you wake up with a blade in your chest." Desmond answered.

On that cheerful note the three of them left to go get cleaned up for lunch. Samson was dolled up like he was ready to audition for the sequel to an *Officer and a Gentleman*. Ortega announced the rest of them should work on elevating their general appearances from Hobo to wartime church service. That was fine with Chris. He'd been wanting to hop back in the shower ever since he was pulled out of it the night before.

Checking himself out in the mirror before walking downstairs Chris marveled at how much he'd changed. He'd been in great shape back when he wrestled. His body had softened up some while he was going to school and working full time. He still carried that self-image around in his head. The one where he was starting to have multiple chins depending on how he held his head. The image that'd driven him to accept the treadmill his mom had spent way too much money on as a present for him. The image that'd made him more than a little bit mirror shy.

That old self-image had just been blasted away. Staring back at him from where five chins had been now stood some male model he'd never met before. He couldn't even bend his head in such a way as to create an extra chin anymore. There were no sections of loose skin. There also weren't any pimples, flakes, oily patches, or anything else marring his near perfect complexion.

Hoping no one would walk in and catch him he pulled up his shirt to check out his abs. Even when he'd wrestled, he'd always had a little bit of a muffin top. The love handles had remained no matter how skeletal the rest of his body got from the exercise and dieting. Not anymore. He rubbed at his stomach to see if the six pack he was seeing was real. It was. Not bad for a guy who hadn't done a sit up on purpose in years.

"Are you checking yourself out?" Benson's unexpected appearance had Chris yanking his shirt down as fast as possible. He could feel the blood rushing to his face. All he needed now was for Ortega to walk in.

Ortega walked in immediately after Benson. His brain locked up with all of the things he wanted to make fun of Chris about in that moment. Why would the moron stand in front of the mirror directly in front of the door admiring his own abs? Why was he checking out his own abs to begin with? Ortega hadn't even considered the vampiric gift being the reason for Chris's improved physique. A year's worth of living on the run in a world where three meals a day was a rare event trumped *Jenny Craig* any day.

"You guys ready?" Chris asked trying to gloss right over the fact that he'd just been caught checking himself out in the mirror.

"You sure you still want to go? Don't need to watch the carbs or anything?" Ortega asked. It wasn't his best, but it was what came out when he opened his mouth.

"I don't even know why you're wearing a shirt. If I had a sexy tummy like yours, I'd just walk around topless all day long." Benson jumped in on the fun.

Knowing it was a fight he had zero chance of winning Chris put his nose in the air and summoned all the dignity he could muster. Ignoring the flood of comments from his companions he walked out of the bathroom with his head held high. He found himself hoping for a zombie attack or something to change the subject. Otherwise, he was going to be hearing abdominizer and Sparta jokes for at least the next week.

The mess hall hadn't changed since they'd been there earlier. Chris had pictured it looking fancier for the commander's visit. Samson had neglected to bust out the fancy tablecloths though. He'd also expected the commander to be taller. The Colonel was only a little over five feet tall. The man they'd watched deliver the orientation video had seemed more imposing. This unshaven shell of that man looked like he had the weight of the world on his shoulders. A weight that was slowly driving him into the ground.

The Colonel came around to greet each of them. The small man grew more animated as he spoke to them. Chris realized he was no longer even noticing the physical stature of the man after a couple of minutes. He was beginning to see how the diminutive commander held the respect of men like Lieutenant Samson.

The Colonel spent the next half-hour listening to Samson report on the horrific events of the day before. Rubrick did interrupt with a few clarifying questions but mostly just listened in silent awe to their story. Listening to it being retold Chris was amazed they'd survived as well. How do you walk through a meat grinder like that and come out the other side whole? The Colonel was extremely interested in hearing more about Greg. The idea of someone being partially infected was horrifying. It opened up the possibility of a cure though. Something which Rubrick was highly interested in.

Once they were done with lunch the Colonel asked them if they'd like to come meet with the special forces unit that'd shown up that morning. Rubrick thought they'd be a great fit into Samson's team. With the recent losses it was a chance to build back to better protect the base and carry out their missions. Desmond asked a few questions about the newcomers. The Colonel didn't have much more information than that it was a handful of guys from a Marine Corps Force Recon unit. Having seen them on video when they were admitted through the gates, he could tell them that the men were dressed in all black.

On hearing the color of the newcomer's outfits Desmond sighed and asked the Colonel to sit back down.

"There's a little bit more to the story sir. I'm going to have to feed you some confidential information that may save the lives of everyone on your base." Desmond said quietly.

Once he had everyone's attention Desmond laid out who he thought the men at the orientation center were and why they all needed to die.

Chapter 17: A Red Day

There were four black clad soldiers at the orientation center. They'd arrived that morning and been allowed in after a quick interview. They'd said they were part of a larger patrol that'd been swarmed in the middle of the night by a mob of the infected. They were the only ones to have made it out. It was a common enough story that it usually wouldn't attract too much scrutiny. What'd given the gate guards pause had been the look of the men. They didn't look like the kind of men who got caught with their pants down.

Following protocol when they were unsure on who to let in, the guards had setup a video call to get a second opinion. Colonel Rubrick himself had ended up on the call to evaluate the men. After a few minutes of back and forth the Colonel had ordered the guards to let them in. They'd been sent to the orientation center and ordered to remain there until the Colonel could meet with them personally.

Chris wanted to drop a couple of mortars on the orientation center and call it a day. They could have the rest of the personnel in the center take a long smoke break or something. The problem was that blowing up those four guys would let whoever was after them know for sure their quarry was in Leavenworth. Desmond was positive these men were a scouting party. If they were just on a fishing expedition, then the worst thing that they could do was kill them. They were going to have to be a lot more subtle.

Desmond had name-dropped high-ranking officers to secure a curtain of confidentiality around Chris's background. Rubrick hadn't fallen in line as easily as Samson had. He was agreeable with verifying the story Desmond was weaving while holding the four men in the orientation center for observation though. The plan was simple. The men would be told that they had to submit to a forty-eight-hour quarantine period. If the men put up any resistance, then they'd go to plan "B". In Chris's head plan "B" ended with the black clad warriors barbecued in a building somewhere on base.

Instead of going straight to the orientation center, the group followed Rubrick to the security office first. That way Desmond could watch a recording of the men entering the front gate. He'd immediately confirmed that these were the type of guys who would've been sent after Chris. The men had the distinctive look of the *Familia* guard. They were probably all humans at least. The real fun would start when members of the warrior caste started showing up.

Not everyone had the right genetic makeup to become a royal. There was another test to see if someone might be able to survive a pharmaceutical cocktail that unlocked a smaller set of genetic enhancements. Those had been fleshed out and defined over the last few centuries. Members of the *Familia* who took this lesser potion and survived ended up in a warrior or scientist caste role. A centuries old member of the warrior caste could go toe to toe with a younger royal and have a good chance of winning in a fair fight. Not that there were many fair fights when it came to the *Familia*.

One of the four men in the room at the orientation center could be a member of the warrior caste. It wasn't easy to tell over video. Desmond didn't think any of them had that oddly perfect look that signaled a member of the *Familia* though. The only way to be sure would be to send Chris in close enough to sniff them out. If a member of the hit squad was a member of the warrior caste though, they'd be able to sniff Chris out at the same time. None of them felt comfortable trying to approach from downwind. Chris wasn't even sure what downwind meant...

"What do we do?" Chris asked Desmond once they'd been able to find a quiet corner to talk. Ortega had walked over to listen in as well. Rubrick shot them a look from across the room but then continued his conversation with Samson.

"We make sure those guys don't see you and we're good." Desmond said almost immediately.

"How long do we have to hide for? These guys could hang out here for months." Ortega stepped right into the conversation. He was right of course. It wouldn't seem odd for the small group of men to remain on the base for a couple of months. It wasn't like travel between bases was easy anymore. You couldn't just hop on Expedia and get yourself a plane ticket.

"We probably need to take off honestly. These guys are like cockroaches. If you can see four of them there's probably another thirty hiding in the walls." Desmond responded.

"Great. What happens if they have some admiral or senator call Rubrick and directly ask him if we're here?" Chris asked. The three of them all looked over to where Rubrick was impatiently waiting to speak to them. They hadn't done anything to earn Rubrick's trust or respect yet. He wasn't interested in handing them over thanks to Desmond's contacts. More importantly the Colonel trusted Samson's judgement of their character.

"Then he'd probably turn us over. He doesn't know us from Adam. He doesn't owe us anything. Best case scenario we disappear, and no one ever even finds out we were here. Plenty of other places we can get lost in." Desmond said.

"Plenty of other places?" Chris asked.

"Absolutely. Not sure why you ended up in Podunk when there're way bigger places still scraping by. We get you to one of those you can hide out until Lynn shows back up. You stay somewhere like this with only a few hundred people you're going to get caught eventually. They may already know you're here." Desmond said. It wasn't reassuring at all the way he said it.

"What if we kill those four guys then disappear?" Ortega asked. He was weighing the options. The way he saw it those guys had brought this on themselves by showing up prepared to kill Chris. Screw those guys.

"They may not be here for you guys." Desmond said quietly.

"You think they're after you?" Chris asked.

"No way to know for sure without asking them. Maybe they're asking around about a black guy. That'd point towards it being me. Unless they're just following me to see where I ended up. They would've had time by now to test the guy they thought was you. The one that Lynn used as your decoy. If they did, then they'll know that you're still out there. They can't be sure the shot killed you, so they'll come looking for you. Or they may just be out here to kill me because I belong to Lynn. *Familia* politics are bloody and confusing as hell." Desmond looked overwhelmed from trying to lay out all the possibilities.

"They know Desmond's here. They don't know we're here. We could take off and leave Desmond here." Ortega whispered. Samson was walking towards them. The Colonel was checking out the video footage for the fifteenth time. Benson was standing beside him nervously running her fingers over her gun. Fighting the baldies was one thing. She'd massacre them without a second thought. Killing people though? Especially in cold blood. She wasn't sure she could do that. Maybe in a war but now she was seeing every human life as infinitely more precious.

"What are you ladies gossiping about?" Samson asked.

"To kill or not to kill..." Chris said before he could stop his mouth from moving. Spilling the beans like that earned him dirty looks from Desmond and Ortega.

"Yeah. It's pretty doubtful that Rubrick's going to authorize a strike on the Marines he invited into his orientation center. Especially when they come with papers saying who they are and why they're here. Papers he's already having our communication's people validate. I don't have any doubts they'll check out. Do you?" Samson asked.

"No. They'll check out." Desmon answered absently. The *Familia* was nothing if not extremely well connected. Even in the midst of an apocalypse their paper pushing cronies could make unbelievable things happen. The massive bureaucratic machine had been in place since the dark ages. It greatly surpassed even the Vatican's extensive network without hardly anyone knowing it existed. Only the *Familia* and their most trusted associates knew the full scope of their wealth and influence. It wasn't healthy for anyone else to find out too much about it.

"I'm going to go meet these guys and feel them out. I'd like Lieutenant Samson to accompany me. The rest of you can stay here for now. At some point in the very near future someone's going to have to give me a better explanation of what's going on if you expect to stay on my base." Colonel Rubrick announced in a vaguely exasperated voice. He wasn't digging all the cloak and dagger.

Samson and Rubrick left the rest of them to watch the video feed of the orientation center. The black clad killers were sitting around leafing through magazines that'd been old before the first of the infected had even gotten the sniffles. They looked like your typical soldiers left to hurry up and wait. A standard state for any group of military men. If they suspected people were staring at them through the video camera they didn't seem to care.

"They don't look evil." Benson said.

"What does evil look like?" Chris asked her curiously. That sounded like a fun topic to kill some time. The communication's officer running the video feed was doing his best to look like he wasn't eavesdropping, but his ears had perked up when Benson said the men didn't seem evil to her.

"Hitler looked like a harmless little nerd." Ortega chimed in.

"Dogs kill thirty times more humans every year than crocodiles do." Benson added. That random bit of trivia earned her some odd looks.

"Why do you know that?" Chris asked curiously.

"Lots of YouTube searches with my nephew. He really liked watching animals fight each other and animal trivia stuff." Benson said with a smile tinged with sadness. Her nephew was most likely dead. The squirming little boy who'd plopped into her lap immediately every time she'd gone to her sister's house to visit.

"The ones by the watering holes are pretty crazy. The way the alligators come out of the water and grab the buffalo and stuff." Chris said to keep the conversation rolling and hopefully get Benson into a happier headspace.

"I think those are crocodiles you're thinking of." Benson said smiling again.

"How have you people survived this long?" Desmond asked gazing around the small group with an amused look on his face.

Before anyone could come up with a smart-ass response, the communication's officer informed them that the Colonel would be walking in the room to meet the men at the orientation center momentarily. The officer did something with the laptop he was sitting at to pipe the audio from the orientation center through the speakers. Now they could hear the men in the orientation center as they sat around waiting. They weren't saying much of anything at the moment.

"I'm Colonel Rubrick. I'm the commanding officer here. How are you men doing?" Rubrick struck a casual pose by the door and waited for one of the men to answer. Samson stood beside his commander looking around warily at the men in the room. He wasn't the only one who'd noted the men didn't pop to attention right away.

"We're fine sir. We're hunting a fugitive though. Perhaps you can help us locate him?" One of the men said.

"Happy to help. First things first though we need to get you men over to one of our quarantine rooms. I'll have Lieutenant Samson here escort you. I just wanted to welcome you aboard personally after hearing what'd happened to the rest of your -" The rest of what Rubrick was going to say was cut off by a barrage of small arms fire. The Colonel crumpled to the ground. Lying on his side in a completely unnatural position the bloody crater in his forehead removed any hope he'd survive. Samson landed face down beside him. A second later the camera went dark.

"That's our cue to leave." Desmond stated immediately.

"They shot the Colonel." The communication's officer said disbelievingly. The man hadn't left the base since everything had started falling apart. Most of his days had been spent either in this air-conditioned space or the small room on the other side of the building where he slept. He wasn't used to this kind of violence. Not like the rest of them were.

"But they did not shoot the deputy." Chris wondered who'd had the gall to say something so stupid. Then he realized the words had come out of his own mouth. That explained why everyone was looking at him in shock. Chris kept his mouth shut. Although he had to seriously fight the urge to throw out a sarcastic *'Too soon?'* The uncomfortable stares struck him as funny. He felt the corners of his mouth twisting into an uncontrollable grin.

"What the hell's wrong with you?" Benson asked staring at him.

"We can figure out what's wrong with him later. Right now, we need to focus on getting off this base." Desmond said. Having spent his entire life around members of the *Familia* he'd seen how they reacted oddly to situations before. Lynn was calm and collected most of the time but every once in a while, something would strike her as funny. It could be as random as the sun hitting the water a certain way. The drugs they took to enable their metamorphosis had some really odd side effects.

"Should I go with you?" The communication's officer stood up to follow them.

"You should be fine here. If they do show up just tell them that you saw me come through the center the other day. If you mention Chris and Ortega here, then they'll probably kill you. I'd keep that part to myself. As a matter of fact, I'd probably find somewhere to hide if I was you." Desmond was not the most reassuring person to be talking to the terrified man.

Not liking what she was hearing Benson asked if the whole base was in danger. To which Desmond responded that the forces aligned against Lynn would keep coming until they were certain Chris was dead or gone. Given that cheerful bit of information they realized that if they just snuck off, they'd be leaving a lot of people to die for them. Including all of the refugee families sheltering at the fort.

"Ok. So, we take some shots at the guys we saw on camera and make sure they see us headed for the hills." Ortega said. He didn't like the idea of engaging skilled soldiers without shooting to kill, but it sounded like that was what they were going to be doing. He'd happily bring the pain to the men who'd just killed Samson in cold blood. He hadn't known Colonel Rubrick well enough to feel one way or the other, but the cold-blooded murder of Samson felt personal.

Taking the keys to one of the golf carts the four of them drove back to the warehouse to grab weapons, supplies, and a better vehicle. If he could find a pony keg of that home brew Ortega was planning on snagging that as well. Sprinting around the barracks they ignored the questions being thrown at them by the small amount of men left in the unit. Ortega finally let them know the base was under attack. When they asked what they should do Ortega ordered them to gear up and stand by. As long as their plan worked the base should be safe.

Out in the parking lot they chose a Humvee with a mounted machine gun and climbed in. Benson took the driver's seat while Ortega squeezed into the turret and cocked the machine gun. In the passenger seat Chris told them to wait when he saw another golf cart pulling into the parking lot with them. Crammed into the back seat Desmond watched wearily as the golf cart pulled in. He could barely move with all the supplies they'd flung into the back with him.

"Is that Samson?" Benson asked squinting at the golf cart.

Several men rushed out of the warehouse to greet the Lieutenant as he pulled up in the golf cart. He had some blood stains on his shoulder and was limping but otherwise appeared ok. Samson ignored the men trying to help him and marched straight over to where Chris was staring at him from the passenger seat in the Humvee.

"Glad to see you made it sir." Ortega called out once Samson was close enough to hear him.

"My body armor caught most of it. Hurt like a bitch but I'm better off then everybody else who was in there. Are you leaving or looking to get some?" Samson asked.

"Some pay back on the way out's the plan sir. Desmond thinks they might leave when we leave. They just need to identify it's us leaving." Ortega called out.

"Give me a minute to grab my crap." Samson shouted over his shoulder as he headed for the door to the warehouse.

"We need to get moving or we're not going to make it out of here. Once these guys start, they don't stop until they've accomplished their mission." Desmond piped up from the back seat. There was no need to get too worked up as Samson reappeared within a minute of asking them to wait. He kept his go bag and extra ammunition right by the front door to the warehouse. The only personal items he cared about were already in his pockets. The Lieutenant waved the rest of the men back into the warehouse before climbing into the back with Desmond.

"My men going to be safe?" Samson asked in a wheezy voice. The body armor may have saved his life, but his chest had still taken a serious pounding. The hole in his shoulder didn't feel great either. The pain was nothing compared to his need for vengeance.

Desmond was about to answer Samson's question when the sound of gunfire drifted to them from the distance. Much closer was the sound of explosions. The steady hum of a helicopter also became audible.

"We've got to go!" Desmond shouted.

"Why don't they just blow up the whole base?" Chris asked. A laser guided missile was well within the wheelhouse of the men they were up against.

"They need a body to test." Desmond reminded everyone. If he had more to say it was cut off by Benson's rapid acceleration of the Humvee. Up in the turret Ortega was steadily cussing as Benson's driving tossed him around inside the hard metal tube.

Chapter 18: Bomb's Away

"What's the plan?" Samson asked after Benson fishtailed out of the warehouse parking lot.

"We shoot our way out. We make sure they see Desmond." Benson answered without taking her eyes off the road.

The adrenaline was getting Chris hyped up as well. For the first time ever, he wasn't tempted to close his eyes at Benson's fearless maneuvering of the heavy assault vehicle. He found that he could feel how the Humvee was balanced on the road. With his heightened senses and data crunching mind he'd know if they were about to crash. Flashing back to riding around with Lynn he now got how she was able to drive so insanely all the time. Her senses would be way more developed than his. What he'd thought was suicidal was just a Sunday drive for her.

A helicopter zipped over the top of them. It wasn't an assault chopper or anything. It looked more like one of the helicopters you'd have seen relaying the latest traffic report on the local news. Back when there was still traffic and local news.

"Shoot it down?" Ortega yelled the question down through the turret.

"Yes!" Desmond, Chris, Samson, and Benson all yelled back at the same time. All they needed was some Rambo with a bazooka up in the helicopter to start lobbing rockets at them. That'd mess up their whole day. Given their normal luck none of them would be surprised if it happened. The helicopter had slowed to a hover and was rotating around.

"Slow down!" Ortega yelled down the hatch at them.

Slowing down didn't seem like the smartest thing to do to Chris. If that news chopper was about to unload a couple of rockets their way, then wouldn't it be better to be moving as fast as possible? Luckily Benson intuited what Ortega was trying to do. She braked hard to come to a screeching stop.

Without the Humvee bouncing all over the place Ortega was able to line up his shots much better. Within a few seconds the helicopter was streaking away from them leaving a trail of black smoke in its wake. Ortega banged on the roof a few times to get them moving again. Not that Benson had needed any signal to know what to do. She was speeding towards the orientation center already. Samson had said the attackers had already left. They didn't know where the attackers had gone though so it seemed logical to Benson to start there. It was also on the way out.

"Head to the communication's shack! They can tell us if those guys have shown up anywhere else yet." Samson was listening to a handheld radio but was loathe to broadcast on it. Decades of counterintelligence work screamed at him not to send anything over open airwaves in the middle of whatever this was turning into. In the distance came the sound of mortars striking the perimeter of the base.

"What are they blowing up?" Chris asked. It didn't sound like they were hitting anything within the base. He never would've trusted himself to identify where the bombs were hitting before. Now it seemed weird that everyone else couldn't triangulate the sounds in their head to figure out exactly where the explosions were coming from.

"A lot of loud noise and a destroyed perimeter barrier." Desmond piped up. He didn't think he needed to explain it any better than that.

"They're going to wipe out the base and let the baldies in to cover it up. All of the refugees will die." Benson stated loudly. Nobody in the vehicle should be able to avoid the moral consequences of whatever they did next. In the distance another helicopter was flitting around. The pilot of that one was keeping their distance. A smart move considering how quickly Ortega had sent the other chopper packing with their tail on fire.

The communication building was on fire. That was going to seriously impede their ability to announce to the rest of the base that they were under attack. On the plus side it gave them a pretty good idea where the men were that they were hunting. The attackers had actually made it easier on them. There was no longer a need to leave anyone alive to report on Chris having left the base. The mission now was to kill every soldier they could find wearing black. They needed to give the refugees time to escape before they hit the road themselves.

"Incoming!" Benson shouted.

Up ahead one of the pickup trucks that'd been parked by the communication building had pulled out on the road. It immediately swung around to race away from the Humvee. Two soldiers in the back of the truck sent some bullets flying in their direction. Benson and Chris were safe enough behind the bulletproof windshield. Up top Ortega ducked down and began what would end up being quite a lot of cursing.

Ortega's cussing was quickly drowned out by the sound of the high caliber rounds the Master Sergeant began sending after the enemy pickup. The heavy bullets carved up the back of the lightweight truck. Both of the soldiers vanished from view as they pressed their bodies as close to the truck bed as they could get them. Ortega kept the rounds flying as Benson closed the distance. The back windshield of the enemy's truck shattered. Some of those rounds found meatier targets inside the cab. The truck spun to the side and rolled over a couple of times before coming to a rest on its side.

Benson drove up next to the smoking ruin to give Ortega time to put a few more rounds into the cab. There was no sign of the guys who'd been in the back of the truck. Their broken bodies were most likely lying-in twisted heaps in the tall brush on the sides of the road somewhere. Even if the men managed to survive, they wouldn't be in any condition to continue the fight anytime soon.

Benson shifted into reverse and executed a three-point turn to point them back towards the middle of the base. If they'd kept going the other way, it would've brought them to the exit. Exiting stage left wasn't an option with Benson at the wheel. Samson would've spoken up as well if they'd tried to leave without assisting the refugees and his men. Up top Ortega's head was on a swivel searching for targets. More importantly he was looking for anyone who was targeting him. He felt way too exposed with his upper body sticking out of the turret. The metal shield that ran around him was good for stopping the average shooter, but these black pajama wearing warriors were playing on a higher level.

Benson swerved across the road to skid to a stop amidst flying gravel and squealing brakes in the parking lot of the warehouse. Samson's men were already outside prepping two more of the Humvees for action. Once they recognized it was Benson's Humvee that'd come sliding back into the lot, they relaxed their trigger fingers. Samson popped out the back to go talk to his men. He'd already dispatched one of his men to go grab some secure radios for them to use.

"You guys aren't feeling like we should just cut our losses and leave? Lieutenant Samson can try to save the refugees before the infected get to them. We're not needed for that." Desmond spoke up from the back. He didn't expect anyone to listen but figured it was worth a shot.

"If you hadn't been followed here then none of these people would be in danger right now." Benson pointed out. Each of her clearly enunciated words was dripping with venom.

"Yeah. We've got to try and help." Chris agreed completely with Benson's sentiment. It wouldn't feel right to leave all these people to die. He didn't think he'd be able to do it even if it wasn't their fault the base was under attack. He no longer had the excuse of trying to save his own life for science. He was beginning to wonder if Desmond had said that the attackers would leave the refugees alone if they left just to get them to leave.

Benson turned the Humvee around and took off in the direction they'd seen the second helicopter going. That was the same direction most of the refugees and base personnel lived in. The muffled sound of more explosions coming from that direction told them the assault was definitely not over yet. Not that any of them had thought killing a few guys in a pickup was going to make the people after them back off.

Up ahead a helicopter shot into the air from behind one of the buildings. It was the barracks building that used to house the students there for training. There was a whole other complex of buildings for the penal side of the base. Those still held some prisoners and a smattering of the infected. There was about to be a whole lot more infected on the base, so they weren't too worried about the ones that'd been locked up for observation.

The helicopter spun in the air as Ortega and the other machine gunners sent a firestorm of bullets in its general direction. None of the rounds did any damage as far as they could tell. The helicopter finished it's spin and flew away with its nose pointing almost straight down. Much more concerning than the retreating helicopter was the whistling sound of incoming mortars. Benson slammed her foot to the floor sending the Humvee zipping forward. Behind them the others did the same.

Off to the side of the road a geyser of dirt and rock flew up into the air. Another explosion ripped half the blacktop off the road in front of them. Those were the kinds of conditions the ridiculously expensive shocks on the Humvees were built to take though. The passengers without seatbelts on didn't appreciate hitting the massive pothole. The unsecured supplies flying all over the place didn't add anything to the comfort factor either. Seconds later they were pulling into a courtyard surrounded by tall buildings.

People were visible in the windows of the buildings. Samson started barking orders into his radio and his men bounced out of their seats to make a run for the various buildings. Samson himself was sprinting full out towards the corner of the parking lot. There were multiple large green buses parked there. Buses that'd been used to transport groups of prisoners in the past. Now the idea was to use them to get the refugees to safety before mortars blew apart the buildings that they were in. The buses were designed to keep inmates from getting out of them. Hopefully they were made well enough to keep the baldies from getting into them.

A series of blasts rocked the courtyard. Superheated chunks of concrete and other debris rained down on them from the buildings being pummeled by rockets. Looking around Chris spotted the increased activity around the entrances to the buildings. Samson had driven the first bus over already. He was running back over to grab another one. Why they kept the buses parked on the other side of the lot was beyond Chris. He really hoped it wasn't because that's where the signs for the bus parking were.

Seeing Samson risking his life to ferry buses over Chris opened his door and hopped out. Ortega looked down from the turret to see why the hell another idiot was getting out of the bulletproof car.

"You want to live forever?" Chris tossed the infamous quote up to Ortega before taking off across the parking lot.

Pissed that he'd let Chris gain the moral high ground enough to throw that line out at him Ortega worked his way out of the turret. Might as well get his head blown off doing something heroic. It wasn't like he was accomplishing anything by staying on a gun when there was nothing to shoot at. Those rockets were coming from multiple directions. Assuming the enemy didn't run out of mortars there weren't going to be many people still breathing in this courtyard in another five minutes. The ones that didn't get blown to smithereens would get to welcome the waves of baldies who'd be converging on the sound of the courtyard erupting.

Chris had started a bus before Ortega had even gotten his boots planted in the parking lot. Not because Ortega was hesitant about joining him. Chris was moving at speeds that would've gotten him full ride scholarships on any sports team for any college anywhere in the world. Full ride scholarships and a barrage of performance enhancing drug tests.

Chris was so attuned to how his body was moving that he didn't even question the crazy speeds he was reaching. He was completely focused on saving the people in the buildings around them. The faster they got them in the buses the sooner they could be convoying away from ground zero. People were finally streaming out of the buildings in mass. The roofs being blown off had motivated them a lot more than Samson's guys pleading with them to leave.

The first bus was rapidly filling up. There was a total of six buses available. If they could get fifty people in each one, they'd be good to go. The buses had less seating inside of them than regular school buses. A lot of space was taken up by the extra fencing to secure prisoners. It made sense they'd want to keep the prisoners away from the guards. They definitely wouldn't want the felons getting anywhere near the driver. There was a separately secured space for the guards as well.

Unsure how many people they were going to need to evacuate Chris parked the bus and went to grab another one. He'd only made it a few steps when a huge explosion sent him sliding face first along the debris covered blacktop. Rolling over on his back he saw that the bus he'd just parked had been blown in half by a mortar. The interior of the bus was on fire. Black smoke was rolling out of it in huge clouds.

Chris shook that off and went to grab another bus. It wasn't like they had much of a choice. Anyone who stayed behind was going to get swarmed by baldies. Anyone who came out and got in a bus had maybe a ten percent chance of making it out alive. Ten percent was better than zero percent. The pricks dropping the bombs didn't seem like they were too worried about conserving ammo.

The other side of the courtyard erupted in a massive fireball. Chunks of burning asphalt landed all around Chris as he pushed himself back to his feet. The world was on fire. Bombs were striking all around him. The smart thing to do would've been to sprint back to the Humvee and take off. Instead, he spit out a wad of blood that included a small piece of his tongue and hopped up in the driver's seat of another bus.

Chris drove across the courtyard towards a building there wasn't a bus parked in front of yet. There was a group of people milling around frantically wondering what to do. One of Lieutenant Samson's men was trying to get them to dash across the open courtyard to make it to the buses being loaded on the other side. When the soldier saw Chris rolling their way, he flipped his focus to getting the group ready to board the bus. Not an easy task amidst all the chaos.

Chris waited impatiently as the group crowded onto the bus. The desperate mob was ignoring the soldier trying to get them to board in an orderly fashion. On the opposite side of the parking lot one of the Humvees exploded. The enemy had scored a direct hit. The longer they stayed in this courtyard the more likely they'd all get hit. They were fish in a barrel here. A small barrel that the fishermen were tossing sticks of dynamite into.

The last of the group had barely made it through the bus doors before Chris stomped his foot down on the gas. Any thoughts of abandoning the bus to rejoin Benson in their armored Humvee had disappeared when several children came clambering up the stairs. He was the best chance those kids had of making it out alive. Wishing he'd grabbed a radio to keep in touch with everyone Chris headed for the exit.

Screams erupted from his passengers when a mortar hit right next to them. The explosive force blasted the bus sideways. The big green machine felt like it was going to flip on its side. Chris deftly worked the steering wheel and brakes to keep that from happening. All four wheels back on the ground they bounced through the torn-up remnants of the parking lot and shot out the exit. A series of massive explosions behind them didn't bode well for anyone else making it out.

Looking in the side mirror Chris saw another bus pull out. The bus had a couple of flat tires and was missing part of its roof. Smoke was pouring out from under the hood. Directly behind that bus a Humvee burst out of the fiery hellscape to join up with them. Chris loved that he'd turned into a master multitasker. Able to drive like a pro while also paying attention to the side mirrors he was able to make out the head sticking out of the turret in the Humvee behind them. If Ortega was alive then Benson and Desmond should both be chilling in the Humvee with him.

They were down to two buses and a Humvee. One of the buses was completely busted up. Getting out of the courtyard was only the first step in getting off the base alive. First things first Chris looked for a place to stop. They were going to have to move the passengers from the messed-up bus into theirs. If they managed to survive doing that then he'd worry about the next step. At some point he really needed to work on ignoring his conscience. That damned cricket was going to get him killed.

Chapter 19: No Rest for the Wicked

Chris hit the brakes hard. After fumbling with the gear shifter for a second, he got the big green machine rolling backwards. Staring in the mirror he turned the wheel slightly to pull up close to the side of the broken-down bus. Rather than parking and waiting for the bus to pull up beside them he was reversing since the other machine was stranded. Moving back towards the danger wasn't a popular decision with most of his passengers. It became even less popular when more mortar rounds rocked what was left of the courtyard that they'd barely made it out of.

"Get them over here!" Chris yelled unnecessarily as he ran around the front of the bus to help. They needed to expeditiously transfer everyone to the bus that was still mobile. Preferably before the people launching the mortars got their location dialed in. A quick nod was all that time allowed for Samson to express his gratitude to Chris for coming back for them. For his part Chris was glad to see that Samson was alive. He'd grown fond of the long-haired bad ass.

A helicopter emerged from the smoke pouring up out of the ruins of the courtyard. Ortega immediately opened fire from his perch in the turret of the Humvee. The helicopter executed an abrupt about face and headed back into the smoke. The pilot maneuvering the bird so fast it was like it'd never even been there. The countdown to this part of the road being blown to hell had just started. They had about twenty seconds to not be there anymore. Otherwise, they wouldn't live long enough to be ripped apart by the zombies that'd be showing up anytime now thanks to all the noise. The Humvee pulled around in front of the bus to blast any bad guys or baldies out of their path.

Chris picked up an old woman and carried her onto the bus. Tossing her to the standing room only crowd he gave Samson a second to get onboard. Samson stepped on the bottom stair with an injured girl dangling off of his shoulder. He still had one boot on the road when Chris slammed his foot down on the gas pedal so hard that he was worried he might have bent it. Pedal broken or not the bus lurched forward with a loud mechanical groan. The big green machine was accelerating way too slowly.

Feeling like he could run faster than the bus was moving Chris offered up a quick prayer that they'd make it a little further down the road. The prayer had barely left his lips when he wondered if turning into a vampire would wipe his faith away. There were all those myths about vampires fearing crucifixes and holy water and such. Deciding he could ask Desmond about that later he looked up ahead to make sure there were no new and exciting issues to deal with. Samson was standing on the stairs beside the driver's seat. The Lieutenant had managed to hold onto a radio to stay in touch with Benson.

The road directly in front of them turned into a concrete cyclone with zero warning. A rocket had struck between them and the Humvee. The front windshield of the bus was blasted out by the concussive force of the explosion. Chris cranked the wheel to the side and slammed on the brakes but there was no way to stop the bus in time. They drove straight into that whirlwind of super-heated cement. The front tires dropped down into the fiery maelstrom. The old lady Chris had helped into the bus went flying out the empty space where the windshield had been.

A couple of others tumbled out alongside the old woman. The girl Samson had been carrying almost suffered the same fate. In an effort to save her Samson swung her around in front of him. This ended with her being smashed against the console with all of Samson's weight bearing down on her. Several of her ribs cracked but she lived.

The heat was unbearable. Everyone was trying to get out of the bus. The vehicle had been built to keep people from escaping though. They couldn't just hop out of an emergency exit. There was an emergency door, but no one had the slightest idea how to make it work. It wasn't like they had time to find a YouTube video showing them how to escape a burning prison bus.

With no way out the panicking people in the back of the bus were surging forward. The people in the front of the bus weren't trying to hop into the molten mess crackling away in front of them. Everyone was pushing everyone else. Children and the elderly were falling down and being trampled. Chris was seeing double. He'd bounced his head off the steering wheel and almost flipped into the lava like section of road in front of them himself. His adrenaline had kicked in allowing him to see the whole wreck in slow motion. His body had known exactly how to position itself to stay alive. It'd still sucked from a pain perspective though.

Between the blistering heat and everyone on the bus shoving each other around it wasn't looking good. Chris used the handle to pop the side door open. He was happy to see that still worked. Staying in his seat he watched Samson gingerly carry the sobbing young girl in his arms to the exit and leap out the open door. The Lieutenant jumped away from the blasted-out area in front of them. It was already cooling off but there was no reason to get any closer than necessary.

Remaining in his seat Chris waited while the rest of the passengers poured out of the bus. The last few out were helping the people who'd been injured. Chris stood up to help a woman struggling to walk on a messed-up ankle. She was trying to explain how someone had fallen on her leg when the bus crashed. Chris didn't care how her ankle had gotten screwed up. He just wanted to get her off the bus before a bomb detonated on top of it. He doubted the guys manning the artillery batteries were completely dependent on the chopper for scouting out targets. There could be someone with a pair of binoculars staring at them right now.

Expecting to be vaporized at any moment Chris rushed the lady off the bus. The refugees had all gathered in the overgrown field beside the road. The large weed covered space had been a manicured lawn at one time. The apocalypse had taken a serious toll on the landscaping. Milling around in the field the survivors were a motley looking crew of the dazed and confused. They were thankful to be breathing but not super optimistic about their chances to continue doing so for much longer.

Benson was parked about twenty yards up the road. Chris was impressed once more by Benson's big brass ones. She knew she was a sitting duck. Sitting there like that when someone was most likely zeroing a rocket in on her in real time took nerves of steel. She wasn't someone you'd want to play a game of chicken with.

"Now what?" Ortega yelled the question over to Chris.

"I was hoping you had some ideas! You're the super soldier!" Chris yelled back hoarsely. He'd inhaled a whole lot of super-heated air when the bomb went off in front of them. His face felt like he'd spent the week at the beach staring up at a blazing hot sun. The burn was going to get a lot worse before it got any better.

Ortega looked like he wanted to make a vampire comment. Considering half the people in the field right now had seen Chris setting Olympic records back in the courtyard it probably wouldn't go over well though. Chris was glad Ortega was able to exercise some common sense and keep his mouth shut. He had no desire to be fending off crucifixes, garlic, and wooden stakes for the foreseeable future.

"Everybody spread out and start walking parallel to the road. Let's get the wounded in the Humvee. We'll drive back to the warehouse and get some more vehicles then come back for everyone else." Samson said. For an off the cuff plan Chris didn't think it was half bad. It beat the hell out of standing around scratching themselves until the enemy got around to dropping ordinance on their heads.

They were helping the walking wounded board the Humvee when the bus Samson had been driving exploded. The orderly line of wounded was overwhelmed by perfectly healthy people frantically trying to crowd aboard the vehicle. Samson had to wade in and knock some people away. He wasn't gentle with the ones who were trying to pull the walking wounded away so that they could climb in. One man was stupid enough to pull out a pistol and demand a ride. Ortega shot that guy in the head with zero hesitation.

Leaving the dead man lying beside the road Benson took off for the warehouse. Samson, Desmond, and Ortega went with her. None of them had room to move there were so many bodies shoved in the cramped vehicle. A couple of the refugees were hanging on to the top of the Humvee next to Ortega. Hopefully they could get to the warehouse and return with enough vehicles to spirit them all away. It was a race now to see if they got back before the bombs or the baldies killed everyone still on foot.

Chris didn't waste any time watching the Humvee bounce off down the cracked pavement. An errant thought struck him that that this could be the last time he ever saw his friends. Of course, if they didn't make it back with vehicles sometime soon, he'd be too dead to care. On that cheerful note Chris started yelling for the refugees to split up and start running. If they stayed in a pack, it'd be too good of a target for the artillery guys to pass up.

Yelling for everyone to put some distance between themselves Chris did so himself. When he caught everyone staring at him, he realized he was moving a little too fast. Fleet footedly dancing through the tall weeds at a speed that would've required special effects to show on the big screen. Purposefully slowing himself down he continued coaxing everyone else to divide up and run. The enemy provided some additional motivation by dropping a couple of bombs on the bus they'd just vacated.

One of the bombs struck the back of the bus while the other hit the part of the field they'd all been standing around in a minute before. The explosions motivated the refugees way better than Chris yelling vague directions. The whole crowd took off running. Within about thirty seconds they were spread out. A combination of athletic ability and panic accomplishing almost exactly what Chris had envisioned.

On top of not wanting to be perceived as a freak Chris realized there was another reason to reign in his uncanny athletic prowess. The watchers were from a paramilitary group employed by the *Familia*. Odds were those guys knew their quarry would exhibit extreme athleticism. By running around like a cheetah-human hybrid he'd be revealing himself as their target. The bad guys wouldn't hesitate to make it rain once they'd positively identified him.

Another explosion tossed dirt all over the fleeing refugees. The people running for their lives didn't notice the tangy smell of the fresh blood mixed in with the smell of the earth. If they had, they wouldn't have cared. They were too busy running for their lives. Chris however smelled it and felt compelled to check it out. Breaking away from the others he ran a lap around the area that'd been bombed.

People had been vaporized in the blast. The only thing left of them was the smell of their blood. Chris expanded his search until he found a man with a pair of completely mangled jeans lying in the tall grass. The man's legs had been completely blown off. The stumps of his legs ended about mid-thigh on each leg. On top of the intoxicating smell of spilled human blood there was the barbeque aroma of burnt flesh coming from the motionless body.

Momentarily tempted to molest the defenseless man by lapping the warm blood from his wounds Chris shuddered in denied ecstasy. The feelings causing him to experience a whole new level of self-loathing. Pulling his pistol, he shot the dying man point blank in the face. Thus, did he provide the man with mercy while also quelling his own demonic urge to plunge face first into the blood drenched flesh. Might as well pull all of his hair out and start running around naked. As far as he could tell the ability to shrug off the blood lust was the main thing that separated the *Familia* from the baldies. That and having hair.

Steadfastly maintaining a brisk jog Chris fled the scene. The area he was in was now a dialed in bomb site. If he was going to die, he'd at least make the enemy have to aim. How dumb would it be to die in the same hole the other corpses were smoldering away in? All it would've taken would've been for the dude dropping the mortars down into the mortar tube to have forgotten to adjust his aim to hit a new target. Hell, it could even be strategy on the artillery man's part. Kind of like the sniper who shoots a guy in the leg then waits to shoot the people who run from cover to try and save the first victim. That'd be one way to kill a bunch of refugees running in different directions. A lot more efficient than peppering acres of overgrown lawn with rocket strikes and hoping they got lucky.

Running swiftly back to where the others were making their way towards the warehouse another thought struck Chris. He'd been assuming there were spotters somewhere calling in coordinates for the artillery strikes. Either that or the helicopters had been taking care of picking out targets. The idea that a drone was spying on them was strong enough that he slowed down and looked up into the sky. He did so despite knowing that any drones would be next to invisible to the naked eye.

Chris easily spotted a pair of drones hovering high above the field. Finding them so quickly reminded him he was no longer hampered by the limitations of your average Joe. He had the same eyeballs that everyone had. The data they gathered was just being more effectively parsed. Effectively enough that he was able to see things that should've been impossible to see. The shot hadn't just given him the ability to run like a roided up gazelle and leap over tall backyard fences in a single bound.

The hunch he'd had to check out the sky had been his subconscious telling him that he was missing something important. It'd be really nice if someone would tell him what all he was able to do instead of having to figure it out by trial and error. A bit of a heads up could save not just his own life but the lives of his friends and the refugees they were trying to protect. For all he knew he might have been able to save the other ones as well. Would it kill the *Familia* to come up with some sort of quick start guide?

Remembering Lynn's ridiculous accuracy with any weapon she picked up Chris wondered if he could shoot down the drone. It was like some part of him had been impatiently waiting for that question. Unfortunately, it'd been waiting to emphatically tell him that it wasn't possible. The drones were way too high for him to have any hope of hitting them with the weapons he was carrying. That internal certainty stopped him from wasting any more time considering that idea.

Up ahead more mortars struck the field. Weaving between the blasts came a half dozen random vehicles. The main similarity between them was that they were all painted Army green. Leading the pack was Benson's Humvee. Behind her was another Humvee followed by a ragged line of pickup trucks, cars, and jeeps of differing sizes. Those were being driven without the bravado apparent in the way the Humvee was shredding its way across the field.

Spurred on by the sight of the calvary coming for them the ragged line of refugees rushed forward. One of the trucks went airborne when a bomb hit near it, but the others emerged from the smoke unscathed. The refugees scrambled onto whatever vehicle got close to them. Chris ran for Benson's Humvee. The escalated barrage of mortars making him care a lot less if someone saw him running at unnatural speeds. Benson saw him coming and skidded to a stop right in front of him.

"Drones watching us!" Chris announced as he slid his sweaty dirt covered self into the passenger seat.

"Yep." Benson said right back. She was working on getting the momentum back she'd lost stopping to pick him up.

"Do we have drones that can shoot them down?" Chris asked. It sounded kind of futuristic but maybe drone killing drones was a thing. He'd watched robot battles on YouTube so who knew. It seemed like the military would have a way of knocking the annoying spies out of the skies.

"Sure do. The guys in the blown-up communications center could have launched them no problem." Benson dead panned.

"There's no way to manually launch them?" Chris asked. He was completely out of this element here. Maybe no one else had thought of doing it manually though?

A sound like thunder rolled over them from their right. A shower of dirt and debris struck the windshield. Benson hadn't bothered answering Chris's question about manually launching a drone to shoot down another drone. She didn't think it was worth the effort to answer it. Chris had to know that wasn't how stuff worked in the real world. Instead of talking about technology that didn't exist, she focused on driving them out of range of the enemy artillery team. Those guys were currently doing their best to total the expensive government issued SUV they were cruising around in.

Chapter 20: Hard and Fast

The lady who'd gotten her ankle sprained on the bus was the only other passenger in the Humvee. Unable to walk without help Benson had told her to stay in the backseat when everyone else scrambled into other vehicles. Not that she'd had much of a choice. They were all part of the rolling motor pool attempting to pluck the fleeing refugees out of the field before they were blown to kingdom come. Each driver had a secure radio courtesy of Samson to help coordinate the effort.

They'd selected their vehicles from the ones that hadn't been hit by the artillery strike on the warehouse parking lot. Luckily the attackers hadn't put too much effort into destroying the place. They'd been able to quickly grab boxes of supplies and fling them in the vehicles. Armed and provisioned the small convoy had rolled out to rescue the people they'd left behind. Bloody and battered everyone who could manage to press a gas pedal and work the steering wheel had stepped right up. Amazing really when you realized they were driving back towards the bombing range instead of running away from it as fast as they possibly could.

Benson had alerted all the drivers to the fact that there were eyes in the sky. She made no attempt to explain how she'd obtained the intel on the drones. Chris was a little surprised no one came back across the airwaves to ask how she knew. Most likely they were all too busy trying to figure out how to deal with yet another complication to their escape. Or they just weren't letting themselves worry about it. It wasn't like a pair of drones flying higher than they could shoot were something they could do anything about.

There were more than enough other things to worry about. The rockets kept on coming. A truck in front of Benson disappeared in a ball of fire. Benson swerved hard right to avoid running into the flaming wreckage. She was randomly cutting the Humvee to the left and right as they slogged through the field towards the exit from the base. The light pickups were making better time than they were. When rockets hit close by though the armor plating on the Humvee was well worth the sacrifice of a little speed and agility.

They bounced up onto the road behind one of the pickups. Wheels on asphalt propelled them forward way faster than wheels slogging through the mud. The rockets stopped for the time being. Chris hoped that meant they were either out of range or the bad guys had run out of rockets. Driving around expecting to die at any second was a trifle unpleasant. Chris was going to have to add that sphincter clenching feeling to the long list of reasons the apocalypse sucked. To think he'd once thought the zombies were the worst part. He'd take a baldie over an incoming missile any day.

Up ahead the front gates finally materialized. The exit was as welcome a sight as could be. The wave of baldies sweeping towards them from that direction wasn't as exciting. Gritting her teeth Benson prepared to slam right into that wave. She was hoping they could duck dive under it and surface on the other side. The alternative was to turn around and cruise back through the bombing range. The guys dropping the bombs had now had time to get the field dialed in. That meant tromping back through those weeds was no longer a viable option.

"Get in the turret!" Benson yelled as she slowed the Humvee down enough to allow Chris to move.

Chris scrambled up into the machine gun turret. Ortega had shown him the basics of how it worked. It'd been a quick lesson, but he'd paid close attention. Even if he hadn't been paying attention his memory had turned photogenic since Lynn had jabbed him. He could've rewatched the lesson from Ortega as easily as rewatching a DVD. Luckily, he didn't need to as he'd paid attention the first time. Based on how his life worked he'd assumed that he'd get stuck up in the turret at some point. It'd be way too pleasant to spend his time hanging out in the air-conditioned front seat.

Up in the turret it dawned on him why Benson wanted him up there. It wasn't to help them escape. It was to help the people in the pickup trucks escape. Benson was busily ordering the remaining vehicles to get out of their way so they could do some damage to the baldies before the rest of them tried driving through. They were going to be the literal tip of the spear. Assuming Chris could figure out how to get a round in the chamber on the big gun they'd clear a path for everyone else.

After some desperate fumbling that resulted in painfully ripping a fingernail off Chris was pounding the incoming baldies with high caliber rounds. His vampiric skills hadn't been a big help with getting the gun loaded but now that he was shooting those skills kicked in big time. He was ridiculously accurate. The world went into slow motion around him as he lobbed round after round precisely into whatever he wanted to hit. Normally the gunner would hit a target with maybe ten percent of their shots. Shooting a machine gun from the turret of a moving vehicle utilized the spray and pray approach. Especially if the driver was swerving all over the place to avoid making them an easy target for rockets.

Chris was hitting a target with pretty much every round. This could've easily been attributed to the large number of tightly packed targets directly in front of them. The real reason for that kind of bullet to target ratio was his newfound skills. His hand eye coordination was simply unbelievable. Down in the driver's seat Benson watched row after row of the baldies get carved up. They were falling down like dominoes with blood fountaining out of their chests. When she'd sent Chris up to man the gun, she hadn't expected him to be some sort of machine gun savant. She'd hoped he'd be able to figure out how to shoot it in the correct direction. This was wildly exceeding her expectations.

His deadly efficiency was creating a new problem. The road ahead was now covered with neatly laid out rows of blood covered baldies. Incoming zombies were trampling over the bloody corpses of the ones Chris was laying out. They were going to have to four-wheel drive over a carpet of corpses to get to the exit now. Corpses with rib bones that could splinter and puncture tires. Bloody skin bags filled with slimy internal organs that were going to make driving almost impossible for the other vehicles in the convoy. The others were going to have to make it through this mess while zombies tried climbing on board their trucks to get at them. This was turning into the monster truck intermission show from hell.

Unable to skirt around it anymore Benson mumbled a prayer under her breath. Seconds later she followed the prayer up with some creative cursing as the steering wheel was yanked in ten directions at once. She tried her best to maintain a trajectory the others would be able to follow. The heavily armored Humvee should grind the bodies up good enough for the others to follow along in her tire tracks. Up in the turret Chris was busily blasting away. Benson figured the worst case with Chris was he might get bit and have to be sick for a few weeks again. His worst case was most people's best case. That was assuming a whole pack of the baldies didn't hop on and eat enough of him to kill him. Reconsidering her initial thoughts, she decided being eaten alive would be the worst case for Chris.

Up top Chris reloaded and continued to blast away. They were blazing a trail for the line of trucks behind them. Everyone in the backs of those trucks was shooting as well. At least the ones who were capable of working their weapons were. Extra rifles had been thrown in the beds of all the trucks. There were people in those trucks who hadn't seen a baldie up close and personal for over a year though. Some of them were curled up in shivering balls of sweat laced fear. Others were barely capable of using a rifle in the best of times. This was not a practice range where they could focus on their breathing while aiming at a stationary paper target.

Being in the beds of those trucks was like being in a raft on a whitewater trip. Except if you fell out then you'd be eaten alive by the vicious monsters surrounding your raft. If the monsters got in the raft with you then you were dead. You were supposed to keep them out by shooting the ones trying to get in while you were bouncing all over the place. The beds of the truck were filling up with a sloshy red mix of the pieces and parts being flung up in the air by the tires of the trucks four wheeling their way through the blood drenched mud course.

When the baldies got too close for Chris to keep them off of him, he slipped down the turret and crawled back into his seat. He wished he had a helmet on since the big machine was bouncing all over the place. If he wasn't able to survive outside, he had no idea how the people in the backs of the trucks were supposed to make it.

"At least the bombs stopped." The woman in the back piped up. It was the first thing Chris had heard her say since he helped her off the bus.

Almost immediately there was a huge roar as mortars struck all around them. Temporarily blinded by the dirt flung across the windshield and deafened by the massive blast Benson kept her foot down to keep them moving forward. Momentum is everything on the battlefield. Chris tried to look behind them to see if the rest of the convoy was still along for the ride. He couldn't see anything behind them except for the settling dirt.

Like a meth addict desperate to make a few dollars a baldie flung itself on the windshield wildly waving its arms back and forth on the mud-covered glass. Once it saw the people inside the big car it snarled and started banging its bald head into the windshield. The monster was so grimy it was impossible to tell if it was a male or female. Benson ended the bizarre snow angel routine by jerking the wheel to the side to send the baldie somersaulting out of sight.

Built for war the Humvee had some pretty sweet windshield wipers. They were able to see again by the time they emerged into the area cleared of zombies by the timely arrival of the bombs. They bounced across that scorched earth with the idea of continuing towards the gates. Up ahead they saw that there were even more zombies coming at them in the next wave. Barking orders into the radio Benson made the decision to take a detour. Cutting to the left she sped along a service road that ran around the base beside the fencing that enclosed the fort. They swerved around another group of baldies to get to the open road.

"Where are you going?" Chris asked. He was looking through the supplies scattered around inside the cab for a wet wipe or something. He wanted to get whatever was stuck to his face off his face before looking in a mirror. Benson glanced over at him and grimaced. Based on the look she gave him he really needed to find a napkin.

"There's only one way out of here where the baldies won't be." Benson answered.

"Yeah, cause the river worked out so well the last time we went that way." Chris replied sarcastically. He was scraping his face with a flap from a cardboard box that he'd found on the floor. What looked like a wart covered flap of skin slid off his face. Completely grossed out Chris used the box to flick whatever it was off his lap and into the floor.

"You have a better idea?" Benson asked.

"Do you know how to fly a helicopter?" Chris asked.

"Nope." Benson answered.

"Then the river it is. Let's just hope the weather's better this time." Chris said.

Tearing down the dirt road Chris kept checking the mirrors until he saw there were at least a few trucks behind them. Benson relayed her plan to the drivers who'd made it through the meat grinder. They all had roughly the same reaction that Chris had. It very well might be the last best option for them to make it out of the fort alive. Samson let them know there were a few vehicles stashed down the river that they could use if they could get there. Chris was ecstatic to hear Ortega and Desmond both agreeing with the plan. Not so much because he was a fan of the plan but because it meant his friends were all still among the living.

Chapter 21: The Ferry out of Hades

Explosions continued to shake the ground as they boarded the last two boats at the dock to head down the river. They must've finally managed to get out of range. Either that or the guys shooting at them had just miscalculated. Rather than stick around to find out Samson and Ortega both pushed the throttles to full ahead on their respective vessels. Not that full ahead was super impressive on either of the old pontoon boats.

Neither of the boats was in great shape which was why they were still sitting there. They were both also on the smaller side. They were better suited for a day of family fishing than evacuating refugees from the fiery hell consuming the base. They weren't even close to large enough to comfortably accommodate the fleeing refugees and their pile of supplies. It was standing room only on both of the vessels.

Chris was helping to organize some of the supplies they'd feverishly tossed onboard when the docks exploded. That answered the question on whether they'd been out of range or the soldiers targeting them had just missed. Maybe someone was still out there listening to prayers. In his darkest moments Chris liked to envision his mom as an angel interceding for him when he prayed. Knowing how superstitious that sounded he kept it to himself. He jealously guarded his memories of her. Praying to her was another way to keep her alive in his heart. It wasn't any more far-fetched than people turning into vampires during the middle of a worldwide zombie apocalypse. If anything, his mom becoming an angel made a whole lot more sense.

The sounds of the base being obliterated faded as they cruised downstream. The bad guys were covering up their tracks by wiping out the rest of the fort. Desmond confirmed that the *Familia* would care more about being in the spotlight than about the loss of human life. Human life was valuable to the *Familia* only in so much as humanity took care of menial tasks for them, served as food for them, and was the source for new members. Chris was still having a hard time understanding how the *Familia* could think he was valuable while at the same time sending kill squads after him. Desmond shrugged that one off as way above his paygrade.

Chris could still make out a pair of drones hovering far above them. That didn't bode well for being able to simply beach the boats and drive away. There wasn't much they could do about it though. They'd just have to keep moving and hope the drones eventually ran out of fuel or crashed or got bored or whatever it was that happened to drones. Between Ortega and Samson maybe they could come up with some kind of special forces magic to escape the spies in the sky.

The muddy banks rolled past with the occasional zombie lumbering along. Between the tornadoes and the bombings, the local undead population had been seriously stirred up. There wasn't going to be a safe place to land the boat and hop in the promised vehicles to leave. No matter where they landed, they were probably going to have to fight. Hopefully that fighting was against a handful of naked cannibals. Trying to make landfall with a group of the black clad mercenaries waiting to greet them wouldn't end well. They weren't equipped to hit the beach against an armed force of professionals. It was a miracle they'd made it this far.

After a harried conversation over the secure radios Ortega and Samson determined there was really nothing they could do besides go fast and hope for the best. Although putting Chris on a dinghy and leaving him bobbing around on the river was tossed around as a possible solution. The *Familia* was after Chris not the rest of them. When Chris volunteered to try it, Desmond was quick to point out the *Familia* would just have the rest of them blown out of the water once they got their hands on Chris. Wrapping up loose ends with finality was a hallmark of the *Familia*.

Samson was lost during large parts of this conversation. Chris felt sorry for the guy. Here Samson was doing his best to protect the people under his watch, and he didn't have the basic information needed to know what the hell was going on. Not that anyone had a really great grasp on why Chris was enemy number one to the Vampire Illuminati. Desmond knew more than any of them, but he was so used to keeping his mouth shut that it was almost impossible to pry information out of him.

"Where do we go after we get the trucks?" Chris asked. He wanted to change the subject now that they'd established him splitting off from the group wouldn't necessarily save them all from being executed.

"Sanctuary." Desmond said out of the blue.

"The creepy mansion place in Rhode Island?" Benson asked. The question earned Chris a hard look from Desmond. Chris shrugged. He'd already told Desmond that he'd let his friends in on pretty much everything he knew himself. He wasn't seeing much reason to keep the secrets of the group trying to murder him.

"Yes. I doubt we'd make it there just driving cross country though. The *Guardia Nera* would figure out where we're headed and get in front of us. We need to shake the drones first." Desmond said.

"*Guardia Nera*?" Benson asked.

"Wow! There's something you haven't tweeted yet?" Desmond blurted out sarcastically.

"Sounds like some kind of beer..." Chris responded with yet another shrug of his shoulders. Everyone around them leaned in to hear Desmond's response. The black clad warriors had come out of nowhere and demolished the base. This was the second time Chris and crew had seen them swoop in like this. Learning more about this new enemy was fast becoming a matter of life or death.

"The *Guardia Nera* is just a name. A generic name to describe the group that's after us. They're specially trained from a young age to serve the *Familia*. The teenagers can hold their own against any special forces operator. They normally operate under a veil of secrecy. Given the current circumstances they've decided to be a little more straightforward it seems." Desmond answered.

"Why are they attacking us?" Ortega asked. He was one of the people who'd been leaning in as Desmond spoke. It was the top question on everyone's mind. Unfortunately, Desmond didn't have a great answer.

"I really don't know. Lynn was trying to stop the elders from wiping humanity off the earth. They can't kill her since she's a royal. They can kill anyone who might end up being her protégé though. Especially if they can get to you before you're formally initiated. There's an additional series of injections you're going to need to reach your full potential." Desmond answered.

The second the words had left his mouth he looked like he wanted to suck them back in. He'd just revealed a lot of information to every prying ear on board a boat full of random refugees. Not that most of them cared. They were much more concerned with getting to a new place where they could work on building some sort of life. The life they'd built at the fort had just been stolen from them by some dark force they didn't want anything else to do with.

"How many men do they have in a typical strike team?" Ortega asked.

"It depends. They have sniper teams made up of three men all the way up to companies with hundreds of men. They've got all the breakdowns in between also. I'd guess they sent at least a couple dozen men out on this mission. Keep in mind each of the elders has their own militias and strike forces and all of that as well." Desmond answered. Chris was beginning to see why Desmond was so tight lipped. Anything he said basically just led to a whole new series of questions. They needed the knowledge Desmond had spent a lifetime accumulating. They didn't have a lifetime though. They had like thirty minutes before they'd be hitting the riverbank.

"Will they be coming after us once they finish leveling Leavenworth?" Ortega asked. He had his eyes focused on the river in front of them. They were following in Samson's wake, but it still paid to pay attention. After everything that'd happened there was no telling what might lie under the water's surface.

"Yes. They're probably already calling up another unit to continue the pursuit. My best guess is they were following me to try and find anyone Lynn might have injected. They've had drones on us to try and find anyone with the traits of who they're looking for." Desmond was struggling to avoid calling Chris out in front of everyone. At the mention of 'the traits' everyone who was listening turned their heads towards Chris. Desmond's attempts at subterfuge weren't working out very well.

"Get ready. We're docking in about ten minutes." Ortega announced. Not that he really needed to. Everyone had clearly heard Samson give him the news over the radio. The boat had gotten pretty quiet while everyone tried to figure out what the hell was going on. As if bald zombies weren't bad enough.

Chris was happy to see the attention shift from himself. He began sorting the gear at his feet into piles that people could pick up and carry ashore. It was going to take multiple trips. Looking up Chris confirmed that at least one of the drones was still watching them. When he put his head back down, he noticed people staring at him again. Probably because he'd been standing completely still staring at the sky for about five minutes. He could locate the drones, but it wasn't like it was easy.

"We still being watched?" Benson asked in a whisper.

"I see at least one up there still." Chris answered. He wasn't bothering to hide his answer. The eavesdroppers had formed a tight circle around them. He'd have had to lean in and whisper to Benson like they were lovers to avoid being overheard. Which would've been a little awkward since they'd formed a very sibling like bond. Benson frequently and affectionately referring to him as her *brother from another mother*. Deep bonds formed quickly when you spent most days side by side fighting for your lives. Your foxhole family morphs into your real family. Brothers and sisters that you'd gladly die for.

Up ahead Samson's boat was pulling up to a floating dock. They'd cruised past the city already. It was even more messed up than everyone had imagined it'd look. The city had already been falling apart before the pair of dueling tornadoes had rampaged down main street. The two boats had attracted a following of baldies who'd tried to keep up with them from the bank. The unwelcome escort had eventually fallen behind as obstructions on the bank cut them off.

"Grab as much stuff as you can carry and follow us once we tie off. Keep the noise down. No talking unless necessary." Ortega ordered in a low voice. Benson was standing at the bow waiting to tie them off when they got to the dock.

The instant the boat bumped the dock Benson, Chris, and Ortega hit the wooden surface boots first. Each of them had packs on their backs but the only things in their hands was their weapons. They'd go with Samson to secure the vehicles while everyone else humped the gear over from the boats to the huge garage that was visible beside the house. Moving in a line they kept an eye out for any errant baldies. If they saw one, they'd try to take it out as quietly as possible. If they saw more than ten of them then it turned into more of a shoot fast and leave the supplies behind kind of situation. Same deal if any of the rifle carrying ninja troopers happened to be waiting for them.

They didn't spot any baldies on the short walk up the gravel covered road to the expensive looking home with the attached RV garage. The home was remarkably intact. Other than the overgrown lawn it looked like it would've looked back before all the madness. Amazing when you considered the number of refugees and baldies wandering the area. Not to mention all of the spiraling portals to Oz that must have passed it by.

Samson went to the garage and began pressing buttons on a mechanical lock. In less than a minute Chris found himself helping to swing the wide doors open. He'd been expecting to see a top-of-the-line RV staring at them when the doors swung wide. Instead, he saw four Ford F-150s neatly parked inside the cavernous space. Motion activated lighting had come on when the door opened to reveal the interior. Looking up in the air Chris wondered if the whole house was on solar or just the garage. His musing was cut short by Samson handing him a set of keys and ordering him to start pulling the trucks out.

Chris pulled the trucks out noting that each one already had crates stacked in their beds. The trucks were cherry. They looked like they'd been driven here new off the lot. Judging by the mileage on each that was what'd happened. Pulling up to where Samson directed him, he asked what was in the crates.

"I tried to put enough stuff in each truck to take care of four guys for a week. Plus, I tossed in some guns and ammunition and whatever else was handy. I've added to it when we've patrolled down here. I'm just happy nobody found it and ripped it off. That would've sucked." Samson answered.

Ortega motioned for Chris to hurry up and get the other trucks ready. The Lieutenant pivoted to jog down to the dock to help the girl with the crushed ribs get up to one of the trucks. It was horrific how quickly the fort had been decimated. Of the hundreds who'd called the base home only a handful were walking up that gravel road from the dock. Some people may still be alive back on the base, but the hordes of baldies and continued artillery assault would make life extremely uncomfortable for them.

While everyone was loading up the trucks Ortega and Chris got sent off to clear out the driveway. One reason the house was still in such immaculate condition was because Samson had camouflaged the entrance. That camouflage turned out to be a number of heavy trees laid out across the entrance. Which explained why he'd sent them instead of doing it himself. By the time Ortega and Chris got finished they were filthy and sweating. On the plus side they had a bunch of brand-new trucks with extra gas and plenty of food. Now if they only had a destination in mind that wasn't full of people who wanted to kill them.

Chapter 22: Chatham Village

The most exciting part of the drive to Chatham was waiting to see if the bridge to cross the Mississippi was going to be there or not. Plenty of bridges had been destroyed in the efforts to slow the spread of the disease. Especially back before everyone realized the disease was already everywhere anyway. One good piece of news was that Chris could no longer spot any drones trailing them. In anticipation of the drone having to eventually go recharge Samson had taken them south at first. Once Chris had confirmed they were out from under the microscope they'd taken the next interchange east.

They drove dangerously fast down the deserted roads. They needed to be as far away as possible before the drones came snooping back around for them. Only a few people had been forced to sit back in the truck beds with the supplies. It sucked to be them at a hundred miles per hour over roads that hadn't been maintained in years. Chris would've felt bad for them if he hadn't been one of them. He had to be out in the open to be able to see if a drone showed up. As he was bouncing around on the hard sharp surfaces, he reflected on the fact that it didn't really matter if he saw it or not since there was nothing that they could do about it. It'd seemed like a good plan standing on the side of the road sipping lemonade flavored water from a Yeti.

Their destination was a small town in Illinois called Chatham. Their road trip destination was based on a rumor Samson had heard that Chatham was one of the few towns to have escaped the infection. Plenty of places had escaped the spread of the disease initially though. Assuming the town had actually escaped the plague and was still standing it could be exactly what they needed to evade pursuit. They planned on buying their way into the village with the supplies in the backs of the trucks. Crates full of MREs were worth their weight in gold. Not to mention the paper products Samson had included as necessary supplies. It was a strange world where toilet paper had become a luxury item.

Chris liked the idea of regrouping in the small town. They could ditch the refugees they had with them and get back on the road with two of the trucks. Or they could be riding into a derelict city with a bunch of baldies tromping around looking for fresh meat. The map showed there was a whole lot of water protecting the small town. If the townsfolk hadn't been all that into getting vaccinated, they may have escaped the worst of the tainted injections. Desmond didn't say anything out loud, but he knew the *Familia* had skipped infecting random cities in each country to keep some humans around. The elders may consider humanity to be a scourge but that didn't mean they wanted to wash their own dishes.

Less than six hours after leaving the house by Kansas City they were passing a sign welcoming them to Chatham, Illinois. Minutes later they were surrounded by a surreal sight. People were walking around a downtown area like nothing had happened. There was food being sold out of different buildings. The people walking around were all armed. Other than all of the visible weapons you had to look closely to see any other differences between now and five years before.

No one did more than glance at the four trucks rolling down the street until they got closer to the downtown courthouse area. Some cones had been set out in the street to stop traffic from going any further. Samson dutifully stopped the pickup and put it in park as a man dressed in a Sheriff's uniform walked up to his window. Glancing around them Chris noted about ten other men in similar outfits. There could easily be others lurking in the surrounding buildings.

"You mind telling me who you are and where you're from?" The Sherriff asked in a cordial tone. Chris had slid over to the side of the truck to listen in. Super hearing for the win!

"Yes sir. I'm Sergeant Dan Bartles. We're on our way up to Chicago to reconnect with our unit. We got cut off by some bandits looking to steal the supplies in the back." Samson made up the lie quickly. Lying well was a requisite skill for any special forces operator. Talking your way out of a situation was typically less dangerous than blasting your way out. It helped avoid a lot of unnecessary news coverage as well.

"So, you're not Lieutenant Samson from Fort Leavenworth?" The Sherriff asked.

"Uh. No." Samson slathered on a big grin and kept right on going with his lie. "We didn't even go by Leavenworth. Didn't make it that far west." Samson drawled. Why the SEAL had suddenly switched to a fake southern accent was beyond Chris.

"Weird. You look exactly like Lieutenant Samson…"
The Sherriff held up a photo of Samson that looked like it
came off his military ID. Samson smiled uneasily and reached
for the printout. The number of armed deputies around them
had tripled. More than enough to overpower them.

"Take the keys out of the ignition. I need you to put
them on the dashboard then place your hands on the steering
wheel. I need everyone else to put their hands on their head.
That goes for all the trucks. You can go ahead and let them
know over the radio. You get one chance to comply." It was
the Sherriff's turn to bust out a big fake grin. The potbellied
older man took a step back. Resting his hand on his pistol
grip the Sherriff waited for Ortega to relay the command.

Samson knew they were screwed. The deputies were
well positioned to mow them down if they tried anything.
Had Samson had been in a truck with just his men, he
might've gone for it anyway. The innocents riding along with
them made him hesitate. That hesitation killed the idea.
Reaching down he pressed the button to stop the engine and
then tossed the keys on the dashboard. Grabbing his radio, he
relayed the Sherriff's orders to the other trucks.

That's how Chris found himself on his knees with his
hands being cuffed behind him on the first well maintained
lawn he'd seen in a long time. The deputy patted him down
after cuffing him to check for any weapons Chris may have
'forgotten' about. The men were separated from the women,
and they were marched over to the basement of the
courthouse. Once downstairs they were taken into
windowless rooms that could be locked from the outside. The
Sherriff had disappeared after ordering them to be arrested.
None of the deputies had a clue what was going on. Or at
least none of them were interested in talking about it.

"Now what?" Chris asked Desmond.

"We wait for the *Guardia Nera* to show up and kill us. Unless someone has a better idea?" Desmond answered.

"There's got to be something." Samson muttered in a frustrated voice. This was his fault. He'd led them here. In hindsight it'd been a hideously stupid move. Of course, if he'd had all the facts he might not have done so.

"If we can get them to open the door, I might be able to fight my way out." Chris mused. If he could summon up his super speed like he did when confronted with baldies, then he should be able to disarm a few guards before they knew what was going on. Then they could take the weapons and shoot their way out. It probably wouldn't work but it was better than waiting to be executed. Now that they'd taken everyone's cuffs off, it might even be doable.

"Why would you be able to do that exactly? What aren't you telling me? If I'd known how important you were then I'd have avoided civilization. Enough with the damned secrets!" Samson exclaimed loudly. His eyes flashed with barely contained anger.

"There's a super-secret race of old rich vampires who basically run the world. They're the ones who let loose the zombie plague. Chris is one of them now. Or close to it anyway. He got a shot and now he's got a lot of their skills. Some of the vampires want to kill him for some reason. Probably cause they're jealous of his super-hot girlfriend vampire. She's over in Europe trying to kill them all or something." Ortega answered. He was right there with Chris on not really seeing why it mattered if people found out about the cranky old demons trying to wipe out humanity. The more people who knew the better actually. Desmond looked like his jaw was going to bounce off the cheap carpet in the room they were locked up in.

"Like seeing drones…" Samson muttered.

"Yep. More important he can move like the damned Flash when he wants to. You saw him take out those baldies back in Kansas City." Ortega said. The rest of the men in the room were staring like they were trying to figure out if this was all some sort of stage show being put on for their benefit.

"The *Guardia Nera* are vampires too?" Samson asked. He was doing his best to wrap his head around this new intel. He had to accept it as true so far since it lined up with his own observations. He trusted Ortega not to pull his leg in this situation. Any other time he'd have been looking around for hidden cameras trying to catch him falling for some kind of really intricate practical joke.

"Nope. They're just a bunch of well-trained assholes with unlimited resources getting paid to kill us." Ortega answered simply. That pretty much summed it up. Desmond looked like he wanted to jump in and add some background but was still fighting an internal war with his oaths of secrecy.

"Ok. So, we just need to get them to open the door then we throw Chris at them?" Samson asked. He understood the plan and wanted to make sure everyone else did as well. A group of unarmed men going up against a bunch of armed deputies needed some sort of a plan.

"I'll take as many down as I can. You guys come after and collect their weapons. We get the girls then go up the stairs and out the back." Chris said. He had his eyes half closed as he talked. He was working on remembering everything that he'd seen as they'd been perp walked through the building. Thanks to his greatly enhanced memory he was pretty sure he knew where to go if they made it out of the basement alive.

"Our trucks?" Samson asked. The way he asked implied he already knew the answer.

"We'll need to find new rides. Whatever we do has to be fast." Chris answered.

"We need to take out their command and control. Otherwise, we're not going to get very far." Samson mused. Everyone waited for more information on how they should do that. Instead of explaining his idea Samson walked over to the door and started banging on it. He was finally rewarded by a voice from the other side telling him to back away from the door. It opened up enough to allow the guard outside to ask them what they wanted. Chris was about to charge the door but decided to wait and see what Samson was up to. Keeping them all in the dark might be Samson's way of getting back at them for keeping him in the dark.

"Can you grab the Sherriff for us? We know there're people coming to get us. We've got a ton of supplies cached a few hours from here. Happy to tell him where they are in exchange for letting us out of here." Samson said his piece and waited. The guard grunted and slammed the door shut.

"Trying to get the command and control to come to us?" Chris asked having finally figured out what Samson was up to. The question earned him a nod from the blond-haired sailor.

"I guess we'll find out. Greed normally trumps everything else. Those trucks that we drove here were full of supplies. Hopefully they really think we may have a mountain of crap hidden somewhere." Samson responded. While waiting they arranged everyone by the position they should be in when Chris made his move.

They'd barely gotten everyone 'casually stacked' by the door when a loud voice ordered them all to stand back. Once more the door was opened a crack. A thick chain lock kept it secure. It'd been put there to prevent someone from doing exactly what Chris was planning to do.

"I heard you boys were looking to make a deal?" The Sherriff asked from outside the door. He had a very large deputy with him.

"Yes sir. We have a big supply cache up the road. If you let us go you can have everything in it plus the trucks and gear that we came here with." Samson answered in a level voice.

"I've already got the trucks and gear that you came here with. What makes you think I'd piss off the people coming to get you by letting you go for some imaginary treasure chest?" The Sherriff asked shrewdly.

"You can send somebody out to confirm it's there. It's booby trapped but I can walk them through getting to the point where they can see the gear. Then you let us go and I give you directions on how to disarm the rest of it." Samson said. The Lieutenant was ad-libbing like crazy. The Sherriff was about to withdraw from the conversation. Only his need for more weapons and supplies kept him there. It was now or never.

Chris struck the door like he'd been shot out of a cannon. His shoulder took the brunt of the impact. The chain was strong though. Whoever had constructed the door hadn't gone down to Lowes and bought one of those generic chain locks that break the first time you forget the damned thing's on there and open the door. Chris bounced off the thick door and landed on his feet next to Samson. The Sherriff and his deputies all skipped backwards a couple of steps. The wall where the chain was connected had splintered but the chain had held.

Ortega charged the door like a pissed off bull who'd just spotted the matador who'd been sticking swords in its ass. The chain gave up and flew out of the wall taking a chunk of the door frame with it. Ortega smashed into the wall on the other side of the door. The Sherriff had only brought a few men with him. The apocalyptic peacekeeper hadn't wanted too many of his minions to hear about whatever valuables the prisoners might be offering up.

Chris lunged for the potbellied Sherriff. The wide-eyed officer of the law was going for his pistol and barking out orders. Chris plucked the pistol neatly out of the Sherriff's hand and smacked him hard in the side of the head with it. He hadn't tried to hit him hard enough to kill him, but he'd absolutely hit him hard enough to ensure he wouldn't be getting back up anytime soon. He wouldn't lose any sleep if the Sherriff never recovered from the vicious pistol whipping.

Another deputy emptied both barrels of the shotgun he was carrying. The birdshot hit the refugees pouring through the broken doorway. The pellets were more of a deterrent than a deadly force. Although the one guy who fell to the ground with a hand clasped over a bloody eye might disagree with how harmless firing birdshot at someone was. The deputy didn't get a chance to drop the shotgun and pull out his pistol instead. Chris was methodically shooting the guards in the hallway faster than they could react.

Ortega and Samson were pulling weapons off the dead and handing out the ones they didn't keep for themselves. Samson had saved one of the deputies from Chris's shooting spree. The man was happily answering every one of Samson's questions as quickly and accurately as possible. Shoving the terrified deputy forward they followed him down the hall to where the females had been locked up. The deputy undid the chain and Benson immediately popped out. A big grin lit up her face as she rushed forward and kissed Ortega on the lips. That move was so shocking everything else stopped for a second.

Wondering how he'd missed the love affair happening right underneath his nose Chris ran past a blushing Ortega to the end of the corridor. The stairs led up to a closed door. Hoping the Sherriff had been subtle about descending down the stairs to talk to them Chris took the stairs five at a time. After their little secret sharing session back in the holding room, he wasn't trying to conceal his 'gifts' from anybody. He'd much rather have people think he was a freak than end up dead.

The door at the top of the stairs was locked. Chris knocked on it authoritatively and someone on the other side opened it immediately without questioning him. The deputy hadn't even bothered looking through the peephole. Chris punched the man in the throat. Waving for everyone to come up the stairs Chris stepped over the deputy who'd crumpled to the ground after being hit. Behind Chris, Ortega took a knee to search the gasping man for weapons and keys. The next door might not be so easy to open.

With no one else in sight Chris headed down the dimly lit hallway towards the back of the courthouse. Without looking back, he knew that his crew was right there with him. The door at the end of the hallway opened to a small set of stairs that led down to another door. That door opened up onto a loading dock. By the dim light of the setting sun Chris saw a wonderful thing. All four of their trucks were neatly parked in a row waiting for them.

Chapter 23: Out of the Frying Pan...

The keys were sitting on the seats in each truck. All of the supplies had been removed but that was the least of their worries right now. They'd gassed up the vehicles before pulling into town. They should be able to make it a decent distance before fuel became an issue. For now, they just needed enough to get the hell out of Chatham. Moving quickly to take advantage of this unexpected stroke of luck, they climbed into the trucks they'd ridden in on.

Everyone with a weapon got into the backs of the trucks. It'd be easier to discourage pursuers that way. The truck Samson was driving led the way out of the parking area. Benson followed closely in the second truck. Ortega, Desmond, and one of the refugees were sitting in the roomy extended cab with Benson. Chris was crouched in the back with a shotgun in one hand and a pistol in the other. The remaining refugees were packed into the last two trucks. Even though Chris had been run out of Leavenworth along with the rest of them he didn't consider himself a refugee. He wondered if he was already getting that ego Desmond had warned him about.

They drove around to the front of the courthouse. From there an access road let them out onto the main street through town. The orange cones didn't slow the four trucks down at all as they raced for the city limits sign. They made it a couple of blocks before a lone deputy stepped out onto the sidewalk to take a few pot shots at them. Other than shattering one of their windows the deputy's wild firing didn't accomplish much of anything. One of the refugees in the last truck sent some lead in the man's direction. The older deputy wasn't into fighting an enemy that shot back. He scurried right back into the building he'd come out of.

They didn't meet any more resistance making their exit. After staring up into the sky for a good ten minutes, Chris was happy to report he couldn't make out any drones. They were looking good until a string of headlights appeared on the road up in front of them. A line of cars was heading towards them from the direction they'd have expected the *Guardia Nera* to come from. It could be a patrol from Chatham that was out and about for whatever reason. Of course, a unit from Chatham would also attack them. They were making friends left and right.

Ortega went with the most likely scenario and assumed it was the *Guardia Nera*. Smoothly turning his steering wheel to the right, he led the line of trucks off road. The Fords rattled and bounced as they traversed from the road to the dirty field they'd been driving beside. It was the type of environment the four by fours thrived in. There wasn't much of a chance that the drivers of the incoming vehicles hadn't spotted them. The possibility they'd be able to slink away that easily was wiped away when the approaching SUVs veered off the road to pursue them across the open field.

A calm descended over Chris. He slipped fluidly into his hyperactive state. The world slowed to a crawl as his brain flipped into turbo mode. He could see everything. It was like he'd recorded the scene of the trucks bouncing across the field in slow motion and was playing it back in 8K on a hundred-inch screen. It wasn't that time slowed it was that he was absorbing and processing so much data so much faster than usual that his perception of it had changed.

Chris recognized the vehicles coming towards them as Cadillac Escalades. The big SUVS had been upgraded with the Secret Service package. The Escalades were going to be able to take more abuse than the Ford's they'd taken from Samson's getaway stash. At least the Escalades didn't have turrets or any of that fanciness though. It was nice to know their assailants would need to roll down the windows to shoot at them. Not that their pursuers would waste a lot of ammunition trying to shoot from the jostling vehicles. The band of professional killers would know most of their shots would just be wasted.

Chris was hoping some of the approaching SUVs would have passengers who were feeling lucky. Your average highly trained Ninja-like assassin might not be able to accurately fire their weapon from a bouncing vehicle at the people in another bouncing vehicle at high speeds, but he totally could. Finding he could flip from super slow to regular slow mode in his head he maneuvered around in the truck to stand up. Completely unaware of how unnatural he appeared he kept himself perfectly balanced as the truck bounced and swerved over the open field on a course to intersect with the SUVs.

Rather than play chicken with them the SUVs turned to the side and sped up to head them off. The brake lights on the Escalades flashed red as all five of the trucks performed controlled skids to come to a stop. Watching everything in slow motion Chris already knew what was going to happen next. He was betting on it actually.

Even as Samson swerved to try and avoid the makeshift firing line forming in front of them the windows on all five of the SUVs started sliding down. In the truck's cab Benson hauled aggressively on the steering wheel to follow Samson. Anyone else would've been hurled right on out if they'd been standing up like Chris was. The passengers up in the cab kept looking back and forth from the line of SUVs to their friend standing up like a drunken sailor in the bed of the truck. How the hell he was still standing was beyond them. Benson expected to see him become airborne at any second.

The soldiers in the Escalades fully expected to hammer the Fords with a solid round of automatic fire as they drove by. The barrels of rifles extended from the open windows like the cannons rolling out on ships from the Spanish Armada. A line of frigates getting ready to blast away at a flotilla of outmaneuvered pirates.

Chris took all this in as he inhaled a single deep breath. On the exhale he killed six of the ten shooters in the SUVs. Another two of the men were knocked out of the fight with wounds that were going to require a surgeon to keep them alive. Good luck on getting an ambulance to pick them up in time out here in the middle of nowhere.

That left two professional killers to rake the line of 4x4's turning right in front of them. Chris hadn't worried too much about those last two. He'd seen that one of the four trucks in their line wasn't going to make the turn. The shooters only got off a couple rounds before that truck T-Boned the Escalade. Neither the refugees nor the *Guardia Nera* in that vehicle were going to wake up feeling great the next day. They'd be lucky to wake up at all.

The Escalades turned and drove off. Except for the one with an F-150 embedded in the side of it. Chris banged on the roof and signaled for Benson to drive back to check on the crashed truck. Benson spun them around and communicated what they were doing to Samson. Chris glanced back towards the retreating SUVs. They were all the way back by the road at this point. One of them tapping their brakes had been what caught his attention.

"We need to get the hell out of here!" Desmond called out from his seat in the cab. He'd opened the sliders in the back window to talk to Chris. He'd tried to convince Benson to make a run for the border, but she'd been intent on following the intuition of the demi-god who could stand up in the back of a moving truck and whip shots off with unbelievable accuracy. It was hard for her to think of that man in the back as her bumbling friend Chris.

"Why?" Chris asked Desmond.

"They know now they can't take you alive. They'll settle for scraping your DNA out of the wreckage." Desmond answered emphatically.

Chris was processing that when he saw that the one SUV had stopped completely. He watched curiously as the back hatch was opened. They were too far away for him to have any hope of hitting them with the shotgun. He was out of bullets for the pistol. Still staring as Benson drove them closer to the wrecked F-150, he suddenly understood what Desmond had been getting at.

"Get us out of here! They've got rocket launchers!" Chris shouted banging on the top of the cab.

Benson reacted immediately. Jerking on the steering wheel she pointed the hood ornament away from the bad guys and floored it. Ortega was on the radio relaying Chris's warning to the other trucks.

The third truck in line exploded in a big fireball. A moment later a rocket whipped through the space Benson's truck had been in a second before. The rocket missed them and slammed into the ground about thirty yards away. It exploded on contact sending a curtain of dirt over the two battered Ford trucks doing their best to disappear into the night.

Chris found himself struggling to remain standing as Benson went into rocket evasion mode. Realizing there was no longer a need to wage a battle against physics he dropped belly first into the truck bed. He was tossed all around as Benson randomly cranked the wheel in different directions with her foot firmly pinning the gas pedal to the floor. It felt like there was never a time when more than three tires were actively touching the ground.

When the truck finally slowed down to something like a normal speed Chris popped his head up to see what was going on. His body hurt from being thrown around in the back of the truck. He could only pull off the slow-motion Matrix moves for so long. It got exhausting after a few minutes. Kind of like a computer with too much stuff open starting to pop up out of memory errors every time you tried to use an application. If he'd known the end of the world was on the way, he'd have switched majors. Some kind of sciences or hard-core biology would've been useful to help him understand what was going on inside him.

"You alive back there?" Benson shouted the question out the open slider. The question broke Chris out of his random thoughts around what courses he could've taken back in college instead of the psychology ones.

"Yeah. I'd say your driving sucked but we didn't get blown up so I guess I can't complain too much." Chris projected his voice so that Benson could hear him up in the cab.

"Damned straight. That was some world class rocket dodging." Ortega jumped in the conversation to compliment his girl. Desmond was leaning back against the door looking carsick.

Chris bit back the teasing remarks he felt like throwing out there at Ortega's obvious pride in Benson. Ortega and Benson were both deeply private people. They'd somehow managed to find companionship. For all Chris knew it was still new for both of them. No reason for him to go throwing darts at their love balloon. Besides, he was honestly happy for them. No matter how much of a third wheel it made him that his two best friends were now a thing…

"Can we get anywhere off roading like this?" Chris asked. It was too dark to make out details of what they were driving over now, but they'd left the relatively flat field long behind in their mad dash to avoid incineration.

"Samson managed to find some random dirt road leading to who the hell knows where..." Ortega answered. The cab went quiet as everyone marinated in those words. It was the first time they'd been said aloud. The realization they were driving down a road to nowhere in the middle of a zombie apocalypse while being tracked by who knew how many professional killers was a little overwhelming.

The road got even more washed out as they beat their way past a trio of grain silos. A couple of minutes after that they followed Samson onto an actual road again. Despite the fact that their enemies could be waiting to ambush them at any moment the smooth concrete felt great after driving over the rough fields. The unfilled potholes didn't have anything over the deep holes and tree trunks that they'd been bouncing over for the last fifteen minutes.

"Ideas?" Samson came over the radio with the question. That one-word query was asking a lot on multiple levels. Desmond was able to answer with an equally powerful word.

"East." Desmon was still focused on getting them to sanctuary. The New England mansion might not be as safe as it once was, but it was safer than anywhere else they might try to hide. The *Guardia Nera* wasn't going to stop coming for them. Now that Chris had revealed himself by single handedly repelling them when they attacked, they'd be coming in force. That force would include some who weren't truly human anymore.

Chapter 24: A Late Checkout

"He's awake!" Benson's exclamation at him opening his eyes seemed a tad bit over exuberant. Chris sat up slowly smacking his lips and rubbing his eyes. His body ached.

"Hey what's up?" Chris asked a beaming Benson.

"You are finally!" Benson answered. Ortega and Desmond had joined her to stare at him. It was all making Chris a little uncomfortable. What was the big deal? Why did his mouth taste like a baldie had puked in it? Why was he lying in a musty motel bed?

"Huh?" Was all Chris could muster.

"You've been sleeping for over a week now." Ortega said looking at him. Chris looked to Desmond for confirmation. Desmond nodded his head.

"It's common. Especially after exerting yourself or when you're going through any kind of metamorphosis. Some of the elders sleep for months at a time." Desmond said. Chris continued to stare at him.

"You know you're keeping secrets for people who want you dead right? You're keeping secrets from me and I'm an uninitiated royal. Whatever the hell that means. Feel free to open up. That vampire trivia rattling around inside your head could be the difference between us living or dying. Like it would've been nice to know that I might be taking weeklong naps." Chris said impatiently. He was over Desmond sticking to protocol. The need for the cloak and dagger garbage had ended when zombies took over the world.

"Sorry. You're completely right of course." Desmond said with Ortega, Benson, and Chris, all giving him the stink eye.

"Cool. So, why'd I just sleep for a week and where the hell are we?" Chris asked when Desmond appeared to need some additional prodding.

"I can't really give you great answers. Remember no one's become a royal for over a decade. They don't really let people outside the *Familia* know too much. I'm a dispensator. My role is to steward for whoever I'm assigned to." Desmond answered.

"You're assigned to Lynn?" Chris asked.

"I was originally Lynn's. I'm yours now." Desmond answered awkwardly.

"You're what now?"' Chris asked surprised.

"Lynn told me I was to be yours if you lived." Desmond answered looking extremely uncomfortable. Chris let that sink in. The statement was a little vague on whether or not Lynn had expected him to survive. Desmond must have thought it was going to be a temporary assignment based on the way he was acting.

It was like pulling teeth, but Desmond gradually gave Chris the information he was looking for. He kept slipping into using formal academic phrases like calling the *Familia* the *Immortalis Familia*. Chris tried to get him to just call a spade a spade. If it looks like a duck and quacks like a duck, why not just call it a vampire? Desmond greatly preferred the more formal terminology though. Calling the beings that he'd devoted his whole life to studying by the same name as the sparkly creatures from *Twilight* seemed to really upset him.

The sleeping was easy enough to explain. Chris was going through a metamorphosis. The drugs he'd been given had opened up parts of his mind that most humans would never access. One of the side effects of the mind being uber enhanced by the treatment was that it had much more control over the different systems in the body. The electrical stimulus sent by the brain to do things like regulate his heartbeat and breathing was becoming more controllable as Chris was being 'rewired'.

During the long periods of sleep the brain was working on enhancing the body to allow it to reach its peak physical potential. Benson had worried Chris was having seizures half the time he was asleep. That was because all of his muscles had been constantly vibrating. Desmond had explained that was why the members of the *Familia* were able to perform crazy feats of athleticism. The big gasping breaths that Chris had taken while out had been to supply the oxygen needed for the muscles to grow. Over time Chris would reach a physical perfection that he'd maintain until he was killed. If nothing came along and killed him then he'd live forever in theory.

It seemed highly unlikely that something wouldn't come along and kill him fairly soon though. The reason they hadn't let Chris crash in the back seat while they stayed on course to reach the sanctuary had been because of Desmond warning them that without Chris awake the next time they were attacked they'd all be killed. The black clad soldiers they'd fought so far were just the foot soldiers. The foot soldiers were cannon fodder.

Chris had sent the *Familia* a very clear message that he'd changed enough to easily handle a patrol or two of the foot soldiers. The way he'd been able to take out the shooters in the SUVs would leave zero doubt that Chris was becoming the real deal. If the *Familia* wanted to stop him, they'd have to send in the big guns. The next group would include an attacker or two with skills similar to Chris's. That's why they were hiding in a motel off a highway to nowhere hoping there wasn't satellite footage or any lingering drones. Without Chris able to fight they were dead meat if a bunch of undead Bruce Lees showed up to take them out.

"I'm thirsty." Chris said once Desmond had answered most of his questions. He had to say it abruptly as otherwise Desmond would've continued his lecture on how the muscles were toned by constant vibrations even when his body was at rest.

"You should be. Your body's been working overtime while you lay there without drinking anything. Normally, you'd be hooked up to an IV and wake up more hydrated than you were before the sleep." Desmond launched into explaining the typical protocol for the hibernation periods. Fearing they'd be killed while they slept the older members of the *Familia* had done things like lock themselves in crypts and barricade themselves inside custom built coffins. It was easy to see how the whole vampire mythos had evolved.

Chris guzzled down a gallon jug of warm water while he joined the rest of the team in trying to absorb all the info that Desmond was dishing out. There was a very pertinent fact that Desmond was avoiding. Looking around at the men and women who'd risked their lives for him several times over Chris decided they deserved the full story. It wasn't a jug full of warm water that he was thirsting for. It was the hot blood flowing through the veins of the people around him.

"I can almost taste your blood. The smell's hot and rich. It'd help me get my energy back a thousand times faster than this water." The nonchalant way Chris put that out there had everyone doing doubletakes. Had he really just said he wanted to drink their blood? Desmond gulped and looked around the room. It was the first time Chris had seen him lose his composure. Even if was just a momentary loss.

"Yes. Blood's full of the exact nutrients you need. You're evolving. You don't really need food. Blood's like a vitamin filled protein shake that'll keep you going. It's something that many of the others have developed a taste for. There's a synthetic alternative that's been developed that's much better for you though." Desmond blurted out the highlights without looking around the room. He didn't want to process the odd looks he knew he'd be getting.

"Damn. You're straight up turning into Dracula." Benson said in awe. No one else had known what to say after hearing about Chris's new dietary preferences.

"Yeah, Lynn mentioned that before. I can control it though. It's not like in the movies where the vampire ends up biting his best friend. Right?" Chris asked the question he knew was on everyone's mind. It was the question he'd have had if he was one of the people sitting around the room anyway.

"As long as you're not so incapacitated you can't control yourself. Like if we chained you to that wall and left you there for a month with no food or water. You'd go into a catatonic state. You'd survive but you wouldn't really be you. If we came back and tried to wake you up, then there's a good chance you'd sink your teeth into whoever was closest. It'd be your body trying to survive. That sort of thing's happened before. The older you get the more disconnected you'll get from humanity and the more likely you'd be fine with snacking on one of us." Desmond answered. The secrets he was telling now could very well get him killed. In for a penny in for a pound though. It wasn't like they could kill him more than once.

"Ok. So, I'm probably not going to eat any of you." Chris said with a nervous smile.

"If he bites us, would we turn into a vampire?" Benson asked curiously. She'd been saving up a lot of questions. There hadn't been a whole lot to do stuck in the hotel room for the last week. Desmond had barely said a word after getting them to agree to hole up in the dilapidated Embassy Suites.

"Possible. If you happened to have the right genetic makeup, then getting his saliva in your bloodstream could cause you to turn. Any exchange of bodily fluids could do it in theory. His body chemistry would be the catalyst to get your body to do what his body is doing. It'd just be a lot slower and a lot weaker than the concentrated DNA enabler the *Familia* has developed. Since only about one in a million people have the potential to be turned though it's not likely. It's how all of this got started though. The original immortals going around exchanging bodily fluids with thousands of people. The biting is what got into popular mythology obviously." Desmond answered. He'd missed his calling. He should've applied to be a lecturer at the top-secret boarding school where his type was educated. He'd have been headmaster of Hogwarts in no time.

"How come everybody a zombie bites changes into one of them then?" Ortega asked. He was right there with Benson on having a whole bunch of questions.

"I didn't turn." Chris interjected.

"We get it. You're special. I'm talking about normal people." Ortega answered without even looking at Chris. Smiling at Ortega's quick dismissal Chris went back to slurping down warm water. He was doing his best not to sniff the air around him to 'taste' the blood.

"I'm not an expert on the zombie virus. I imagine the chemists in the *Familia* modified the drugs they use to enable the DNA in the potential *Familia* members. They could've broken it down to the lowest common denominator as far as being able to transfer it. That'd explain why any exchange of bodily fluids and the disease spreads. The baldies have that same ability to sit around forever in a catatonic state without dying. They've also got that sense of smell like Chris does, but they don't have the ability to hold back when they smell the blood. That trait must've been engineered in along with the craziness to make sure it'd spread." Desmond answered. He'd spent a good bit of time thinking about the similarities between the *Familia* and the zombie plague. It made sense to him.

"All of this is great, but don't you guys think we should get back on the move again now that I'm awake? We need to hole up somewhere safe before the bad guys find us, right?" Chris asked. He stood up to test his legs. It made him a little woozy but nothing that wouldn't go away in a few minutes.

"That might be easier said than done." Samson joined the conversation. He'd been hanging out in the hallway connecting the living room area of the suite to the bedroom part. He'd been listening like everyone else. His mind had been far away though. Stuck in the hotel room for the last week had given him way too much time to dwell on his recent failures.

"How come?" Chris asked.

Instead of answering the question directly Samson gestured at Chris to follow him. The blond-haired warrior led Chris to the living room section of the hotel room and put his finger to his lips. Chris nodded to show that he understood the request to keep quiet. Samson bent down and moved a couple of towels away from the bottom of the door before unlocking the bolt and pushing the door open. He swept his arm out to indicate Chris was free to walk outside.

The Embassy Suites had a huge courtyard in the center of the six-story building. The hotel rooms all opened up to a landing that ran around each floor showcasing the huge open atrium in the middle. The lobby was full of fake plants, a mold covered pond, artfully decorated nooks, and lots of zombies. It was standing room only down below for the mob of monsters. All of whom were staring up at the level Chris and team were on. A few of the baldies were moving around on the lower-level landings as well. He didn't see any on the higher floors. The towel had worked well to block out the smell. Now that he was out on the balcony, he couldn't believe he hadn't noticed the stench sooner.

Samson pulled him back into the room. One last glance showed the undead were getting overly excited from the faint odor of humanity drifting down to them.

"What if we went down the wall on the outside of the hotel?" Chris asked. Taking the elevator down to the lobby didn't seem like a great idea.

"They're outside too. They just showed up the other day. The whole mess of them. They don't look like they're planning on leaving any time soon either." Samson answered.

Chris sat down on the musty couch in the living room. Everyone was looking at him anxiously. As if he had any idea how they were going to crowd surf over that massive mosh pit of madness downstairs. Ignoring their questioning gazes, he put his head down and rubbed his temples. Normally that helped him think. This wasn't a normal problem though. There weren't many normal days anymore.

Chapter 25: The Only Easy Day Was Yesterday

"You think he can get us out of this mess?" Benson asked. She'd gone through the connecting door into the room she thought of as the honeymoon suite. The last week may have been miserable for everyone else but her and Ortega had made the most of it.

"I don't think we should put too much stock in his superpowers. End of the day he's an untrained civilian with a great sense of smell and an unbelievable vertical leap." Ortega said. He was pulling on his boots and suiting up. They normally walked around all the time with weapons strapped on ready to rumble or run as needed. He'd let his guard down a little bit over the last week. His chronic athlete's foot was almost completely gone. It was amazing how much less grumpy he was when his feet weren't constantly itchy. A fact that Benson had pointed out at least five times a day for the last three days.

"He's also a magician with any weapon you hand him." Benson reminded her foot fungus free lover.

"True. It's nuts watching him work. It's like something out of the *Matrix*. It might get a little rough this time though. We have way less bullets than there are baldies." Ortega responded. Itch free or not he was slipping back into his standard pessimistic state.

Benson kissed her man and finished shoving her stuff into her pack. The two of them had really managed to nest the room up in the week they'd been there. She knew once they walked through that door the honeymoon was over. Chris wasn't going to want to hang out another few days to think about what to do. Thinking things through wasn't really a strong suit of his. The rest of them were ready to check out as well. The undead convention wasn't something any of them had bargained for when making their reservations.

None of them had anticipated getting stuck up on the sixth floor for this long. They'd come in and chained the doors shut to the staircases like they always did. The third morning they'd woken up with the guys who'd pulled sentry duty telling them to be quiet and stay in their rooms. A quick peek below had revealed why. Next, they'd wet some towels and shoved them everywhere they saw that air might escape their rooms. They'd hoped the herd would wander off as quickly as they'd wandered in. That hadn't happened.

How the baldies had managed to get up on the first three floors was beyond Benson. The doors to the staircases were chained. All she could figure was that some of the zombies had managed to jump and climb. Maybe when they got excited enough, they were able to summon up the same adrenaline-fueled powers Chris had. Whether or not the baldies might eventually be able to leapfrog up to the sixth floor was less important than the fact that they were out of food. They'd been out of food for a good two days now. The water they'd been drinking was a gift from the dark storm clouds that'd been building up overhead for the last few days.

"You know he's going to want to jump off the ledge and go in guns blazing right?" Benson said putting her hand on Ortega's stupid large bicep to stop him from opening the door.

"That's cool. I could use a snack." Ortega said turning around to smile at her. Benson got the message immediately. The Delta soldier she might at some point admit to being in love with had summed it up nicely. They could either stay where they were and starve to death or bust out. Busting out would be a lot easier while they still had energy. From what they'd learned earlier it was also a really good idea to keep Chris well fed.

"You guys ready?" Chris asked when Ortega and Benson emerged from their impromptu lovers retreat. Benson was impressed with the restraint Chris exhibited in not saying anything about them having shacked up. Little did she know he'd been working on something witty to say ever since he'd noticed the sleeping arrangements. Thanks to the brain fog from his long nap, he hadn't come up with anything yet that he thought was good enough to get punched for. Desmond had mentioned that after these long sleeps it'd take some time to snap back to normal. It was only natural to be a little groggy after that kind of body building hibernation.

"Ready for what exactly?" Benson asked. She wasn't trying to be a smartass. She was honestly curious what Chris was thinking. It came out sounding a little harsh though. Evidently, she could use some food as well. Rainwater may keep you alive, but it wasn't anywhere close to filling. She'd woken up that morning dreaming about a cheeseburger.

"Ready to get out of here. The room service sucks." Chris answered her. He wasn't put out at all by her attitude. He wasn't in the best mood himself despite spending the last seven days taking a nap. It didn't help that he kind of wanted to rip everyone's skin off and lick the blood off their gooey insides. He needed to get out of here and find himself a steak somewhere.

"We need a distraction." Ortega said. He'd been mulling the problem over in his head ever since the army of the dead had shown up in the lobby.

"We fling a bunch of bloody rags and noisemakers out of a window on the other side of the hotel." Chris said. He was surprised they didn't already have this planned out. It seemed like the standard 'get the baldies to run one way while we run the other' scenario to him. He was already cautioning himself to stay far away from the bloody rag creation part of the process. He'd felt himself getting a little overexcited thinking about it. He hoped he wasn't going to spend eternity starting to drool every time he walked past a discarded tampon.

"How are we going to get a bunch of bloody rags?" Benson asked curiously. Was Chris talking like a quick cut and slap a bandage on it to throw over the side or did he think they needed buckets of blood. How much of the red stuff was required to chum up the other side of the hotel? It had to be enough to distract the school of zombies long enough for them to sneak over to the trucks.

"You're going to need to figure out that piece on the other side of the hotel. I don't want anything to do with it." Chris answered seriously.

"Will they be able to smell it from inside the hotel?" Samson asked.

"That's why we have to make a lot of noise. The noise will attract them, and the blood will keep them interested. Unless anybody has a better idea? I just climbed out of my coffin like thirty minutes ago." Chris's attempt at levity came out sounding a little 'hangry'. No one had ever accused him of being a morning person.

"I was thinking we go down a few floors and hop out on the car port roof. We just need to get the zombies standing around down there to go somewhere else. Like we could try to get them all to go inside the hotel. Easy enough for one of us to stand on the balcony and yell or bleed or whatever gets them excited." Ortega completely ignored Chris's condescension. The much better plan he'd just put out there took all of the sting out of it anyway.

"How do we get from the carport down to the ground? It's still like a two-story drop. This is the zombie apocalypse you know. You don't want to end up with bad knees." Benson said. She had her head stuck out the open window staring down at the covered area off the main entrance that Ortega was referring to.

"Throw some beds down there to hop out onto? Once we're exposed on the roof, we're not going to have a ton of time to setup a ladder or anything. We'll need to be moving fast." Samson said. He'd walked over next to Benson to join her in staring down at the parking lot below. A parking lot with way too many shuffling shapes moving around it. From this height it kind of looked like they were being surrounded by a drunken nudist convention that catered to bald people.

"Why can't we just take the stairs to the first floor and go out that window?" The young female refugee with the broken ribs that Samson had been taking care of asked. It was a legit question. Especially since she hadn't been out of the room since they got there.

"There's a mess of zombies on the first and second floor already. We're going to have to deal with the ones on the third floor to get from the stairs to a room we can get down from. We're going to have to do this in stages." Samson answered. Chris was happy to see the girl was still alive. It helped that she had the body double for Thor as her personal protector.

It was decided that the first step would be to clear the baldies quickly and quietly off the third floor. Then they'd see if they could do the same for the second floor. The first floor was so crowded that there must be some sort of access stairway or something that they'd missed. The third floor was lightly populated by comparison. A dozen of the man-sized monsters were visible listlessly lumbering around that landing.

Chris, Ortega, and Samson took the stairs down to the third floor. They'd talked about doing it at night instead but using flashlights would stand out more than just going during the day. It wasn't like they were super visible during the day anyway. The only light was what filtered down through the green tinged skylights up above. It should be enough for them to engage and kill the dozen or so tangoes they needed to deal with though.

A dozen was too many for them to take on all at once, so they'd come up with the idea of popping out a door and killing the ones closest to that door then darting back into the stairwell. They'd go up a floor, see where the baldies had ended up at then go to whatever corner made sense for the next strike. They'd try to do it all as quietly as possible to keep the baldies below from getting too stirred up. None of them could figure out how the baldies had managed to spread to the second and third floor. They didn't want to find out the answer to that mystery hard way.

"You ready for this?" Benson whispered the question to Chris. It was like the fifth time she'd asked him. Someone needed to remind her about the no talking rule. On top of possibly attracting the zombies the repeated questioning was starting to stress Chris out. How did somebody know if they were ready to pop out a door and murder a bunch of zombies with machetes? It was the kind of thing you'd see a video game character doing and think that there was no way anyone would ever survive doing something that stupid in real life.

"I guess we'll find out." Chris whispered back nervously. Without the slightest clue how to 'flip the switch' to put himself into that hyper aware combat mode Chris walked out the door when Samson opened it for him.

Trying to focus on slowing down time he found himself humming that *Lose Yourself* song by Eminem. The real Slim Shady may be tough in a rap battle but he bet the super star wouldn't stand as firm if he had a couple of bloodthirsty baldies sprinting for him. With that oldie but goodie rap song still rattling around in his head Chris stepped towards the snarling monsters running towards him. Behind him he heard his friends engaging another target. His super hearing was as good as ever. It was just his combat mode that needed a reboot.

He skewered the first bald headed, sore covered, mess of a man right through the stomach. That was a rookie mistake. His arm was half-wrenched out of its socket as the baldie spun trying to get its teeth into Chris. There may be a massive amount of pain involved in the jumbo-sized belly button piercing Chris had just given the monster but none of that pain was reflected in the glazed over eyes of the infected man trying to get at him.

Those eyes revealed a deep hatred of all things human. Chris had wondered if his transformation into a vampire would eventually make the baldies ignore him. His smell must still be more human than zombie. This freak was definitely not ignoring him. Out of the corner of his eye he saw the freak's friend leaping towards him. Shoving the handle of the machete he had embedded in the first baldie as hard as he could Chris stepped backwards to get away from the gnashing teeth.

A fire axe descended in an arc embedding itself into the zombie's head. Infected blood splattered Chris's face. It was like he was on the front row of a demonic Gallagher show. One where they used human heads instead of watermelons and didn't allow ponchos. On the plus side his combat mode finally kicked in. Time slowed and his situational awareness went through the roof.

Stepping backwards he swung his second machete in the air hard enough to partially decapitate the skinny psycho who'd made the dive for him. The body hit the floor without even twitching. The journey had ended for the worldly bodies of those two infected people. Chris had stopped humming the Eminem song. His mind off on another tangent now. He'd noticed he never really thought of the humanity behind the monstrosity anymore. The fact that those two mostly headless bodies had once been regular people.

Benson punching him in the arm brought him back to reality. She gave him a look that left no doubt as to her opinion of his taking a break to daydream in the middle of an operation. Slightly embarrassed Chris followed Benson back through the door into the stairwell. Samson and Ortega came in immediately after. They'd left a dead baldie on their side of the hallway as well. The sledgehammer Samson was carrying reeked of corrupted baldie blood.

Flipping a flashlight on Benson shined it over each of them to make sure no one was bitten or otherwise incapacitated. Sensing she was about to ask him if he felt like he was up for continuing Chris headed her off. Once again breaking the rule for keeping quiet. As long as they just whispered in the stairwell, he didn't see a big problem with it. He kept his public service announcement hushed and succinct though since he didn't know if maybe the baldies were able to hear stuff as good as he was.

"Took a little bit to kick in but it worked. I'm good. Let's keep going." Chris gently pushed the flashlight out of his face. Benson had kept it there long enough that he could still see a bright white circle when he blinked. Her expression showed she had serious doubts about his statement. There wasn't much they could do about it now though. Time to play four corners until everything on the third floor was good and dead.

Chapter 26: A Leap of Faith

Having almost died multiple times attempting to clear the dozen deadheads on the third floor they were revising the plan. Staring down from a third-floor window at the dirt covered roof below they discussed how to get down there in hushed voices. None of them wanted to attract the attention of the zombies on the floors below them. The second floor had about fifty of the shuffling shamblers walking around. The first floor was standing room only. The lobby had filled up to capacity as they'd cleared off the third-floor balcony.

The fire code violating mob down in the fake tree covered lobby were staring upwards waiting to see if any more humans made an appearance. The way they got to the first floor had been revealed during all the madness. There was a big rock pond looking water feature set in the corner of the lobby. Stairs were hacked into the fake rock behind the plastic palm trees to allow for changing out filters. The creatures simply marched up that staircase then jumped for the railing on the first floor. Only about ten percent of them made it, but ten percent of a lot equals a lot.

As to how they spread to the other floors that remained a mystery. They were spending as little time out on the landing overlooking the atrium as possible to avoid stirring up the standing room only crowd below. Smart money was on the baldies simply climbing up on the railing and stretching out until they could reach the railing above them. Maybe only one in a hundred could figure that out but one percent of a lot…

Samson had sent everyone out to gather sheets from the other rooms. He was now in the midst of a craft project. They needed to weave together a couple of sheet ropes. One to go from the third floor to the roof of the carport. A second one to get down to the ground from the top of the carport. When asked why they didn't just do this from the sixth floor Samson admitted he wasn't entirely sure it was going to hold. In which case falling twenty feet was better than falling eighty feet. Chris got the impression a few of them had hoped he'd wake up supercharged and just kill all the zombies so that they could walk out the front door. He'd need to work harder to live up to his own legend.

With a couple of people working on making the bed sheet ropes the others focused on the best way to cause a distraction. Chris came up with simply walking to the other side of the hotel and opening fire on the baldies below. That'd make maximum noise and let them kill some of the monsters who were focused on killing them. Chris was pretty sure he could just hop out the window then hop off the roof below to get in the truck without having to use the rope if he had to. He was the only one with a hope of making it out if everything went to hell.

Most likely everything would go to hell.

"How much longer to finish your giant friendship bracelet?" Chris asked a visibly frustrated Samson. The man was busily threading strips of sheets into and out of one other. Beside him Ortega had given up. Basket weaving wasn't a course taught at Delta school evidently.

Benson and the girl Samson had taken responsibility for were jamming along. Braiding hair and braiding sheets were turning out to be very similar in scope. Others were moving around the room making sure everything was positioned for a quick getaway. Desmond was standing by the bathroom door looking bored. There wasn't a whole lot of use for an executive assistant with exhaustive knowledge of vampire lore at the moment.

The group was moving as fast as they could, but it was well after midnight before they were done. They had two bed sheet ropes. One that was about thirteen feet long and another that was almost eighteen feet long. They'd started over a few times as they figured out the original methods weren't working as well as they'd hoped. The end results looked very much like long braided ropes. Which was good since that's what they were supposed to be. An impromptu game of tug and war showed the ropes were fairly strong.

Chris was all for rolling out immediately. Desmond and a few others agreed that they might as well get moving. They were overruled by everyone who'd worked on the home-made ropes. None of them were able to move their hands. Benson swore her forearms were going to fall off at any second. No way any of them wanted to climb down the ropes then fight their way to the trucks. It wasn't like they were on a time crunch. They'd found a family size bag of staler than hell Tostitos in one of the rooms when they were gathering sheets. An equal helping of the cardboard flavored triangular hunks of fried lard should ensure none of them starved to death overnight.

They used the next day to put together some creative ways to secure the ropes so they could be climbed down. At the risk of having to hear her complain about her forearms some more Benson was asked to add a few more feet to the rope they planned on using to get down to the car port roof. They were all pretty sure there was a name for the place where you pulled up your car to hand the keys to the valet. None of them had a clue what it was though. Car port was the term they'd ended up settling on so they could stop making up names for it every time they discussed the plan.

Come dusk they were ready to put their plan into action. While everyone else huddled around the open window Chris and Ortega walked out the door and looked down to see hundreds of eyes staring back at them. The packed crowd of baldies below began to get more and more excited as the two of them walked around to the other side of the hotel. They weren't trying to be quiet now. The wanted the zombies to see them. They wanted the ones outside to come in to see what was going on.

The panting, shrieking, and obscene grunting from the monsters below kept Chris from speaking to Ortega. He poked him in the arm and pointed instead. Across the open lobby he'd seen the baldies on the first and second floor were trying to climb up to the third floor now. A bunch of them were missing their marks and stage diving into the crowd below. Chris wasn't worried about the stage drivers. There were quite a few who looked like they were going to be able to pull themselves up and over the railing to join them on the landing though.

Shoving their rifles into their shoulders Ortega and Chris went to work. Looking to cause maximum damage and make the most noise possible Ortega dropped a frag grenade off the landing into the lobby. Pressing their backs against the wall they waited until it'd gone off to get back to the railing and continue picking off the baldies who looked like they might actually be able to climb. Once they'd gotten those taken care of Ortega pulled out another grenade and they repeated the process.

After dropping six grenades Ortega pulled out a handful of Ziploc bags that had blood covered toilet paper rolls in them. Everyone had taken a turn getting cut then using the toilet paper to stop the bleeding. Chris did a solo revolution around the landing while Ortega tossed the blood-soaked toilet paper rolls down into the lobby. Despite the fact that he was still shooting the monsters as he walked none of them paid him any heed. Their blood lust had them much more focused on Ortega tossing around the aromatic toilet paper.

Stopping by the room they were using as their staging area Chris got a thumbs up from Samson. That meant the zombies from the parking lot were making their way into the hotel. At least the ones they could see were. They'd parked their two trucks under the carport to keep any enemy drones or satellites from spotting them. Unfortunately, it also meant that they had no clue if the two trucks were covered in the undead or pleasantly zombie free. They wouldn't know until they had boots on the ground. Unless they could tell while they were dangling from the bedsheet rope like an oversized pinata for a baldie birthday party.

Chris signaled for Ortega to head back to the room. They'd be going out the window soon and he was going to be needed on the ground. Especially if it turned out to be a hot landing zone. Once they were on the ground there wouldn't be any turning back. No way they'd be able to shimmy back up in all their gear before a baldie sank their teeth into them.

Chris could smell the blood in the air from the toilet paper rolls. He'd gone up a few floors and stuck his head out a window while the others had been mutilating their fingers to get the blood on the rolls. He told himself he wouldn't have done anything if he'd been there watching them squeeze the warm red elixir out of their fingers. It was the same thing alcoholics told themselves about being able to hang out at a bar without being tempted to have a drink. Luckily Chris was self-aware enough to take himself out of a situation where he may bite off one of his friend's fingers.

Walking sideways around the landing Chris went by the set of glass elevators that would've taken him down to the lobby back in the days of free omelet bars and manager sponsored happy hours. Now the big glass boxes were just obstacles to lining up shots on the zombies bouncing around like Adderall addicts in the front row of a music festival. All they really needed to complete the picture would be for Chris to toss down a gigantic, inflated beach ball or two.

Not that he could see them that great. Ortega had hung one of those lantern flashlights on each end of the rectangular shaped landing. The lanterns cast enough light to throw up huge shadows and make the place even creepier. The combined body odor wafting up from the crowd would've been enough to send a pre-apocalyptic Chris running for the nearest porcelain throne to toss his cookies into. At least a handful of tortilla chips wasn't going to do much damage to the plumbing.

Ortega stopped to briefly clasp hands with Chris before continuing on towards the room. Chris felt a powerful urge to follow Ortega out. No one had thought to factor in the creepy factor when coming up with a plan that left Chris alone in the hotel. The hotel with a lobby straight out of Dante's inferno. Leaning over the edge Chris sent a few bursts from his M-16 into the crowd below. Letting his brain sink into that analytical slo-mo state he picked off a few of the zombies who must have had rock climbing experience from their pre-zombie days. Not that the creatures flinging themselves at the railings then windmilling their arms like crazy before crashing to the ground looked like contestants on American Ninja Warriors.

Chris was supposed to give the rest of the group twenty minutes then head back to the room. In twenty minutes, the plan was for the rest of the group to be standing on the top of the car port. Chris would join them and be one of the first over the edge to clear out any lingering baldies. Benson and Samson would each grab a truck and pull it over closer to the ropes. Everyone would get in while Chris and Ortega provided cover fire. Once in they'd haul ass for the highway. It wasn't the best plan ever, but it beat sitting on the sixth floor until they starved to death.

Keeping up his part of the plan Chris tossed out the hand grenades he'd been given then started in on the flash bangs. They had two of those as well. The blood smell from the toilet paper had pretty much dissipated. The zombies had devoured the rolls as fast as Ortega could throw them down. There was the slightest hint of uninfected blood wafting up off of one of the rolls that'd landed on top of a fake palm tree. It was overpowered by the corrupted blood of the zombies ripped apart by the grenades they'd tossed down. A warm river of infected blood was running down the center of the lobby.

Pacing himself Chris methodically emptied another magazine into the howling demons below. The noise and the blood were getting them even more riled up. Not that the demons had a whole lot of variable settings. They were normally either catatonic or coming right for you at full speed with their mouths wide open. Chris thought about cutting his hand and wiping some blood on the wall to provide that uninfected blood smell. He couldn't cut himself now though. Otherwise, when he got outside the human shaped bloodhounds would follow him out there. This whole plan depended on the zombies staying inside the lobby.

Running out of things that went bang he resorted to yelling every time he sent a bullet into the lobby. If the baldies had the ability to filter noises like he did, then they'd be able to hear him. He doubted that they had the same level of abilities though. That was fortunate since they'd be much better hunters if they did. Or maybe they did but they were too crazy to use them. There was obviously a whole bunch of noise going on in their heads.

The twenty minutes took forever. When it was about time, he used up the bullets in the magazine he'd been working on and slammed in a fresh one. He put his flashlight into disco mode and set it on the ground. Why flashlights had a mode where they rapidly flashed was beyond him. Hopefully it mesmerized the infected enough that they wouldn't notice him slinking back around the landing to get back to the staging area.

Chris got in the room and shut the door behind him. In case he was followed by one of the baldies who could navigate the railings he locked the door and slid the couch in front of it. There wasn't much he could do about the big interior windows other than pulling the curtains across them. Getting around the room without his flashlight wasn't a big deal. Even in complete darkness he was able to stroll around with confidence thanks to the juice Lynn had shot him up with.

He got to the open window just as Ortega dropped onto the roof of the car port. He looked up and saw Chris staring down at him. Since no one had been in the room when he started down the rope the sudden appearance of a face in the window almost earned Chris a three-round burst from Ortega's AK-47. Luckily the Delta soldier was able to process information on a battlefield in real time. It wasn't quite as impressive as how Chris processed data, but it kept Ortega from pulling the trigger and painting the inside of the hotel room with Chris's brains.

Chris was oblivious to how close he'd come to getting an extra nostril shot into his face. Scanning the rooftop below he saw that everything was going according to plan so far. No one looked hurt from climbing down to the roof. Samson and Benson were over on the side of the roof staring down at the parking lot below. Desmond was looking up at the window to make sure Chris made it out. Everyone else was quietly waiting for the signal that the coast was clear in the parking lot below.

Chris considered untying the bedsheet rope and taking it down with him so they could get everyone off the roof faster. The problem with that would be if they needed to climb back up to the third floor later. Like if the coast didn't turn out to be clear below. He opted to climb down the rope instead of just hopping down from the window. That decision was more about not making a thump when he landed than anything else. Legs dangling in the air he instinctively knew that dropping down to the roof below wouldn't be an issue for him.

Making quick work of scurrying down the thick rope he hurried over to where Benson and Samson were trying to tie the other rope around a protruding piece of concrete. There really wasn't a great place to secure the rope. From up above the concrete sticking up from the roof had looked like it stuck out more than it actually did. There were other places they could tie the rope to, but they needed it as close to the edge as they could get it.

Squatting by the edge of the roof Chris peered into the darkness below. There was a nice breeze blowing which helped explain why they hadn't been sniffed out by the baldies already. They needed to get a move on though. Eventually one of the zombies stumbling around the parking lot would look up or smell them. Once one of the monsters caught wind of them it'd start getting interesting.

It was a long enough drop down to the pavement below that no one other than Chris felt good about just going for it. They'd all stared down at the ground they'd be dropping down onto enough in the daytime to know there wasn't much they needed to worry about landing on. As long as they stuck to the middle part of the roof, they should be good to go. Even with the rope they were still going to have to drop down a good six to ten feet. Plenty of distance to screw up your ankles if you landed wrong. Ortega and Samson had led some 'how to fall' classes up in the room earlier that day based on their extensive jump training.

Chris waited impatiently for the next phase of the plan. The cloud covered sky was a blessing as well as a curse. The darkness they were operating in made tying knots and sliding down the sides of buildings a lot more difficult. On the flip side it made it a lot more difficult for anyone, including the infected, to notice them up on the roof. They hadn't counted on the weather being so cooperative. Their appreciation of the weather soured some when the first drops of rain struck their upturned faces. No one who'd survived the dueling tornadoes in Kansas City wanted to repeat that experience.

Those first few drops turned into a downpour in no time flat. That was going to make this operation even more entertaining. As miserable as they may be the storm would provide them a lot more cover than they'd have otherwise had. Ortega tapped Chris on the shoulder and pointed down. Chris gave Ortega a second to grab the rope and swing himself out over the edge of the roof. Once Ortega disappeared over the side Chris took a step forward and casually hopped off the roof after him.

Landing neatly on the pavement below Chris stood silently in the rain waiting for Ortega to join him. Together the two of them stepped out of the rain into the shelter provided by the roof in front of the main entrance. The trucks were two big shadows sitting right where they should be. They were surrounded by other shadows that Chris really wished weren't there. Not all of the zombies had decided to go hang out inside the lobby after all. Chris twisted his wrist a few times to limber up his machete hand. He had his combat knife in his other hand to supplement the machete. Ortega was still rocking the fire ax.

There were too many of the shadowy shapes in front of them for Ortega and Chris to step in yet. Mother nature was on their side for once. Samson and everyone came down to stand behind them in the rain. Samson and Desmond helped the people who slipped trying to come down the rope. The girl with the broken ribs was one of the last to come down. She slipped and fell almost the entire distance. Samson managed to catch her before she smashed face first into the concrete. Her screams of pain from her ribs being abused for a second time easily overrode the low rumble of thunder in the distance.

It was almost impossible to make out what the shapes underneath the carport were doing in the darkness. Until they all surged towards the extremely human sound of the girl crying out in pain. No time for everyone to make it back up the braided bedsheets now. Stepping froward Chris swung his machete at the first baldie he saw darting towards them. In the infamous words of Tallahassee from *Zombieland* it was time to nut up or shut up.

Chapter 27: Nut Up or Shut Up

The machete connected with the side of the zombie's head. The sharpened metal edge embedded itself about three inches into the possessed man's skull. Chris's foot lashed out striking the bald menace in the chest. Simultaneously Chris ripped his machete out of the battered baldie's skull sending a warm wet gush of skull juice spraying on the ground. The baldie was undeterred. It'd keep coming until it was dead. Chris's other arm darted out and severed the monster's windpipe. Going into meltdown mode from the massive bodily trauma the diseased creature collapsed on the ground. The body twitched as it continued to try to get up. The virus still struggling to spread itself to the uninfected.

They went in with edged weapons. Right now, they were fighting the stragglers who hadn't made it into the hotel yet. The noise from firing a gun would see them caught up in an avalanche of the undead. They needed to avoid any loud noises to keep the mob from crashing out of the hotel lobby. There'd come a time very soon when they'd go full auto. They had to get to the trucks first.

Chris was scary. He was moving too quickly for the others to follow his motions. A trail of mortally wounded baldies lay in his wake. Ortega, Samson, and Benson walked that bloody trail swinging their weapons of choice. Chris was performing a bloody ballet, but he wasn't able to kill all of them. As fast as he was, he could still get overwhelmed. There was plenty of mayhem to go around.

Ortega had switched back to a hatchet and knife combo. Samson had his axe. Benson was wielding a carpenter's hammer and machete mix. The rest of the group timidly emerged out of the rain to join in the fun. Desmond was leading them. He'd been charged with making sure the walking wounded made it into the trucks. He'd accepted that responsibility knowing that everyone understood there were no guarantees.

Weak with hunger Chris nevertheless found his body reacting faster than ever. He only had to think of hitting a target and his arm was lashing out like a striking cobra. He was taking in every bit of data to form a complete picture of the situation. He knew which zombies he was going to kill and how he was going to do it. He also knew which ones were going to get past him. Those his friends would have to deal with. He could process sensory inputs like a supercomputer and his body was reacting better than the best trained athlete. There were plenty of limitations to what he could do though. The shot hadn't turned him into Superman. Passing as one of the lesser Avengers was a possibility though. He was way more impressive than that one guy with the bow.

A quick hop and he was standing in the back of one of the trucks. A baldie scrambled over the tailgate to get at him and Chris whacked it in the head with the dull side of the machete. The monster landed in the truck bed and didn't move. Two more of the undead came over the side with outstretched arms. Chris put a steel toed boot into an attacker's forehead hard enough to feel the crunch as the skull fractured. Spinning on the heel of his other boot he swooped down and came up with his combat knife deep into the other one's neck.

Pulling the serrated blade out of the dead zombie released a flood of infected blood. The stench of the corruption made him gag. Most people would just smell the typical coppery smell of blood. To Chris it was the smell of maggot covered feces. To think that vile smelling liquid was pumping through the veins of the infected was obscene. No one could maintain their sanity with that evil bile clogging up their systems.

Samson made his way between the trucks. Chris could sense more than see him in the darkness. An image popped into his head of the blond warrior swinging his axe like a serial killing Paul Bunyan. Easily jumping over Samson into the bed of the other truck Chris slid his knife and the machete back into their respective sheaths. He was going to need new sheaths if he couldn't get that awful smell out of them. Pulling the stock of his M-16 up to his shoulder he stood tall in the bed of the truck closest to the entrance to the hotel.

Samson popped open the door to the truck Chris was in and started the engine. The other truck came to life a second later once Benson got situated. Ortega had climbed into the truck bed next to Chris. Putting the barrel of his AK-47 on the lip of the truck bed Ortega made sure he had a full magazine. Now that the truck engines had started it wouldn't be long before they were facing a demonic stampede.

Chris waited until the first wave of rage filled baldies surged out of the broken hotel entrance. The automatic sliding doors had been pushed aside until they were bent and broken. The remnants of those doors did little to stem the flow of human shaped devils spewing out of the lobby. The lustful cries of the undead masking the sounds of gunfire as both Chris and Ortega opened up on the wave of flesh coming for them.

A couple of fully automatic large caliber machine guns may have been able to stop the mob from getting to the trucks. The small arms fire from Chris and Ortega barely slowed them down. The few seconds they did gain were long enough for Benson and Ortega to get them rolling out from under the carport. Those two had been picked to drive because they could both be trusted to stay calm under fire. One thing they absolutely didn't need was for someone to panic and drive into a concrete bench or something.

Benson had pulled out first since the back of her truck had been where Aubrey, the girl with the broken ribs, and the other refugees had been loaded. She hadn't pulled out until Desmond hopped in the passenger seat and gave her a thumbs up. Samson pulled out right behind her. Ortega and Chris were in the back of his truck using every round they had to hold off the hounds of hell.

Aubrey was totally stoked to have made it into the back of Benson's truck. Her body hurt like hell from all of the additional stress put on her shattered ribs. Against all of the odds she was alive though. Her and the tiny group of people in the back of the truck were all that was left of what'd been a stronghold against the infection. Fort Leavenworth had been coping well with the end of the world. She couldn't figure out why anyone would've attacked the base. It made no sense to her at all.

Holding her side Aubrey tried to regain her breath by taking shallow breaths to minimize the pain from her broken ribs. Cold rain drops struck her face like tiny needles made of ice. The body of the baldie Chris had hit with the unsharpened side of the machete had been shoved to the back of the truck. The first thing they'd do when they stopped would be to open the tailgate and roll the body out. A soldier from the fort had stepped up to supervise the people in the back once Desmond had deserted them for the comforts of the dry cab.

Wanting to make sure the zombie was actually dead the soldier crawled on his knees towards the tailgate. He picked the exact wrong second to let go of the side of the truck. Benson swerved to avoid a baldie that lunged at them from out of nowhere. The soldier slid across the wet floor to smash face first into the wheel well. Tasting blood in his mouth he tried to determine if he'd bitten his lip or taken a small chunk out of his tongue. Distractedly running his tongue around the inside of his mouth he missed the sight of the body in the back twitching.

Whether it was his mouth or tongue bleeding didn't matter to the baldie Chris had knocked out. The aromatic smell of warm uninfected blood had worked better than the finest smelling salts to bring the infected woman back to life. Rain pouring off her naked body she fastened her mouth on the soldier's face in a passionate kiss. Her teeth clamped down on his cheek as she ripped and tugged at his skin. In a total panic the soldier pulled his pistol and started shooting. He began yanking on the trigger well before the pistol was pointed at the woman trying to French kiss him through the brand-new hole in his cheek.

The Smith and Wesson nine-millimeter standard magazine holds ten rounds. The soldier was using the extended magazine which holds thirteen rounds. He managed to put three of those bullets through the sliding glass window in the back of the cab. Benson didn't continue plowing straight ahead through the rain when someone started blasting away at the back of her head. She pulled the wheel hard to the right and slammed her foot down on the accelerator before yanking the wheel back in the opposite direction.

Fish tailing through the rain at high speeds didn't do anything to improve the panic-stricken soldier's aim. The wildly fired bullets struck some of the people in the tightly packed truck bed. Ironically enough the soldier even managed to shoot himself in the foot. Against all odds he did finally sink a couple of bullets into the possessed woman's leg. The two bullet holes in her thigh didn't do much to diminish her passionate moans. Sun blistered face glistening with fresh blood she plunged her teeth into the screaming soldier's neck.

A refugee with a bloody hole in his good hand thanks to the dead soldier's shooting spree fired his pistol at the zombie cradling the blood covered corpse of the soldier. The bullet nicked the infected woman's shoulder. The sudden pain meant nothing to her. All the shot had really accomplished was to remind her that there were other people in the back of the truck to eat. Using her good leg to propel herself across the wet truck bed the zombie dove onto the man's leg.

Ripping himself away from her the refugee jumped backwards from the rapidly accelerating truck. His neck and half the other bones in his body snapped like twigs when he slammed into a steel streetlight post at sixty miles per hour. Benson glimpsed the man being wrapped around the beam in her rearview mirror. Benson yelled for Desmond to figure out what the hell was going on in the back. Twisting around in his seat Desmond saw the demonic visage of the rage raptured baldie as it attacked Aubrey.

"Stop! Baldie in the back!" Desmond yelled. He pulled his pistol to line up a shot but with the rain and Benson's erratic driving it was impossible. The zombie and Aubrey were wrapped around each other like a couple of drunk newlyweds.

Benson deciphered what Desmond was trying to tell her and slammed on the brakes. Both doors flew open as her and Desmond leapt out to try and save the people in the back. When the baldie stuck her head up over the lip of the truck bed Benson put a bullet in her skull.

"Are you ok?" Benson asked Aubrey. The whimpering girl ignored her. Everyone else in the back of the truck was very much dead. The guy who'd leapt out of the moving truck and face planted into a streetlight was a goner. They were idling in the middle of a highway next to a deserted gas station. Lightning crackled in the sky as the rain poured down on them in big cold drops. Killing off most of the humans on the planet had seriously screwed up the weather.

"What's going on?" Samson asked them through his window. He'd pulled up his truck beside theirs.

"There was a zombie in the back somehow." Desmond answered.

"How's Aubrey?" Samson asked fearfully. He put the truck in park and jumped out with a worried expression on his face. He'd been looking out for Aubrey ever since he saved her life on the bus back in Fort Leavenworth. Even with all his other failures he'd managed to save the girl. He'd broken a few of her ribs doing so but she was still on the right side of the ground. He'd done something right at least.

"Not sure." Benson answered. She'd climbed up into the back of the truck to check out the young woman. Boots sloshing through the bloody water trapped in the truck bed she squatted down next to Aubrey. Some of that bloody water splashed over the two of them when Samson hopped up into the truck.

"Are you ok?" Samson asked leaning in close to Aubrey's face. The girl was in shock. Her lips were blue from the cold. She was shivering. Her eyes stared sightlessly out into the night. Her drenched hair hung down around her face. Samson pulled out a light and began shining it over his young charge's body looking for injuries.

"Her ear." Benson whispered directing Samson's hand to cast the light on the side of Aubrey's head. The side where an odd lump of flesh was visible through the scraggly curtain of drenched hair. A bloody flap of skin was all that was left of Aubrey's ear. The rest of it was in the dead baldie's belly.

"Did it bite me?" Aubrey's clear voice startled Benson and Samson. Neither of them had expected the girl to say anything. Not when her glazed eyes and slack jawed expression screamed out that she was in a major state of shock. How else would she not realize most of her ear was missing?

"It did honey." Benson said reaching out to hug the girl. Aubrey leaned in to accept the embrace. Her state of shock shattered as she shuddered with uncontrollable emotion. Tears streaming down her face she struggled to breathe while Benson held her tightly. Samson squatted beside the pair awkwardly trying to figure out some way he could help. The big soldier lost it when Aubrey reached up and began feeling around to figure out what was wrong with her ear.

Big tears welled up in Samson's eyes. Unashamedly he wept for the young girl whose life was effectively over. The rain washed the tears from his face as fast as they appeared. The big blond SEAL didn't lose his composure in any way other than the tears. Externally he was a rock. Internally he was falling apart. First his base, then his men, and now this girl he'd sworn to protect. Everything was falling apart.

"Will I change into one of those things?" Aubrey asked.

"Not right away." Benson answered running her fingers through the girl's hair. Samson was beyond thankful that Benson was there. He had no idea what to say. He'd failed Aubrey so horribly. He'd do anything to switch places with her.

"I don't want to turn into one of them." Aubrey said. She was on the verge of a panic attack thinking about it.

"We won't let you." Samson said firmly. The tears in his eyes didn't translate to any trembling in his voice. He'd be her rock. He'd failed to keep her safe. He could at least make sure she died well.

"Can I get warm first?" Aubrey asked in a calmer voice. The voice of a young girl asking for a favor. A voice that broke everyone's heart.

Samson scooped Aubrey up and handed her down to Ortega. Ortega cradled her while Samson hopped out of the truck to reclaim her. He carried her through the rain to sit her inside the cab of his truck. Blasting the heat, he drove over to the gas station.

The two trucks parked by the gas pumps to get out of the rain. The pumps had long since been rendered nonfunctional. Most likely the gas had been drained out of them in the early days of the pandemic. Not that any of them spent too much time worrying about where they were going to find the gas that they needed to fill up the trucks. Right now, it was all about Aubrey.

"Maybe I'm immune?" Aubrey looked around hopefully. Samson glanced over at Chris. Chris shrugged. It was possible. It was winning the lottery three times in a row possible, but it was possible.

"You could be honey." Benson said sliding up to Aubrey and holding her arms out for another hug. An embrace Aubrey desperately slipped into.

"I feel like I'm at my own funeral." Aubrey declared when she'd regained control of her voice again. No one knew how to respond to that. She'd pretty much nailed the mood.

They stood around watching the rain pour down in thick sheets around the edge of the shelter covering the pumps. At some point Aubrey asked if she could rest. Samson set her up in the truck. Benson climbed in the driver's seat to keep her company. Holding hands, the two of them both slipped off quickly into an exhausted slumber. The traumatic events of the night were enough to override Aubrey's fear of turning and Benson's fear of waking up next to a flesh-eating monster.

"I'm sorry man." Chris put his hand on Samson's broad back. With the body armor, backpack, and assorted weapons the gesture was purely symbolic. Samson was staring through the truck window at Aubrey peacefully sleeping in the passenger seat. Her hastily bandaged ear wasn't visible from this angle. All of the worry and fear fell away from the young woman in her sleep. It made her look more like she would've looked if the world hadn't gone to hell.

"She's got maybe a week, right?" Samson asked quietly. His eyes never left the young girl's innocent face.

"Something like that. Maybe more. Maybe less." Chris answered thinking back to his days in the quarantine facility. Locked inside that gym with all of the other freshly infected he'd seen some turn in a few days. Others had taken weeks. Not that he'd been able to keep a close scientific watch on any of it since he'd spent most of the time black out sick.

"Don't worry. I'll do it when she starts showing symptoms. No one else touches her. We'll give her until the symptoms pop up. Sanctuary can wait." Samson spoke the words with finality. There'd be no arguing with him. Chris nodded along knowing the others wouldn't have a problem respecting his wishes. It wasn't like they had anywhere they had to be. Might as well see Aubrey off in style.

Chapter 28: Nibbling on Sponge Cake

"There's a Gettysburg in Ohio?" Chris asked through the open slider. He'd stuck his head up to read the road sign when he felt the truck slowing down. Given his obvious prowess at riding in the back Chris had been stuck back there again.

They'd consolidated down to a single truck to save on gas. Even with the gas they'd been able to salvage from the homes and shops they'd broken into they'd barely been able to scrape together enough to fill the tank of the gas guzzling Ford. A Ford that was no longer recognizable after Ortega had decided they needed to change it up to keep from being easily recognized. Inspired by a case of purple spray paint they'd found when they were searching for gas, he'd immediately given their ride a ghetto paint job.

Aubrey hadn't started showing any symptoms yet. She was beyond depressed while Samson nurtured a flame of manic hope. He kept feeling her forehead and staring at her for the first tell-tale signs of a rash. Chris couldn't believe Aubrey hadn't snapped at him yet. He could tell Benson was close to losing her patience with Samson. It wasn't fair to give Aubrey too much hope. It wasn't fair to Samson or the rest of them either. There was almost a hundred percent chance Aubrey's hair was going to start falling out within the next week or so.

The truck had the feel of a mobile hospice. The young patient being mostly whole and healthy looking somehow made it worse. What was left of Aubrey's ear was scabby and nasty looking when they removed the bandages to clean it. She'd thrown a fit about wasting their limited medical supplies on her ear. When Benson had said they didn't want it to get infected Aubrey had pointed out they were going to have to kill her pretty soon anyway. Next to that what was a bit of an ear infection? Maybe it'd help her not hear the bullet they'd have to put in the back of her head.

Things had gotten even more tense after Aubrey's outburst. No one wanted to say anything that'd set her off again. Benson had been surreptitiously smashing up antibiotic pills and putting them in the drinks she offered up to Aubrey since then. Samson had even stopped touching the doomed girl's forehead for a few hours following that scene. Driving in silence had eventually become way too morbid. Not that Aubrey breaking the silence by collapsing into a crying jag and declaring they should just kill her already and get it over with helped at all.

To pass the time Benson began asking Aubrey questions about her past. Questions about her childhood. She wanted to make the ride more pleasant for Aubrey, but it was a serious downer for everyone else. Benson should've known better than to try opening up the can of warms that was asking anyone about their past. There were very few happy endings. In Aubrey's case they got to hear about how her mom had shot her dad then swallowed a bottle of sleeping pills after telling Aubrey how much she loved her.

The mom had swallowed the pills about half a mile from the entrance to the refugee center at Fort Leavenworth. With her hair already falling out in big patches the mom knew she wasn't getting in and wanted to make sure her daughter did. Too afraid to put a pistol barrel in her mouth she'd instead chosen to take the pill route out. The mom had imagined herself watching Aubrey toddle off down a street lined with flowers towards the security of armed soldiers and tall walls. The mother would then lie down on top of a grass covered hill and slip blissfully into a forever sleep.

In reality it was raining when they drove up to Fort Leavenworth. A long line of cars was snarled in a massive traffic jam with people trying to reach the perceived safety of the base. The armed soldiers guarding the front gate didn't appear friendly at all. They looked scared. Young men and women in uniform dealing with a situation they'd never been trained for. Rifle waving refugees were leaving their cars and demanding the soldiers let them in. What'd eventually happened was a scene that'd played out at hundreds of militarized checkpoints across the world.

Push came to shove, and a refugee shot one of the guards. The rest of the guards instantly opened up on the mob. The uniformed guards blasted away at men, women, and children indiscriminately. Both sides fought to protect themselves as well as they could. In the middle of all that chaos Aubrey's mom had turned. Spinning around to flee from the gunfire Aubrey saw her mom squatting over the writhing body of a young boy missing a good chunk of his cheek. While the boy's parents fled in terror Aubrey's mom bent down and bit into her victim's nose. Shaking her head around until she'd worked off enough flesh to make a mouthful she chewed viciously on the bloody skin.

In shock Aubrey had watched her mom chew the boy's nose off his face. The yelling, screaming, and gunfire caught her mom's attention. Looking up the monster that used to be her mom had locked eyes with her daughter. Aubrey hadn't seen even the tiniest sliver of recognition in those eyes. They'd transformed into the merciless eyes of an apex predator. They were flooded with the raw rage of a rabid dog.

"My mom looked at me and I thought I was dead. I thought she was going to come over and eat my face next." Aubrey told the truck full of rapt listeners. Each of them able to connect with her story as they had similar ones of their own. Ones they'd never shared with anyone.

"What happened?" Benson finally asked when Aubrey seemed content to end her story there.

"A soldier came out of nowhere and shot her. He shot my mom without even thinking about it. Not that I blame him. He saved my life. Then he walked over and shot the boy with no nose right in the head. Made sure he was good and dead. That's what you do when someone gets bitten right?" Aubrey looked around to see if anyone would challenge her on that. Samson was the only one who chose to speak up.

"Or you ride around with them for a few days to see if maybe they'll be one of the lucky ones. If you do pull through you only lost an ear. You've got another one right on the other side of your head." Samson responded with a tightlipped smile. It was an attempt at levity that fell flat. It did help change the course of the conversation though.

"I probably won't though. I get that. Thank you all for trying to give me a chance though." Aubrey said. She appeared to be coming out of her funk at least. Not that anyone blamed her for being in the funk to begin with.

"I think you need something to cheer you up. What sounds good?" Benson asked out of the blue. The question hung in the air long enough that she thought she wasn't going to get an answer.

"A strawberry margarita with real booze in it? My mom sometimes let me have a sip of hers." Aubrey asked after thinking about it for a minute.

"Done." Samson said immediately.

"Yeah. All we need is a liquor store, some ice, salt for the rim.... Piece of cake." Benson said. She said it energetically though. If there was one thing the crew in this truck was good at scavenging it was booze. They might end up walking because they ran out of gas, but they'd be sipping on various whiskeys and lugging along lots of ammunition while they did it. They should all get matching bullets and booze tattoos when this was over.

A sign up ahead pointed out a corner market in good old Gettysburg. The village had been home to about 513 people based on the 2010 census results proudly displayed on the welcome sign they'd passed. Small towns with small populations were generally deserted. This one was out of the way enough where they'd need to keep their eyes open though. Baldies were always angry but regular people didn't take too kindly to people coming in to scavenge off their land either.

The corner market was a big disappointment. Not only didn't it have any booze sitting on the shelf that was plainly meant to display booze it was devoid of any other useful supplies as well. Someone had come in and completely cleaned the place out. There weren't even any drink cups left in the dispenser by the soda fountain. A search of the storage room turned up equally disappointing results. The only highlight being when Ortega screamed like a little girl and came hopping out of the room backwards after running face first into a gigantic spider web.

"How about a crystal light packet mixed with some warm Jack Daniels?" Ortega asked once everyone was done making fun of him.

"Yeah, that sounds just as good as an ice-cold margarita alright." Benson said giving Ortega an appraising look. She wasn't sure if he'd brought it up to try and appease Aubrey or if he just wanted to reclaim some of his manhood after the whole spider web incident. It was probably a little bit of both. She wondered if Ortega bothered mixing his lemony concoction with water. Knowing him he was probably just pouring the packets straight into the JD to make his very own, very alcoholic version of Lynchburg Lemonade.

"Screw that. We'll drive around town until we find some." Samson said.

"Almost out of gas." Benson reminded him.

"We'll walk around town until we find some." Samson immediately flipped the script to accommodate their current fuel situation.

"It's ok. Let's just look for gas and get out of here." Aubrey said.

"Yeah, this doesn't seem like the best place to hook up a frozen beverage." Chris agreed. He was disappointed as well. He'd been looking forward to a nice cold drink. Although he'd also been wondering how the hell Samson was planning on pulling it off. He'd hoped the man had some sort of special forces training in margarita recon or something. Developing a course like that would've been a solid use of taxpayer dollars as far as Chris was concerned. Especially when you considered the other ways the government blew through everyone's money.

"Nothing says we can't look for both." Samson said with a grin. He knew no one there was going to argue too much about rooting around for some tequila and margarita mix. They'd worry about the ice part of the equation once they had the base ingredients.

Desmond was the only one growing impatient with all the delays. He wasn't as used to the rest of them at roughing it. He'd spent a good portion of the apocalypse in relative comfort thanks to his status. The *Familia* and their associates had access to a whole other world of solar powered lodging with supply caches it'd take decades to run through. It was like he was stuck sleeping in the terminal when he normally had access to the 24-hour Crown Club. The only thing keeping his impatience under wraps was the very real possibility that as soon as he showed his face at the proverbial Crown Club someone was going to kill him.

They began conducting their typical salvage operation by clearing homes then searching them. It was important to make sure there was nothing waiting to kill you before you started checking the cupboards for dried goods. That really old cannister of oatmeal wasn't going to do you any good with a baldie gnawing on the back of your head.

The houses were devoid of any danger. They were also devoid of any supplies. Someone had cleaned out the whole front row of homes. It wasn't uncommon for them to look through a dozen houses and not find anything useful. It was weird to search though a dozen homes and see everything removed so neatly though. Normally the places that'd been looted were completely tossed. Furniture all over the place, clothes strewn across the floor, and the lingering smell of rotting food or forgotten corpses in the air. There was none of that in any of the houses they spent the afternoon searching.

"There's something weird going on." Chris said for about the fifteenth time. Everyone felt it. They'd all been thrown off by the cleanliness of the looted homes. With his hyper acute senses Chris had been more thrown off than the rest of them. Not only had all the houses been looted they'd been cleaned after being looted. The furniture smelled like pledge. There was minimal dust. If anyone had died recently in any of the houses their smell hadn't lingered enough for Chris to detect it.

"Yeah, if we had gas, I'd say to cut our losses and see what the next town down the road has to offer." Samson said. His faith in finding the ingredients for a strawberry margarita was being severely challenged.

"We've got a few gallons in the tank. We'll make it a few towns down the road at least." Benson said. She turned around to start the long walk back to the truck. The houses here were spread out. People had real yards. It wasn't your typical suburbs with the zero lot lines. This place was a Norman Rockwell kind of neighborhood.

"Hold up." Chris whispered. They'd been walking for a couple of minutes and were coming up on the curve that'd take them back to the general store. Chris had caught the hum of conversation in the air. He didn't know where it was coming from. Only that it wasn't them talking. They stood there for a good ten minutes before slowly moving forward again. They'd dropped into the formation they used to travel in a hot zone. Weapons were locked and loaded. Aubrey was in the middle with Benson while Ortega and Chris took point. Desmond and Samson fell back about ten yards to watch their backs.

Chris held up his hand when he got near the corner. He could hear people up ahead. The way they were trying to keep quiet basically screamed the word ambush. Chris signaled for everyone to fall back. Eyes scanning the neighborhood he noticed something on top of a roof that he'd skimmed right over before. He jogged across the street to get a better look.

"We're being watched." Ortega said. He'd come over with Chris to see whatever it was Chris was looking at. They both stood there staring at the camouflaged black disc on the roof of the home. It'd been stuck on behind an old satellite dish. Looking carefully Chris was able to trace out the path of a wire that ran up into the branches of a tall tree. Somewhere up there was most likely a solar panel that fed into the camera. Undoubtedly there were cameras all over town. They'd probably been under observation ever since they attempted to loot the local Jiffy Mart.

Up ahead of them a group of a dozen men appeared wearing riot gear and carrying assault rifles. The other group Chris had heard was also now scurrying through the yards around them to encircle their position. They'd walked right into a trap.

"Into that house." Ortega ordered running towards the front door of a home they'd searched earlier. Another odd thing about the houses was that none of them had been locked. Chris was wishing he'd listened to his inner voice earlier and made them leave.

They crashed into the house and spread out on the second floor. It was a large enough home that they had to rely on their walkie talkies to communicate. Looking out his window Chris watched as a dozen men took up firing positions on the other side of the street. He had no doubt they were being completely surrounded. Hopefully the special forces dudes he was stuck in the house with were better at this than they were at finding the ingredients for frozen beverages.

Chapter 29: Blaze of Glory

"I guess that makes us officially surrounded." Samson broadcast over the walkies after everyone confirmed they could see the enemy outside their windows.

"Can Chris kill them all?" Benson asked from her position in a spare bedroom on top of the garage. The room was so clean she felt kind of bad for not having wiped her boots off before coming inside. There was nothing in the room except furniture. The bed had mattresses on it but no sheets. She'd opened up the window to watch the men moving around in the street below. Backing away quickly when it occurred to her that if she could see them then they could see her.

"If they didn't know he was coming then maybe. Surrounded like this with them expecting us..." Desmond answered for Chris. The way he ended his statement was like sending an audible shrug. Before Chris could ask if they were thinking about chucking him out the window in a luggage chest to take on all the bad guys *Young Guns II* style a voice boomed out from the street below.

"We have you surrounded! A few of you looked like professionals so you understand what that means. Come out with your hands up!" The man below had a megaphone. He was standing on the other side of a fence that wrapped around the backyard of the house on the opposite side of the street.

"How about you take a quick walk around the block! We'll hop back in our truck and get the hell out of here. If you happen to have some gas, we'd appreciate it." Samson yelled back in a neighborly voice.

"Come out or we'll be forced to open fire!" The man called back on the megaphone.

"What do you guys think?" Samson asked over the walkie talkies.

"They'll kill Aubrey the second they see that she's bitten." Benson blurted out. They all knew she was right. No one was going to suffer some infected stranger to be near them if they could help it.

"One of you guys are going to have to kill me in like a week anyway. Why not just let them do it?" Aubrey asked. Her efforts to spare them the pain of having to kill her just made them want to protect her even more.

"Screw that. We're not letting these assholes take away your last week. We still owe you that drink." Ortega answered immediately. No way was he letting Aubrey get killed by strangers. When the time came to do it then they'd do it themselves.

"They've got some kind of grenades." Benson announced over the radio. The men on the street below were passing around green cans with tabs on top of them. They were either smoke or tear gas. It looked like they were trying to take them alive. Which actually made this whole situation a little scarier. Why'd these neat freaks want to capture them alive? Benson resolved to fight to the death. She didn't want to know what happened once they were captured.

"They're popping smoke." Samson called out. All around the house the assailants were tossing smoke grenades. Thick orange smoke began billowing out of the cannisters. It'd make it much harder for them to sight in on anyone approaching the house.

"Last chance! Come out or we come in!" The megaphone voice called out.

"We've got grenades to." Ortega reminded everyone over the walkies. He was hoping someone could toss one at the moron on the megaphone.

"On three." Samson said. He already had a grenade in his hand. This would work best if they all tossed them out at the same time. He'd long since moved to sit beside the window so no sharpshooters outside could take him out. He counted to three and tossed the grenade out the window. All around the house other grenades started going off. The loud noise from the fragmentation grenades exploding was followed by the sounds of men screaming in pain.

Bullets peppered the house from every direction. The glass in the window next to Chris shattered throwing sparkling fragments all over the floor. Standing up carefully in the small bedroom he'd been squatting in he announced over the radio that he was going for a quick walk.

With his M-16 gripped firmly in his hands Chris hopped neatly through the ruined window. Slipping like a ghost into the smoke-filled backyard he stood up and got his bearings. The smoke didn't slow Chris down at all. He navigated through it the same way he could navigate a dark room. His spatial sense kicked in alerting him to where the enemy was. The moans of pain were also a good indicator of where the bad guys caught by the round of grenades were at.

Chris slew the men immediately outside the house with ease. The smoke tilted the advantage firmly in his direction. A shadow among shadows he quickly lapped the entire house leaving a trail of dead bodies on the overgrown lawn. In full combat mode he turned his attention across the street to where the bulk of the enemy was. Chris had taken about ten men out in the smoke. All of them had been moving forward to break windows and toss in cannisters of tear gas. The men had been wearing masks and moving like they knew what they were doing.

Emboldened by his success Chris bounded out of the smoke's protective cover to charge the men standing across the street. Too late he realized that the men on the other side were anticipating he may do that. They may not have been expecting anyone to come out at the superhuman speed he was moving at, but they were ready enough to send a hail of bullets in his direction regardless. Indecisiveness got the better of Chris. Even with his decision-making skills amped up he was debating the best course of action. That questioning was enough to make him hesitate in the middle of the street.

Bullets struck his vest knocking the breath out of him. He tried to disappear back into the smoke, but it was almost gone already. Despite the cover fire he heard kicking up from behind him he couldn't make it back to the house. A round found his calf putting him painfully down on the ground. Putting his head down he tried wriggling across the lawn to get away. The gun fire reached a crescendo as well over twenty men went full auto. The firing line blasted away at a crawling Chris as well as his friends up on the second floor of the house.

Chris was struck several times in his legs and feet. He compartmentalized the pain and kept dragging himself towards the house. If he could make it inside, he could regroup and retake the offensive. Hands grabbed him and dragged him backwards. When he tried to fight them, he was struck repeatedly in the head. The men who grabbed him were wearing full-on riot gear. It was SWAT team issued which explained why they all had the police issued collapsible metal rods they were using to beat him with. He was out cold by the time they cuffed his hands behind his back and tossed him on the ground.

"They got Chris." Samson broadcast over their commando communicators. They were all still in separate rooms. Gathering together would make it easier for the bad guys to concentrate their fire to kill them all at once.

"Is he alive?" Desmond asked from his position hugging the floor in the loft at the top of the stairs. He'd been posted there to serve as a lookout. He was supposed to warn them when the enemy breached the front door and came pounding up the stairs. Not that it'd do them a lot of good to know the overwhelming well-armed militia was making their move.

"I think so. It was hard to see with all the bullets flying around. It's about to get really hard to breathe in here." Samson warned everyone in anticipation of the tear gas he assumed was coming next. He pulled out a bandana and tossed it over to Aubrey. She was sitting with her back to the wall on the interior side of the room as far from the window as possible. After instructing Aubrey to use the bandana to cover her mouth and nose he let himself relax while he waited for the inevitable. The only good thing was that they were on the second floor. The first floor would get the worst of it since the reactive agents in most of the gasses tended to be heavier than air. It was still going to suck though.

The acrid odor of tear gas hit Samson's nostrils a minute later. If all they had to deal with was a couple of cannisters going off downstairs, then that wasn't too bad. He'd barely finished that thought when a cannister came crashing into the room he was in. It was followed by a whole lot of bullets meant to dissuade him from picking it up and throwing it back out the window. Dragging Aubrey out into the hallway Samson met up with the others. Snot and tears running down their faces they tried to dampen the effects of the gas with moistened t-shirts and bandanas.

The assault didn't let up. More cannisters crashed into the rooms. Bullets pinged around throwing up splintered wood and stirring up clouds of white plaster. The rounds easily punched right through the drywall. Hardened warriors or not there was no way any of them were going to be able to hang out in the bullet riddled, tear gas filled house for much longer. The enemy would be able to snap a couple of gas masks on some toddlers and send them in with Nerf guns to finish them off if this lasted much longer.

"Let's get out of here." Ortega announced loudly. He had to be loud to be heard over the sounds of Desmond and Aubrey puking their guts out. Not to mention the bullets flying all over the place.

"Fight?" Samson asked. He didn't know if they'd be able to put up much of a fight with their limited ammunition. The blindness and extreme nausea due to the tear gas wasn't going to help much either. He'd expected their new friends to come charging in through the front door with gas masks by now. Evidently, they thought they could just wait outside for them to give up and come out. They were probably right. Marinating in tear gas sucked big time.

"I can't stay in here. We have to go outside." A miserable Aubrey struggled to get the words out around bouts of barfing.

"They'll kill you once they see your ear." Samson reminded her. Aubrey didn't respond. She was too sick from the gas to care.

"Shoot her ear." Desmond said. He had to repeat himself to be heard over the noise. Ortega felt like an idiot. This was a very face palm kind of moment. Of course, they could just camouflage the bite mark by strategically putting a bullet through Aubrey's ear. It might not hold up under close inspection, but it should get her past the guys down below. Assuming any of them got past the guys down below.

Pulling out his tactical shotgun Ortega started blinking rapidly to clear his eyes. Samson had moved over to help. Neither of them could see and their skin felt like someone was constantly pouring hot wax over it. Not an ideal situation to try and pierce Aubrey's ragged ear flap with a twelve gauge.

"Drop your weapons!" A voice boomed out behind them. The guys from across the street must've finally got tired of waiting.

Not knowing where the shotgun was pointed exactly Ortega didn't dare pull the trigger. Worried about what was going to happen to Aubrey Samson spun and started to stand up. He caught the butt of an assault rifle across the bridge of his nose. When he didn't immediately go down, he was struck again by the guy who'd just whacked him in the nose. Ortega grabbed the guy beating on Samson. The Delta warrior took the assailant down with a head and arm technique. Wrapping himself around the gas mask wearing bully Ortega put his back to a wall and his combat knife up to the man's jugular.

"Everybody gets civilized right now or I'm going to put a stain on this carpet that'll never come out." Ortega croaked. A world of pain wracked his body, but he still felt pretty good about taking down the goon who'd been beating on Samson. It was always a good day when you did something you could hold over the head of a SEAL. He'd need to hold it over Samson pretty soon though since they'd most likely be dead before they saw another sunrise.

The bandana Ortega had wrapped around his nose and mouth were soaked with mucus. His eyes were sealed shut with some sort of gunk he'd never known could come out of his eyes before. As part of his training, he'd been subjected to all kinds of discomfort. Tear gas had been one of the many things he'd had to endure. Never for this long though. This was torture. It was his muscle memory and reflexes that'd allowed him to snag his hostage. Unless these guys were complete idiots, or he'd managed to snag a VIP the hostage wasn't going to help a whole lot.

As if to prove the point that the hostage taking had been an empty gesture one of the men stepped over and kicked Ortega in the face. The man continued doing that until Ortega let go of his hostage. Ortega leaned back against the wall letting the blood from his shattered nose pour down onto the floor. On top of the blood there was slime oozing out of every orifice in his head. His last coherent thought was to wonder why the guy hadn't just shot him in the face. If someone had been holding one of Ortega's friends at knifepoint, then he sure wouldn't have messed around trying to take them alive.

Beat to hell and choking on their own snot they were shackled and tossed in a trailer attached to the back of a golf cart. Benson was the only one well enough to be able to look around. A blood covered Chris was on the bottom of the golf car trailer dog pile. Aubrey and Desmond were both just happy to be breathing fresh air. Doing her best to note what was going on Benson watched as they were driven past the houses they'd searched earlier. From her vantage point atop the dog pile, she had a great view of a road and some trees.

The trees abruptly ended. The cart kept on pulling them down a dirt road that ran through a corn field. A corn field that just kept going. The tall stalks blocked her view of anything else. A hole in the dirt path made the cart bounce hard enough to shift the dog-pile around. Benson went from the figurative top of the world to face down on top of Ortega. Unable to wiggle back to her previous position Benson closed her eyes and willed the burning sensations left over from being exposed to the tear gas to go away. She hoped she hadn't made the wrong decision in changing her mind and letting these men take her alive.

Chapter 30: Quarantined

"Are you ok?" Benson asked when Ortega started shifting around.

"Good to go." Is what everyone thought Ortega said. It was hard to tell since he sounded like he'd overdosed on Novocain. His face looked like he'd stuck an air pump up his nose and gone to town. Every visible part of it was turning black and blue. Not that the rest of them looked much better.

Chris was out cold. Desmond didn't think he'd be waking up anytime soon. Chris would need some time to recover from exerting himself. Not to mention the time needed to recover from being shot multiple times. Aubrey had been smacked around enough that their captors hadn't even noticed half of her ear was missing. Samson looked like he'd challenged Mike Tyson to a boxing match. Benson had read the room and let the cuffs get slapped on her without any fuss. Judging by everyone else's faces she'd made a wise decision.

Benson had been the only one coherent enough to pay attention to what happened to them once they were dragged off the trailer. A small group of men had used wheelbarrows to transport the unconscious group to a back room in a large warehouse. Benson had been marched in under the supervision of a gun toting local wearing a police uniform. Casually looking around while she walked, she'd seen enough to get an idea of what they'd gotten themselves into.

There were rows of bunk beds with shackles hanging off of each bed. For everyone she saw walking around with a badge and a gun there was someone else walking around in an orange jumpsuit. Some of the prison pajama wearing peeps were sporting ankle bracelets as well. The nightmare scenarios she'd imagined when she'd promised herself to fight to the death were playing out right in front of her. On the plus side by deciding at the last second to not fight to the death she still had all of her teeth. All she'd have accomplished by resisting would've been getting her ass kicked like her muscle headed comrades.

They were chained up in a nasty smelling room. It smelled like someone had dumped a barrel of lemon pledge into a port a potty and stirred around the mess at the bottom on a hot day. The horrible scent made since once she understood better what the room was used for. Chains had been added to the walls with manacles and shackles set about six feet apart from one another. The door opening to the hallway was made of heavy wood and looked solid as hell. Light was provided by a couple of overhead LED strips. Benson had seen the solar panels on the roof of the warehouse. At least they'd have power.

Once they'd all been chained up one of the guards had told Benson that someone would be back with food and water. When she'd asked him how long they were going to be stuck there for he'd just shrugged. The customer service in this holding cell was horrible. If she could get on the WIFI she'd destroy them on Yelp.

"We need to get out of here." Desmond said looking over at Benson.

"I agree completely." Benson replied sarcastically. Eyes wide to emphasize she was screwing with him she saw that he was serious. He must've gotten hit in the head pretty hard.

"We'll need to wait for Chris to wake up." Desmond whispered conspiratorially. He'd totally missed the sarcastic way Benson had leaned into answering him. He'd also totally missed the security camera mounted above them. Benson pointed it out and Desmond immediately stopped talking. Relieved he'd taken her non-subtle hint Benson leaned back to close her eyes and focus. She completely agreed with Desmond's instinct to get out of there. They just needed to work out the details. It was going to be fun trying to plan something out with that camera directly above them.

Three hours later no one had come to check on them yet. Everyone except Chris had recovered enough from their beat downs to be sitting upright. Chris was still lying in the same position that he'd been in when the men had fit the shackles to his leg.

"Interesting they put us in a room with a big drain in the middle of it." Samson commented. The statement was a way to break the silence after they'd wrapped up discussing which parts of their bodies might be broken versus just hurt. The consensus was that it'd be worth it to pay the deductible to get the X-Rays done. Not that there was much they could do about the parts that were broken. The apocalyptic dental plan consisted of occasionally brushing your teeth and hoping no one hit you in the mouth really hard with the butt of their rifle.

"It's probably how they're gonna clean us to inspect us for bites." Desmond said matter of factly. He seemed so sure of the answer that everyone turned to stare at him.

"Been in a lot of rooms with drains on the floor?" Benson asked.

"Not really. It makes sense though. When they capture people, they chain them up in here until they're sure they're not infected. Probably going to make us strip while they inspect us for bites and rinse us off with buckets of water." Desmond responded. He didn't get why everyone had immediately jumped to the conclusion that he was used to being locked up in dungeons that you could easily wash the blood out of. He'd still be sipping brandy in an armchair by a fire next to a window overlooking the Pacific if Lynn hadn't sent him out on this doomed mission. He was beginning to wish he'd forgotten to charge his sat phone.

"What do you think they do if they find someone with a bite?" Aubrey asked nervously. She'd already forgotten about the whole camera above them thing.

"Well, if I was running the place and someone presented with a bite mark, I'd let them sit in here a couple of weeks to see if they turned or not. Always the chance the person's not infected or even the chance they're immune. If they're immune, you could use their blood to come up with a cure." Benson stepped in quickly to answer Aubrey's question. If someone was listening, then hopefully that would keep them guessing as to if any of their prisoners had been bitten or not.

"They should give us yoga mats or something." Samson complained as he tried to get comfortable on the hard, cold concrete.

"I'm gonna use the drain." Ortega broke his silence to announce his intention to turn their new home away from home into a public urinal. He wasn't the easiest person to understand with his swollen jaw and chipped teeth. You just had to pay close attention and kind of know what he was probably saying anyway.

Once Ortega had broken the seal it turned into a pee party. Aubrey and Benson both predictably complaining about how much harder it was for girls. In this case it was a matter of distance. The boys had a definite anatomical advantage when it came to this particular activity. Benson was happy to see that the drainage in the room ensured that anything in liquid form made its way down to the drain eventually. None of them wanted to spend a lot of time thinking about what to do with stuff in solid form. After living in close quarters through an apocalypse they didn't have many secrets from one another. There was still a certain level of privacy one wanted when answering certain calls of nature.

"I see you're making use of the drain." A man in a pair of the prisoner PJs had opened the door in the middle of their tinkle fest.

"Where do we wash our hands?" Benson asked sarcastically. She was attempting to achieve some degree of modesty by yanking her pants back up while maintaining a squatting position. It wasn't working out very well.

"Save the passive-aggressive for the guys running this place. I'm just here to get you rinsed off and changed into some stylish new duds. My name's Tony." The long-haired man with a scruffy beard turned and pulled a cart into the room. It'd been an AV cart at one time but was now being used to transport buckets of water. He'd managed to fit six large buckets on the cart.

"No loofahs?" Benson asked. She wasn't looking forward to stripping naked while some strange hippie looking guy dumped a bucket of water over her head. It was like an R-Rated Tik-Tok challenge. Her nervousness was expressing itself in her trying to be funny and failing miserably.

"Sorry, but I need for all of you to strip down. Once you're naked you get a quick hobo shower. The doc will come down to do a quick physical then you get your fancy new jumpsuits." Tony waited expectantly for them to eagerly start stripping.

Being tasked with rinsing off the fresh meat meant Tony had to stand there until they all started wriggling out of their clothes. The manacles were staying on which made it really hard for them to get their clothes off. As they got into situations where they needed help getting a sleeve removed or something Tony began going around with a pair of scissors cutting off the material. No one complained since he'd already told them their clothes were going to be thrown away anyway.

The only exception was the body armor most of them still had on under their clothes. The obvious stuff had been taken off when they were taken prisoner. Tony carefully set aside the body armor to be collected and cleaned later. That would end up going into the armory to be used by the militia that guarded this little slice of paradise. The strip search uncovered some weapons a few of them had managed to squirrel away. Even unconscious Ortega and Samson had gotten in a couple of knives and a small handgun between the two of them. There was no keeping the weapons hidden when they were stripped naked.

No one bothered trying to resist Tony. He'd made it clear he had no access to the keys to their manacles. He'd also told them that while he was in there a guard would be watching them from the main security room. Pulling their clothes off over their bruised and battered bodies was the other reason it'd taken such a long time. Tony had to strip Chris down since no one else could reach him and Chris was still out cold.

Once they were all undressed Tony used a bucket of water on each of them. The water had a few drops of liquid soap mixed in to help them smell a little bit better. The water wasn't warm. It was actually really cold. The room they were in was really cold. The sound of chattering teeth was very audible when Tony disappeared outside and came back in with a towel for each of them. The towel was an unexpected luxury. It was very appreciated since none of them had been looking forward to the air-drying alternative.

A man wearing a pair of jeans with a flannel shirt on showed up after they'd all finished toweling themselves off. Standing around awkwardly with towels wrapped around themselves they waited to see what fun surprises this new guy had in store for them. Tony had moved to the side to wait and help with whatever this non-orange jumpsuit wearing guy needed. Another man appeared to stand in the doorway. This man had a pistol in his hand. He was wearing a standard khaki police uniform on top of a pair of combat boots.

"I'm Doctor Jameson. I'll be looking each of you over for any obvious signs of infection. You will comply immediately with my orders, or you will be shot. If you make any sudden movements towards me, you'll be shot. We would've been by sooner, but I've been busy trying to help the officers you wounded in town." Dr. Jameson concluded his little speech and immediately ordered Ortega to drop his towel.

The doctor inspected each of them in turn. It was the standard spot inspection of their skin along with yanking on their hair that they were all used to. They were each covered in multiple contusions, scrapes, and cuts making it impossible for the doctor to conclude that any of them were infection free. Aubrey went with her ear being shot off in the gunbattle at the house the previous day. The doctor didn't seem to believe her but that didn't really matter. Everyone who gets bitten pretty much lies about it. What this place did was to keep everyone quarantined for at least two weeks. Anyone who had any suspicious wounds spent even longer in isolation.

The doctor explained the quarantine policies briefly before leaving. The man in the doorway remained. The reason why became obvious a few minutes later when he handed Tony the key to the manacles. Tony needed those to help each of them get dressed in one of the infamous orange jumpsuits. After getting each of them dressed then passing out bed pans Tony gave them all a cup of water and a bowl of corn mush. The corn mush was fresh and delicious. The water not so much.

"You think they ever turn these lights out?" Aubrey asked a little later. Tony had left and they were all just sitting around in their new jumpsuits staring at the walls. Not a lot to do when you're chained to a wall in a building full of men who'd have no problem shooting you on sight.

"Why is that corn mush getting to you?" Benson joked. They were going to be in the room for a couple of weeks together. At some point someone was going to be the first to make use of the bedpan. None of them wanted that honor.

"No, I just don't see how we're supposed to get any decent sleep chained to the wall." Aubrey complained. No one had a great answer for that. When they got tired enough, they'd sleep.

"Chris still breathing?" Benson asked from her side of the room. Chris had been put in the opposite corner. Ortega was the closest one to him. It was almost like they'd arranged them in order of who was the most physically messed up.

"Looks like he's breathing. He's going to have a stiff neck for the next five years after he wakes up though." Ortega answered. Chris was lying in the same position Tony had left him in after cramming him into that bright jumpsuit. When they'd uncuffed Chris to get him dressed everyone had tensed up half expecting to have to fight. It would've been awesome if Chris had woken up in the middle of that operation to rip Tony's head off before going for the guy in the doorway. Having seen how fast Chris could move when he was motivated there wasn't much doubt that he could easily overcome the guard.

Things continued in that general vein for the next few days. Tony showed up sporadically to empty out bed pans before feeding and watering them. The water always tasted funny while the corn was always delicious. No one else had shown up since the doctor had inspected them. Nothing of note happened until Aubrey caught all their attention by loudly hyperventilating while she stared at her hand. The hand that was full of hair that'd just fallen off in her hand when she ran her fingers though her hair.

"I'm sorry. Now what?" Aubrey croaked through her tears after pulling some more hair out of her head. Benson and the others tried consoling her but there was only so much they could say. Aubrey was going to turn then their hosts would shoot her. If their hosts even bothered to wait. Her hair was falling out and half her ear was missing. It didn't take a forensic pathologist to put that together.

When Tony showed up with a plastic jug full of water and a bag full of boiled corn, he immediately noticed Aubrey sobbing against the wall. He passed out the corn including carefully sliding a plate over to Aubrey who completely ignored it. When he was done passing out food, he told them he was sorry about Aubrey and left. No one tried to talk him out of what they knew he was going to do. It had to be done.

The next twenty minutes were spent awkwardly continuing to try and console the inconsolable. Aubrey knew what was happening to her. She told the others that she welcomed it. She'd been in constant pain since Samson had cracked her ribs. She missed her family. She hated always being scared.

The same man who'd guarded the doors while they were being rinsed off for the doctor showed up to take care of Aubrey. He told her he was sorry and actually seemed to mean it. Then he aimed the pistol at her head and pulled the trigger. Where a vivacious young woman had been there was now just another dead body. A lifeless hunk of meat in an orange jumpsuit with her blood slowly making its way down to the drain.

Tony came with a wheelbarrow and under the watchful eyes of the guard uncuffed Aubrey and rolled her out of the room. The only reminder that she'd been there was the stains on the floor from her blood. That'd get cleaned up and washed down the drain with their piss and sweat. No one felt like talking for a long time after that.

Chapter 31: That Line from Forrest Gump About the Shrimp Except with Corn

Ortega was sweating like crazy in the chilly shed. He was stacking trash bags full of dried corn into the crates on the top shelves. Samson stood below tossing the bags up to him. Neither of them talked more than necessary since there was a cop standing about ten feet back from them. The cop watched them suspiciously the entire time they were working.

The cop had good reason to be weary. With their combined combat training it wouldn't take much for the two special ops guys to take him out. The youngish man with the shotgun in hand had barely been out of the academy when the world turned upside down. The two sweaty jumpsuit clad men packing the shed for winter had both been fully certified bad asses well before the young guard had graduated high school.

As miserable as an honest day's work was, they were both stoked to be out of the concrete pit they'd been forced to live in for over two weeks. Time had ceased to pass for them as the twenty-four hours a day of LED lighting threw off their internal clocks. The sudden bloody end to the girl they'd all been vested in protecting had made the room feel more like a crypt. There'd been nothing to look forward to except Tony's daily visit to bring them each some water and a random corn-based meal.

Chris had finally woken up towards the end of their stay. What should have given them all renewed confidence had only served to make the situation worse. He'd woken up extra hungry and it wasn't the golden colored cream corn he had on his mind. All he could smell was the blood of his friends trapped in the room with him. Waking up when he had was very fortuitous. Tony had been watching him for signs of death for a while. The doctor couldn't fathom how Chris could still be alive unless he was infected. They'd been on the verge of killing him just to be on the safe side.

The last time they'd all been together was when they were pulled out of the quarantine room to attend their orientation. Leaving behind the safety of that old slaughter room was strangely disconcerting. When you got used to being under bright lights in a small concrete room with your body chained to a wall it was weird to walk out into the real world again. It was weird even to walk.

Samson had led them in daily exercises to keep their health and spirits up. Once a day after Tony had shown up to feed and water them the blond SEAL had done his best to motivate them to exercise for an hour or so. Ortega cracked a bunch of jokes at first about SEALs and their love for push-ups, but he joined in. He knew how important it was to keep up morale. Men in his line of work received plenty of POW training in case they were ever captured.

Thinking back to the orientation video at Fort Leavenworth the group had expected similar at Fort Corn. The locals still called their town Gettysburg but among the five of them the corn puns had gotten out of control. Other than the SEAL Zumba sessions Samson led there hadn't been much else to do during their captivity. In between wallowing in self-pity and trying to be as casual about using the bed pan as possible, they had a competition going to come up with the best corn puns. The game had taken a dark turn following Aubrey's execution.

In the orientation session they'd been told they were now the property of the sovereign city-state of Gettysburg. The city was ruled by a duly elected sheriff. All free citizens got to vote on a new sheriff every six years. There were no checks and balances. What the sheriff said was considered law. There were three classes of people in Gettysburg. The cops were there to defend the city and enforce the laws. Civilians were free men and women who took on other occupations as assigned such as the doctors and mechanics.

The five of them were to be part of the third class. The prisoner class. The orange jumpsuits and police officer outfits had made that kind of obvious. Each of them would even be 'tried' by the judge. The judge happened to be the same man as the sheriff. If convicted of resisting arrest and the murder of the men they'd killed while resisting arrest they'd be sentenced to a lifetime of hard labor. The trials had happened one by one as they were let out of the orientation room.

They'd all been found guilty. They each got to look at pictures of the men they'd killed. Some of the men had gotten married and started families. Many of them had close friends. All of those people showed up for the trial. After they were each found guilty the judge let any family of the men killed line up and take a swing at the freshly convicted killers. The only rule was that they couldn't do any permanent damage. The prisoners were what made this 'life of leisure' possible for everyone else.

The five of them were split up into different areas. Every morning they were assigned a work detail. They were required to wear ankle bracelets as they were considered 'lifers' so more likely to make a run for it. Others who had shorter sentences could expect to earn their way into the civilian or cop class if they worked hard and kept their nose clean. They wore the orange but weren't considered flight risks. Their sentence was more like community service than the hard-core manual labor the lifers were charged with.

There were a few hundred people living in the tiny town. The population had only dropped by a couple hundred since the dark days of the infections. A lot of the people living there had been lackadaisical about any sort of preventative vaccinations, so they'd missed the infected time capsules that'd been delivered to the rest of the world. The town's main physician had advocated for natural remedies over big pharma produced medication. The naturalist leaning doctor's logic had been extremely flawed, but it'd worked out well for them in the end.

Furthering that survival had been the militant way the local law enforcement had stepped up to declare martial law. Looters had been slammed into the first batch of orange jumpsuits. They had a trailer full of the brightly colored outfits courtesy of a truck driver who'd pulled over on their stretch of highway after overdosing on oxy. Overdoses were common in the early days of the outbreaks.

At the end of the day the structure the sheriff had put together was working. They kept the original town cleaned up to eventually move back into. For now, it was a honeypot to lure in travelers so they could capture them and use them to perform manual labor. They had cameras everywhere courtesy of the county's former IT director. He'd come up with the idea of mounting solar panels to power the devices. With the help of a few electricians and the raiding of every Best Buy in a two-hundred-mile radius they'd been able to build out a wireless network that covered a good portion of the town and surrounding farms.

It was a decent life for everyone. The cops and civilians benefitted from the prisoners manual labor while also doing their own jobs. The prisoners had learned not to complain. They weren't sent out on looting missions or anything. A lot of the people in orange were happy with their lot in life. They got their three meals a day, worked hard, and had a safe place to sleep at night. It wasn't where any of the five of them wanted to end up. Being a lifer wasn't a position they were suited for.

Any of them could've escaped on their own. Chris saw a thousand openings a day where he could easily snag a guard's weapon and make a run for it. The problem was that they'd been split up. The fact that they fought well as a team had been noted by the men who attacked them. That was used against them now. By making sure no more than two of them were ever together they ensured none of them could do anything without risking the others being singled out for punishment. They'd been told if any of them escaped then one of the friends they left behind would be put to death to pay for it.

It put them in a bad spot. A spot that Chris spent a lot of time thinking about. He didn't have the training or background in search and rescue operations like Samson and Ortega did. What he did have was his crazy ability to analyze data. The area of his brain unlocked by the chemicals in that concoction Lynn had shot into his butt cheek didn't just kick in when he was in combat mode. He could close his eyes and watch his memories like he was watching a movie on Netflix. Not only could he watch his memories he could zoom in and out on them. He could filter sounds to hear just the conversations he was interested in.

Within a week of working the fields Chris had determined the only way for them to escape was going to involve killing an excessive number of the cop class. The next time he was assigned to a work party where he could talk to someone it happened to be Desmond. Desmond was good with Chris killing everyone there so they could escape. Oddly enough so was Chris. He wondered if he should have more of a problem with it.

The next opportunity Chris got to mention his plan was with Benson. They'd both been assigned to spend the day mopping out the main warehouse. That was where the bulk of the corn was stored. It was also where the majority of the prisoners spent their nights. Benson didn't have much of a problem with Chris killing everybody either. She'd taken to calling her guards 'Master'. Her guards didn't appreciate the connotation. To prove they weren't really bad people they'd whipped her. On one occasion one of the guards had tried to do more than beat her. That guard was still in the infirmary. It was doubtful he'd ever be able to have children.

The abuse Benson had suffered at the hands of the guards was more than enough to motivate Chris. He wasn't willing to turn a blind eye to his friends suffering. Not when he had the power to do something about it. Wishing he could get them a message somehow Chris decided that it was time to leave. They'd break out that night. The darkness would work in his favor from a combat perspective. It was also the only time of day when Chris would be able to know for sure where each of them were.

Spending the day tweaking and finalizing his plan he was able to flash Benson and Desmond a signal. Whether or not they'd noticed his raised eyebrows and the way he mouthed the word 'tonight' remained to be seen. Chris hadn't had a better signal worked out since he hadn't expected to see them. Ortega and Samson had been kept in another building and mostly worked the field, so he never saw them up close. Those two weren't going to need any kind of advanced warning. They'd jump right into shit creek whether they had a paddle or not.

After spending the day walking down golf cart trails with a machete to beat back the weeds Chris was ready to go. Thanks to his autonomous workouts where his mind basically caused his muscles to flex and unflex all the time he had virtually unlimited stamina. The guard following his group on a golf cart would run out of battery long before Chris got tired.

Back at the warehouse when the day was done Chris gulped down as much water as he could without getting sick. A major reason Gettysburg had ended up becoming a slave state was because of their abundance of food. The acres of corn fields easily fed the people who worked them. With no gas for tractors the agricultural work all had to be done by hand. Electric vehicles charged up by the sun's rays were lined up behind the main warehouse. Everything from Teslas to a couple of electric scooters.

After eating his fill of boiled corn Chris slowly walked towards his bunk. The guard watching over his group was looking to make sure each of them got next to their bunks and held out their arm. Once their arms were out one of the prisoners was assigned to go down the row and lock everyone in. The key to the cuffs was kept outside the door to the section of warehouse they were in. A section that smelled like a mix of corn and the contents of the bedpans they were issued to answer the calls of nature while they were locked up at night.

Chris was ready to kill someone just to get access to indoor plumbing. It was amazing how quickly the human race had descended back into emptying chamber pots out each morning. Chris smiled at the thought of people riding down those old cobblestone streets. Knights and damsels carefully dodging the streams of excrement being flung from the windows. What amused him was the fact that he was about to go medieval on this whole base.

He was outnumbered and without any resources other than his chamber pot and a couple of uneaten kernels of corn. This time he had surprise on his side though. This time he wasn't pinned down in a house with dozens of men on every side of it just waiting for him to emerge from the smoke. Grinning enough to show his teeth Chris approached the guard by the door and asked if he could get some more water.

The guard was about to tell him to get back in line when Chris casually leaned forward and shoved his thumbs into the man's eye sockets. With his bloody eyeballs dangling by a fleshy strip of nerves the guard gasped and fell over backwards. Before the guard could remember how to scream Chris stepped forward and slammed his booted foot into the man's throat. Voice box completely crushed the man lay on the floor spasming out. A strange noise was coming out of his mouth, but it wasn't loud enough for Chris to worry about it.

"If you leave the room you'll probably die. Either way stay quiet, or I'll kill you myself." Chris addressed the roomful of his wide-eyed fellow inmates. Most of them had been looking forward to climbing into bed after a long day of work. None of them had expected to see the nice guy they'd been working beside walk up to the guard and casually pop his eyes out.

Chris had considered whether he wanted to add to the confusion in the night by letting his bunkmates charge out of their holding cell or not. For his plan to work he needed silence in the beginning then chaos towards the end. With no clue if his little speech would achieve that objective or not Chris stooped down to grab the guard's shotgun. The key for the handcuffs was hanging on a peg outside the door on a long lanyard. Chris tossed that around his neck and kept on moving.

The common areas of the warehouse were well lit. Chris knew that Desmond and Benson had been placed in a room like his about thirty yards down the corridor. Stomping towards them in his bright orange suit he wondered if he should've taken the time to throw on the uniform from the guard he'd blinded. When he'd been planning this out, he'd been more focused on speed than camouflage. Now that he was actually walking around in the orange suit, he realized just how noticeable it really was. Which was of course the purpose of making the prisoners wear the bright orange suits in the first place.

Two guards emerged from one of the doors up ahead and noticed the prisoner walking towards them with a shotgun. One of them went for his pistol while the other one raised his own shotgun. Chris shot both men. He'd really hoped he could've kept the gunfire out of the mix for the first few minutes anyway. This meant he needed to speed up.

The room the two guards had emerged from was a room that looked identical to the one Chris had been in. The handcuffs with the extended chains were looped through steel hoops on the posts to secure them to the bunkbeds on one end. The other end was fastened around each inmate's wrist. The inmates were all staring at the door when Chris sauntered in. Flipping on the light switch he quickly spotted Desmond and Benson. The two of them looked as surprised as everyone else to see Chris.

"Didn't you see my signal?" Chris asked as he unlocked their handcuffs.

"Are you talking about when you walked by today doing that weird double eye blinking thing and whispering to yourself? How the hell is that a signal?" Benson asked. The second her cuff was off she was at the door stripping the guard of his weapons. Desmond ran over to help her.

"Here. Free yourselves. It's going to be a fight though." Chris handed his cuff key to a man he'd worked beside in the fields. Jogging out of the room to rejoin Benson and Desmond he grabbed the handcuff key that was hanging outside the door to this room and put that lanyard around his neck.

"What now?" Benson asked.

"There's the carpool right behind us. The keys are in the security room. We take it and take the keys. You two grab us a car and meet me over at the other building where Samson and Ortega are. Sound good?" Chris asked.

"Why not. Let's do it." Benson said with a grin.

"Yeah, we might still be able to take them by surprise." Desmond said wrapping the dead guard's webbed belt around his own waist. He'd already checked to make sure the magazine in the pistol was full. For a glorified secretary he was getting pretty good at the day-to-day soldier stuff.

Both Benson and Chris gave Desmond a hard look when a loud gonging alarm started going off. The loud noise had started immediately after Desmond jinxed them by saying that they might still be able to take the security booth by surprise. Breaking into a fast jog they ran under the domed security cameras towards the small room holding the keys and the video monitors. If they could take that room, then they should be good. That was a mighty big 'if' though now that they'd lost the element of surprise.

Chapter 32: A Bad Plan Well Executed

The security center was somewhere up ahead. Chris had spent a lot of time trying to decipher where it may be based on how the base was setup. The room would need to be in a space with plenty of power. The main warehouse had the most solar panels. There were large bundles of cable he'd noticed heading down one hallway. A hallway that they were never taken down when they were sent out to work. He'd seen a uniformed cop sweeping the corridor one day. That'd settled the matter for Chris.

There was always the chance that the operations center was in one of the houses or another building. There was always the chance there were multiple operations centers. There might not even be an operations center. They had no way of knowing. Chris was basing all of this on eavesdropping and working to put all the data he'd gathered together. He'd spent a lot of time in his own head. Hopefully it paid off.

Rounding a row of corn storage areas, the corridor in question appeared. Thanks to the blaring alarm there was an armed guard in riot gear standing at the end of the hallway. He had an assault rifle and a headset with a mic on. Before he could bring the rifle to bear Chris, Benson, and Desmond, all lit him up. He should've taken the time to wear the matching riot helmet. They were going to need to fingerprint him now to verify his identity.

"Stay here and put his gear on. That should buy you some time out in the parking lot." Chris told Desmond.

"I'll cover him while he's doing that. You got the ops center?" Benson asked loudly. The alarm was really blaring in this part of the base. Anywhere else in the world she'd have been worried about the noise attracting all kinds of zombies. Here they seemed to have a large enough zombie free buffer around them that it didn't matter. If it weren't for the slavery and rapists in positions of power this might even be a tempting spot to settle down.

"Yep. Be back in a few seconds. Try not to die." Chris said turning and running up the corridor. Benson was a fan of that advice. She put her back to the wall and raised the shotgun to fire at anyone who came around the corner while Desmond took the riot gear off the corpse.

Chris slipped down the corridor towards where he hoped the room that he was looking for would be. Eyes on the big bundle of yellow network cables running along the ceiling he slid to a stop when they disappeared into the wall above a nondescript wooden door. The door had a camera right outside of it. There was also an intercom. The door looked super solid. The wall just looked like the rest of the wall.

Bringing his shotgun up into his shoulder Chris shot the camera first. He didn't want the people inside to know what he was up to. He only had seconds to get inside. The people he was attacking would be on the horn getting every available cop to converge on this room. Ignoring the door Chris started shooting the wall with the tactical shotgun. Once he had a sizeable hole blasted through the wall, he stuck the barrel of the assault rifle through and sprayed the room on the other side down.

Wishing he had a grenade he settled for continuing to make the hole in the wall bigger. He hid behind the door when the people inside the room returned fire. The return fire finished the job of blowing away enough of the drywall for Chris to be able to charge into the room. Hoping he timed it right he did just that.

A bullet hit him in the top of his shoulder as he somersaulted through the wall into the operations space. Flipping into the room he crouched on the far side with the assault rifle in three round burst mode. Before the plaster dust had settled from his entrance, he'd killed the four men in the room. Two had been turning to fire on him while one had been running for the door to escape. The fourth man had died at his station desperately screaming into a handset for someone to come help them.

The room was lined up with video monitors showing different parts of the base. The images changed on the monitors in a pattern that seemed random to Chris. The cops were running to the stations they were supposed to man when the alarm went off. There were dozens inside the warehouse already. This escape attempt was going to end badly if they didn't get moving. Going to the lockbox on the wall Chris grabbed all the keys. He dumped out a little box full of hard candies he found on a desk and tossed all the keys in the box instead. Deciding it was worthwhile he logged a few more valuable seconds taking as many weapons off the dead men as he could.

One of the men had a machete on him. Hoping he didn't end up electrocuted Chris began hacking at the mass of cables snaking into the room. The video monitors all went dark. Satisfied he opened the heavy wooden door and stepped over the dead guard to leave. A man in riot gear was running towards him with shotgun in hand.

"Here's the keys. No time for any more uniforms. I'm going to go get Samson and Ortega. If it gets too crazy, just take off." Chris said tossing the box of keys over to Benson. If he hadn't still been in battle mode, he might have shot Desmond in the face. That'd been his initial instinct when confronted with an armed man in riot gear running towards him. Luckily his brain had kicked in. Noticing Benson tagging along reminded him Desmond had stayed behind to don a dead man's gear.

"See you out there." Benson said turning to run down the hallway leading to the carpool area.

Chris immediately turned his attention to the group of armed men he heard running towards them from the other direction. He couldn't just run along with Benson and Desmond, or these guys would catch them. He needed to take out this group then head over to bust out Samson and Ortega. Making sure his weapons were good to go he knelt down beside the wall and waited. It was time to turn this corridor into a morgue.

He didn't have to wait long. A group of men in police uniforms came running around the corner with weapons in hand. Used to bullying unarmed prisoners the men weren't ready for a phenomenon like Chris. He blasted away at them with ridiculous accuracy. The tight confines of the hallway made it easy for him. The men in the uniforms were mostly untrained. Many of them had cited military experience to get the privilege of wearing the uniform. That military experience had mostly been in things like aviation electronics or personnel. Ratings that didn't necessarily translate well to gunfights in tight dark corridors.

Chris looked like an old-time pirate with muskets, machetes, and pistols hanging all off of him. As he ran out of ammunition, he was tossing weapons on the ground. When the people shooting back started getting a little too close, he ran to the side and did a backflip off the wall. Avoiding the wildly fired rounds now coming from the few men not busy bleeding out on the floor Chris yanked out the machete he'd been using on the network cables. Machete in hand he somersaulted into the middle of the people still shooting at him.

On the floor he slammed the blade of the machete into a combat boot hard enough to sink the blade halfway through the guy's foot. Yanking the blade out he stabbed upwards directly into another man's crotch. The blade sank deep. The man made a noise unlike anything Chris had ever heard before. Abandoning the machete to the newly minted eunuch Chris pulled out a combat knife to use on the last person standing between him and leaving.

The last person was a woman in a cop uniform. She didn't seem super excited to be in a position where she had to fight the man who'd just slaughtered the group she'd come running in with. Chris stepped forward to finish her quickly. Wisely enough she didn't try to go for a weapon. Rather she stuck both hands in the air and fell to her knees saying repetitively that she surrendered.

"Why shouldn't I just kill you?" Chris asked. He didn't have time for this.

"I've never hurt anybody. I just watch the monitors." The lady cop blubbered the words. Snot and tears making her speech sound like she was trying to swim and talk at the same time.

"Turn around." Chris said.

Expecting to be executed the woman slowly complied. Chris couldn't help but think of all the time this was wasting. Time was something he didn't have much of. The second she was turned around he took the cuffs he'd taken off a dead officer's belt and cuffed the woman's hands behind her back. For good measure he hit her in the back of the head with the hilt of his combat knife to knock her out cold. She may or may not wake up. She had a fighting chance now though.

Feeling oddly proud of himself for ripping apart a group of men and putting a woman into a coma Chris ran down the hall. He needed to get out of the main warehouse and break into the secondary facility. Ortega and Samson were chained to beds somewhere inside that other building.

On the way out of the building Chris ran into another man in uniform. Running full out Chris put all his weight behind slashing his knife across the man's throat. He hit him hard enough to almost decapitate him. With his spine barely holding his head on his body the blood spouting man was dead before he had the chance to realize he was being attacked.

Chris made it out the front doors and sprinted across the open field. When bullets began following him across the open space, he picked up the pace as much as he could. Running fast enough to cause the men shooting at him to pause to make sure he wasn't on a motorcycle or something he approached the building he needed to get into. Bullets were kicking up dirt all around him. There was no time to try and figure out a way into the building.

Vaulting on top of the building Chris ran across the roof to the other side then hopped down to find a door. On the far side of the building four cops stood staring at the spot on the roof where they'd all just seen a man jump. A fifteen-foot jump at least. It took them a minute to remember to use their radios. It took another minute for them to convince the sheriff that a man had jumped on top of the building. With the operations center destroyed the sheriff was using the radios to take command of the situation.

Almost landing on a cop who picked that second to come running out of the secondary warehouse Chris twisted around when his feet hit the ground. The cop was turning around to figure out if he'd just seen what he thought he saw. Before the cop could do anything, Chris shoved six inches of serrated steel into the man's throat then yanked it back out. It was gross but effective.

In the dark with no one around to see him Chris pulled the dying man close. Shoving his face into the hot warm blood gushing out of the man's neck Chris drank his fill. It satisfied him like nothing else had ever done. The blood didn't flow long with the brain dead. When the heart stopped pumping the delicious red nectar up into Chris's waiting mouth, he dropped the body to the ground.

Supercharged by his nocturnal snack Chris ran through the door that his blood donor had just emerged from. A pistol in each hand he searched the space for doors like the ones in the other buildings. In the brightly lit space, he was able to easily target any cops who were dumb enough to stick their heads up. It appeared that most of the men willing to run towards the sound of gunfire had already been killed.

Finally spotting the door that he was looking for he turned the handle to open it after moving the bolt out of the way. Snagging the key for the handcuffs off the little peg outside the door he stepped into the room and flipped on the lights.

"About time." Samson grumbled from his position in the top rack at the end of the room.

"You've got red shit all over your face." Ortega said when Chris came over to uncuff him.

"Please tell me you stopped to grab some spaghetti on the way here." Samson said staring hard at Chris.

"Not the time. We need to get the hell out of here." Chris announced avoiding the obvious question in his friends voices.

Tossing the key to the handcuffs to one of the other men in the bunks Chris took off out the door with Ortega and Samson struggling to keep up. Both men were fast but neither of them was vampire fast. Right back out the back door Chris led them around the perimeter of the warehouses. Sticking to the cornfields they got to the road where Benson and Desmond were supposed to be waiting for them.

There was no one there. Chris turned and started jogging up the road. He was hoping they just needed to go a little further in order to find their friends. All he could see in his mind's eye was Benson laying cold and dead in the parking lot behind the warehouse. Why hadn't he gone with them?

Chris was on the verge of telling Ortega and Samson to keep going while he ran back to the warehouse to look for Benson and Desmond when they turned a corner to see a couple of Tesla sedans waiting for them. Desmond and Benson waved at them from the driver's seats of each. The expressions on their faces showed they hadn't really expected to see Chris come jogging down the road with Samson and Ortega either.

Walking quickly towards the cars Chris aimed for the one with Desmond assuming Ortega would hop in with Benson. Samson would most likely climb in with Chris once they got there. After the long separation they were all thinking Benson and Ortega may have a lot of catching up to do. None of them wanted to be a third wheel with that happening.

Reaching for the door handle Chris felt a chill go down his spine. Shouting for everyone to hurry he looked back down the road and saw headlights rounding the corner. A convoy of golf carts and other electric vehicles came flying quietly around the curve in the road. That quiet didn't last long. The men on the golf carts immediately opened fire at the sight of their quarry.

Pistol in hand Chris stood his ground picking off the drivers of each of the vehicles. A couple of them drove off the road into the corn. Either because Chris had shot the driver or because the driver was opting not to be a target. Chris noticed a man in a fancier uniform than the others. That cart pulled into the corn before Chris could sight in on the legendary sheriff. That was a bummer as Chris would've loved to give the prisoners that they were leaving behind the gift of sniping that evil bastard.

Chris snapped off a few more shots before diving into the Tesla's back seat. Bullets buzzed around them like angry hornets. The men attacking them were shooting blindly from behind the stalks of corn. Desmond wasted no time in putting as much distance between them and the men shooting at them as possible. They drove for a few minutes before coming to a gate. Ortega jumped out and opened the gate.

Just like that they'd escaped. Not only had they escaped they'd managed to score a couple of sweet rides. Even though they weren't actually going to be able to charge them back up without finding a house with solar panels and the special charging plug already installed. That was a problem they had around three hundred miles before they had to worry about. For now, they put the windows down and enjoyed the taste of freedom.

Chapter 33: Are We There Yet?

Driving through the next town on the highway after Gettysburg gave them a pretty good idea what the sheriff had done to keep the town safe. The town of Covington had been burnt to the ground. It could've been an accidental fire but none of them believed that for a second. What made sense was that the Gettysburg looters had stripped the town of everything useful then burnt the place to the ground.

The looting would've happened after everyone in the town had been shot or taken prisoner. The police force from Gettysburg was non-discriminatory. It hadn't mattered if you were infected, not infected, or somewhere in between. To establish a buffer zone, they'd simply killed everyone in the town. Plenty of people would argue with that approach. Well, they would if they'd still been alive to argue. Ruthlessness was a common trait of successful leaders in the apocalypse. The sheriff's forces had continued to expand the buffer zone. The survivors they found were taken back to Gettysburg to be put to work.

"We need to find a phone somewhere." Desmond announced once Samson and Chris had gotten done bandaging up one another's bullet holes.

"I don't think the app that shows the charging stations is going to be working." Chris responded. He'd been thinking about how they were going to recharge the cars. He wasn't convinced they'd escaped the clutches of the sheriff yet.

"I meant to call Lynn with." Desmond said.

"You think she'd be able to get to us?" Chris asked. The last he'd heard Lynn was somewhere in Europe dealing with a bunch of really old vampires who had no use for the human race. At least not as anything other than walking juice boxes.

"If she knows where we are she can get to us. She has tons of resources. The *Familia* has always been prepared to pull the trigger on crippling human society if they needed to." Desmond answered curtly. He still felt funny about spilling the secrets he'd sworn up, down, and sideways to never share.

"So, we need a phone or a charging station. Both would be the bomb dot com." Chris responded. He wasn't willing to bet they'd find either anytime soon.

"If we're not further than these cars can go on a single charge before the sheriff sends his men after us, we may not need to worry about finding a phone." Samson reminded them. He talked a lot less lately. Ever since the guard back at the warehouse had blown Aubrey's brains out in front of them. If it was up to him, they'd find a gun shop, load up, then go back to Gettysburg to continue kicking ass. All he needed was a hunting rifle with a decent scope and he could take out the sheriff without breaking a sweat.

They continued to pass the burnt-out husks of houses. On the edge of the next decent sized city, they spotted a house that hadn't been burnt down yet. Benson must have noticed something interesting about it. She'd put on her turn signal and pulled off the highway to drive over to it. Desmond followed her down the paved driveway to the front of the big house.

"Solar panels." Desmond announced pointing at the top of the house.

"I bet she thinks we can charge up the cars here." Chris said.

"We're still pretty close to Gettysburg. I'm not sure hanging out here is such a great idea." Samson was scanning the house to see if he saw any obvious signs of a threat.

Benson had parked and gotten out of her car. Pistol waving around in front of her she approached the garage. Ortega followed her with a shotgun he'd picked up somewhere. The sight of them both strolling around in the bright orange jump suits reminded Chris that they needed to go clothes shopping soon. The stupid jumpsuits didn't even have pockets in them. Probably so that prisoners wouldn't have an easy place to hide their shivs.

"Want to help me clear the house?" Chris asked Samson. Samson shrugged and opened the car door. Desmond didn't have a working weapon so stayed behind. Benson and Ortega joined the two of them up on the porch. The two of them had failed at being able to get the garage door up from the outside.

Ortega broke the decorative window next to the front door. They waited the requisite thirty seconds to see if a baldie was going to come tearing down the hall. When nothing showed up to eat them Ortega reached through the broken glass to get the door unlocked. Kicking down doors was great in the movies but less so in real life. Unless you wanted to end up with back problems at an early age. They'd all experienced the joy of kicking a door with everything they had and bouncing off it like a kid's rubber ball.

Door open, they stacked up and went in. The home had power and was a comfortable temperature. They hadn't noticed from outside but there were even some lights on in the foyer. Seemed like a waste of good electricity since it was the middle of the day. Spreading out to clear the house they stopped when they heard a rumbling noise from the door leading out to the garage. A second later there was a loud honking sound from outside.

"Is that the garage door?" Benson asked. They'd all frozen in place when they heard the noise start.

The sound of guns going off came from the front yard. The beeping from the Tesla grew more frantic. The four of them rushed to the porch to take some shots at the sporty Ford truck backing out of the garage. It was one of the new electric ones. Chris remembered seeing the commercial for them while he was running on the treadmill his mom had bought him back in his old apartment.

A woman was driving while a stocky looking man was crouched in the back shooting at the cars that they'd left parked in front of the house. Desmond was nowhere to be seen. The horn kept beeping so Chris assumed Desmond was ducking as low as he could get in the front seat while he honked away.

Staying low the four of them began pouring rounds into the truck. The driver floored the accelerator to reverse faster. She did it too fast though and missed the turn. The truck went backwards into a deep drainage ditch. Chris was the first one to the wreckage. He hopped backwards when the driver started shooting through the side window. The rest of the group caught up with him as he squatted down in front of the truck. It was sticking up at such a steep angle that they could've remained standing and still been invisible to whoever was in the cab.

Ortega gestured to indicate he'd go around the driver's side with Benson. That left the passenger side to Chris and Samson. Holding up his fingers Ortega did a quick countdown from three. Ortega didn't screw around. He took one step around the truck and started pumping buckshot into driver's side. The second blast caught the driver directly in her face. The woman dropped the revolver she'd been trying to reload and began screaming. The pain of having most of the flesh on her face blown off was too much for her to take. A third blast shut her up permanently.

The four of them searched frantically for the guy they'd seen in the back of the truck. Benson could almost feel the man aiming his rifle at her. It turned out the guy didn't even know where his weapon was. He was doing his best to drag himself along the bottom of the drainage ditch to get away from them. Chris spotted him and worked with Ortega to pull the man up and out of the ditch. The bottom half of the man's leg was wobbling around sickeningly. He didn't stop screaming the whole time they were pulling him up the briar infested embankment.

"Dude. Shut up. You weren't screaming like a little bitch when you were trying to crawl away from us." Samson said poking the man in the chest with his rifle.

The man stared at the rifle. He'd stopped screaming and moved on to a kind of hyperventilating continuous sob. It was making Chris feel bad. Like they'd run over a dog and then stopped to take its chew toy away. Shooting the guy in the head to put him out of his misery seemed like the humane thing to do.

"Should we just leave him here?" Benson asked.

"I try not to leave people behind who've shot at me. It's been a winning strategy so far." Ortega quickly provided one of his apocalyptic life hacks.

"Maybe he's got information." Samson said poking the man in the chest again before ordering him to shut up. They were all surprised when the man actually shut up. Pushing his luck Samson asked the man to tell them something useful. When the man just stared at them Samson poked the barrel of his gun right above where the man's leg was no longer connected correctly. That started a stream of pained cursing.

"How's Tonya?" The broken man asked when he'd finally gotten himself back under control.

"She's been better." Ortega answered after glancing over towards the front seat of the truck. A couple of rounds of buckshot to the face had made it look like Tonya's torso was topped with a gigantic raw meatball wearing a cheap brunette wig. The broken man started sobbing again then broke out in insane laughter when Samson poked him in the leg again.

"You got anything for us?" Samson asked the man again. This was getting super awkward.

"You're all dead!" The man said it with such sincerity that Chris actually looked around to see if maybe this guy had some other friends who were about to take them out.

"You're a lot closer to dying than us. You want to give us some useful intel and we'll put you in bed and give you a bunch of painkillers? Let you go out with a nice buzz?" Samson asked. He felt like that was a solid trade. Better to float out on a blissful cloud of codeine in a nice comfy bed than choke to death on your own blood in the dirt by a drainage ditch.

"Take me to the bed and I'll tell you." The man called Samson's bluff.

"You might as well take him. There actually is a charger in the garage." Benson said. She'd walked over to check. She grabbed Desmond to help her move the cars over to see if they could get them to start charging.

Samson and Ortega looked at each other. Not having anything better to do Samson bent forward and scooped the dirt covered cop off the ground. The man was wearing jeans and a t-shirt, but it was obvious what he would've been wearing back in Gettysburg. Going back into the house they moved carefully up the stairs to the first bedroom they found. Ortega opened the door so Samson could put the man down on the bed.

Chris went around patting the bed to make sure there wasn't a gun concealed beneath a pillow somewhere. He shook his head when Samson looked over at him to make sure it was safe to back away from the bed. Samson and Ortega started coaxing the man into talking some more while Chris began digging through the dresser and closet in the room. He was anxious to get out of the prison clothes and into something a little less conspicuous.

Ignoring the interrogation happening on the bed behind him Chris tugged on a pair of jeans that were noticeably too big. Looking at the size on the tag he smiled to himself. The jeans that were way too big were the exact size he'd been buying for the last three years before the apocalypse. He'd thought wrestling was a great way to stay in shape. Evidently, he should've hopped into a zombie apocalypse every time he needed to make weight for a meet.

Chris was tugging on a pair of sneakers when he caught something being said that caught his attention. Turning around he listened as Samson counted out pills from a bottle he was showing to the man on the bed. He was promising the guy morphine while showing him whatever random crap he'd snagged from the bathroom medicine cabinet. Too far gone to notice their prisoner had started giving up secrets. The biggest one being if they looked in the other bedrooms there was an open phone line to Gettysburg.

"We've got to go!" Ortega called out from down the hall.

Ortega had found the simple field phone in a bedroom closet. The wire coming out the back of it most likely ran all the way back to Gettysburg. The happy couple in the house were here to watch the road and report what they saw back to the Gettysburg operations center. Chris had left that center all shot up, but it wouldn't have been too hard for them to get the phones working again. For all they knew the phones didn't even go to that room.

"Did you tell them we were here?" Samson asked the man in the bed who was happily dry swallowing every pill the big blond SEAL handed him.

"Yeah. They're on their way." The man answered without bothering to look up.

Samson stood up and fired a round into the man's face then another into his heart to be sure. The blood splattered onto the jeans and t-shirt Chris had just pulled on. It smelled wonderful.

"Dude change shirts." Samson said with a look of disgust on his face. Chris realized he'd been caught sucking the blood off the t-shirt. Completely agreeing with the disgust he'd seen on Samson's face Chris grabbed another shirt out of the dresser. Throwing one to Samson and grabbing an armful of clothing for everyone else Chris hustled past Samson to head downstairs. He and Samson avoided eye contact for the time being.

Downstairs they got some more bad news. A lucky shot had done something to one of the Teslas, so they now just had one working vehicle. With no time to waste they all piled into the remaining Tesla. Benson spun the wheel to get them back out on the highway. If a patrol had been sent out as soon as the people in this house had spotted them then they didn't have much time. Benson got them on the highway then punched it to rocket them away from Gettysburg as fast as the mobile tax break could go.

Chapter 34: Hot Pursuit

"They're behind us." Chris said. He'd been told to stare out the back window since he was the guy who could spot drones from the ground with just his naked eyes.

"They must have sent a few cars out right after we got away." Ortega said.

It made sense. The Sheriff couldn't just wave goodbye to the people who'd made a mockery of his whole setup. The prisoners who'd risen up out of their chains to trash the plantation. It wasn't going to help their case that they'd left two more dead bodies in their wake. The more insult they added to injury the less likely the sheriff would ever pull his forces back.

Chris almost asked how they'd have known which way they were going. There was only the one highway though. Thinking back to the large motor pool the Sheriff could've dispatched five cars in each direction. That would've still left a few in reserve. Any more than that and they'd have been cruising after them in golf carts though. There must not be a spare golf cart on any courses for a hundred miles based on all the carts back around the warehouses and cornfields.

"We've got to get word to Lynn somehow." Desmond said while nervously looking back over his shoulder at the barely visible group of cars coming after them.

Thanks to Benson's driving their pursuers were falling behind. That wasn't going to last forever though. It was surreal to think that their lives could be measured by the battery indicator on the dashboard. Once it hit zero, they'd be dead in the water. This time they wouldn't be up against a bunch of bored guards confined to tight hallways. They'd be up against a highly alert patrol armed with lots of automatic weapons who'd be highly motivated to shoot them all as quickly as possible.

"We hear you man. This thing didn't come with a car phone though." Samson responded to Desmond's reminder that they needed to get in touch with Lynn. The SEAL was on the verge of getting annoyed. The tense situation they were in wasn't helped by Desmond constantly whining about wanting to call his 'mommy' for help.

Desmond got the hint and shut up. He'd keep bringing it up as need be though. The muscle heads in the car might not get it but there were much scarier things out there than the racist morons in the cop convoy behind them. Not that he could really call them racist. They practiced plenty of diversity in picking who got to be a cop and who got to be a prisoner. It was refreshing to see such progressive thinking in a group of people who were ok with forcing other people to work for them in chains. Refugeeism?

"We could setup an ambush." Ortega mused out loud trying to come up with a way that they got out of this alive.

"How many rounds do you have left?" Samson asked.

Ortega got the point. They only had the weapons they'd stolen in the last hours' worth of fighting. Those weapons had come with limited rounds. Those rounds had mostly been expended to get them to where they were now. They had enough left over to maybe take on a few trained troopers. There was nowhere close to enough ammo for an extended gun battle with multiple cars full of well provisioned militia. Even with Chris's scary stupid accuracy they'd be setting themselves up for a serious beatdown if they forced an engagement.

"Find somewhere to hide?" Benson asked.

"I think they're expecting that. Wouldn't be shocked if they had a drone or two in those cars with them." Ortega answered. He was sitting in the passenger seat holding Benson's hand. It was a measure of how much he'd missed her that he'd take one of her hands away from the steering wheel while she was driving like a bat out of hell with a bunch of people intent on murdering them riding their bumper. It was sickeningly sweet that she hadn't pulled her hand away yet.

"They can't track us with these can they?" Desmond asked holding up his leg where the ankle monitor still had a red glowing dot on it.

"They didn't take yours off to charge?" Ortega asked. In the room he'd been locked up in the bracelets were rotated around to the convicts the guards considered most likely to run. They were put on a charger every night. It turned out in the room that Desmond and Benson had been in the guards had been pretty lax about charging the devices. Pulling out a large kitchen knife he'd snagged back at the house they'd just made a pitstop at Samson got to work on getting rid of the monitor for Desmond.

"They can't track us this far out anyway. I think those were all hooked up to the WIFI. Whatever network guy they had working for them was a genius. An evil genius but still a genius." Samson said as he carefully poked and sawed at the thick rubber band wrapped around Desmond's ankle.

"We could lose them in a big crowd of the infected." Chris said. He was envisioning driving through town making as much noise as possible to alert all the local baldies that he was bringing them some meals on wheels.

"You might be on to something there. Looks like they cleared out this whole area though." Ortega said looking out the window. They all ignored Desmond cursing at Samson. The big SEAL was doing his best to wedge the blade of the kitchen knife in between Desmond's skin and the thick bracelet without cutting him. Benson's one-handed drag racing down the highway wasn't helping though.

The city of Piqua had seen better days. From the highway they could see the scorched concrete where the buildings had been burnt after being looted. The people of Gettysburg were serious about maintaining a buffer zone. Little did they know that if the baldies got it in their heads to go running down the highway, then the buffer zones wouldn't do much more than just keep the monsters moving along.

"Interstate coming up." Ortega announced. He was flipping through the console of the pricey modern vehicle. GPS was super spotty but there were still maps to look through. Ortega had zoomed in on their current location.

"North or south?" Benson asked glancing down at the console. She'd finally been forced to let go of Ortega's hand. The further they got from Gettysburg the worse the roads were getting. She'd never been part of one, but she'd heard the other prisoners talking about pulling 'chain gang' duty to work on keeping the roads up. They must be reaching the outer band of where those road crews maintained.

"Dayton's south. I've never heard of any of the cities to the north. At least not any of the ones we're able to reach before we have to find another charger. If we want a big city that's probably crawling with baldies, then south it is." Ortega said. Normally they'd have been trying to avoid places covered and smothered with the infected. Now the baldies might be their best chance at ditching their unwelcome escort.

That seemed to settle it. No one spoke up with any other ideas at least. Benson took the southbound on-ramp at a completely unsafe speed and kept the pedal to the metal. In the back Desmond cussed Samson out when the SEAL got tired of screwing around and just started hacking away at the ankle bracelet. He drew some blood, but the bracelet finally gave up its hold on Desmond's ankle.

"You're staring." Samson waved his hand in front of Chris to break him away from staring at the blood pooling on Desmond's ankle.

"I thought you said the blood sucking part was mostly myth?" Chris asked Desmond in a low voice. No matter how subtly he brought up this particular topic it got everyone's attention. Not that Chris cared if the people in the car listened in. They were practically family at this point.

"You won't want it as bad once you're on a regular diet. That diet includes supplements that do the same things for your body as drinking blood does but are way more efficient. Those supplements have only been around for the last couple of centuries. Before that there was a whole lot more blood drinking." Desmond answered.

"So, when you said it was a myth you really meant it was history?" Chris asked.

"Yeah basically." Desmond admitted.

"Is he going to lose his mind and try to suck us dry?" Benson asked. She could always be relied on to cut to the chase.

"Only if he's hurt really bad or seriously malnourished." Desmond answered to Benson's obvious dissatisfaction. What she'd wanted to hear was a resounding 'No'. Desmond looked a little miffed as he'd already told them all this at least once.

"We need to stock up on Gatorade. That way we can make sure Chris doesn't get dehydrated and start nibbling on us." Benson's oversimplification of the issue was making Desmond want to break out into lecture mode. This was neither the time nor the place though. They really needed to call Lynn. Getting those supplements was a big part of the reason for that. The only other place they'd be able to get them was at the sanctuary. The sanctuary wouldn't be safe though. The factions hunting them down would have it under twenty-four-hour observation.

"Bad guys!" Ortega called out.

Up ahead one of the fancy Fords was idling on the side of the road. Even as Ortega pointed it out two men popped up out of the truck bed to blast away at them. Not even Benson could get the car to dodge bullets at such a short range. Rather than try to go around them and get riddled with bullets she chose another tact.

"Everybody down!" Benson yelled slipping down into the driver's seat. She'd pointed their car straight at the truck and stomped on the gas pedal. Not that the pedal had that much further down it could possibly go.

Their windshield was torn apart by machine gun fire. A couple of seconds later they t-boned the truck. The sounds of screeching metal accompanied the taste of blood in their mouths as they were all tossed around. Broken glass was everywhere. Chris had positioned his body in such a way as to absorb most of the impact. He was the first one out of their car after the crash. Ortega and Benson were groggily dealing with being punched in the face by the airbags. Desmond and Samson were seriously messed up. Neither of them had been wearing their seatbelts. A serious apocalyptic error.

Chris climbed out and immediately went over to see how their enemies had handled the impact. There was a cop in the front seat of the enemy truck dealing with his own airbag issue. That guy looked up in time to realize he had a lot more to worry about than whiplash. Chris casually shoved a kitchen knife through the man's eye socket. He did that a couple of times before the man finally did the decent thing and fell over dead. Which was odd since Chris would've been willing to bet a pallet of spam that the quickest way to kill someone with a kitchen knife would've been to do what he'd just done. Live and learn he guessed.

The shooters in the back of the truck had been thrown completely off the interstate. The truck had been parked on the side of an overpass that was a good thirty feet off the ground. Looking down at the road that passed underneath the interstate Chris saw a baldie nosing around the broken bodies of the two men who'd been shooting at them. Looking in the back of the truck Chris saw something even better.

The back of the truck was loaded down with ammo boxes and spare weapons. There was even a crate full of frag grenades. Chris happily held up an M-16 set to fully automatic for Samson when he saw the man had finally gotten out of their totaled Tesla. Everyone climbed out and wobbled their way unsteadily over to the truck. Benson and Ortega pulled the body of the man Chris had stabbed in the eyes out of the driver's seat. Benson climbed in to try and get the truck running after they unceremoniously tossed the former driver's body off the side of the overpass.

Samson tossed an unconscious Desmond in the back then climbed in to join Chris. Ortega walked around with a rifle he'd snagged out of the cab. Feeling much better now about ambushing their pursuers they got lined up behind the truck. Samson took all the grenades out and lined them up where everyone could reach them. That way they'd all have a couple to fling at their assailants. The people coming for them would also be well armed. They just wouldn't be the same caliber of soldier as the people setting up the ambush.

"The truck's running. We could just drive away." Benson brought up as they settled in.

"Let's just go ahead and kill them now. I'm tired of running." Samson said.

That sounded like a plan. A few minutes later they heard vehicles coming down the road towards them. The cars all slowed down when they saw the accident scene in front of them. Watching carefully from around the front of the truck Ortega held up his hand to show the number three. He'd been waiting to make sure all the cars got within range and stopped. The hand gesture was to tell them to countdown from three then attack.

Chris cheated a little and only counted to two. Finished counting he sprinted across the road to draw as much of the enemy fire as he could. Tossing grenades as he ran, he enjoyed seeing the shock on the faces of the enemy as they realized they'd been had. The shock turned to fear and pain as bullets ripped into them and the grenades began going off. This pursuit was not ending as the pursuers had hoped.

Chapter 35: Aim High

"Air Force Base." Samson blurted the words out.

They were cruising through downtown Dayton on the interstate trying to figure out what to do next. The eventual plan would no doubt include getting as far away from Gettysburg as possible. They were working on putting some distance between them and the weird prison farm commune as they figured out their next step. The truck was roomy enough for four of them. Chris had once again been delegated to the bed of the truck thanks to his ability to surf and shoot from back there.

At least his shooting ability was the reason everyone said he should be volunteered to be in the back. Chris suspected that admitting to their blood smelling delicious was also a turn off for everyone. The whole blood all over his face and getting caught sucking blood stains out of his clothes hadn't helped. Not to mention Desmond admitting that people with Chris's 'condition' did indeed enjoy a spot of fresh AB+ now and again.

"You want to extrapolate a little on that? I can find you some crayons somewhere." Ortega was never one to skip an opportunity to tease the big SEAL.

"Wright brothers. White Petersen. Right, something?" Samson said staring at the ceiling trying to remember what the hell the local Air Force base was called. He knew it was a big one.

"Wright Patterson?" Ortega asked.

"You've heard of it?" Samson nodded his head to indicate that was the right name.

"Never been there. Wouldn't have remembered the name if it hadn't just shown up on the GPS." Ortega said pointing at the map on the screen between the driver's and passenger's sides of the front. The screen was smaller than the one in the Tesla, but it made up for it by being in a vehicle that wasn't totaled. Ortega had been manually moving the map screen around to get an idea of where they were at and what was around them.

"It's one of the biggest bases the Air Force has. This close to a large population center where we're already seeing baldies pop up, I doubt they're still there. Wouldn't surprise me to find a working phone there though. Not to mention weapons and gear." Samson explained. That sounded good to everybody else.

It took them a lot longer than it should've to make it to the base. The base was out past the city proper. They had to drive through densely populated parts of the city to get to it though. They could've gone the long way around but weren't sure the battery would make it. Plus, they wanted some charge left in case they needed to leave the base in a hurry.

The roads were covered in trash and bones. The flesh had been picked off the dead by the carrion eaters. The crows must've had a feast when the infected mobs from the city clashed with the armed military police from the base. There were small hills made of the mummified remains of the dead surrounding the different gates leading onto the base. This on top of the destruction apparent in the city from what must've been massive outbreaks. The citizens of Dayton must have doubled down on flu shots then went back for a booster.

Next to the interstate there'd been some signs of the scavenging operations they'd seen in the other towns. A few buildings had been burnt out. No one had come close to making Dayton baldie free yet though. Another major advantage of going electric was that it was a million times quieter than rolling through downtown in a diesel-powered truck would've been. That kept the majority of the infected in their hidey holes. They were hibernating in the buildings and wouldn't wake up unless they sensed prey outside.

The baldies they did see they ignored for the most part. About half of the baldies ignored them as well. Chris had ducked down in the back and the windows up front were tinted. The ones who opted to tag along behind the truck would need to be dealt with quietly once they got to their destination. Luckily there was a convenient case full of bladed weapons in the truck bed to help with that chore.

Benson had been worried about how they were going to be able to get on the base. With everything going on the Air Force would've been in lockdown mode. That would've included shutting gates and throwing up razor wire everywhere. Machine gun nests and roadblocks would've been erected. It was surprising when they followed the signs to the main gate to find nothing stopping their path forward except for a simple hand operated gate blocking the entrance.

Chris hopped out of the truck and raised the gate for them to go through. Thinking ahead to when they'd inevitably be running for their lives to get off the base Chris went ahead and left the gate up. He'd love to believe this place was going to be their sanctuary away from the actual sanctuary but given their track record he doubted it. He hopped back in the truck and slapped the roof to let Benson know she could keep going.

Driving though the main gate they turned the corner into a scene from a classic zombie movie. The entire street seemed to shift around as inanimate bodies came to life. The creatures had been laying every which way on the blacktop. Like they'd all been rampaging around looking for human flesh and decided at the same time that they should just drop to the ground and lay there for a year or so. It was weird enough that not even Benson reacted quickly to the otherworldly ambush.

By the time Benson hit the brakes they were almost completely surrounded. In the back Chris grabbed a rifle and a box full of ammunition. Taking a couple of steps, he jumped on the roof of the truck then immediately bounded up on the roof of the building next to them. Scanning the roof, he made sure nothing was going to surprise him then turned around and got to work.

There were at least a hundred baldies crowding around the truck. Benson was rocking the vehicle back and forth between reverse and drive trying to escape. There were so many zombies surrounding them now that she couldn't get the momentum needed to break free. Not without someone clearing a path. Which is where Chris saw himself coming into the picture. It sucked that he was going to have to sound the dinner bell multiple times to clear a path, but he didn't see much alternative. He'd already dismissed the bladed weapons. No way he could hack his way through that many of those things.

The zombies were already working on smashing their way through the truck windows. Chris began methodically shooting the beasts in the head. He'd planned on working outwards from the truck but the second he shot one another stepped in to take its place. He could've just kept the gun aimed at the same place and pulled the trigger every second and been fairly effective. The problem was that he had to keep acquiring different targets as they tried to break into the truck. He almost let the mob of maniacs crack a window or two. If the zombies broke the passenger window, then Ortega could waste some of the walkers instead of him having to do it all.

Chris kept shooting until he was out of ammunition. The truck was surrounded by corpses with holes drilled through their heads. It was hard to miss when you had superpowers and were only like twenty feet away. It helped that the targets were packed so tightly together that even once he started getting a little sloppy no one was ever going to notice the difference. Last magazine drained Chris took stock of the street below, pulled out a knife, and hopped off the roof.

The three baldies still standing were all facing the truck. Chris crept up behind the infected as they tried to navigate around the pile of dead bodies surrounding the vehicle. A knife thrust through one side of the throat and out the other did the job. The first two never even noticed Chris behind them until it was way too late. The third one turned around and got the knife blade though the front of his throat instead of the side. It was just as effective from that angle.

The others had to climb out of the truck through the windows. The bodies were piled too high to open the doors. Chris had been picking off the baldies as they crawled all over the truck. Once everyone was out, they began sifting through the dead bodies trying to gather what weapons they could carry. They needed to get moving again as soon as possible. With all the noise Chris had just made there'd be a lot more zombies showing up soon.

Chris reloaded and shot two baldies that came running down the street towards them. It was time to go. The truck was buried in biohazard. They'd have to give it up for now. If they couldn't find another vehicle, then they could give it a few days for everything to calm down then come back and shovel the truck out from under the pile of cadavers.

"Let's go!" Ortega hurried along Samson and Benson who were trying to fish more supplies out of the truck.

When a seasoned warrior like Ortega yells that it's time to go then the party's over. That was even more true now than it'd been the rest of the Delta soldier's eventful military career. Samson and Benson immediately abandoned their search and began climbing down the cliff of corpses surrounding the truck. Hopefully neither of them had any open wounds because they were covered in the noxious juices of the contaminated dead.

Ortega waited for them to get down. Once they were on solid ground he set out at a fast clip towards the other end of the street. They needed to disappear around the corner before 'Death Alley' filled up with more of the infected. The second they were out of danger he totally planned to work that 'Death Alley' quip into the conversation somehow.

At the end of the street, they ran into another baldie. This one still had on a badly stained flight suit. Ortega whacked it hard across the face with the sharp side of a machete. The machete split the nose of the zombie in half and got stuck in its sinus cavities. The baldie made a nasally noise then tried to jump on top of Ortega. Chris came from behind and shoved the flight suit wearing beast down on the ground. Ortega stepped forward and curb stomped the back of the creature's scabby bald head. That pushed the machete the rest of the way into the monster's melon.

Choosing to leave the machete right where it was Ortega continued running around the corner and down the road. His entourage followed closely behind. They made it out of 'Death Alley' right as dozens of infected from outside the base began streaming into it. Behind those dozens were hundreds more who'd heard all the ruckus and gotten up to investigate. Those hundreds were attracting the attention of the thousands who'd been nesting in the buildings surrounding the base. The buildings voided their ghoulish residents out into the street like pale white hairless rats fleeing a flotilla of sinking ships. The shambling mob began converging on the Air Force base from every direction.

Unaware of the hopeless situation they were getting themselves into the five of them picked up the pace to stay out of sight of what they assumed was a few dozen baldies at the most. They were still thinking they'd be able to find a building to wait out the sudden surge of the infected. Once that surge ebbed, they'd go back and dig the truck out from under the bodies covering it. In the meanwhile, Ortega still had their main mission top of mind. They needed to find some dial-tone with international access.

Seeing signs for the base medical complex Ortega led them in that direction. When they finally reached the medical center Ortega was impressed by how large it was. Observing the sweat pouring off each one of his heavily breathing companions reminded him that this was a fairly large base. It made sense they'd have a decent sized hospital.

"You could at least pretend to be tired." Benson said shooting Chris a dirty look. Chris was standing off to the side looking like he'd just enjoyed a leisurely stroll through a park.

Ortega ordered them all to keep moving before Chris could come up with a suitably snarky comeback. The truth was that his own stamina kept surprising him. It hadn't even occurred to Chris that he should be tired after hopping up on a building to slaughter a hundred zombies then murdering his way a few miles across a base at a full-on sprint. Not that it'd been a full-on sprint for him. If he'd really poured on the speed, he'd have left everyone else in the dust. It'd been more of a 'valet jog' for him.

The main doors to the hospital were locked with chains wrapped around them. Not wanting to make a bunch of noise by breaking in they began circling the complex. The main entrances were all heavy-duty doors that'd been secured with chains. The easiest way in was going to be through one of the windows on the patient room side. Those windows were heavy duty as well. It took multiple strikes to get one of the windows to crack from that awkward angle.

They'd also had to sacrifice silence to get in. They'd tried wrapping the butts of their rifles in their sweat-soaked shirts but that hadn't seemed to do anything other than make a different kind of noise when they hit the window. In the dead silence of the deserted base the sound of rifles beating their way through glass resonated. The monsters who'd been shuffling around aimlessly upon discovering the empty alley perked back up. Their heads all snapped in the direction of the distant noise. Once again filled with malevolent purpose the mob moved as one towards the hospital.

Chapter 36: Phone Home

"Dark as hell in here." Benson commented once she'd been boosted up into the hospital room they'd broken into.

"They have solar. We'd just have to find where the breakers are at." Ortega said shining his flashlight around. With the whole effort to stabilize the climate the government had gotten all kinds of carried away with windmills and solar. It was hard to find a federal facility that hadn't spent way too much money on some sort of renewable energy source. They were never going to get a decent return on that investment now that everyone was walking around insane and hairless. It was a good thing for the survivors though.

The hospital room was dusty but otherwise pristine. This base must've been evacuated early on in the crisis. There'd been a lot of shifting people around as the higher ups tried to navigate the unknown waters of the undead scourge. Moving people to places where they thought they could better protect them. Then watching as those places got infected and fell like dominoes.

"You think the whole base is like this?" Benson asked as Ortega helped Desmond into the room. She gestured with her hands at the room to indicate what she was talking about.

"Unless someone tried to stay in any of the buildings. Otherwise, if it's sealed up tight the baldies won't bother." Desmond answered. He was a little late to the conversation. It was a topic they discussed frequently though. Hearing a snippet of it was enough to know what was being talked about.

"I don't know that we're going to find a way to contact Lynn in a hospital." Chris said. He'd been the last one in. Rather than reaching for anyone's hand he'd just neatly hopped through the broken window.

They decided to lay low until the handful of baldies walking around outside got bored and left. Ortega's main contribution to the planning was finally getting his 'Death Alley' pun out there. Making the decision to not try and get the power turned on they went in search of the cafeteria. Turning the power on could attract the attention of the infected. It wasn't worth triggering an avalanche of baldies just so they didn't have to use their flashlights.

"This place is creepy." Benson whispered after they'd spent a few minutes walking down the long empty corridor. Their footsteps echoed with every step they took. Gurneys and medical equipment had been pushed to the side. It was like the personnel working in the hospital had been told to leave but expected to come back in a few days. The place was locked up tight on the outside and had been cleaned and sanitized on the inside.

"Agreed. Super creepy." Ortega whispered back. Deserted hospital corridors were featured in lots of horror movies precisely because they were creepy. Or maybe they were creepy because they were featured in so many horror movies. Ortega's pontifications on the origin of hospital hallways being so unsettling were interrupted by Chris waving his light to show he'd found something.

The five of them crowded around a sign next to a trio of elevators. The elevators weren't going to do them much good but the stairwell next to them could be useful. What they were looking for in addition to food was the pharmacy. It was never a bad idea to stock up on painkillers and antibiotics. A bottle or two of anti-depressants wasn't a bad thing to keep around either. In this case the pharmacy and café happened to be in the same direction.

Desmond had only mentioned trying to find a sat phone once since they got in the hospital. He'd brought it up immediately after picking up the phone in the patient room they'd entered the building in. Upset when he didn't get any dial tone, he'd reminded everyone they needed to find a way to get in touch with Lynn. Knowing he sounded like a broken record didn't stop him. He didn't get the sense that the others were as focused on getting ahold of Lynn as he was. They were understandably more interested in finding supplies than letting an international vampire cabal know their current location.

"You know we need to get in touch with Lynn, right?" Desmond sidled up to Chris and whispered the question. He knew Chris would be able to hear him even if he whispered so quietly that no one else could.

"Yeah. There should be somewhere on the base where we can find a phone that'll work. We'll have to figure out how to charge it up. We can grab some supplies and crash here a few days. Once we've got some antibiotics working on the infections from our multiple gunshot wounds then we can get out there and look." Chris responded. He didn't bother keeping the annoyance out of his voice. Desmond was starting to get on his nerves as well. Lynn's ex-personal assistant must not be used to being separated from her for this long. Or maybe he just wasn't used to being out in the field for this long. The whole prison farm thing had been pretty traumatizing.

"I don't think you have to worry a whole lot about infections." Desmond said.

"Yeah, but the rest of you mere mortals do. I need everyone to stay alive until I've mastered all my superpowers." Chris said. He meant it as a joke. It came out weird though. Earning him some odd looks from his traveling companions.

"Hopefully they've got a lot of garlic in the mess hall so we can shut you up." Ortega responded almost immediately to Chris's comment.

"How long have you been working on that one?" Chris asked.

"The 'Death Alley' one was way better." Benson commented with a worried smile. Something didn't feel right. She noticed Chris looking around anxiously as well.

"You guys hear that?" Chris asked.

They'd located the mess hall. It was conveniently located right where all the signs said it should be. More importantly they'd located a massive pantry that still had canned and dried food in it. There was a lot of empty shelf space. The pandemic had been pretty rough on the supply chain. Especially towards the end of it all. When the people from the base had been relocated, they hadn't bothered stripping the place completely. Whether they were in a hurry or just overly optimistic they'd left behind shelves full of canned vegetables for the taking.

"Hear what?" Samson asked. He'd been walking around inside the pantry inventorying the various food items.

"I think we may need to take some cans to go." Chris said. Before anyone could ask him what he was talking about, he took off out the door. No one bothered following him. He was moving way too fast.

"Anyone else still freaked out by the way he goes running around in the pitch black like that?" Ortega asked.

"Shut up and help me get this stuff into my bag." Benson said. The way Chris had torn out of here she was thinking they'd be exiting quickly. She wasn't leaving without at least one can of peaches.

Chris was back before they had a chance to do much more than shove a few of the oversized cans into their packs. He didn't need to tell them what was up. They could all hear it now. The sound of bare flesh slapping the windows of the building they were in. An inhuman drumming that chilled them all to the bone.

"There's too many of them in the front. We've got to go now!" Chris waved at them all to hurry. How to fit the oversized cans into their packs had just become the least of their worries.

They ran back the way they'd come from. Desperately sprinting down the corridors in a race against terror. A race against being trapped in the creepily sanitized facility while hundreds of the demonic undead smashed their way in. Visions of slowly starving to death while monsters tried to get at them in their tiny hiding spaces flashed through their heads. The impending claustrophobia encouraging them to run even faster.

Their hope for an easy escape was crushed when they heard glass breaking from the direction they were headed. The moans and cries of the damned washing down the dark corridor stretching out in front of them. Chris shook his head when Samson looked over at him. Desmond's eyes were desperately going back and forth. He was not the seasoned warrior that the people surrounding him were. On the verge of hyperventilating, he ran over to the stairwell door and pulled it open.

Agreeing with the path Desmond had chosen Chris ran over to hold the door for the rest of the team. As soon as they were all through Chris let the door shut behind him. The baldies weren't great at opening doors they had to pull on so that should buy them a little time at least. They needed to find some chains or something to secure the doors with though. Otherwise, one of the zombies would eventually pull on the door while another one was leaning on the lever to open it. It was the whole hundred monkeys typing on a hundred typewriters scenario.

Chris flew up the stairs. He was taking five or six steps at once. In no time flat he caught up to the others. They'd huddled up around the third-floor door. Samson had wanted to wait for Chris to show up to tell them if they should open it or not. He was thinking they might be able to get to the parking garage. If they could then there was always the possibility of getting a vehicle started and using it to get the hell out of there.

Chris listened at the door for a second then shrugged. He wasn't hearing anything coming from the other side. It was a thick metal fire door though. Not the best possible scenario for him to tell what was on the other side. Samson leaned forward and pushed the door open slightly so Chris could hear better. There were definitely sounds coming from the hall outside, but it was hard to tell from exactly where they were coming. Up this high there shouldn't be more than a handful of the monsters roaming the halls yet.

"Might be our only chance." Samson hissed. The others nodded.

Moving down the hallway with weapons in hand they headed towards the parking garage. There was a really good chance the parking garage was already filled to capacity with the man-eating monsters, but it was worth a shot. They could always turn around and get back in the stairwell.

It was a quick walk over to a door marked *'Parking Level 3.'* It was another fire door in a building designated as a tornado shelter. Once again, they were forced to open it blind since Chris couldn't get a great read on what was on the other side of it. Samson once again pushed it open just a crack so that Chris could get a better sense for what was on the other side. The dim light from the parking garage filtered in around the sides of the door. Desperate to escape before it was too late Desmond pushed the door all the way open to get out.

Chris's arm snaked out. He grabbed the back of Desmond's shirt and yanked him backwards hard. Even with his enhanced speed he wasn't fast enough. Several arms shot through the open door before Samson could pull it shut. Ortega blasted the arms with a shotgun and tried to grab the door handle. A dozen more arms were shoved in the door to wrench it open. The snarling faces of a crowd of enraged baldies materialized in the doorway.

"Run!" Chris yelled unnecessarily. Ortega and Samson blasted away at the open doorframe to keep the monsters at bay while Chris shoved Desmond in the correct direction. Together they ran down the hallway back towards the door leading to the stairs.

The baldies were right on their heels. Benson already had the door open and was waiting for them. Samson and Ortega threw themselves into the stairwell. Chris slowed when he felt a hand grab his ankle. Kicking the hand off him he leapt for the door. Desmond and Benson both lunged for the door at the same time. Ortega grabbed Benson to pull her away from the open stairwell door. Chris helped Desmond through. Before anyone could close the door all the way, the baldies were already inside.

Expending every last bullet, they tried to force the monsters out of the stairwell. All it did was buy them enough time to retreat up the stairs. Hearts pounding, they made it out onto the roof. Ortega and Samson leaned against the door while the rest of them looked for some way to secure it. Otherwise, the zombies would be out on the roof within the next few minutes. Once the baldies were on the roof, they were all dead. Chris might be able to save himself, but he'd have to leave his friends behind to do so. He wasn't willing to do that without a serious fight.

Seeing some two by fours neatly stacked in the corner of the roof Chris ran over and grabbed two of them. Working with Ortega he got the boards propped against the door then went back to get some more. They ended up propping six of the long pieces of wood against the door with another two on the ground to help brace the ones against the door. The whole setup required at least two people to lean against parts of it or the zombies would be able to knock it over.

"Well, this sucks." Samson announced from his position on the ground holding one of the braces in place.

"Better than being eaten alive." Benson said as she watched the exit door vibrate each time the zombies inside surged against it to try and get on the roof.

"There's got to be a way out of this." Desmond said pacing around the roof. The baldies had completely surrounded the entire complex. The hospital was an island in a sea of the dead.

"Not for at least two of us." Samson responded. As soon as the people holding the two by fours in place left their post the roof would fill up with baldies. Even if there was a way to escape someone was going to have to stay behind. It wasn't looking good.

"Well. I don't think we're going to have to worry about finding a way to escape for too long." Chris said staring up at the cloudy sky.

"How come?" Ortega asked.

"There's a drone checking us out." Chris responded with one hand shielding his eyes.

"That's good right? It could be Lynn." Desmond said. He stood up and tried to locate the drone in the sky as well. No one had the heart to tell him that it was more likely the same elite unit that'd blown-up Fort Leavenworth. Trapped like they were all they could really do was wait for the bombs to start falling. It was going to be a long day.

Author's Note

Life as a slowly evolving superhuman in a post-apocalyptic America isn't all that different from the lives we all lead. There's not really that much more death. It's not like any of us get more than one chance anyway. Whether you die from a zombie chomping down on your face or because you decided to read a text message while doing ninety down the interstate, we all die eventually.

Another big similarity is that we never know where our journey will take us. Every day you wake up and proceed to make a thousand tiny decisions that impact the way the rest of your life's going to work out. Those little things add up. For me lately it's been this fantasy I have of waking up early to work out every day. I think of all the positive impacts it'll have on my life and it's a no brainer. At six in the morning those benefits don't seem as important. As a matter of fact, over the last two months I've been doing this I've only managed to work out early like once.

I'll keep trying though. I want to survive long enough to see all my children get a good start on their lives. A few grandkids sound good now that I'm getting older too. Not too soon but at some point, it'd be cool to have kids you can play with and then return. So, waking up early to work out would make me healthy and it'd give me an extra hour in the afternoons to spend with family. Which brings me to a subject I feel like might make a pretty good book. Something around the theory that Satan holds the patent on the snooze alarm. Maybe more of a short story but I think you can see where I'm going with that. □

Chris doesn't know where he's going. He knows his body is changing. The world is changing. He faces an uncertain future. But what I love about him is that he faces it. He doesn't shirk his responsibilities. No cowering in the corner. Or at least not for very long. He's adapting to a world that's gone completely to hell. He's adapting and he's taking his companions with him. Is it out of loyalty or just a need to try and hold tight to some reminder of his own humanity?

Book 3 for this series is in the works. Expect the pace to continue to pick up as the world continues to slide towards the point of no return. The future of humanity is in the hands of beings who are no longer really human. I can't wait to continue on this journey. Thank you so much for coming with me this far. I hope to see you again soon!

For those who've kept up with all these notes and might be curious. All the kids are fine and no more are currently expected. (Give us a month or two) **THANK YOU** so much for reading these books and helping support them. If you do get a moment, please leave a review, and toss me a few stars. It's VERY appreciated.

To leave a review click here:
https://www.amazon.com/Exploited-Blood-Book2-Turn-Merritt-ebook/dp/B09Z9RV6W3

Thank You!

R S Merritt

Other Books by R S Merritt

Try an excellent 7 Book series built around a Zombie outbreak:

Zombies!

Need more Zombies? Check out the **hilarious** 6-Book Zournal series:

Zournal

Looking for some fantasy set in a modern-day world? Try the Son of the Keeper series:

Son of the Keeper

Need another epic thriller series set in the end of the world?

Crawlerz

Printed in Great Britain
by Amazon

21464048R00224